DEATH
IN SHANGHAI

M J LEE

ONE PLACE, MANY STORIES

HQ
An imprint of HarperCollins*Publishers* Ltd.
1 London Bridge Street
London SE1 9GF

This paperback edition 2017

1
First published in Great Britain by
HQ, an imprint of HarperCollinsPublishers Ltd. 2015

ISBN: 978-0-263-92773-3

Printed and bound by
CPI Group (UK) Ltd, Croydon, CR0 4YY

For my mother, Margaret Lee

February 22nd 1928.
The 31st day of the Year of the Earth Dragon.

CHAPTER 1

In the middle of Soochow Creek is a sandbank known by the locals as 'the Beach of Dead Babies'. On a bright, cold Shanghai morning, there were no dead babies lying on it, just a dead blonde.

Inspector Danilov stamped his feet on the cobblestones of the bank, trying to force some life into his cold toes. He pulled his old coat around his thin body and searched its pockets for his tobacco tin. Blowing some warm air on his fingers, he opened the tin and rolled a cigarette with one hand. The first breaths of smoke choked his lungs, producing a series of deep, barking coughs like the alarm cries of a deer. A spit of black tar filled his mouth, the remains of the opium he had smoked the night before. He spat it out and watched it land in the mud at the edge of the creek before it was swallowed by the lapping, grey waters.

His colleague, Charles Meaker, the District Inspector from Hongkew, walked to the middle of Zhapu Bridge, scanning the area as if getting his bearings. At the centre of the bridge, Meaker located the position of the blonde stretched out on the sandbank. From a pocket, he produced a linen measuring tape and laid this along the stone parapet of the bridge.

After an age of measuring, a smug smile spread across his pale face. 'I believe it's one of yours. It's on your side,' he shouted. Then he rolled up the measuring tape and put it back inside his jacket pocket, taking the opportunity to hitch his trousers over his large stomach.

He strolled over to Danilov on the city side of the bridge. 'Floaters are always a nightmare. Hate 'em mesel'. Looks like this one topped hersel' upstream, and the body floated down. Enjoy it.' He tugged at his moustache. 'Another chance to enhance your reputation.'

Danilov took a long drag of his cigarette, savouring the bitter tang of the tobacco. 'Thank you, Inspector Meaker, have you finished?' He turned back, looking for his new constable in the large crowd that now lined the banks. 'Stra-chan, come here, will you?'

'It's Straw-aaan,' said Meaker, the "ch" is silent. But you Russians wouldn't know anything about that, would you?'

The young detective ran up. 'Yes, sir?' He had a shock of black hair, an eager smile and eyes that gave away he was half-Chinese.

'Stra-chan,' Inspector Danilov emphasised, 'go down to the sampans and check if anybody saw anything.'

'Good luck with that. Hear no evil. See no evil. Speak no evil. Just do evil. That's what this lot believe.' Meaker mimed the actions of the three monkeys ending with an expansive gesture that took in all the watching Chinese.

Inspector Danilov ignored him. 'Go and check them anyway. Somebody may have seen something.' Strachan began to turn away. 'Don't forget to send a man to the pathologist. The morgue is just across Garden Bridge on the other side of the river. Let Dr Fang know there's a body coming in.'

'Yes, sir. Anything else, sir?' Strachan stood to attention awaiting any further orders. He was new to the detective squad, and this was his first case.

'Hurry up, we haven't got all day,' said Danilov. 'The feet feed the wolf, as we say in Minsk.'

'Er . . . yes, sir, right away.'

'I'm off back to Hongkew for a nice cuppa. Good luck with the floater, Danilov. Rather you than me, heh?' With a long, pipe-stained chuckle, Meaker twisted his moustache and walked back across the bridge to his own district.

Danilov looked down once more at the muddy, murky water eddying around the foundations of the bridge, Inspector Meaker and his jibes already forgotten. His eyes drifted across to the sandbank where the body lay half submerged, its arms stretched out to the sides. Like Jesus on the Cross, he thought. And then the image of a long-forgotten triptych came back to him, its central panel a Jesus with sharp ribs and blood pouring from a wound in his side.

He smelt the rich fragrance of incense, a smell that was only found in the Orthodox churches of his youth. He lifted his nose to the wind and looked around him. A hawker had already set up his stall on the banks of the creek, taking advantage of the crowds that had come to see the body. The hawker was stirring his pot of charcoal and sweet potatoes with a wooden paddle. Each time he stirred, the unmistakable smell of incense filled the air. How strange, thought Danilov, how very strange.

The body still lay there on the sandbank, only thirty yards from shore but a whole lifetime away. The long blonde strands of hair, washed by the muddy waters, writhed in each ripple of the creek. The blondness contrasting vividly with the bleached greys of the sampans that lined the banks tied up to each other, sometimes three deep. A child, its head as round as a football, ran to the prow of one of the boats, where it was joined by a small dog, both fascinated by all the fuss. On his right leg, the child had a rope tied around his ankle. Danilov smiled to himself. Tied to a life on his boat for the next forty years. Just like all of us.

He heard Strachan run up and stand quietly behind him.

'Time and tide wait for no man, the English are fond of saying, are they not?'

'I suppose so, sir.'

'Well, then, let's get going. Our body is waiting for us, and the tide will change soon. Find the photographer, he should be around here somewhere.'

Followed by a long line of people, Danilov walked through the crowd towards the sampan like the Pied Piper leading a gaggle of curious children.

***

He was watching from the crowd. He saw the pantomime performed by the tall detective with the absurd moustache, wearing a suit that was too small for him. The measuring, the sighting, the rushing around to achieve nothing. God, they were idiots! Why had he been forced to endure such morons all his life? But they kept him safe, he knew that. Their stupidity allowed him to hide among them, to hide in plain sight. In Shanghai, it was so easy to pretend to have a veneer of sophistication, a veil of normality. Here, surface was everything, shallowness exalted. Everybody had a secret. Everyone knew that somebody was hiding something. It just didn't matter.

Well, he would make it matter. He would throw light on their shallowness, on their dark secrets. The city of shadows could not hide from him. Those flickering images that pretended to be real concealing their evasions, lies, and dissembling. He would shine a light on them all. He would show them up for what they were. He had already started, but now it was time to really go to work.

He caught the aroma of sweet potato on the air. An ugly vegetable with a beautiful core of sweetness within. A bit like Shanghai he thought, but in reverse.

* * *

Danilov stepped on to the old sampan. It rocked drunkenly beneath his feet as he was joined by Strachan, two Chinese constables who would lift the body from the river, and a photographer.

An old woman stood at the rear of the boat, her back bowed like the branch of a mulberry tree. She reached out her hand with its deeply creased palms and short, stubby, dirt-encrusted fingers. 'One dollar,' she said, thrusting her hand closer to Danilov. He reached into his pocket and gave her 50 cents. She glanced at it, smiled toothlessly, and placed it carefully in a cotton drawstring bag around her neck.

She leant on the oar that stuck out from the back of the sampan. Slowly, rhythmically, she swayed from side to side, her gnarled feet gripping the deck of the boat, only moving her upper body. The boat swam forwards towards the sandbar in short, rolling jerks.

Along the banks, the watching faces were mostly Chinese, but with a smattering of Europeans dotted in the crowd. Their taller size and sharp, white faces stood out against the round heads and Chinese gowns of the men, the elegant *chi paos* of the female office workers, and the thin vests and blue trousers of the dockside labourers.

At one side, the hawker stirred his pot of sweet potatoes. It was amazing how quickly the hawkers turned up whenever a crowd formed. It was as if they sensed that something was going to happen and were drawn to the scene like flies to sticky paper.

The boat was closer to the sandbank now. He could see the naked body quite clearly. The blonde hair was longer than he thought, the muddy water hiding its length as it waved like yellow seaweed just beneath the waves. The breasts and shoulders were small, almost undeveloped. The face was thin and angular, with traces of mascara around the eyes and a thin smear of lipstick on the lips. The arms were kept in place by weighted stones. Thin sisal ropes wrapped around the wrists ensured they stayed in place, anchored to the sandbank.

Danilov thought for a moment. This was no suicide. Not a person driven to such despair that they had thrown themselves into the river rather than face life.

Then he noticed the long nails with their bright purple nail varnish. Claws rather than nails, he thought, weapons for inflicting damage. He never understood why such nails were seen as beautiful or beguiling in a woman. For him, they appeared like the weapons of a predatory insect.

A flash went off as the photographer manoeuvred to get a better shot. More flashes and more rocking of the boat. He took one last look at the body lying half submerged on the sandbank and gestured for the constables to take it out of the water. They reached over the prow of the boat. One constable untied the ropes from the wrists while the other held the body steady. The constable handed both ropes and the stones to Danilov. He felt their weight. About three pounds, he guessed. Enough to keep the arms outstretched even in the face of the tide.

Both constables leant out and grasped the naked blonde underneath the shoulders. As they did so, the body came free of the water and a torrent of snakes issued from the stomach. The constables dropped it back in the river and jumped back into the boat. Danilov leant out and saw the body floating now, the blonde hair still waving in the water. For a moment, all he could see were snakes, their heads raised as if to strike. Then he realised that he was looking at intestines, which had fallen out from a vast dark hole where the stomach had once been.

The constables were next to him, chattering loudly in Shanghainese. The old lady looked at the body and spat a long stream of brown juice into the river. Strachan was just staring fixedly at the naked corpse, his mouth slightly open.

Danilov reached down and lifted the body by the shoulders whilst one of the constables took the feet. As they lifted it into the boat, the other constable pushed the intestines back into the stomach cavity with his hands. But still the guts wriggled out beneath his fingers, slithering away from his touch.

Strachan watched, unable to move, fascinated by the paleness of the corpse, its whiteness in stark contrast to the murky grey of the water. The others ignored him as they heaved it into the boat, where it lay there like a dead fish, the intestines still alive as they oozed back out of the cavity.

Danilov knelt down and examined the body at his feet. The stomach and thighs had been slashed with deep, frenzied cuts so all that remained was a dark emptiness where life should have been. Surprisingly, though, there were no rat bites. In a city teeming with rats, even they had avoided this particular feast. On the chest, or what remained of it, two Chinese characters had been carved. 'Stra-chan, come and look at this, will you?'

Strachan wiped his mouth with the back of his hand, and slowly inched his way across the deck, keeping his eyes fixed on the pale body.

'What do you make of this?' Danilov pointed to the characters sliced into the flesh. Strachan's face went bright red as he finally looked away from the body and its intestines lying on the deck.

He reached out and touched Strachan on the hand. 'Everybody reacts differently, the first time they see a dead person up close.'

Strachan nodded and forced himself to look back at the body. 'It's "justice", sir. The characters for "justice".'

'Thank you.' At a nod from Danilov, the photographer moved into position. Flashes exploded, capturing the body from every angle and every side as he struggled with the rocking of the boat to get his shots.

When he had finished, one of the Chinese constables inched forward to cover the body with a loose tarpaulin. The old woman began to sway backwards and forwards again, propelling the boat towards the shore. Her mouth, with its graveyard of teeth, still held its smile.

'When we get to shore, fingerprint the body and send it to the morgue. Come back to the station when you've finished.'

'Yes, sir,' Strachan answered, wiping his mouth with the back of his hand.

'You'd better get used to bodies, you'll see many more before you finish working with me.'

***

'The Chief Inspector's been asking after you. Just thought I'd let you know.'

Danilov thanked Sergeant Wolfe, and walked behind the desk of Central Police Station, past two Sikh guards, into the inner sanctum of the detectives' office.

The desks were arranged in two neat rows, one behind the other like a deck of cards laid out for a game of patience. Behind each desk was a detective. Some were going through old files. Some were on the telephone. Some were pretending to read old reports. A few were asleep, their heads nestled in the crooks of their arms.

Danilov put his tobacco tin and keys on his desk, walked up to Chief Inspector Boyle's office and knocked.

There was no answer. He knocked again.

He heard the faint shuffling of chairs and a loud, 'Enter!'. He opened the door and took off his hat. A tall, rather dapper man sat behind his desk, two white tufts of hair above his ears contrasting sharply with a florid face. The curtains were half closed, giving the room a dark, cave-like atmosphere. In the corner, a putter and ball leant up against the eau-de-nil wall, a colour that seemed to cover every wall of every British office he had ever entered. Why they loved this particular colour, he was yet to discover. Perhaps its sickly paleness reminded them of home?

Boyle coughed. 'Inspector Danilov, do take a seat.' He indicated the only chair in front of him. It was small and hard, forcing all those who sat in it to feel like a penitent schoolboy.

The strong smell of Boyle's cologne dominated the room. '4711,' thought Danilov, as he took one of the more comfortable seats from its place along the wall and set it down noisily in front of the desk.

Boyle reached forward to open the large silver box in front of him. Inside was a choice of cigarettes: Turkish for smokers who loved a rich aroma, American for the sophisticated and, of course, British Woodbines for those who had acquired the habit in the trenches. Danilov took a Turkish cigarette, lighting it with the onyx lighter that lay next to the cigarette box.

So it was going to be one of those meetings, he thought. Boyle had a particular style: no offer of a seat was going to be a dressing down. A seat and a cigarette was a 'quiet' chat. A seat and a cigar was an understanding that Boyle wanted something that only the person blessed with the cigar could provide. All the police dreaded the seat and the glass of whisky, for that meant the miscreant was going to be transferred to some obscure job in the nether reaches of the police universe, where the offender would spend the rest of his life arresting dog eaters and night soil collectors.

Danilov inhaled the rich earthy smoke of the Turkish. Fine tobacco, a little elegant for his taste but still a fine smoke.

'Or would you like a cigar?' Boyle opened the other wooden box that lay on the table, revealing a selection of the finest Havanas and Dominicans.

'Thank you, sir. A coffin nail is fine for me.'

Boyle chuckled. 'Coffin nails. That's what we used to call them during the War. Long time ago though. Lost a lot of good men, too many.' He blew a long cloud of blue smoke out into the office. 'You didn't fight, did you, Danilov?'

'No, sir, I was in the Imperial Police in Minsk. We weren't sent to the Front.'

'I was a Captain, Manchester Regiment, you know. The scum of the Earth from the back streets of Hulme but damn fine men, if you get my meaning.

'I understand, sir.'

Boyle stared into mid-air. Above his head, a print of a Chinese street scene hung at a slight angle. Hawkers sold food from banana leaves placed on the ground. People wandered through examining the wares. On each building, Chinese characters blared the names of the proprietors of the shops.

Not a traditional choice for a head of detectives, thought Danilov. He stubbed his cigarette out in a bronze ashtray already full of stubs.

The movement seemed to pull Boyle out of his remembrance of the past. 'Jolly good. I've asked you here today for a couple of reasons, Danilov. Firstly, how was the body that you found this morning?'

'How was it? Dead, sir, extremely dead.'

'Suicide?'

'No. Not unless this one decided to kill herself by slashing her stomach and thighs to the bone, tying her wrists with stone weights, rowing out to a sandbank and then jumping into Soochow Creek. No, sir, I think suicide is out of the question.'

'Shame that. I had Meaker on the phone. He thought it was, but as it was on our side of the creek, he was going to leave it to us. He seemed rather pleased at the idea.'

'Inspector Meaker is entitled to his opinion, sir, but it's not a suicide. Far from it. Murder I'm afraid. A brutal one as well.'

Boyle shuffled the papers in front of him. 'Well, get it over with as quickly as you can. Upstairs gets its whiskers in a curl when Europeans are murdered. The murder of European women particularly seems to excite them. Got to maintain our prestige. The Chinese depend on us maintaining order. Without it, where would we be? Solve it quickly, Danilov.'

'The body is on its way to the pathologist now, sir. Dr Fang will do his usual thorough job.'

Boyle harrumphed and lifted a piece of paper from the top of his pile. 'There's one other thing that requires a delicate touch. You did rather well with the Bungalow Murders last year and that awkward affair with the American Consul in '26. As for your time with Scotland Yard, well, enough said.'

'Thank you, sir.' Danilov recognised when he was being buttered up. 'But my two years in London were wasted. We never found the anarchists we were looking for.'

'At least it meant you could polish your English. You speak it better than most of my English chaps.'

'Thank you again, sir.'

'As I was saying, you handled those delicate situations rather well. The thing is, we've had a strange note from the French. The French Head of Detectives actually, a Mr . . .' he glanced down at the paper he was holding, '. . . a Mr Renard.'

'Is it the note that's strange, sir, or the fact that the French have sent it?'

'It's both, Danilov. Last time we talked to them was spring last year, when we had that little problem with the communists. Anyway, a meeting has been set up for tomorrow morning with him. Usually, I'd go myself but I've got a Council session and it can't be postponed. Can't stand the frogs anyway. Had enough of them in the war. Far too dramatic for my tastes. Quite like the language, though, became quite good at it, even if I do say so myself. Damn fine wine too, if my memory serves me right.'

'Where is the meeting, sir?'

'Oh, yes, that would help wouldn't it?' He scanned the note quickly, his lips moving as he read the words.

'Ah, here it is, Avenue Stanislaus Chevalier, at 10 a.m. Their HQ, it would seem.'

Danilov took out his notebook and wrote down the details.

'Do report to me afterwards, Danilov. Can't have those frogs sending you off on a wild-goose chase. "*Une poursuite de l'oie sauvage,*" if I remember my French.'

'A better translation, sir, might be, "*un ballet d'absurdités,*" or more simply, "*une recherche futile.*"'

'Well, that's as may be. French never was my strong suit.' Boyle closed the cigarette case, always a sign that the meeting was over. 'Clear this blonde case up quickly, Danilov.'

'I'm going to see the pathologist right away, sir.'

'Good. It's probably just a lovers' quarrel that's gone too far.'

'It went too far, sir, of that I am sure, but it's more than a lovers' quarrel. I believe it's far darker and more dangerous than that.'

***

Inspector Danilov returned to his desk after the interview with Boyle. He stood in front of it for a long time, realising that something was wrong. The ink bottle was in a different place, and the pencil was half an inch out of alignment. He reached down and put them back exactly where they should have been.

Behind him, he could hear the muffled sniggers of the other detectives.

'Wha's up, Danilov, somethin' not right?' This was from Cartwright, a detective with the imagination of a bull and the wit of a dinosaur. 'Out of whack, are we?'

Danilov turned back and addressed Cartwright, but actually talking to all of them: 'I'd rather you didn't touch anything on my desk in future.'

'Always so prim and fuckin' proper aren't we? I thought you Russians were rougher and tougher, like the girls in Blood Alley.' More sniggers from the detectives.

'Not all of us are the same, Cartwright. Just like you English, we are different, too.' He looked him up and down. 'You, for instance, had an egg with two slices of bacon this morning for breakfast. I had just one cup of coffee. You had an argument with your wife last night and this morning it continued. I live alone. And your house boy has left, as well. I prefer to do without servants. Your . . .' he stopped here, looking for the right word, '. . . paramour . . . is also two-timing you with . . .' he swivelled round and pointed at another detective, Robson, 'sitting to the left of you, Cartwright. Such women, of course, do not interest me.'

'Wha' the fuck? How do you know . . .?'

But Cartwright was already talking to the back of Danilov as he walked out of the detectives' office.

'You'll get your comeuppance one day, you mark my words. You may speak bloody English but you'll never be an Englishman. Bloody Russian prick!' Cartwright shouted to the closing door.

Danilov had already gone next door to see Miss Cavendish, the office secretary. She was an old maid who had been born in Shanghai and lived there all her life, but still didn't speak a word of Chinese. 'Well, there's no need, is there? They all speak English. Or at least the ones I have to speak to. Or they speak pidgin. And I'm frightfully good at pidgin. Second language to me it is.'

Danilov stood in front of her desk and coughed. She glanced up and he caught a waft of her scent. French and very floral. 'Miss Cavendish, could I bother you for the file on the French Head of Detectives? A Mr Renard, I believe.'

'Actually, it's Major Renard, Inspector. I'll have it on your desk in an hour.' She leant forward and whispered, 'I couldn't help but hear what you said about Cartwright – he will be upset.'

'Cartwright can't be upset, Miss Cavendish. That would indicate an ability to feel. He is either totally happy or totally drunk. Those are the limits of his emotions.'

'Was it true?'

'He has the same breakfast every morning because he can't be bothered explaining to his cook he would like something different. He wasn't wearing his normal pungent eau de cologne, which only happens when his wife locks him out of the marital bedchamber after an argument. She was still unhappy with him, so he was unable to splash more on this morning. You may have noticed he is still wearing the same clothes as two days ago. Hence, the boy is no longer providing his services.'

'But how did you know about his . . .' she leant forward and returned to whispering: '. . . paramour?'

'That part was easy. I observed her with Robson on Nanking Road two nights ago. It seems she has switched her favours recently. And everything I said about myself was true.'

'You are a proper Sherlock Holmes, aren't you, Inspector Danilov?

'I admire your famous detective, Miss Cavendish, but I always believed he missed the patterns in crime. The patterns are everything. Once we understand them, everything else falls into place.'

'A bit like my knitting, without the pattern I'm lost.'

'Precisely, Miss Cavendish. All criminals have patterns through which they reveal themselves. Our job is to discover the pattern. It was one of the first things they taught us at the Imperial Police Academy.'

Miss Cavendish was the ears of all gossip in Central. If he wanted to know anything about the station or its inhabitants, Chinese, English, Russian or Japanese, he just asked her. She was better than any stoolie on the street, and she was free, which was even more important.

'I would look out for him if I were you.' She indicated the closed door of the detectives' room. 'A bit of a bull in a china shop is our Inspector Cartwright. Or a bull in a China police station, I should say.' Miss Cavendish giggled at her own little joke as she played with the pearls that encircled her neck. Danilov wondered if she were flirting with him.

She popped a sweet into her mouth from the packet that lay on her table. She offered one to him. For a moment he was tempted but then shook his head. His hands lay on her desk, the scars that creased the skin above his knuckles vivid red against the pale white, a legacy of the education his father had given him years before in Minsk. He quickly hid them behind his back.

'Inspector Allen from Intelligence gave these to me.' In her left hand, she waved her packet of purple sweets. 'Haven't had these French sweets since before the War. He's such a nice man. He left this for you.' Her right hand held a large brown internal envelope marked private and confidential.

He took it, ensuring his hands were palm upwards. Inside was a white sheet of expensive writing paper. 'Too predictable, Allen.'

He took out a large fountain pen and wrote P X QKN below Allen's last line. Folding the paper, he returned it to the internal envelope.

'Secrets and secret notes, Inspector Danilov.' She thought for a moment and then said, 'I've been meaning to ask you something for a long time.'

'Ask away, Miss Cavendish, if I am able to satisfy your curiosity, I will be happy to oblige.'

'How is it you speak such good English? For a Russian, I mean.'

'Two years at Scotland Yard, Miss Cavendish, looking for some Russian bombers. We never found them so it was a wasted time. It did give me a love for your language though. Such a less stoic tongue than my native Russian.'

'Well, you are a card, I must say. Scotland Yard, indeed. Who would have guessed?'

'Thank you, Miss Cavendish. If you see Detective Stra-chan, please tell him to meet me at the morgue.'

'Now, that's an invitation nobody could refuse.'

Danilov stood there for a moment, nodded once and left. He would never understand the English sense of humour.

CHAPTER 2

Elsie Everett strode across the classic wood-lined lobby and entered the Grand Ballroom. A resplendent peacock dominated the stage above the band, couples shuffled around the dance floor and waiters danced between the tables, carrying drinks and plates of snacks.

She couldn't see Richard. Was he late again? There was Margery Leadbitter. She would have to sit with the viper. Richard was so annoying; if it wasn't for his money, she would . . . well, she didn't know what she would do, but she would have to bring him under control quickly.

She dodged the dancing waiters and presented herself in front of Margery, leaning in to kiss her on both cheeks. She felt a slight stickiness from the woman's skin and it gave her a frisson of disgust. 'Where's Richard?'

Margery picked at something that lay on her bottom lip and examined it closely. 'I don't know. He was supposed to have been here half an hour ago. Alfred's late too.'

'Typical men. What are you drinking?'

'An Old-Fashioned. I can't face anything bubbly today.'

Elsie caught the eye of one of the waiters. 'Another Old-Fashioned, with a maraschino cherry and no lemon.' She turned back to Margery. 'How's Alfred these days?'

'I don't see much of him any more. He always seems so busy. I was surprised he wanted to come this afternoon.' She paused for a moment and then continued, 'Maybe it was because I told him you were coming.'

Elsie didn't know how to respond, so she lit a cigarette and studied the room. It seemed to be the usual crowd of wasters, good-time charlies and hangers-on. On her left, a young Chinese man with closely-cropped hair like a military helmet was surrounded by three extremely young and giggly women. In one corner, an elegant Chinese grandfather in a long Mandarin coat sat all alone drinking tea. Across the dance floor, she caught a fat, bald European staring at her, his gaze averted as she noticed him through the dancers.

Then she was seized in a big bear grip and kissed on the cheeks. He was always a little rough, like a colt who had just learned to walk, but she enjoyed the hard bristle of his moustache against her soft skin.

'Look who I met outside. He was prowling around like a cat looking for a sparrow.' Richard stepped back to reveal the long, lean silhouette of Alfred. 'Good afternoon,' he said, bowing slightly from the hips.

'Don't be so stiff, Alfred. Give her a kiss on the cheeks. You remember how we used to do it in France, don't you?' Richard rounded the table and reached over to kiss Margery. She accepted as if it were exactly what she was supposed to receive, nothing less, nothing more.

'I'm so thirsty, I could drink Lake Tai.' Richard raised his hand and instantly a waiter appeared at his elbow. 'Champagne?'

'Not for myself and Margery,' said Elsie.

'But you'll join me, won't you, Alfred? Can't drink champagne alone.'

'I'll join you too,' said Margery, looking pointedly at Elsie.

The waiter ran off to fetch the bottle. 'Sit down, Alfred. You're making my neck tired looking up to you.'

Alfred pulled out the cane chair and placed himself between Richard and Margery, opposite Elsie.

'How was this morning, Richard?' She emphasised her refined vowels, taught at considerable expense and even more pain by Madame Tollemache all those years ago. Pain that had been worth it, as she had long lost the nasal twang of the streets of Salford.

The waiter brought the champagne and poured out three glasses. 'Here's to life, liberty and the pursuit of drunkenness.' Richard drained the glass in one gulp and indicated for more to be poured.

'As I was saying, Richard, you really need to get that pony of yours into better shape. You have a real chance at the races this Easter.'

'I can't be bothered getting up early and exercising the bloody thing in the wee small hours of the morning. I'd rather wallow in my pit.'

'Well, it's your loss . . .'

'I just hate it when men ignore us, don't you, Elsie?' Margery's voice cut through the music from the band, and all the other conversations at the tables nearby.

'Well, I . . .'

'Elsie's far too polite to complain, aren't you, dear?'

'Of course she is,' said Alfred quickly, 'the manners of an angel and a voice to match. I was in the audience the other night at the theatre. You were perfect in the Novello song. What was it called?'

'"The Land of Might-Have-Been",' said Elsie, 'a lovely tune, almost as good as "I Can Give You Starlight".'

'Thank you, Alfred, we all know how you admire Elsie's . . . attributes,' said Margery, finishing her champagne.

A hush enveloped the table like a damp sea mist.

'Let's dance, shall we? I love this new one from Harry Horlick.' Richard held out his hand to Elsie.

They stepped out onto the brightly lit dance floor. A woman glided past them with a manic grin on her face, her partner a stiff, small man with the shiniest hair Elsie had ever seen. The band seemed to get louder and gayer.

'Thank God, I got you away from them. Alfred's fine, but Margery's becoming a little shrill, a shrike with claws.'

'She's fine, Richard, she means well.' Elsie had decided to play the shy innocent girl for all she was worth. It was going to be her best role.

'Just like you to say something kind about Margery, when she's been such a witch.'

'No, she hasn't.' She leant away from him, beating her little fist playfully on his jacket. He laughed, pulled her closer and together they shimmied across the dance floor.

* * *

'Good afternoon, Inspector, good to see you again, even if it is always under the most trying of circumstances that we meet.' The voice was elegantly patrician, the Received Pronunciation even more pronounced than usual.

Dr Fang was dressed in his normal working attire: bright red bow tie with a fine gold weave, a crisp, rather old-fashioned shirt with wing collars and a beautifully tailored dark-green tweed suit. On his small feet, polished brown brogues peeped out beneath the turn-ups of the tweed trousers.

Dr Fang had been educated in London, then studied under Locard in Lyon, which he never tired of telling people. He believed in Locard's principles religiously. Procedures were to be followed to the smallest detail because every contact leaves a trace, however minute. There was no room for speculation, no margin for error. It was the facts, just the facts, that were important.

'Come into my parlour.' Dr Fang opened the door to the morgue. The pungent smell of formaldehyde hit Danilov like a Shanghai tram. And, as always, he was transported back to the sweets of his youth. He never knew why the smell of formaldehyde had this effect on him, bringing back memories of running down the streets of Minsk, his shoes clattering on the cobblestones, an aunt, elegant, austere, reaching into a large jar of sweets and bringing out a soft pink bonbon that melted in his mouth, covering his teeth in sticky sugar.

But he wasn't in the Minsk of his youth now. He was in a brightly lit white-tiled room that ached of loneliness and solitude. In front of him lay six stainless steel tables, each covered with a white sheet.

Dr Fang stood next to the nearest of these tables and removed the cover revealing a white, bloodless corpse. The body had a Y-shaped incision on the chest that had been crudely sewn up with large, even stitches. The stomach and lower body was a mass of nothingness, revealing glimpses of pale meat hidden in the dark emptiness.

He heard Strachan coughing behind him.

'Is this your first post-mortem, young man?' asked Dr Fang.

'Yes, sir,' answered Strachan with a voice that was much stronger than Danilov expected.

'If you're going to be sick, please do it outside. There's a pail placed there precisely for the purpose. I will not have my clean floor covered in the acids of your stomach, is that clear?'

'I'm not going to be sick, sir.'

'I'm glad to hear it. Shall we begin?'

Danilov nodded.

'Good. I would like to thank you, Inspector Danilov. As ever you have given me a most interesting specimen to work with. Found in Soochow Creek wasn't it?'

'That's right, sir. Early this morning, floating on the "Beach of Dead Babies". It must have been washed down the creek on the ebbing tide,' said Strachan.

Dr Fang gave a loud sniff as if he had just inhaled a large dose of formaldehyde. 'Oh, I doubt that, young man, it's . . .?'

'Detective Constable Strachan, sir.'

'Well, Detective Strachan, we are here today to deal in facts, not idle suspicions, rumours, conjectures or suppositions. Is that clear?'

'As the Soochow Creek, sir.'

Dr Fang sniffed once again. 'Let us begin, with just the facts this time.'

Danilov watched as the doctor tugged at the end of his nose, letting the pause add to the drama, playing the game of silence.

'As I said before, a most interesting case. Of course, a cursory examination of the body would conclude the victim had died from a deep incision across the lower abdomen and the pubic region.' He indicated both areas with a retractable metal pointer. 'But one would be wrong to leap to such an erroneous conclusion.'

Here he stared pointedly at Strachan. 'I'm quite sure the cuts were made post-mortem. See, there is no bleeding from the wounds.' He pointed to the deepest slash across the base of the stomach.

'But wouldn't the creek have washed away the blood?' asked Strachan.

'For a layman, that would be the most obvious inference,' sniffed Dr Fang, 'but examining the capillaries under the microscope indicates no blood flowed through them when these cuts were made. Ergo, the victim,' again he pointed to the body lying naked on the slab, 'had already been dead before the wounds were made.'

'Approximately how long had the victim been dead?'

'I'm afraid it's impossible to say. Being in water makes the time of death uncertain.'

'So the victim could not have drowned?'

'It seems, Detective Strachan, you have quite a lot to learn about forensic science. The first thing you should learn is that we will complete these examinations more quickly if you keep quiet and not ask so many damn fool questions.' Dr Fang adjusted his red bow tie and sniffed once again.

Danilov held up his hand to prevent any response from Strachan. 'Please continue, Dr Fang.'

'As I was saying, the victim couldn't have drowned because there is no water in the lungs. Interestingly, this medical phenomenon was first reported by a Chinese physician. His name was Song Ci and he produced a fascinating book called *Xi Yuan Lu* or *The Washing Away of Wrongs*, in 1248, during the Song Dynasty. I'm presently preparing an English translation which I would be happy to let you read, Inspector Danilov.'

'I would be delighted, Dr Fang. But to return to our present investigation . . .'

'Of course. I'm sure that the victim was killed before entering the water. An examination of the skin shows few signs of wrinkling, it wasn't in the water for long.'

'But there is one sign that indicates this more than anything else, isn't there, Dr Fang?'

'As ever, Inspector Danilov, you have noticed that something is missing.' Again, the doctor paused for effect. 'There are no rat bites. Normally, when a body ends up in any of the creeks or rivers surrounding Shanghai, our friends, rattus rattus and rattus norvegicus, like to partake of a little spot of luncheon or supper. One can usually estimate the length of time in the water from the number of bites. Of course, this can depend on the time of year and the exact place in the river they were found, but an absence of rat bites indicates the body was not in the creek long enough for our friends to gather a party for luncheon. In fact, after a thorough examination, I only noticed one bite, here . . .' he pointed to the right side of the body closest to him '. . . and possibly one more, here on the intestines.'

'Hmm, interesting and very illuminating, Doctor,' said Danilov. 'I thank you for the depth of your investigation.'

Dr Fang beamed like a schoolboy who had just received a gold star for having spelt hypothalamus correctly. 'But, there is more, Inspector. You see the bruising around the neck, here and here . . .'

Danilov leant in to take a closer look. The dead eyes of the victim stared up at him. Cornflower-blue eyes, he noticed. Such a beautiful colour. He forced himself to look closely at the marks on the victim's neck.

'You will notice bruising on the neck. I would say with certainty this victim died from strangulation.'

'The bruising seems to go all the way round.'

The doctor nodded.

'So it wasn't manual strangulation?' Inspector Danilov demonstrated by holding his hands out in front of him, grasping an imaginary neck.

'I would say not. More likely to be mechanical or ligature strangulation, but using something soft, not hard or abrasive. There is incomplete occlusion of the carotid arteries and the skin is not broken.'

'A garrotte then.'

'I couldn't say, Inspector. All I can say with certainty is the victim wasn't strangled with the hands. There are no finger or thumb impressions or bruising.'

'Thank you, Doctor. The facts are just what we need.'

Dr Fang sniffed again. 'There are four other facts that may interest you, Inspector.'

'Please continue, my ears are on the top of my head, as we say in Russia.'

'That would be interesting anatomically, Inspector, but a little painful when it rains.'

Strachan laughed and received a warning glance from Danilov.

'As I was saying, four facts. Firstly, here, on the inside of the wrist, the faint mark of a tattoo. Somebody has tried to remove this, but the words are still clear.'

Danilov leant forward once more and inspected the inside of the wrist. He reached into his pocket and produced a pair of wire-framed glasses. 'Suffer the little children to come unto me,' he said out loud.

'Luke, chapter 18, verse 16,' said Strachan, looking pleased with himself.

'I'm sorry, Stra-chan?'

'Luke, chapter 18, verse 16: "But Jesus called them unto him, and said, suffer the little children to come unto me, and forbid them not: for of such is the kingdom of God." Sunday school years ago, sir. Comes in handy once in a while, all those years on my knees, learning the bible. But I think everybody knows these particular verses.'

'I suppose they do, Detective. But why would our victim have a tattoo like that? Not so common is it?'

'Not common at all, sir. Usually, it's a tiger. Or a heart with Mother written in the middle.' Strachan seemed to think a little more. 'Or even a naked lady. One time . . .'

'Yes, yes, Detective, we don't have time to hear about your experiences with naked ladies. I have two more bodies I have to examine before supper.'

'Please continue, Dr Fang, we wouldn't want to keep you from your bodies. Or your supper. It seems you have three more pieces of information to give us?'

'Thank you, Inspector. The second is that the victim's hair was dyed.' He pointed to the long locks of blonde hair, now dry, that flowed from the head of the body. 'Recently dyed, I would say. No traces of new growth coming through at all. The third is the characters carved into the chest with a knife or similar instrument. The characters are those for "justice". Neatly cut, almost like a stencil. I will try to ascertain what type of knife made the strokes of the characters when I have time.'

'And the final piece of information?'

Now a smug smile passed across the lips of Dr Fang. 'This is probably the most interesting thing I discovered in my examination of the body. Most interesting indeed.'

'And what is that, Doctor?'

'Well . . .' Dr Fang dragged out the revelation, playing the moment for all it was worth, 'our victim was a man, not a woman.'

'But the hair? The breasts? The make-up?' said Strachan.

'Yes, detective, all there. But this is, without doubt, a man.'

'How can you be sure?'

Dr Fang sniffed as if the imparting of secrets of his profession was beneath him. 'There are noticeable physical differences between the male and female bodies. The most obvious, the genitalia, are how most laymen distinguish between the sexes.' Here, he stared at Strachan. 'But there are other indicators. The first is bone size. Males tend to have larger bones then women. Next, I would look at the pelvic region, here . . .' he pointed to the area around the body's missing stomach, '. . . but with this particular corpse, that area has been devastated by the murderer.'

Strachan leant over to look closely. Dr Fang sniffed once more and pointed to the skull. 'Then, I would look here. In males, the chin tends to be squarer. Females tend to have a more pointed chin. If you look closely, our corpse has a quite pronounced square chin. The last giveaway is the supraorbital ridge . . .'

'The what?' said Strachan.

'The brow, for our young Detective Constable. In males, it tends to be much more prominent. Finally, if all else fails, I check the fingers. On women, the index finger is longer than the third finger. The reverse is true of men.'

Danilov couldn't stop himself from checking the hands of the victim.

'This, taking everything into consideration, gentlemen, is most definitely a man.' Dr Fang folded his arms across his chest, daring Strachan to question him any further.

'Now that is interesting,' said Danilov.

***

Elsie glanced at her Vacheron Constantin watch, a present from Richard. 'I've got to be off now, back for the evening show.' She took one last swallow of her Old-Fashioned, draining her glass.

'Such a bore,' said Margery.

'Terrible isn't it? But a girl's gotta do what a girl's gotta do.'

'Can I give you a lift?' said Richard.

'Don't worry, you stay here and . . .' she looked straight at Margery, '. . . enjoy yourself with your friends. I'll see you this evening at Ciro's. Shall we say 11 p.m.? Don't be late, it's no fun sitting there all alone.'

'I'll pick you up from the theatre if you want.'

'Don't bother. Trevelyan gets awfully jealous when he sees any of his girls with somebody else. You know how old theatrical poofs get, more possessive and catty as they age. That one has the claws of a female tiger with cubs to protect.' She looked at her watch again.

With a blown kiss to Richard thrown over her shoulder, she dodged the white-jacketed waiters and ran out of the ballroom. With luck, there would be a taxi waiting, hang the expense. Anything was better than another dressing down from Trevelyan.

She stepped out of the hotel, and immediately a taxi started its engine and pulled up in front of her. Maybe my luck has finally changed, she thought.

Elsie Everett didn't notice that a man had followed her out of the hotel.

She didn't notice that he nodded to the driver of the taxi as it picked her up.

She didn't notice that there was no meter in the taxi.

***

He watched her leave, stepping past all the waiters and the scum who frequented these cesspits. How the smell of them disgusted him. The sharp odours of stale perfume sprayed on liberally to smother the even sharper stench of sweat. The powder spotting the women's faces, clumping in small white boils as they pranced to the beat of the band. And the raucous laughs, hollow red-framed mouths showing nicotine-stained teeth. All laughing too hard, too long and too falsely.

He saw all the dancers and their escorts, the waiters and waitresses, the musicians and their shiny dinner jackets, and he knew they couldn't see him. Couldn't see him for what he was. He blended in so well, like a chameleon in human form, he was changed by wherever he was, melting into the background, hiding in plain sight.

If you never want to be noticed, just be bland, be ordinary. It was the same at the Front, just wear khaki like all the others and nobody could ever see the real you. Just another soldier they would say. Never noticed his face they would say. Well, you don't, do you? Just notice the rank not the man, they would say.

Here, in Shanghai, he needed to cleanse the city of its degenerates, to remove the bloated maggots that fed on its flesh. He had made a start in other places, of course, but somehow, it never felt right. Meaningless deaths to salve an itch. There was no pleasure in it. But here, he had found his reason to exist. Perhaps the city had fed it, like a mould growing on a petri dish, concentrating the need like never before. And, strangely, Shanghai had made it so much easier to act. Here, everything was allowed, nothing forbidden, not even him.

He took out another cigarette and lit it with his gold Dunhill lighter. Time to play with her now. She deserved not to be kept waiting.

***

'Are you both leaving? Just as I was beginning to enjoy myself. The dance doesn't end for at least another half an hour.'

'I need to check in at the office,' said Richard. 'You know how I'm expected to show my face every day. Ah Ching will have already finished everything, of course.'

'And I'm feeling incredibly dirty, like I've been swimming in Soochow Creek. Horrible feeling,' said Alfred.

She pouted, placing another cigarette in the ivory holder, leaning forward for Alfred to light it. 'I'm not happy, but you can both make it up to me tonight at Ciro's. It's going to cost you a bottle of Belle Epoque and Lobster Thermidor.'

'Can I at least give you a lift back to your place?'

'No, thank you, Richard. If you two are both leaving me, I think I'll do a little window shopping. Dimitri has some new Art Deco pieces in from Paris. There's this wonderful titanium bracelet that shouts my name every time I see it.'

'I'll get this.' Richard took the silver plate off the table and checked the bill: $13.50. He quickly signed the chit, adding a dollar from his pocket as a tip.

All three got up and ambled towards the door. The waiters still danced frenetically around the tables. A black trumpeter, having received a smattering of applause for his solo, sat back down on his seat as the rest of the orchestra took up the melody. There were fewer dancers now but the short, shiny-haired man and his tall, grinning partner still beat their merry path round the outside of the dance floor, magically avoiding all the other dancers.

Before they had even reached the door, the waiters had removed the glasses, plates, tablecloth and half-drunk bottle of champagne, replacing them with a fresh supply of tableware from behind the counter.

The money had gone too. It had been removed first, of course.

CHAPTER 3

Danilov stared out over the creek and onto the now empty 'Beach of Dead Babies'. The sun was just going down over the post office on the other bank, casting an orange haze over the river.

'I always like to come back to the scene of the crime afterwards, Stra-chan. It lets me see it as the murderer knew it, without the crowds and the rest of the watchers.'

Life in the creek carried on as usual, despite the excitement of that morning. The sampans wobbled in their ungainly way up to the Whampoo or down into the interior. The wharves bustled with sweat and energy as cargo was unloaded from the lighters that served the ships in the harbour. The young boy still sat on the prow of the boat, playing with his dog, the tether attached to his foot.

The waves continued to lap the shores of the 'Beach of Dead Babies', where just eight hours before a body had lain with its belly slit open.

The hawker, with his fragrant pot of sweet potatoes, had vanished though, gone to ply his trade somewhere else.

'It's quiet, sir.'

'It is if you ignore all the bustle and noise of the river.'

'I meant compared to this morning.'

'That's the point, Stra-chan.' He rolled a cigarette with tobacco from his tin. 'I can see it as it was when the

M J Lee

murder was committed.' He brought the cigarette up to his mouth and took a long drag, coughing as he exhaled, clearing his lungs. 'But, of course, this wasn't the primary murder scene. The body was carried here.'

Strachan stared out into the river. A sampan swam past the 'Beach of Dead Babies', almost touching the edge of the sandbank.

'See the sampan, how close it gets to the area where the body was found?'

'Yes, sir.'

'Our victim didn't just float there. It was carried out to the "Beach of Dead Babies". Somebody must have seen it being taken there.'

'I asked the local river people. Of course, nobody saw anything. But I've put the word out. Perhaps somebody will come forward.'

'Remember there were no rat bites. It means the body hadn't been in the creek for long. Thirty minutes at the most. Ask people if they heard or saw anything from 5.30 a.m. to 6 a.m.'

'I'll get the local sergeant on it, sir.'

'Make sure people know there is a reward for information. Five dollars should be enough.'

'More than enough, sir.' A lighter chugged past, its thin funnel sending out acres of grey smoke that stank of half-burned coal. Strachan flipped open his notebook, checking what he had written earlier that morning. 'The victim's body was weighted down with stones and placed on the sandbank.'

'Interesting, you say "placed", Stra-chan, because it *was* "placed". We were meant to find it. The creek is one of the most open places in Shanghai, with constant river traffic. The body was bound to be found. In both senses of the word. The killer weighted it with stones so we would find it there. He didn't want it to be washed down into the Whampoo. Why did he do that? What's he trying to tell us?' He exhaled a long stream of cigarette smoke and coughed again. A glob of spit formed in his mouth.

'I don't know, sir.'

'But that's what we have to find out, Stra-chan. That's what they pay us to find out.'

'I thought they pay us to find the killer, sir.'

'We won't be able to do that until we know why he does what he does, Stra-chan.' He rolled another cigarette with tobacco from his tin. 'I wonder why it's called the "Beach of Dead Babies".'

'I asked the locals, sir. They told me it's because of the local currents. All the unwanted babies placed in the river inevitably end up there.'

'Like Moses.'

'Exactly, sir. The river people adopt the male children as their own.'

'And the girls?'

'Apparently, they get taken to the orphanage, sir. Girls are just extra mouths to feed.'

'Thank you for that, Stra-chan. Remind me never to introduce you to my daughter.' As soon as the words were out of his mouth, Danilov knew he had made a mistake. He looked away, pretending to examine the wharves behind them. It was nearly four years since he had last seen her. Four years on April 26th. Strachan was still staring at the 'Beach of Dead Babies'. Perhaps, he hadn't noticed? Time to get him working. 'The doctor said our victim was a male with a female appearance.'

'I believe there are a few clubs catering for those sorts of tastes, sir. I could check them out. Show a few photographs around once they come back from processing.'

'That's a start. Check the registry of doctors. This man was already showing female characteristics, maybe he was already seeing a physician. Did you notice the absence of body hair?'

'Could have been shaving, sir.'

'Hair continues to grow after death. Yet there was none.'

'I'll get onto it when we go back to the station. I was also thinking about the Chinese characters carved into the chest.'

'And?'

'I suppose it means we are looking for a Chinese killer, sir.'

'You suppose wrong, Stra-chan. Anybody can write or copy a character, even you.'

'I suppose so.'

'Let me do the supposing, Stra-chan, you just concentrate on the facts.'

'Yes, sir.'

'Next steps are: you will follow up on the doctors and the boatmen. I would like your report on my desk by tomorrow morning.'

'I'll do it before I leave this evening, sir.'

'Good, then you can accompany me to meet our Frenchman tomorrow morning.'

'As long as we don't have frog's legs for breakfast, sir.'

'Most certainly not, Stra-chan. It will be a strong coffee and a croissant in the French Concession. Frog's legs would only be served for luncheon or dinner.'

'It was a joke, sir.'

'I see you have an English sense of humour.'

'I picked it up at school, sir.'

'Well, put it down when you are with me, Stra-chan, is that clear?'

Strachan looked out over the river. For the second time that day, he gave the same response. 'As the Soochow Creek, sir.'

***

Her head ached. She shook it to try to clear the fuzziness.

Where was she? Another night drinking too much? She tried to remember what happened but nothing would come. She had got into a taxi but then . . .?

She tried to lift her arm to brush away the hair from her eyes, but it wouldn't move. She tried again. It was like both her arms were gripped around the wrists by coarse, hairy fingers.

She shook her head once more and looked down. Both her arms were strapped to a wooden chair with lengths of thin rope. Twisting left and right, she leveraged her body against the back of the chair and twisted her arms. The ropes cut into her wrists, drops of fresh blood flowed down her hands and onto her leg.

Tears ran down face. Her head lolled forwards. Memories flashed into her head. Leaving the Astor, Getting into a cab. A bald head. Driving around Shanghai. Stopping. Bitten fingers. A red livid scar across the top of his head. Reaching for her. A cloth over her mouth. Darkness.

How did I get here? Why me? A great wracking sob seized hold of her chest. Her head lolled forward again, the tears dripping down onto her dress where their warmth and wetness seeped into the fabric.

She tried to rock the chair backwards and forwards, but it wouldn't move. It was made from solid, thick wood, bolted to the floor. Like an electric chair without the current, she thought bitterly.

She lifted her head and peered into the gloom that surrounded her. Not much to see, just a drab brownness that seemed to be walls. From them, a dark, dank smell like the earth of a graveyard suffused with the stench of fish, drifted towards her.

She felt the wood of the chair arm beneath her fingers. There were marks there. Something hard buried in the wood. She picked at it, digging it out. There was a crescent moon of opaque whiteness on the tips of her fingers. What was it? She felt its sharp edges and realised straight away.

A fingernail.

She screamed and struggled against the ropes. Got to get free. Got to get out of here. The ropes clung to her wrists, tightening their grip.

Who'd taken her? Why was she a prisoner? She hadn't done anything wrong in Shanghai. What were they going to do with her? Another sob wracked her chest and more tears flowed down her cheeks.

A shroud of self-pity enveloped her. All she wanted was her turn in the limelight. She shouldn't have been here at all. Diane had been chosen for the part. But she had an accident on the Underground. Elsie had tried to save her but . . . it was too late. Everybody creates their own luck, don't they? It just wasn't Diane's day or her part. She deserved what happened. And Elsie deserved her chance as an actress. One of them had to be disappointed. It just wasn't going to be her.

She struggled again against the ropes. They seemed to become tighter. She stopped, exhausted.

Her head sank onto her chest. I wonder if they are white slavers? Like those people she'd read about in the Sunday papers. One of them had seen her on the stage and kidnapped her to sell into slavery as the mistress of a Chinese warlord. Or maybe the moll of a famous gangster? But why tie her up here? In the newspaper reports, the star had been kidnapped, imprisoned in the lap of luxury, waited on hand and foot by a charming manservant. But she was tied to an old chair in a dark, dank place which stank of rancid fish and putrid earth.

She twisted her head to one side. For some reason, she sensed a presence. 'Who's there?' The words harsh against the darkness.

Nobody answered, but she knew somebody was there. Over to her left, in the midst of the blackness, there was something even darker. She stayed very still and controlled her breathing, taking a quick intake of air and holding it, listening for any noise.

Silence.

But there it was, on the left, the soft whisper of someone else breathing. Deep, controlled breathing.

She fought against the ropes. Once again, they seemed to get tighter the more she struggled to wrench herself free. 'Who's there? I know somebody is there.'

Still no answer.

Above her head, a single bulb hung from a black flex in the ceiling. The light didn't penetrate to the gloom that enveloped the rest of the room. She realised the only thing it illuminated was her. Finally, my own spotlight, she thought bitterly.

She stopped struggling and listened again. She was sure she heard soft breathing from the depths of the darkness. 'I know you're out there,' she shouted, using her theatrical voice to project more confidence than she actually felt.

There was movement. A chair being scraped back, someone standing. Then she caught the memory of a smell. The sweet, delicate aroma of a scent. Where had she smelt that before?

Footsteps coming towards her. No, the echoes of the room were playing with her hearing. They were moving off to her right. The creak of an old door opening, no light coming through the entrance though. The click of a switch. She was in darkness. Alone in the darkness.

She screamed and screamed and screamed, but nobody came.

CHAPTER 4

'Hello, George, what's your poison?'

'A large Scotch with a drop of the wet stuff. I hope you're buying, Charlie?'

'Wouldn't want you to reach into your pocket, George, don't know what you'd find there.'

'A lovely little bit of stuff from Kiev, last time I looked.'

Meaker waved at the barman standing in the corner, staring into space. Reluctantly, he stirred himself and strolled over to them. It was like a thousand other joints in Shanghai: a long mahogany bar, a stack of bottles behind the counter, many covered in dust, sawdust on the floor and a gaggle of bored girls in the corner.

The barman poured their drinks from a bottle of Johnnie Walker, leaving a jug of water with a brightly painted piper and the legend 'Bonnie Scotland' next to their glasses.

'I hope it's real,' said George Cartwright, smelling his whisky.

'Nothing's real in Shanghai, you know that.'

'Well anyway, down the hatch. If it doesn't touch the sides, it can't hurt.'

They both finished their drinks in one long swallow. The waiter ambled over again to refill the glasses. 'I wouldn't go too far, pal, it looks like George has got a thirst on.'

'I've always got a thirst on. Runs in the family. A thirsty throat, that's what all the Cartwrights have, according to my dad.'

'Bottle, him seven dollar,' said the barman.

'Leave it. Saves you troubling your legs.' Meaker reached over and snatched it from the barman, pouring another large double for himself.

'So what's this about, Charlie? I'm sure you haven't asked me here just to drink your whisky and dazzle you with my sparkling repartee.'

'Sparkling repartee is not your strength, George.' He poured him another whisky.

Cartwright picked it up and drained the glass. He wiped his mouth. 'So?'

'How's home life?'

Cartwright smiled ruefully. 'As good as it gets. The wife refuses to speak to me. The servant has run off. And the kids, well, they think I'm just a piece of shit on the end of a stick. Other than that, everything's hunky-dory. Why are you asking?'

'Like to make a few bob on the side?'

'Now you're talking, Charlie.'

Meaker took a sip of his whisky. Cartwright filled his glass from the bottle, adding just a splash of water for the health of it.

'I'll put my cards on't table, George. Hongkew's a dead end. I've been stuck there for six months . . .'

'You went there after working with Danilov, didn't you?'

'Sent there, not went there. Boyle thought it would be better if I "spent some time in a smaller station". Silly old fart.'

'Danilov dobbed you in, didn't he?'

'Strung up like a kipper, I was. Fuckin' Russian. Always has his tongue up Boyle's arse, cleaning his teeth from the inside.'

'You know how I feel, Charlie. Can't stand the little fucker, with his smug smile and neat desk.' He took another long swallow of whisky and wiped his mouth. 'I screw with his desk every day. Just to annoy the little fucker.'

'Anyway, I'm looking to come back to Central but . . .'

'Danilov's in the way. What do you want me to do?'

'Nothing. Yet.' Meaker took a sip of his whisky. 'Just let me know what he's up to. He's got that creek body to handle at the moment.'

'And Miss Cavendish tells me Boyle has him working with the French.'

'Rather him than me. If there's one lot I can't stand more than the Russians, it's the French. Wanted nowt to do with 'em when I was in the trenches, unless they were female and horizontal.'

'What's in it for me, Charlie?'

'A few bob on the side. Plus a nice cushy number when I come back to Central. I'll look after you.'

'Sounds good.' Cartwright downed another glass of whisky in one long swallow. Meaker took a sip of his.

'Well, are we kicking on? The Handle Bar is just getting going. Got a new load of Russians in from Siberia. Fresh meat for the grinder.' He thrust his hips forward.

'You go on, George. The missus will kill me if I'm out late again.'

***

'Richard, you've finally made it. I've been sitting here like a lonely jam tart at the Mad Hatter's tea party waiting for Alfred. What's happened to the man?'

'I'm supposed to know? You're the one engaged to him.'

'Engaged to nothing. You know that was just for his family and mine. Kept them both off our backs.'

The band finished their number and there was a smattering of applause from the dancers. Like a flock of errant sheep, they returned to their seats surrounding the wooden floor. Ciro's was the most elegant place in town. No luxury had been spared no matter how frivolous: Italian marble, French glassware, an American band, the latest dancers from across the world. All because its owner, the richest man in Shanghai, David Sassoon, had once been refused entry at another club.

Sassoon was now sitting in his usual place, to the left of the band, at the front of the dance floor, surrounded by his latest harem of young women. Richard smiled and waved. Sassoon waved back but quickly returned to his girls.

'Sassoon's here with his FOBs.'

'I do wish you wouldn't use that term, Richard. I was "Fresh Off the Boat" once. Anyway, he can do what he wants. He owns the bloody place.' She glanced across at Sassoon, hoping he wouldn't notice she was looking. 'The FOBs are getting younger. Either that or I'm getting older.'

'Still as fresh as a cherry blossom to me, Margery.'

She leant over and kissed him on the cheek. 'Always the charmer, Richard. What would I do without you?'

'Probably every man in Ciro's, knowing your appetites. Somebody has to keep you in check.'

'Somebody has to keep me in alcohol.'

Richard took the hint. 'Champagne?'

'The Belle Epoque. It feels like a *fin de siècle* sort of evening.'

He raised his arm and was immediately served by two waiters. 'A bottle of the Belle Epoque.'

'Certainly, Mr Ayres.'

'Here's Alfred now. God, he's bumped into that awful man, Doyle. I do hope there isn't a scene.'

Richard turned and craned his neck towards the door. He could see Alfred apologising profusely to a one-armed man, brushing the man's jacket with his handkerchief. Doyle did not look too pleased, and kept waving Alfred away with his one arm, finally turning on his heels.

Alfred stood there a moment before carefully wending his way through the tables. 'I just met the most awful man.'

'Don't you know who he was?'

'Am I supposed to?'

'That's one-armed Doyle. He's American, bodyguard for one of the warlords. General Sung, I think. He's supposed to be a killer.' Margery took a drag at the cigarette in her ivory holder. 'I hope you apologised profusely.'

Alfred went a strange shade of pale.

'Sit down. Here comes the wine.'

Alfred coughed once and pulled out a chair. 'Where's Elsie?'

'I don't know.' Richard glanced at his watch. 'She should have been here half an hour ago. I thought I was going to get the cold shoulder for being late again.'

The waiter returned with the glasses and a wine cooler filled with ice. He opened the champagne with a satisfying pop and filled three glasses to the brim. Richard lifted his and said, 'Let's drink to my good news.'

'Good news?'

'I'm going to be married.'

All the glasses froze in mid-air, except Richard's. He drank his champagne in one long swallow, and reached for the bottle to pour himself another glass.

Margery was the first to react. 'Married? To whom?'

'Elsie, of course. She doesn't know yet so keep it a secret. I'm going to ask her tonight. The band is primed to play our favourite song.'

'It's a bit sudden, isn't it? You've only known her for a few months. And Susan only passed away last year,' said Alfred.

Margery's glass slammed on the table. 'Don't be a bloody fool, Richard. You know nothing about her.'

'I know I love her. That's enough for me.'

'But she's an actress '

'Yes, and a bloody good one, too, so you keep telling me, Alfred. But let's not talk about it now. It's a done deal, I've made my mind up. *Rien ne va plus.*' He took the bottle from the ice bucket and poured the champagne, filling his glass right up to the rim.

They danced a little. Drank another bottle of Belle Epoque. Argued about Elsie again. Danced some more. And had yet another bottle of Belle Epoque. The dance floor was becoming a little less crowded, the band a little more subdued. All three of them had gradually slipped into a lassitude that comes from too much to drink and too little to say.

It was Alfred who broke the ice. 'She's not coming.'

'Perhaps she heard you were going to ask her to get married,' said Margery.

'You're drunk, Margery. Go home.'

'No, Alfred, I'm not drunk. Just getting started actually.'

'She's probably just a little tired. Gone straight home I expect. I'll go to see her tomorrow morning,' said Richard swallowing the last of his champagne.

'I thought you were off to Nanking tomorrow?'

'I'll put it off. Father will be angry but I can handle him.'

'Do you want me to go to the theatre tomorrow?'

'Alfred, always keen to see little Elsie, aren't you?'

'Margery, you're drunk.'

'But tomorrow I'll be sober and you'll still be trailing after Elsie like a lovelorn lamb.'

'Margery, that's enough.' Richard's voice was sharp and cutting.

Margery raised her glass. 'Let's have another bottle of bubbly for the road. Just one more won't hurt. To celebrate Richard not getting engaged tonight.' Margery drained it and fell forward onto the table, her hair resting on the remains of a plate of Lobster Thermidor.

'I think it's your turn to take her home,' said Alfred.

'I'll do it. Don't worry about the theatre tomorrow, I'll go. She's my fiancée, after all.'

'Not yet she isn't,' said Alfred.

Richard stared at him through the blur of champagne. He couldn't quite work out what he meant.

* * *

Strachan found the Registry of Doctors filed behind the desk of Miss Cavendish. It was dated 1927 – he would have to ask her if there was a more recent copy. He knew she would be annoyed with him for taking it, but he didn't care. It was more important to give Danilov his report tomorrow morning, rather than later in the day. He would soften her up with a box of chocolates from Loewenstein's. He knew she had a particular weakness for nougatine.

He took the registry back to his desk and switched on the light.

'Working late, Strachan?' asked one of the night shift officers. He didn't know his name.

'Need to get this finished for Danilov by tomorrow. The Soochow Creek murder.'

'You're working for him? Poor bugger. Daft as a brush that one is. And Russian. Can't trust 'em. You should try to get into Charlie Meaker's team in Hongkew. Cushy number that is. Charlie knows how to play the game.'

'I'll remember. Thanks for the tip.'

'And you might try Serendipity at Easter.'

'I'm sorry?'

'Another tip.'

Strachan frowned, still confused.

'The Easter races. I'd put a few dollars on if I were you.'

'Thanks again. I'll remember.' He opened the registry hoping the detective would take the hint.

'You'll be working all hours with Danilov. Never lets a body have a moment's peace that one.' The detective walked away to get himself a cup of coffee from the canteen.

Strachan opened the registry, scanning the specialisations of all the listed doctors. These were just the ones trained in Western medicine, there was no registry of traditional Chinese medicine. If there were, it would be a book of more than 1,000 pages. He would have to concentrate on the Western doctors.

Danilov was a queer fish, the others were right. Such a prim and proper man, different from the other White Russians he had met. But as they were all madams, ex-Tsarist soldiers, conmen or call-girls, he knew his knowledge of them was limited. But did Danilov have to be as frosty as an arctic winter?

He wasn't used to such treatment. Of course, a few of the English had been difficult at first, looking down at him because he had a Chinese mother, but they usually came round when they found out his father had been a copper.

He never talked about him to any of them, but he knew the story was well known in the station. His father had been called to a robbery in the middle of his beat. Three hoodlums raiding a jewellery shop just off Haig Road. Before he had even taken his pistol from its holster, he was dead, shot through the heart.

That day always stayed in his memory. He was just seven years old. Strange people filled all the rooms of the house on Amoy Street. His mother was wailing in the bedroom. He tried to comfort her, to stop her crying, but he couldn't. He didn't even find out why she was crying until later.

He still missed his father. It was like an ache that was always going to be there, deep within him, missing the warmth of his body when he came home in the evening. Always missing that warmth.

He'd joined the police as soon as he was old enough, passing through the training course with flying colours. His mother was disappointed, she wanted him to go to University and become an architect but he knew this was what he wanted to do. It had been difficult at first. The English police had been wary of him whilst the Chinese just shunned him. But he had soon won the English over, drinking, fighting and taking down the bad guys as well as any of them. The Chinese were harder but their love of food helped. None of them could resist his mother's soup.

The detective came back from the canteen carrying two steaming mugs of coffee. 'You're gonna need one of these if you're working with Danilov. Never stops, that one.' He placed a mug down in front of Strachan.

'I know what you mean. Look at this.' He pointed to the directory. 'He wants a report on his desk tomorrow morning.'

'Rather you than me.' He went back to his desk, sat down and opened his newspaper to the sports pages.

Strachan began to scan the registry, turning the pages quickly as he read the doctors' names and their particular fields. One entry caught his eye. Dr Teuscher, specialising in the psychiatry of sexual disorders. He wrote the address and the details down in his notebook.

But what to do about the traditional Chinese doctors? Perhaps he could ask Uncle Chang?

His uncle was the only member of his mother's family who had kept in touch with her after the marriage to his father. The rest of the family had treated her as if she didn't exist. She was no longer invited to family gatherings for grandfather's birthday or Chinese New Year. No longer welcome in the family home in Wuxi with its single peach tree in the courtyard. No longer a member of the family.

She would be waiting for him to come home now. Every night, when he returned, she would get up and bring him his bowl of soup, sitting by his side as he ate it. There were no servants, there hadn't been for a long time. He had often asked her to get a maid from the country to help with the washing and cooking, but she had refused. It seemed her penance for marrying his father was to spend the rest of her life cooking, cleaning and caring for his son.

He returned to the registry of doctors. Another entry caught his eye. Dr Ian Halliwell, an American, newly arrived from New York, and specialising in genito-urinary infections. Well, he would certainly be kept busy in Shanghai. He added the doctor to his notebook.

He took a sip of the coffee, but it was already cold. What time was it? He glanced up at the clock on the wall: 10.15. Just a few more pages to go.

On the second to last page, he found another entry that was in the right area. Dr Lamarr, sexual dysfunction with particular reference to androgyne conditions. He wrote down the address. The clinic was not far from where the body was found, on Canton Road.

Interesting. He wondered if there were a connection.

He heard the clock chime eleven as he finished the last page of the registry. Enough for tonight. Time to go home, drink my soup and tell Mother about the day. He would miss out some of the details though. He didn't think his mother would enjoy the story of a body almost severed in two, belonging to a man pretending to be a woman.

* * *

Danilov opened the door of his apartment in Medhurst Gardens. It was small with one bedroom, an attached living room and bathroom, and servant quarters. There were no servants though. He didn't need looking after.

He switched on the light. The bright whiteness of the walls always stunned him. He walked in, took off his hat and coat and hung them behind the door. The living room was bare. There was an old leather sofa which he occasionally sat in to read, facing an even older fire that was never lit, even in the depths of winter. If it was cold, he just kept his hat and coat on in the flat. Above the fire was his sole possession, a clock. He had bought it with his first salary from the police. The ticking was a constant reminder that life without his family was continuing. The only other furniture was a small table with a telephone, installed by the police commissioner to ensure he was always available. In the two years he had lived here, it had rung just once.

He didn't like the flat. In fact, he hated it. But he stayed because he wasn't there often, only returning to sleep each evening, like a bear returning to its cave. In this case, an empty, white cave.

He walked into the bedroom. The single bed was neatly made from this morning. Beside it was an old, rickety table with a light and a chess set. He switched on the light and removed a white pawn from the board. 'You are going to be in trouble, Mr Allen,' he said out loud to the white walls.

He had first met Allen at the promotion board two years ago. They had discovered a mutual love for chess and had been playing by correspondence ever since. He knew Allen was in Intelligence, anybody connected with Special Branch had to be, but that was none of his concern. All he cared about was Allen's next move. Checkmate was just four moves away unless he was very careful.

He took off his brown jumper, folding it carefully on the rattan chair at the end of the bed. He sat down and removed his shoes. He fingers were slightly stiff, his left shoulder aching. He no longer had the energy or the *joie de vivre* of his youth. Where had all the years gone? He wondered.

He opened the door of the bedside table and took out a tray. On it was an opium pipe made from bamboo with an ivory bowl, a spirit lamp, silver lighter, small ebony box and a silver pin, all placed neatly in their usual positions.

He took the lighter and lit the spirit lamp on the tray. The flame spluttered briefly before glowing brightly, throwing a shadow on the wall of the bedroom. He picked up the pin and rolled the pea-sized ball of opium in the flame, heating it all over. He watched the shadow changing shape on the wall as the opium ball reacted with the flame.

The first breath of the opium filled his lungs. Immediately, a soft wave of ease, like being caressed by an eel, flowed across his body. He exhaled, smelling the sweet, ashy fragrance of the opium freshen the stale room.

Another mouthful of smoke, seeing the little ball of opium flare briefly before going out and returning to black ash. The smoke again filled his lungs and a renewed sense of ease filled his body. Less intense this time, but still there, still flowing into every cell and dancing around, relaxing every fibre of his being.

He placed the pipe next to the chess set and lay back on the bed. Images of his wife and children flashed through his mind.

A white dress, cinched at the waist, sun setting behind his wife's shoulder, silhouetting her hair.

A dance, music playing, her body held at arm's length, her head back, laughing.

A child sitting on a table in the kitchen, jumping down and running to greet him, nothing but joy on her face.

Waving goodbye at the station, her tears, his children shouting, him leaving to go to Moscow.

How he missed them. Their hugs, their joy, their love. Would he ever see them again?

The fleeting images softened. Filtered light through the leaves of birch and needles of pine. He was at home again, running through the forest, discovering a natural pool, diving deep within in it, feeling the chilling warmth of the water. Then the wriggling energy of his son beside him, just learning how to swim and moving with all the grace of a hippopotamus. His beaming smile wondrous at defying the attempts of the water to keep him in its embraces. Afterwards, teeth chattering like the heels of a Spanish dancer, they smelt the sweet aroma of hot chocolate beside a pine-scented fire, and devoured the warm soup of piroshki.

Home.
Softness.
Sleep.
No more worries.
No more nightmares.
Not tonight.

***

In the dark basement of a building not far from the life and bustle of the Bund, Elsie Everett screamed her lungs out for most of the night.

Nobody heard her.

February 23rd 1928.
The 32nd day of the Year of the Earth Dragon.

CHAPTER 5

Inspector Danilov and Detective Constable Strachan stopped in front of the ornate stone building on Avenue Stanislaus Chevalier. They could have been in front of any building in any department of France. Two Doric columns soared to a heavy tiled roof, punctured by three mansard windows. Two sitting lions guarded each side of the elegant entrance. The whole place had the aroma of suburban France; cooking chicken, red wine, rosemary and garlic.

It was only the presence of Annamese constables, flowing in and out of the tall oak doors, that destroyed the image of rural France.

They walked up the granite steps and approached a gendarme sitting behind a bleached walnut desk. 'We have an appointment with Major Renard,' said Danilov.

'And who shall I say is calling?' replied the gendarme in fluent, if accented, English.

'Inspector Danilov of the Shanghai Municipal Police and Detective Constable Stra-chan.'

Strachan winced visibly as he heard his name pronounced by Danilov.

'Certainly, Inspector, this *fonctionnaire* will take you to the office. Please follow him.'

The *fonctionnaire* was Annamese, dressed in an eighteenth-century costume of brightly coloured satin waistcoat and trousers, accessorised with a white powdered wig. Following closely behind him, they walked up sweeping marble stairs. On either side, pastoral scenes of an idyllic France, with pretty shepherdesses guarding placid sheep, decorated the walls. They passed under a low arch etched with LIBERTÉ, EGALITÉ, FRATERNITÉ in strident gold letters. A long corridor stretched before them.

'A bit different from our HQ,' whispered Strachan.

'The French always have a hint of the baroque in their public buildings. It's meant to intimidate the masses,' said Danilov.

'It's certainly working.'

They passed heavy wooden doors on either side of the corridor. All of them were closed with no sounds coming from within. The silence of the building was interrupted by the echoes of their boots on the marble floor and the soft shuffle of the slippers of the *fonctionnaire*, a slipping, sliding sound that slithered off the walls.

Danilov tried to make less noise as he walked, but he couldn't. The nails embedded in the heels of his boots clattered against the floor with every step.

Eventually, they reached the end of the corridor. The *fonctionnaire* knocked softly on a double door that stretched all the way to the ceiling.

'*Entrez.*'

The *fonctionnaire* opened one side and stepped back, allowing them to enter first.

In front of them, two immense sash windows filled the room with light. Behind an ornate desk sat a young Frenchman in what appeared to be a military uniform. He got up, walked around his desk and approached them with his hand stretched out.

'Inspector Danilov, I presume?'

'It's good to meet you, Major Renard.'

The officer laughed. 'I'm not Major Renard, I'm his assistant, Lieutenant Masset.' They shook hands and he indicated a pair of chairs, placed against the wall. 'Major Renard will see you in a moment, Inspector. He's a very busy man. Can I get you some coffee?'

'Thank you but no. We've drunk enough coffee to float the Ile de France this morning.' Danilov took his seat against the wall and proceeded to roll himself a cigarette. The Lieutenant returned to his chair behind the desk and continued with his paperwork. Behind him, a large ormolu clock, with two naked cherubs holding up the face, ticked loudly.

As he rolled his cigarette, Danilov looked around the room. The furnishings were decorated in the style of *fin de siècle* France. As if they had been purchased thirty years ago and remained in this room ever since. The ceiling was at least fifteen feet high, and had a rounded corbel that was peculiarly French. Another painting of rural France dominated one wall, while the other had a large, faded tapestry of a hunting dog surrounded by autumn foliage.

The clock behind the Lieutenant ticked remorselessly on.

Lieutenant Masset abruptly stood up. 'Major Renard will see you now.' Danilov checked his watch. Twelve minutes since the time they had entered. A pre-arranged time to keep guests waiting, he thought. How typically French; just like the headmaster of a school, keeping the errant pupils waiting for their punishment.

The Lieutenant walked to another pair of double doors that stretched up to the ceiling, opening both of them to reveal a room three times larger than the antechamber. At the end, a small French gentleman sat behind an immense oak desk.

The Lieutenant guided them across a thick oriental carpet and past cabinets containing exquisite Sèvres porcelain. They were directed to sit in two wooden chairs placed in front of the desk. Major Renard did not get up.

'I presume you do not speak French, Inspector. Major Renard does not speak English so I will translate. Forgive me if I make any errors.'

Major Renard stared at both of them. He was small with an elegant goatee, combed and manicured into a silvery point. His white hair was brushed back to reveal a high forehead. His eyes were perched above a long, beak-like nose that dominated his face. When he spoke, Danilov was surprised to hear a high, excitable squeak rather than the deep voice he was expecting. The contrast was very disconcerting, like discovering the bull one had hired to service a field of cows was only interested in other bulls.

After a long speech in French, the Lieutenant began talking in his accented English. 'The Major had asked for Chief Inspector Boyle to attend this meeting. You are not him. You are not even English.'

'The Chief Inspector sends his apologies. Unfortunately, given the short notice, he is indisposed at this time.'

The Major grunted at this without it being translated.

'I am Inspector Danilov and this is my assistant, Detective Constable Stra-chan.'

Again, the Major launched into a long speech in French. 'The Major supposes that you will have to do but he is surprised the English Head of Detectives does not give this matter the attention it deserves,' the Lieutenant translated.

'It would be difficult to give it any sort of attention without knowing what it was.' This time the Major turned to Masset for a translation. There was a brief discussion between the two of them before the Lieutenant continued. 'To save the Major's valuable time, he has authorised me to give you an outline of the matter.'

The Lieutenant brought his thumb, index and middle fingers together and blew as if moistening them before turning the pages of a book. Danilov thought it was a very interesting idiosyncrasy. The action of a clerk, rather than of a policeman.

'This is a very difficult situation. There have been murders.'

'Murder is unfortunately fairly common in all parts of the city. It is a problem we are facing all the time,' said Danilov.

'Monsieur, this is different. These are particularly brutal murders.'

The Lieutenant let his words lie on the table between them. The Major embarked on another long speech in French.

The Lieutenant continued speaking, but it was obvious to Danilov he was no longer translating. 'In the French Garde Municipale, we believe the murderer comes from the International Settlement.'

'How can you be so sure?'

'A witness saw the murderer's car leaving the scene of the crime. It had a number plate from your district.'

'What was the number?'

'The witness couldn't remember. It all happened so fast you understand. He just knew the car was from the International Settlement.'

'How can we assist the Garde Municipale?'

Lieutenant Masset blew on the ends of his fingers. 'When I explain the murders to you, Inspector, then you will understand.'

Danilov leant back in his hard-back chair. The Major began another long speech in French. But before he could get into the flow of his speech, Danilov interrupted him.

'*Je comprends que cette situation est vraiment importante, Monsieur le Chef, comment pourrait la Police Municipale de Shanghai vous aider?*'

Both the Lieutenant and the Major watched him in silence. Eventually, Major Renard said in English, 'Your French is quite good, Monsieur.'

'As is your English, Monsieur le Chef. Now we've got that out of the way, how can we help?'

The Major nodded at Masset. 'We expect you to find the murderer and return him to us so that he may be put on trial. The honour of France is at stake.'

'The honour of France?'

'One of the victims was an official of the French government, killed without mercy. This 'orrible murder must not be left unpunished.' The Major pronounced 'horrible' in a very French way.

'And the other victim?'

'A Russian prostitute. A woman of no consequence in society, but nonetheless we believe the murders are related.'

'Why?'

'Lieutenant Masset will give you all the details but there was one feature that appeared in both murders. They both had Chinese characters carved into their bodies.'

Danilov looked across at Strachan. 'We are also investigating a similar death in the Settlement at the moment. A killing without mercy. Could I see your case notes?'

'Masset will give them to you. The killing may be just be another vicious gang war over opium but—'

'We doubt it,' interrupted Masset.

The Major glared at him. He tapped the table three times with a well-manicured fingernail. 'You must understand, monsieur, when one of our officials is attacked, the nation of France itself is under attack.'

'We will do everything in our power to help find the murderer.'

The Major pulled the end of his white goatee, sharpening it into a point. 'I do not need to remind you of the consequences of failure, do I, Inspector?'

'No, sir, you don't.'

'Good. Find him and deliver him to us.' Once more, the Major tapped his desk three times, then waved his feminine hands. Masset stood up immediately.

Danilov understood that the interview was over. 'Thank you for your time, Major. We will catch this man.'

There was no answer. Just another wave of the hands.

CHAPTER 6

'Can I help you, sir?' The old concierge stretched his arm, blocking the narrow back entrance to the theatre.

'I'm looking for Miss Everett,' said Richard.

'You and everybody else. Didn't turn up last night. Not good, not good at all. The artistes always turn up. Once, we had Mr Mayhew here, wonderful actor, magnificent Lear. He turned up with a broken leg one day. Still went on. Had to do the heath scene in a chair but he did it anyway. What a trouper, if you catch my drift.' He tapped the side of his nose with his finger. 'Can't say the same for Miss Everett though.'

'I was supposed to meet her last night . . .'

'I thought I'd seen you before, but there are always so many chaps waiting for the girls, I can't tell 'em apart. Here's Mr Trevelyan, the director. Miss Everett is not in his good books, if you catch my drift.'

'You're looking for Miss Everett?' The director was a bulky, florid man with red-veined cheeks and a large spotted handkerchief sitting like a toadstool in his top pocket. 'Aren't we all. She was supposed to be here last night at six o'clock for rehearsals. Didn't make those and didn't make the show either. Miss Davenport had to take her place. Heavy calves, Miss Davenport. Doesn't have the lightness of foot for the part.'

'I was supposed to meet her last night after the show. She didn't turn up.'

The director shrugged his shoulders and sighed. 'So you were stood up too. Typical. A girl gets infatuated with some man and her standards drop quicker than her knickers. Well, if you see her, tell her not to come back. She's been replaced by Miss Smith.' He leant forward conspiratorially. 'Between you and me, she was getting a little past it anyway. They all have a sell-by date those sort of girls. And hers had been sold a long time ago.'

'So she didn't come here yesterday evening?' Richard persisted.

'That's what I've been telling you, my dear. Didn't see a hair of her once pretty little head. I hope she enjoys her little fling because the final curtain has been lowered on her career. The only place that will have her now is Little Piddling rep, on a Wednesday night, in the middle of February.'

'But she said she was coming here. We were at the Astor . . .'

'Drinking again, was she? I warned her about that. Ages actresses dreadfully does the booze. The skin never recovers, you know.' He glanced at the clock in the concierge's office. 'Is that the time? I must be off to see Harold about his shimmy in the third act.' The director looked at Richard and his voice changed, adding an edge to his words. 'If you see Miss Everett, tell her not to come back. She's been sacked. Given the elbow. Shown the curtain. Danced her last chorus. She won't be paid either. We don't pay those who let us down, do we, Mr Harcourt?'

'No, we don't, sir,' the concierge said smiling.

'Anyway, I have a dance number waiting. Goodbye.'

With a little wave, the director flounced off into the darkness of the theatre.

Richard took out his pocket book and quickly wrote a note for Elsie. 'Would you be good enough to give Miss Everett this, if you see her?'

The concierge took the note, leaving his hand extended, palm upwards.

'Oh, yes, of course.' He gave the man a dollar.

'Thank you kindly, sir. Very generous. But between you and me, I don't think we'll see her again. There was another gentleman who used to hang around here waiting for her. If I were you, I would forget Miss Everett. Not your type at all, if you get my drift.' And, once again, he touched his finger to the side of his nose.

The concierge pocketed the dollar and returned inside his shed guarding the theatre door.

At the bottom of the alley, a hawker was selling newspapers. In his hand was a copy of the *North China Daily News* with a bold headline:

WOMAN'S BODY FOUND IN CREEK

Richard shivered as if someone had just walked over his grave.

***

'Both occurred in the last eight days?'

Lieutenant Masset nodded. 'We found the second body three days ago, over towards the old Chinese city, on the borders of our Concession. At first, we thought they were gang related.'

'What changed your mind?'

'They lack the simple brutality of a gang killing. With the gangs, it's either a shot to the head or long, painful torture, followed by dumping the body in the street.

Both are there to set an example. To discourage the others, as you English are fond of saying.'

'It's actually to "encourage" the others, and it was used first by a Frenchman,' said Strachan.

Danilov held his hand up for silence. 'But you think something else is happening?'

The Lieutenant again brought his three fingers up to his mouth and blew on them. 'It's almost as if the bodies had been put on show. Like an art gallery. We were meant to find them, to see them, as they had been displayed.'

Danilov reached into his pocket and pulled out his tobacco tin. He took one of the papers from the tin and laid it on the table, adding a few strands of tobacco. Then he closed the tin, placing it on its side on the edge of the table, adjusting the angle until it matched the lip of the wood. That felt better. The tin was in perfect alignment. 'Tell me about the bodies,' he said.

Masset opened the case file. 'The first victim was one of our resident magistrates, a lawyer by training, Monsieur Flamini. The body was found on the steps of the courthouse, hands tied behind his back. He had been strangled. That was eight days ago.'

'He could have been killed by a gang. Perhaps he had jailed one if their members,' said Strachan.

'That is true,' agreed Masset, pausing for a moment for effect, 'but why was the body frozen? As hard as ice it was. The weather has been cold recently but not cold enough to freeze a body.' Lieutenant Masset stared into mid-air. 'I'll always remember the way the man's lips were parted from his teeth. Pulled back in a snarl like a scared dog.'

He took out a silver case and lit a cigarette. The aroma of Turkish tobacco filled the room. 'It was a grimace, the look of a man who had seen something terrible at the point of his death.' Masset took a long drag on his cigarette. 'I was at Verdun, Inspector, and I'll tell you, I never saw anything like the look on the magistrate's face.'

He took another drag on the cigarette. 'And we found a ten dollar note frozen in the man's hand, his fingers gripping it tightly. Our pathologist thought he had been alive when he was frozen.'

'Could I see the body?'

Masset shook his head. 'It has already been returned to his family. I believe it is on its way back to France.'

'That is disappointing.' Inspector Danilov looked down at his hands. 'Had Monsieur Flamini been threatened in any way?'

'Not that we know. He had been a magistrate here for four years. He was known as diligent in his work. A wife and two children in France. A mistress in Shanghai but that is common, is it not? Even among the English.' Masset shrugged his shoulders in a way only the French know how. 'We checked all his recent cases to see if someone with a grudge would want him killed but he handled property related work rather than criminal law. There was a suggestion of small irregularities in some of the recent property cases that came up before him. But nothing could be investigated or proven. If we arrested every official for "small irregularities", we would have none left to do the work.'

Again he shrugged his shoulders. 'It was when the pathologist undressed Monsieur Flamini that he found the strangest piece of evidence. There were Chinese characters carved into his chest. The characters for "vengeance".'

Danilov took the Lieutenant's lighter and lit the cigarette he had been holding in his fingers. He inhaled deeply and blew out a long stream of blue smoke. 'Now, that is interesting.' He glanced across at Strachan. 'And the second murder?'

'A Russian prostitute. Not high class and not a street walker. Just another Russian prostitute.' Masset stopped speaking, suddenly realising that the inspector in front of him had the surname Danilov.

'Just another Russian. Please carry on, Lieutenant.'

'She was found outside the abattoir close to the old Chinese city on Rue Albi, floating in a barrel of pig's blood. For making *boudin noir*, you know.'

Danilov nodded to encourage the Frenchman to continue.

'According to our pathologist, Dr Legrand, she was alive when she was put in the barrel. He found blood in her lungs and trachea.'

'How did she die?' asked Strachan.

'She drowned. According to our pathologist, she had been lying in the barrel of blood for at least two days before she was found.'

Danilov took another drag on his cigarette. 'Her time of death?'

'He couldn't be certain. The warmth of the pig's blood you see . . .' Lieutenant Masset stopped talking. He blew on his fingers once more and then continued. 'Her hands had been tied with a thin rope. There was one other thing. She also had Chinese characters carved into her chest. But this time, they were different. They were the characters for "damnation".'

'Were the characters carved in the same style?'

Lieutenant Masset shrugged his shoulders once more. 'I think they were, but I can't be sure. I didn't spend a lot of time with the body. You'll find the coroner's report in our case files.'

'Thank you, Lieutenant Masset, I'll read it.'

'We have no real leads to the killer. To be frank, our detectives are more used to managing brothels and opium dens than investigating murder.' He brought his fingers up to his mouth and blew on them. 'You seem to be very interested in these murders, Inspector. Why?'

Inspector Danilov stubbed out the end of his cigarette and immediately rolled another. The office was now a warm fug of blue smoke, the whispers of fumes caught in the bright light from the sash windows.

'We may have a similar murder ourselves. A young woman, or should I say a young man, found in Soochow Creek, his body nearly cut in two, his stomach and genitals slashed to ribbons.'

'You think they're connected?'

Danilov shrugged his shoulders, copying the Frenchman, but not achieving the same Gallic elegance. 'I'm not sure, but they do show similarities: hands tied, Chinese characters carved into the chest. And it is strange that all three murders should occur within such a short space of time. If it were the usual gangland squabbles, we would see shootings and very public displays of revenge. These killings, brutal though they are, seem very personal.'

He took another long drag on his cigarette. 'A message from the killer to the world, perhaps. Could I see the body of the second victim?'

'I'm afraid not. Nobody came to claim her, so she was cremated according to French law. It's one of the few areas in which we are remarkably efficient.'

'Then her clothes may give us some clues.'

'She was naked when she was discovered.' Masset thought for a moment. 'We still have the barrel in which she was found. It's in the cellars beneath here.'

Danilov stubbed his cigarette out in the ashtray. 'Let's take a look, Lieutenant.'

* * *

Lieutenant Masset led them through a maze of corridors in the basement of the building. Here, the richly painted walls of the floors above had been replaced by rough grey brick. It many areas it was badly finished as if the builders couldn't be bothered with any surface that their bosses were unlikely to see.

Danilov realised that not many people were invited down to this part of the building.

'I think it's this way, Inspector.'

They passed an open room filled with junk from past investigations. It was all piled in the room in one heap, without any thought for filing or organisation. Danilov looked inside and shuddered.

'I think it's in here.' Lieutenant Masset pointed to another room across the corridor. He opened the door and switched on a light. A bare bulb hung from a black-and-white flex in the middle of the room. Danilov could see that it was just half-filled with junk, evidence from investigations and props from a Christmas party. A lack of cobwebs indicated that most of these things had been left here recently.

'It should be in the corner.'

He picked his way around the remains of a lion's head. The kind used by the martial arts troupes at Chinese New Year when they dance their blessing of good fortune on a business or shop. The body of the lion was nowhere to be seen.

Masset removed a dust sheet. Underneath was a wooden barrel. Its appearance was nothing out of the ordinary. Just another wooden barrel, used to store wine or vinegar, about four feet tall and with the classic round waist and tapered top and bottom.

Nothing about it indicated that it had once stored the body of a dead Russian prostitute.

Strachan coughed. 'This makes our filing system look modern, sir.'

Danilov raised his hand. 'This is the barrel in which she was found?'

Lieutenant Masset nodded.

'What happened to the pig's blood?'

'It was poured away in order to retrieve the body'

'Was it saved? Or filtered to see if anything was trapped in it?'

Lieutenant Masset shook his head. 'I'm afraid not. The first constables on the scene thought she was still alive. They poured it away and tried to revive her.'

'But your pathologist said she had been dead for at least two days.'

'We can't fault them for enthusiasm. And anyway, the coroner may have been wrong. He wasn't certain of the exact time of death. The warmth of the pig's blood had affected the onset of rigor mortis.'

Danilov grunted. He walked over and examined the barrel. In the thin light of the bulb hanging from a flex in the ceiling, he could just make out the red stains down one side. 'Did the pathologist notice anything else?'

'As I told you, he thought she was alive when she was put in there. The top of the barrel had been sealed with pitch. A small air pocket above the blood may have allowed her to breath for a short while. Not long. Gradually, she would have used up the air and . . .'

'Drowned.' Strachan was writing in his notebook. He stopped and lifted his head. Both men were staring at the barrel.

'Not a pleasant death,' whispered Lieutenant Masset.

Danilov ached for a cigarette. Anything to get him out of this cellar and away from the tomb of his fellow Russian. 'I think we've seen enough.' He turned to go and stopped. 'Lieutenant Masset, do you still have the lid of the barrel?'

'It's somewhere around here, I think.' He scanned the ground at his feet. The lid was propped up against the lion's head. Masset picked it up and handed it to Danilov.

It looked like a normal lid, around twenty inches across. At the edges a thick layer of pitch or tar had created a black ring that stuck to the top and side.

'The pitch would have made the seal airtight. She must have used up all the air that remained in the barrel before gradually sinking into the pig's blood,' said Masset. 'I don't think I'll ever be able to eat *boudin noir* again.'

Danilov turned the lid of the barrel over to look at the underside. He could see traces of red staining the wood where the blood had lapped against the lid. He walked over to the centre of the room, avoiding the evidence from the countless other cases strewn on the floor. He examined the underneath of the lid, tilting it left and right under the harsh light.

There was something, Scratches, faint marks against the grain of the wood. 'Stra-chan, come here. Your eyes are better than mine. Look at that.'

Strachan rushed over and took the lid, holding it up to the light. 'There seems to be something scratched on the lid, sir. Two words, I think.' He tilted the lid so that the

light shot obliquely across it. 'The first letter is an "H",
sir. Then, there's an "A".' He brought the lid closer and
then moved it away, squinting with his eyes as he did
so. 'Then there seems to be a "T" and an "E". Spells
"HATE".'

'Thank you, Stra-chan, even I can work that one out.'

'The next line is not so clear. An "A", I think. Then
an "L" and maybe another "L". But the last letter is
very faint, sir. It's hard to see down here, sir.'

'"HATE ALL", that is interesting,' said Danilov.

'A message from the killer, sir?'

'It looks like it, doesn't it, Stra-chan? Lieutenant
Masset, you didn't notice these scratches?'

The Lieutenant shrugged his shoulders once more.
'We thought they were marks from the makers. Not
important.'

'I think you were wrong.' Danilov put his hat back on
his head. 'Let's get out of here. I need the fresh air of a
smoke.'

CHAPTER 7

'Come, Stra-chan, we're close to Moscow cafe.'

They walked down the crowded streets of the French Concession. Despite the cold, both sides of the road were a hive of activity. Hawkers sang the praises of their wares. Gamblers, wrapped up in jackets and mufflers, surrounded the mahjong tables on the pavement, watching and understanding every nuance of the play. Shoppers dawdled at shop windows, admiring the latest trinkets imported from France. Chauffeurs chatted, sharing a smoke as their idling cars pumped exhaust into the street.

'We need to examine the lid of the barrel more closely, Stra-chan.'

'Lieutenant Masset said he would send it over just as soon as he had cleared it with Major Renard.'

Danilov threw his cigarette into the gutter. 'Bureaucrats. They have nothing better to do than to give themselves permission to do nothing. Why can't they just leave me to get on with the investigation?'

Strachan kept silent. They crossed the street opposite a Russian Orthodox church, its golden dome glistening in the haze of the morning sunshine. Danilov turned down one of the lanes off the main road and entered a narrow *lilong* on the right, past a watchman in front of his grate, snoring loudly. He pushed through a glass door and stepped into the warm fug of a cafe.

The room was small, no more than six tables. On their left, two chess players lifted their heads, annoyed at the interruption. Ahead of them, a large copper samovar hissed a jet of steam and hot water.

A small, elf-like woman approached them. She had fine, almost porcelain features and moved with the elegance of a dancer from the Kirov. 'Good morning, Pyotr Alexandrevich, what a pleasant surprise.'

'Good morning to you, Elena Ivanova.' Inspector Danilov stepped aside to reveal Strachan standing behind him. 'May I present to you Detective Constable Stra-chan. This is Princess Elena Ivanova Ostrepova.'

'I'm pleased to meet you, Detective.'

The Princess held out her hand. Danilov expected Strachan to kiss the hand or at least shake it heartily. Instead, he leant forward and just touched the tips of the elegant fingers.

She turned to Danilov. 'This detective has such good manners, not like the last one you were with.'

'Inspector Meaker was a little . . . clumsy, Princess.'

'Clumsy? The man was a bear, a boor and a bore.' She lifted her old-fashioned pince-nez to her eyes and examined Strachan. 'But this one I approve. Most charming.' She turned back again to Danilov. 'So, is this visit business or pleasure?' She pointed to an empty chess board at a nearby table.

'Business, I'm afraid.'

'How tiresome. Never mind, at least we will have some tea and snacks together, yes?'

'That would be most welcome.'

She led them to a large wooden table covered in glass and topped with an intricate lace cloth. She clapped her hands and immediately a waitress began to set the table with fine china plates and glass tea cups.

'Please sit. If it's about your family, Inspector, I'm afraid I have heard nothing more since our last chat. My "little ears" have heard not a pin drop.'

Danilov coughed, hoping that Strachan hadn't heard. 'Stra-chan, the Princess has the finest network of "little ears" in Shanghai. There is nothing that goes on in the French Concession she does not know about.'

'You flatter me, Pyotr Alexandrevich. You must be after something very important.'

They both laughed. 'As usual, Princess, you see through me as clearly as a drop of melted snow.'

The food and snacks began to arrive. Danilov paused while the waitress served them, pouring the tea into glasses. He inhaled the aroma, picked up the glass cup by its metal holder and took a little sip of the scalding brew. 'As perfect as ever. Just like Minsk, only better.'

'It's good enough. The water isn't the same, you know. In St Petersburg, there, we used to drink tea.'

Danilov saw a momentary 'oh' of happiness cross the face of the Princess. He imagined her younger self flirting with dashing officers, dancing the night away, laughing like there was no tomorrow. The look vanished to be followed by one of sadness and regret.

'You said you had business with me, Inspector?'

'I did, Princess.' He took another sip of the tea. 'Recently there have been two murders in the Concession.'

'A terrible business.'

'Terrible indeed. The first was a French magistrate, Monsieur Flamini. Found on the steps of the courthouse . . . frozen.'

The last word was spoken after a long pause. The Princess stared back at him. 'And what do you want from me, Inspector?'

'Have your "little ears" heard anything?'

'A few whispers here and there. But whispers are very hard to hear, they get caught in the breeze and vanish into the air.' She snapped her fingers softly.

Danilov looked straight at the Princess. The elegant old lady with her rather old-fashioned Edwardian dress and beautiful, porcelain skin had been replaced by something much harder, like a sleeping cat that had just revealed its claws.

He smiled. 'You are quite right, Princess. Whispers are such fleeting things. Here one moment and gone the next. Only the bad rumours fly on wings. I heard one such rumour recently.'

'Did you, Inspector?'

'About a club on Chu Pao Street. A Russian club it appears. Our friends in the Shanghai Police may raid it soon. Illegal activity apparently, girls and opium. The usual vices.'

'Such vices are everywhere in the city. Mankind loves its vices more than it loves its virtues.'

'Unfortunately, that is true, Princess.'

'But without mankind's addiction to its vices, you wouldn't have employment, Inspector, would you?'

'That is unfortunately also true. It is the great paradox of my profession. We are dependent for our existence on the continuation of the vices we are employed to eradicate. If we are ever successful, we have no job.'

'I wouldn't ever worry about your employment, Inspector. Not in Shanghai anyway.'

Danilov was enjoying the game. Like chess between two evenly matched players, the opening moves had been made and now the players were exchanging pawns.

'Do try the pirogi, Inspector. The chef used to work in the Winter Palace. Before the Reds arrived though.'

He picked up the round meat-filled dumpling. The skin was as translucent as fine paper. He bit into it and immediately the warm comfort of a long-forgotten memory from the past filled his mouth. 'Beautiful, Princess, a taste of home. Or rather a taste of what home should taste like. The home of one's dreams.'

'Thank you, Inspector, they are quite pleasant, aren't they?' The Princess took a long sip of tea. 'The French magistrate you spoke of, found in a rather Siberian manner, was, of course, an upstanding member of the community. But recently, it seems he had been making demands of certain property developers.'

'Demands?'

'The usual. Extra surcharges for signatures, more charges for the dismissal of cases, even more charges for the approval of developments. He had become a little too demanding recently. A young mistress is, apparently, an expensive proposition.'

'You think this had something to do with his death?'

She raised her hands in a courtly gesture. 'My "little ears" do not know. Nor have they heard anything concerning the identity of the people involved. Give them time and they may be able to find out more.'

Danilov took another sip of tea. 'And the second murder?'

'Much closer to home, as you can imagine. Her name was Maria Tatiana Stepanova. From Moscow, originally. Came to Shanghai in 1926. I'm afraid the usual story. No money. No skills. Nothing to sell except that which women have always sold.'

'She was not one of your "little ears"?'

The voice became hard again. 'No, Inspector, she would not have met such a fate if she were.'

'I'm sorry for offending you, Princess, please accept my apologies.'

The Princess glared at Danilov over the rim of her tea glass. 'She was an independent, working from home, protected by a thug, Victorov, I believe his name is.'

'Not much of a protector.'

'Not much of a man. I believe he fled Shanghai after the murder, nobody knows where. The Garde Municipale are looking for him, but they won't find him. That sort knows how to hide.' The Princess swore in Russian. Then her face softened. She leant closer to the Inspector. 'Danilov, whatever she was, whatever she had become, she did not deserve to die like that. Like an animal in a slaughterhouse.'

'Princess, we will find the man who did it, I promise you.'

'If I hear anything, I will inform you in the usual way. For now, I see my customers need me.' She stood up and smoothed down her long green skirt.

Again, Danilov could see the steel shrouded in the wool.

CHAPTER 8

Sergeant Wolfe, the duty officer, sat up behind a high desk looking down at all the arrivals in Central Police Station. He was surrounded by two Chinese constables and three young interpreters, each of which spoke the local Shanghainese dialect, Mandarin, the national language, and one of the myriad other versions of Chinese originating in Chekiang, Shantung, Anhui, Canton or Fukien.

So many interpreters were necessary because each region specialised in a particular form of thievery. The Cantonese were pickpockets and shoplifters. The Teochews from Fukien were opium smugglers, dominating the now illegal trade through their numerous guilds. The Shantungese were big men, the armed robbers and street thugs for hire. When there was a fight, they were never far from the action.

Finally, there were the Shanghainese themselves, the organisers of all the mayhem that the Shanghai Municipal Police, like the Dutch boy and his dike, just about kept under control. For Shanghai was the big city. The magnet that attracted all the riff raff, scoundrels, bad eggs, ne'er-do-wells and thugs from all over China, drawn like moths to an illegal flame for its vice and its money.

Above all, for its money.

'Looks like we've got a right one, here.' Sergeant Wolfe pointed to the shuffling giant of a man before him, dressed in rags that had been repaired a thousand times with cloth that had come from half as many sources.

'What do you want?' the sergeant asked him in Shanghainese.

The Giant just smiled back and shifted his woollen hat from hand to hand as he shuffled his feet.

'What do you want?' the interpreter asked in Mandarin. The Giant smiled again and launched into a long speech, punctuated by actions and pointing.

'Don't know this dialect. It's not Shantungese or Teochew. Or even Hakka.' The interpreter leant over the desk and inspected the Giant from head to toe. 'He's a big one though. Wouldn't like to meet him on dark night in a narrow alley.'

The interpreters covered most of the dialects that entered through the doors of the station, but occasionally even they were baffled by a minority language. That rare eventuality was covered by Sergeant Wolfe's little black book, with its list of interpreters and their various specialisations. Only once had he been stumped. It was by an old lady from one of the mountain provinces in the south who only spoke a special women's language. She had been arrested for selling some exotic herbs in the street the night before. Wolfe let her off with a caution. He used English. It was just as unintelligible to her as any other language.

'From his clothes, he could be off one of the boats. See the feet.'

The sergeant looked down at the bare feet, shuffling on the floor of the police station. They were large, black with dirt, and had a slight webbing between the toes.

'Could be from one of the boats on Lake Tai or in the rivers. Haven't a clue about their dialect. Looks like he doesn't speak anything else.'

Sergeant Wolfe sighed. Another bloody nuisance. Why couldn't they just speak one language instead of hundreds of bloody dialects? At least the written language was the same. 'See if he can read?'

The interpreter quickly wrote the characters for 'What do you want?'

The Giant smiled, grabbed hold of the pen and wrote three shaky characters.

The interpreter picked up the paper. 'It's his name. Probably the only thing he knows how to write.'

Sergeant Wolfe sighed again. It was going to be one of those days. Picking up his little black book, he leafed through it, looking for somebody, anybody, who might speak the dialect from Lake Tai. He found a Mr Huang Shu Ren, who might fit the bill. He picked up the phone, but there was no dial tone. 'Somebody plug the bloody phone back in.'

It was going to be one of those days.

* * *

'Chief Inspector Boyle would like to see you, Inspector.'

'Thank you, Miss Cavendish, I'll see him presently.'

'I think he meant as soon as you returned to the station.'

Danilov took off his hat and coat and hung them on the hat stand next to her desk.

'The fingerprint report has come back. There is a positive match to a Mr Henry Sellars.' She handed the report over to Danilov. 'I thought the body in the creek was a woman.'

'So did we all, Miss Cavendish.'

He glanced at the report. Positive match to Henry Sellars, aged 20. Three previous convictions, two for theft and one for importuning in a public place. He would check the files later. Meanwhile, Boyle was waiting.

He knocked on the door.

This time, the word 'Enter' came quickly, as if Boyle had been waiting just behind the door for him. He stepped in and was greeted by a fog of cigar smoke. Havanas by the smell, and expensive.

'Ah, there you are, Danilov, we've been waiting for you. I think you know Allen, don't you?'

'Good to see you again, Danilov,' said Allen, from his position lounging in the couch in the corner. Danilov could just make him out through the haze of smoke. 'I do enjoy our games of chess. One day, I may even beat you. By the way, my next move is KxR. You've lost your rook now, Danilov.'

'Good afternoon, Mr Allen.' He bowed slightly from the waist. 'A pleasure to see you too. Even if you are a rather blurred figure through all this smoke. I will respond to your courageous move with Q-QB3. I think you will find it's mate in three moves.'

'Really? I must go back and check the board. I don't think you can win that easily.'

'Join us in our smoke, Danilov,' said Boyle. He held up the maple box covered in intricate marquetry. 'Or would you prefer Turkish? I seem to remember coffin nails are your preference.'

'A coffin nail would be perfect.' Danilov took the Turkish cigarette, noting the blue logo of a dancing gypsy on the white paper as he rolled it beneath his nose to catch the aroma. He lit it, inhaling a rich, redolent lungful of the finest tobacco.

'How was the meeting with Renard this morning?'

Boyle was as direct as ever, thought Danilov. He glanced at Allen, quietly puffing at what remained of his cigar. Boyle caught the look. 'Don't mind Allen. He's in Intelligence, he knows everything anyway.'

'You flatter me, Thomas. I merely know nearly everything. And anything else, I ask you.' They both laughed like two members of a private club sharing an in-joke at the expense of a non-member. Danilov was acutely aware the non-member was him.

'The French have a number of problems,' he began.

'Being French is one of them.' Boyle laughed at his joke, joined again by Allen from his perch in the corner.

'I'm sure it is,' continued Danilov, 'but at the moment there are other, more pressing problems.'

'Which are?' The question was from Allen and there was no joke in his voice.

'Two murders. Both brutal.'

'What's that got to do with us?'

'They believe the murderer is based in the International Settlement.'

'On what evidence?' snapped Boyle.

Danilov detected a tone of indignation in his voice as if he were affronted by the idea murderers might be operating in his jurisdiction. 'Based on information received. My guess is the French have been putting pressure on their own criminal gangs, the Green Gang in particular, to find out who is behind the killings. That gang has pointed the finger in the direction of the International Settlement.'

'Poppycock.'

'Perhaps, sir, but the French seemed sure . . .'

'The French are always sure until they are not sure. During the war, it was always the same,' said Boyle.

Danilov ran his fingers through his hair. Be patient, he thought, explain what is happening, help him understand. 'There have also been two murders in the last couple of weeks. A French magistrate and a Russian prostitute.'

'I suppose they were together at the time,' said Boyle.

Allen held up his hand again. 'Gangland murders?' Danilov noted Allen seemed to be asking all the questions now.

'I don't think so. Too clever, too vicious and too personal for a gang. The magistrate was strangled and then frozen in ice.'

'Our murderer sounds very cold-blooded.' Boyle laughed at Allen's joke as a long stream of cigar smoke blew past Danilov's face. He continued anyway. 'The Russian prostitute drowned in a barrel of pig's blood, her lungs filled until she could breathe no more.'

He waited for the inevitable joke. He heard nothing except the creak of leather on a chair as Boyle shifted position.

Danilov took a deep breath. Now was the time to take the plunge and actually say what had been swimming around in his head since this morning. 'I think both murders are related to the killing in the creek, sir.'

'Oh,' said Allen, 'why is that?'

'There are some rather obvious coincidences. All three victims were bound with the same thin ropes, and all of them had Chinese characters carved into their bodies.'

'Chinese characters?'

'The characters were carved with some sort of knife, sir. It was neatly done, almost as if they had been copied from a book. The characters for "vengeance", "damnation", and "justice". Not common words at all.' Danilov ran his fingers through his hair once more. 'On the bottom of the barrel lid, we found something even stranger. The words "HATE ALL" were scratched into the wood.'

Allen's eyebrows were raised in surprise. 'Strange words, indeed.'

'So that's the basis for your belief that the murders are related,' Boyle snorted, a cloud of cigar smoke expelled from his mouth.

'More than that, sir, I think we could have a serial killer on our hands.'

'What's a "serial killer" when he's at home?' Boyle sneered, looking to Allen for support. 'Someone who kills wheat? Or corn, perhaps. Maybe he uses a machine gun on a sheaf of oats.' His shoulders chuckled along with the rest of his body.

Danilov continued anyway. 'It's a new theory. From Ernst Gennat, director of the Berlin Police. He calls them "*Serienmörder*". Literally, serial killers. It's when a murderer kills more than one victim. I met him at a conference in Berlin in 1922. We spent a long time discussing his theories. An example would be Jack the Ripper.'

Boyle stopped laughing. 'So now we're listening to Germans. Had enough of them during the war. They did a lot of serial killing then, let me tell you.'

Allen was quiet for a moment. 'Do we know the names of the victims?'

'The magistrate was a Monsieur Flamini and the Russian prostitute was . . .' he opened his notebook '. . . Maria Tatiana Stepanova. The victim in Soochow Creek was a Henry Sellars.'

'The man who had the appearance of a woman?' said Allen.

Danilov stared at him for a long time before answering. 'Yes.'

'Strange people. Knew about them in India, of course. Hijras they were called. Popular at weddings and the like.

But didn't know they existed here too.' Boyle flicked the ash from his cigar into the ashtray.

Allen glanced down at his watch. 'Got to go, I'm afraid. Careful with the French, Danilov, they can be unpredictable to say the least. Let me know if you need any help with the murders. Intelligence can be useful, sometimes.'

Danilov stood up to take the opportunity to leave as well.

'Goodbye, Mr Allen.'

'I'll look into that move of yours. It's mate in four for me unless you're careful.' He popped a sweet into his mouth from a packet he kept in his pocket. 'Don't want to breathe cigar smoke all over the secretaries upstairs. Do you want one? Got into the habit in France.'

Danilov shook his head. 'It's mate in three for you.'

'We shall have to see, Inspector. Bye, Thomas, see you at the club.' Allen left the room. Before Danilov could follow him out, Boyle stepped in front of him.

'Do take Allen's warnings about the French seriously, Danilov. Upstairs . . .' he gestured with his thumb, '. . . don't want any mistakes on this. Do you understand me?'

'Yes, sir, I understand.'

'And solve the killing in Soochow Creek quickly. If a prostitute and a Frenchman have been murdered in the French Concession, that's none of our business. Let them solve their own problems.'

'But, sir—'

'Solve the murder in the creek. Quickly. Do you understand? I want it sorted and the case closed.'

He put his arm round Danilov's shoulder and led him to the door. 'And let's hear no more talk about "serial killers". Bunch of poppycock, if you ask me.'

He opened the door and Danilov walked out.

'Solve it soon. Do you understand?'

***

Danilov rearranged his desk again. The lamp had been placed on the left side, touching the desk blotter. His pens were now stacked on the right. Children, children, children, he thought. 'Just carry on, Stra-chan, while I deal with this.'

Strachan checked his notes, finding his place with his finger. 'From the registry, I discovered three European doctors who could have been dealing with our victim, sir: Dr Teuscher, Dr Halliwell and Dr Lamarr. I checked the files on them. We arrested the first one two years ago for performing an illegal abortion but he was released without charge. We had nothing to go on and the young woman involved refused to co-operate.'

Danilov sat down, his desk exactly how he wanted it. Now he could concentrate.

'He died six months ago. Our registry appears to be out of date. Whilst Dr Halliwell is now in Peking. He fled there after the fighting a year ago. Looks like he was tagged by Special Branch as a Comintern agent.'

'Our victim had seen a doctor recently, Stra-chan, so we can rule him out. Let's pay a visit to Dr Lamarr. No phone call. Let's surprise him. Have the photographs come in?'

'Here they are, sir. I've passed copies over to Chief Inspector Boyle already.'

'Have you now? And who told you to do that?'

'Miss Cavendish. Apparently, they asked for the photographs to be passed to them.'

'They?'

'Chief Inspector Boyle and Mr Allen, sir.'

Danilov leant forward and took a long drag on his cigarette. The politics was already starting. They were muscling in on his investigation. He stared directly at Strachan. 'Next time, you pass nothing to nobody without my approval. Is that understood? If they want the photographs, they can get them from the lab directly.'

'Yes, sir, I . . .'

'Nothing to nobody.'

'Yes, sir.'

Danilov examined the photos one by one. 'Let's go and see this doctor now. Where is he?'

'Just behind the Bund, sir. On Canton Road, number 131.'

Danilov opened the desk drawer to place the photographs inside and found a set of keys. They had a note attached to them from Miss Cavendish. 'Can you drive, Stra-chan?'

'I've passed the Police Advanced Driving course, sir.'

'Your apparently boundless range of skills never ceases to amaze me. Well, we are in luck. Apparently, Chief Inspector Boyle has been kind enough to bless this investigation with a car.' Danilov tossed the keys to Strachan.

He caught them in his right hand and looked for any identification marks. 'Which car is it, Inspector?'

'I don't know Stra-chan, but I presume it will be a black one.'

'They're all black, sir.'

'Then work it out, Stra-chan. Use your detective skills.'

Strachan thought for a moment. 'I'll ask Miss Cavendish, sir. She's bound to know.'

'There's hope for you yet, Stra-chan.'

CHAPTER 9

Lamarr's office was in a building known as the surgery because of the number of doctors who congregated there. All ills were catered for, from athlete's foot to polio, septicaemia to hair loss, typhoid to in-grown toenails.

After taking a lift to the third floor, they walked down a long, sterile corridor. On each side, glass doors had the doctor's name stencilled in various typefaces. Some even had the specialisation beneath the name: hypnosis, osteopathy, paediatrics, bowel movements. Others preferred a long list of abbreviations and full stops: Ph.D., M.D., F.R.C.S., P.P.A.D., were just a few Danilov recognised.

They stopped outside room 323. The name was there in large, simple, sans serif letters. Dr I. P. Lamarr. No abbreviations with full stops or any specialisations were listed beneath the name.

Danilov knocked and entered. A receptionist in a light blue nurse's uniform sat behind a neat desk, with nothing on it except a green lamp, desk diary and telephone. The room was elegant in an understated way. A light-green carpet, four comfortable armchairs, lighting from two tall lamps. On a side table, a stack of magazines threatened to topple over. Danilov glanced at the magazines. Some were in English, some in Chinese, all were over a year old.

'Can I help you?'

'We would like to see Dr Lamarr.'

'Do you have an appointment?' She was looking in the desk diary. From where he was standing, Danilov could see it was empty.

'I'm afraid Dr Lamarr is busy today. Can I make an appointment for you?'

Danilov walked up to the desk, standing as close to it as he could so his body loomed over the petite nurse. 'I would like to see Dr Lamarr now. Please tell him the police have an appointment.'

The nurse quickly closed the desk diary and got up. 'I'll see if he's available.'

She tapped gently on another glass door, waited for a quiet 'Enter' and went in.

When she was gone, Danilov went behind the desk and opened the diary. He leafed through the appointments for the last week. There were six names that appeared two or three times each, all written in neat handwriting. The desk itself was beautifully arranged, everything in its place and a place for everything.

The nurse appeared in the doorway. 'The doctor will see you now.'

Danilov closed the diary and walked into the next room, passing the nurse on his way in. If looks could kill, I've just been stabbed a thousand times, he thought.

If the waiting room had been comfortable, Lamarr's office was opulent. But opulence that whispered money quietly rather than shouting obscene wealth from the rooftops. A wealth that shows its ostentation through a lack of ostentation.

Danilov admired the precision of everything. The desk was exactly where it should be. A leather couch was just the right shade of brown. The chair beside it at exactly the right angle, comfortable yet stylish. All was clothed in soothing, muted colours to relax even the most nervous patient. The only block of colour was behind the desk. A Kandinsky perhaps, he thought. Evidence again of taste. And of wealth. Lamarr's practice must be extremely lucrative despite the lack of patients.

The good doctor was sitting behind his desk, wearing a clinician's white coat. He was writing in a notebook. Danilov noticed the fluid script and the beautiful mauve ink.

Lamarr looked up as if he had just noticed there were some people in his office and he needed to talk to them. A disturbance of little consequence.

'Hello, there, my receptionist didn't get your names.'

'We didn't give them,' answered Danilov bluntly. 'But this is Detective Constable Stra-chan and my name is Danilov, Inspector Danilov of the Shanghai Municipal Police.'

'Good afternoon, gentlemen.' An avuncular smile crossed the fleshy lips of the doctor. Danilov could see the skin was pale and shiny around his face, glossy almost, as if a fragile coat of oil had been applied just before they entered.

'Do sit down, gentlemen.' Lamarr indicated two comfortable chairs in front of the desk. 'How can I help you?'

'I wonder if you have ever seen this person.' Danilov took a picture of the victim and passed it over the desk to Lamarr. He glanced at it briefly before putting it back down.

'I have seen this person.'

'His name?'

'I'm afraid I can't disclose that information, gentlemen.'
The same avuncular smile appeared again on the doctor's

lips. 'As you are no doubt aware, such information falls under doctor–patient confidentiality.' He opened his arms in the classic 'I'm awfully sorry but there's nothing I can do' pose. Again, a smile crossed his lips.

Danilov was looking down at the hat in his hands. When he spoke, it was quietly. 'Doctor Lamarr, I don't understand.'

'I'm sorry if I haven't made myself clear. You must understand my patients have a right to privacy.'

'I understand that. What I don't understand is why you are practising medicine in Shanghai. You may be registered, but you have not been licensed, has he, Stra-chan?'

'No, sir, registered but not licensed. I checked with the Medical Council before we came.'

'And if you are not licensed, then all this,' Danilov waved his hands in the air indicating the elegant office, 'just vanishes in the blink of an eye.' He snapped his fingers.

The doctor stared at the fingers. A bead of sweat formed on his forehead and ran down the oily skin.

'So, what was that about doctor–patient confidentiality? I don't think I understood it.'

The doctor pulled a white handkerchief out from his pocket and began to dab his face, pulling at his collar as he did so. The loosening of the collar also seemed to loosen his tongue. 'Everything I say will be confidential?'

'Naturally, it's just between these four walls and six ears. A fool's tongue runs before his feet.'

'I'm sorry, I don't understand.'

'It's a saying from Minsk. In Russia,' said Strachan.

'Thank you, Stra-chan. Please continue, Doctor.'

The doctor picked up the fountain pen and began to spin it nervously using the tips of his fingers. He glanced down at the photo once again. 'This is one of my patients. Henry Sellars. He also goes under the name Harriet Sole.'

'I don't understand, please explain,' said Danilov.

The doctor ran his fingers through his hair and sighed. 'Henry Sellars came to me about six months ago. He had some worries . . .'

'He used to dress as a woman?'

'More than that. He thought he was a woman. And in his mind, he was. It's an interesting condition. He was an androgyne.'

'An androgyne?'

'A man who believes he is a woman. Not as rare as you would think. Kraft-Ebbing estimates that one in every three hundred men has this belief. According to him, their psyches, tastes and manners are more or less conspicuously feminine. On the sexual side of life, the ultra-androgyne desires as far as possible to pass for a woman. The ultra-androgyne feels himself to be a female and is attracted only towards the ultra-virile or tremendously virile, males.'

The doctor stopped speaking and the pen started to spin in his fingers again.

'And how were you treating him, Doctor?' asked Danilov.

'A few injections. The permanent removal of hair. He wanted me to remove his sexual organs.'

Out of the corner of his eye, Danilov could see Strachan cross his legs. 'Is that common?' he asked.

'Not common but possible. Hirschfeld in Germany has perfected a technique for the operation.'

'Chinese history is full of examples. The Imperial Eunuchs are rumoured to have kept their severed members in a jar beside their bed, looking at them every night before they went to sleep. The Empress Ci Xi . . .'

Inspector Danilov held up his hand. 'Thank you, Stra-chan. Please continue, Doctor.'

'Of course, I have never performed the operation in Shanghai. I'm not licensed.' The smile had returned.

'But you have performed it in America.'

'Yes, on three occasions.

'And the patients?'

'For them, it's life-changing. Literally.'

'How did he come to you?'

'I'm well known in the community. Most of my patients get to hear of me through word of mouth.'

'Oh, and where would one hear such words? Where would one see such mouths?'

'I'm sorry, I don't understand.' The smile had vanished again and more beads of sweat had formed on the doctor's forehead.

Danilov remained silent.

The fountain pen was now revolving like a spinning top caught in a hurricane. After an age of spinning, the doctor spoke. 'Most of my patients go to a particular club.'

'Which "particular" club?'

'The Paresis Hall on Foochow Road. Most of the androgynes go there. There's a small number of gynanders too. But I don't treat those.' A look of distaste crossed the doctor's face.

'Gynanders?'

'Women who want to be men. I don't treat them. Not my field.'

'Good, we will pay them a visit.'

'Please don't tell them that I told you, my business . . .'

The doctor had reached across his desk and touched the Inspector's arm. Danilov looked down at the hand on his sleeve and gently removed it, placing it back on the oak desk. 'Mr Sellars had a tattoo on the inside of his wrist. A verse from the bible.'

'He asked me to help him get rid of it. Something he had done when he was a member of some religious group. The Children of God. American missionaries. I tried to remove it, but tattoos are difficult . . .' He shrugged his shoulders.

'Thank you, Doctor. You have been most helpful.' Danilov stood up and strolled across the room to the door. Just before he opened it, he turned as if remembering something. 'One last question.'

'Yes, Inspector,' answered Dr Lamarr. The pen was spinning again.

'It's strange you haven't asked me what happened to Mr Sellars.'

The pen began to spin faster. 'I thought you had arrested him and maybe he had given you my name.'

'No, Doctor. He never mentioned you. Mr Sellars is dead, you see. Murdered. Not far from here, in Soochow Creek.'

Danilov opened the door and left, followed by Strachan.

The doctor sat behind his desk, his mouth open. The spinning pen fell from his fingers, splattering the elegant oak desk with drops of expensive mauve ink.

CHAPTER 10

Ah Yi Kao decided to go to the park that afternoon. It was a wonderfully clear day, the sun was shining and a slight breeze had blown away most of the coal smoke that clouded the skies during the winter. It would be good to get out of the house. The child was fretting and fidgeting, unable to run around. And how this child loved to run.

This was the third child she had looked after for the family, cooking the young ones' food, enjoying afternoon naps with them, keeping them amused while the father made money and the mother spent it. The other two children were away at school now. She had just the one child left to look after. A proper handful he was turning out to be.

It would be good to get out of the house this afternoon. She packed a flask of warm *congee* and a few dough sticks for the child. He might get hungry when they were at the park. He was two years old and had just discovered he had legs – they were very useful when you wanted to run and, if you moved them quickly, they took you to places Ah Yi didn't want you to go.

The mother wasn't too keen when she told her she was going out that afternoon, but she didn't say no. When it came to children, Ah Yi Kao always knew best. Better than any mother, of that she was sure.

She put the food, a small ball, and a bag full of towels, water, cloths for wiping his face, and an extra coat into the rack beneath her pride and joy; the pushchair. None of the other Ah Yis had anything like it. It had been imported from the USA, and she often paraded up and down outside the house in Sichuan Street, just to show off its shiny chromium wheels and handle, and the bright yellow hood. How she polished the pushchair. It had to look its best when she went out with her child.

She dressed the child in warm clothes even though it wasn't cold outside. A blue jumper she had knitted herself topped with a crimson padded jacket and matching trousers. She placed a warm, knitted hat on the child's head, tying it beneath his double chin. Better to be safe than sorry. He stared up at her with his big dark eyes and round rosy cheeks, anticipation etched on his face. He loved going out. She pinched one of his cheeks for good luck.

'Time to go, Xiao Ming,' she said in Shanghainese. He struggled a little as she picked him up but as soon as she put him in the pushchair, he sat there as quiet as Buddha.

They left the house, turning right at the end of the road and walking down Pékin Street towards the Bund. At that time in the afternoon, the roads weren't busy. Above her head, the clear blue sky shone through the twisted arms of the plane trees that lined the road. She pulled the yellow hood down so Xiao Ming could see what was going on. Better for him, she thought. He twisted around and smiled at her. What a charming little smile he has. A proper ladykiller in the future.

At the end of the road, she smelt the wonderful aroma of roasting sweet potatoes. A hawker was standing on the corner with his bike and oven, stirring the charcoal.

She went over and ordered two. The boy would be hungry after running around and they both loved the rich taste of sweet potato.

The hawker wanted 60 cents each. Shame on him. She knew the right price, offering him 30 cents and scolding him for being a dirty thief. Eventually, they agreed a price of 40 cents. It was a good bargain. Near her house, the hawkers charged 50 cents for each piece and they weren't nearly as big as these. She would have to come this way again.

She turned left at the Bund and walked a short way until she reached the entrance to the public garden. She hesitated a moment before going in. It wasn't so long ago the gardens were reserved for foreigners and their children. My child is as good as any of theirs, she thought, wheeling the pushchair into the park.

She expected a guard to jump out from behind one of the bushes, scold her and demand to know what she was doing there. It didn't happen so she relaxed, walking the pushchair further into the gardens. She smelt the first scents of spring in the magnolia blossoms that clung to one tree like dumplings cling to a fat man's fingers. She reached up to one of the flowers, bringing it down to inhale its aroma. She let it go and lifted her face to drink in the sun. The garden was just beginning to show the first signs of spring. Buds glistened on the bare branches, birds frolicked in the undergrowth, a squirrel clawed its way up to the crown of a tree.

The boy screamed from his pushchair. She looked around. The other maids were at the far end of the park and a tall European man was walking away from her. It would be safe to let him run around here.

She lifted him out of the pushchair, placed him on the ground, tucking his jumper into his padded trousers.

He toddled off with a wonderful self-assurance, his body swaying from side to side as he lifted his left and right legs. He let out a whoop of joy at being free from the house and the pushchair. To the Ah Yi, it seemed as if a round, red ball had let out a cry of delight.

And then he was off. She was amazed how quickly he moved with his short stubby legs, running down the path and disappearing around the corner.

She walked the pushchair after him. There he was, already thirty yards ahead of her, turning another corner on the path. She ran after him as fast as her chubby legs could take her. Imagine the shame if a child fell over in her care. How would she explain the grazed knees or, even worse, a cut head to her mistress? The thought sent a shiver through her body. She moved the pushchair even more quickly, turning the corner as fast as she could.

The boy had stopped running now. He was talking to a European woman who was sitting on a park bench. Baby talk with lots of pointing and shaking of fingers.

Ah Yi Kao relaxed. He was fine, complaining about her, she expected. He had a habit of talking to strangers. She would soon put a stop to that behaviour.

She pushed the stroller towards them. The woman didn't react to Xiao Ming at all. Usually, people would lean forward and listen, pretending to understand the gibberish the boy was speaking. This woman didn't, she just sat there, staring into the distance.

As she got closer, the Ah Yi noticed the woman's clothes. They were short and thin, even for such a warm day in late February. The sort of clothes only the worst type of Chinese women wore. Her skin was red too as if she had been sitting out in the cold too long. But the woman was foreign and you never knew the strange things foreign women got up to.

The Ah Yi moved forward to pull the boy away. He shouldn't talk to such women, you never knew where, or with whom, they had been.

The Ah Yi kept her eyes averted when she reached down to grab the boy's hand. It was only as she pulled him away that she noticed the feet. The woman wasn't wearing shoes. How strange in this weather. The woman's legs were also covered in thin red stripes, looking as though they were weeping.

She pulled the boy to her. She could see all of the woman now. She noticed the blue eyes first, strange eyes that looked as if they couldn't see. She saw the deep red gash of the woman's throat and the red soup that had flowed all over the woman's dress.

It was only then that she screamed.

***

He watched the Ah Yi screaming from the undergrowth. People came running from across the park. Soon, there was a crowd surrounding the body. Her beautiful body, how he would miss her. But he had to leave her here for them to see. They had to be able to see his work, otherwise how will they know what to do? How will they know they have to change?

The cops arrived quickly. 'Keystone Kops', running around here and there like a pack of demented mice. He loved to watch their stupidity. Trampling the ground around the beautiful body, despoiling his tableau. One of them even had the temerity to go up and touch her on the side of the head. Of course, she fell over to lie down on the bench.

How dare they? How dare they disturb her repose? Why didn't they just leave her as he had placed her? Idiots! All idiots!

He would have to show them even more. He knew who his next lesson would be. He would show them the errors of their ways. They didn't know yet. They didn't see yet. But they would soon, of that he was sure.

Eventually, he would have to judge them all. Or at least, all of them who had lied, cheated or stolen. Maybe he would spare the children. The pure, unadulterated children. Not those who had already been maculated by the touch of this society.

There were so many still to judge. But at least he liked his work. He didn't know whether he was supposed to take pleasure in it. The writings said nothing about pleasure, just about judgement.

Elsie had been tougher than he thought. He must remember not to underestimate the will to live. An extremely strong instinct. A primeval instinct, the will to survive. He had survived, lying out there in no man's land, surrounded by rats and mud and death. He had survived, but the rest had not. They had been judged and found wanting. They had lied and cheated, but he had been pure. That's why he had survived.

Over the years since then, he knew what he needed to do. But it had only become clear when he came to China. It was only here that he understood the rightness of his cause. It was only here he knew the Chinese had been practising his justice for millennia. Here, he had come alive like a caterpillar turning into a butterfly. Now, he acted just as he was meant to act. Just as he was guided to act.

He knew who would be next.

***

A small man with a thin, caterpillar moustache stood in front of Sergeant Wolfe's desk. 'I'm the interpreter, Mr Huang. You rang for me?'

'We've got a strange one.' The sergeant pointed to the Giant standing in the corner, examining one of the pockets of his threadbare clothes. 'Can't understand a word he says. Thought he might be one of the river people.'

The interpreter began speaking a dialect to the Giant, all sibilant esses and long, slithering sounds. The man replied quickly, again going through his pantomime of pointing and gesturing.

'You were correct, he's from the river. His boat is moored at Soochow Creek,' said the interpreter.

'Ask him why he's here.'

The interpreter spoke a few words and received a lengthy speech in return, complete with pointing, waving and a peculiar demonstration of something. Sergeant Wolfe scratched his head.

'A voluble people, the river dwellers. Storytellers all of them,' said the interpreter shrugging his shoulders. 'We could be here a long time.'

'Tell him to get on with it, I haven't got all day.'

Once again, the interpreter spoke only a few words to the Giant. This time, the answer still had all the previous gestures and pointing but was considerably shorter. Meanwhile a newcomer entered the reception area and noticed the desk sergeant.

'Hello, Jim, you seem to be busy today.'

'George Cartwright. Long time, no see. I thought you'd be skiving off somewhere this time of day. Isn't it time for your afternoon refreshment?'

'Funny man, you are. I'd never do that on duty, would I?' Cartwright stared down at the small interpreter and up to the ragged Giant standing beside him. 'What you got here then?'

The interpreter took his chance to speak. 'The man here said it's about the body, yesterday. The police were asking if anybody saw anything.'

'Which body?' asked Cartwright.

'The one in Soochow Creek. The man wants to see Detective Strallan or something like that.'

'Probably Strachan, him and Danilov are handling that case.' Sergeant Wolfe turned to the interpreter. 'They're not here now. Ask him to come back later.'

'Don't worry, Jim. I said I'd help out on that case. Do you have a room where we can talk quietly?'

'Take that one, George. Thanks for this, I've enough on my plate already with this little lot.' He indicated the crowd of people who were waiting to see him.

'You owe me one, Jim. A large one with a splash of water in it.' Cartwright pointed at the Giant and the interpreter. 'Come this way and have a chat with Uncle George.' He winked at Sergeant Wolfe and led them to the interview room.

After they were seated, Cartwright got right down to business. 'Now then, what's all this about?' He had made sure there was as much distance as possible in the confines of the room between himself and the Giant. He'd heard stories in the bars of the terrible diseases some of the river people carried. It was enough to make your toes curl. Better have a few stiff ones after this, just in case.

The Giant kept shifting around on the wooden police chair, obviously unused to sitting on such a hard seat. He turned this way and that, finding some semblance of comfort by putting his right leg up on the chair, jammed against the haunch of his bottom.

A dirty toenail stared right at Cartwright. He tried to look away but kept being dragged back to its hard yellow cap with a thick layer of black beneath. 'Ask him what he wants,' he stammered, finally dragging his eyes from the foot and its webbed toes.

The interpreter, who was also sitting as far away from the Giant as he could, let forth a slither of sounds.

The Giant began to reply slowly, gradually gaining pace and expression as he became more involved with his tale.

The interpreter kept up a running commentary. 'He had got up early that morning . . . to catch *Lei Man* . . . it's a small river fish . . . lives in the mud . . . used in *congee* . . . he sells them to the restaurants on Foochow Street . . . gets a good price . . .'

'He just needs to say what happened, not give his bloody life story.'

The interpreter rapped out another trilling song of dialect. He tapped on the table for effect at the end of his speech. The Giant began to speak again, this time more slowly and precisely.

The interpreter continued: '. . . he was just washing the bow of his boat when he saw two men rowing out to the sandbar.'

'He was certain it was two men?'

The interpreter asked and a sing-song reply came back from the Giant which even Cartwright recognised was an affirmative.

'What did the men look like?'

'He couldn't see their faces . . . one was tall and the other was short.' The Giant used his hands to show the difference in height. 'The tall one was nearly as tall as him.'

'How does he know?'

The interpreter asked the question and immediately began translating the answer. 'Because when they reached the "Beach of Dead Babies" – I think that's what he called it – when they reached there, the two men stood up in the boat.'

Cartwright was about to ask another question when the interpreter reached across and touched him on his hand. He pulled it away immediately, taking out his large white handkerchief to wipe the spot where he had been touched.

The interpreter carried on anyway. 'They took something quite large from inside the boat which they threw over the side onto the beach . . . he thought they were just dumping some rubbish.'

'At that time in the morning?'

This time the interpreter answered the question without referring to the Giant. 'On the river, you don't ask many questions, so nobody tells you any lies.'

The Giant started speaking again. The interpreter translated: '. . . they spent about two minutes over at the beach, leaning out from the boat, arranging their parcel.'

'He didn't ask them what they were doing?'

The interpreter's eyes fluttered to the ceiling. 'These people don't. None of their business what anybody else does. They value their lives.'

The Giant carried on: '. . . he says they rowed back to the bank and got into a big car. The bald-headed man drove and the tall one sat in the back.'

'Bald-headed?'

The interpreter and the Giant demonstrated with his hands. 'He says the man's head was totally bald, like a winter melon except his head was pink not green.' The Giant laughed and both shoulders lifted almost to his ears as he did so. When he had finished, he carried on talking. 'He then went out with his net just below Garden Bridge to fish for *Lei Man*. When he came back two hours later, the police were everywhere.'

Cartwright glanced up at the clock on the green wall of the room. Nearly five-thirty, time for his evening pick-me-up at Coco's. 'Anything else?' he asked.

The interpreter spoke once again. The Giant shrugged his broad shoulders and shook his head.

'It seems that's it,' said the interpreter.

'OK, thank him for visiting the station today. You know, the usual polite rubbish you people enjoy hearing from each other.' Cartwright started to get up when the Giant started speaking once more, this time holding his right hand out, palm upwards.

'He says he wants five dollars,' said the interpreter.

'What?'

'Five dollars. The reward that was promised.'

'Reward?'

'For information. The policeman told all the boat people.'

'I know nothing 'bout any reward. Tell him to come back later. You can get your chit from Sergeant Wolfe.' Cartwright got up and rushed out of the room. God, he needed a drink.

The interpreter tried to explain about the reward. The Giant did not look a happy man.

***

The local police had closed off the park at all the entrances, but that hadn't stopped a crowd of sightseers from gathering around the metal railings.

Inspector Danilov drew up in the black sedan driven by Strachan. They had gone back to the station after the interview with the doctor, only to be greeted by the news of the discovery of another body.

'Afternoon, sir, we've closed the gates and sealed off the park.'

'Well done, Sergeant. Who found the body?'

The sergeant pointed at the plump, well-fed Ah Yi, sitting on a bench just inside the gates. She was shouting and crying to the police in loud Shanghainese. Her young charge sat quietly in his pram, enjoying all the activity going on around him.

'I have to go home. I'm late. The family will be worried, his parents will sack me,' she wailed.

'Stra-chan, interview this woman quickly, then get her a police escort home before she wakes the dead. I'll deal with the body.'

'Yes, sir.' Strachan moved quickly to the woman's side, kneeling down next to her and touching her softly on her arm. 'Is this your child?' he said quietly in Shanghainese. The woman stopped crying and nodded. 'He's well behaved. You've taught him well.' She nodded again. 'We mustn't get him worried though.' Again his arm touched hers lightly.

'No,' she answered.

'Just tell me what you saw and then we'll drive you and the boy home.' He tickled the boy under his chin. The young child responded with a large smile, his eyes vanishing into the fleshy cheeks.

In between gasps for breath, she began to talk, Strachan encouraging her with little nods of the head.

Danilov scanned the park. It was caught in that wonderful time between winter and summer, the buds beginning to show on the trees and signs of life bursting through the brown earth. It was a time he loved in Minsk, when the crocuses were pushing through the hard ground, little fingers of green with blue highlights, thrusting themselves into the world.

Over to his left, an English lawn stretched to a wooden bandstand. Its wooden stage lay empty and forlorn, just memories of hot summer nights and waltz music to keep it warm in winter.

The crowd behind him, four or five deep in some places, had gone silent, straining to hear the testimony of the Ah Yi as she talked to Strachan.

Another crowd, another public spectacle.

Danilov lifted his nose to the breeze. There it was again, the lilting scent of incense in the air. Again, he was taken back to a church in Minsk, walking down the aisle with his new bride-to-be, the chants of the monks a counterpoint to the echoes of his footsteps, a priest in ornate golden robes and white flowing beard waiting for them at the altar.

He turned around quickly and scanned the faces of the crowd behind the iron railings. Young and old, round and gaunt, short and tall, European and Chinese, they all stared at the plump Ah Yi giving her statement.

And there he was. The hawker with his cauldron of charcoal and sweet potatoes, reaching for his paddle and stirring the white embers in the base. The aroma of incense wafted through the air again.

The sergeant touched Danilov's arm. 'It's this way, sir.' He led him down a narrow path, past a magnolia tree in full blossom, round a corner and there she was.

'Please wait here, Sergeant.'

She was lying on a park bench dressed in a light pink camisole, a vivid splash of red glistening on her chest. Her hands were neatly crossed in front of her and her eyes were open.

Blue eyes. Cornflower-blue eyes. The same as Henry Sellars. They had a peculiar lack of life in them, like glass eyes lying on a tray in an ophthalmologist's shop.

He moved closer. He could see red lines scarring her arms and legs. Sharp, slicing cuts that contrasted with the great red gash that used to be her throat. But something seemed wrong to him. She wasn't as posed as Henry Sellars had been.

He walked back to the sergeant. 'Has anybody touched the body?'

The sergeant looked down. 'I'm sorry, sir, one of the lads touched her face to see if she was dead. I'm afraid she fell over onto her side. We didn't want to move her.'

Danilov lifted his hat and ran his fingers through his hair. Would they never learn? Well, the damage was done now. 'Please inform Dr Fang that another body will be coming to the morgue today. If he could look at it as soon as possible . . .'

'Yes, sir.'

'And ask Detective Constable Stra-chan to join me as soon as he has finished.'

'Yes, sir.'

The sergeant marched back towards the gates. Danilov scanned the park again. A pretty place, quiet but open. There would be people here at all times of the day. Why take the risk to be seen? And why were the bodies displayed so openly? What message was the killer trying to send?

Perhaps that wasn't the right question. 'Ask the right questions and they will eventually lead you to the solution.' He remembered his training from the Imperial Police Academy, Muller, the old instructor, always intoning, 'To find the right answer, look for the right question,' in his German accent.

He had not asked the right questions yet.

A cough announced someone was behind him. 'What is it?'

Strachan stepped forward. 'The woman found the body at 4.30 p.m., sir. She had just come to the park with her child for a stroll before dinner. The boy ran away from her. She chased after him and thought he was talking to a woman on the bench. It was only as she got close that she realised the woman was dead.' Strachan glanced down at the body lying on the bench. 'Strange though, she said the woman was sitting upright. She was clear about that. She said it was just like the woman was taking a tea break on the bench.'

'Hmmm, nobody else reported seeing her?'

'Nobody so far. The local police cleared the park so we don't know who was here when she was found.'

'Ask around, will you? Perhaps they are still watching from over there.' He pointed towards the crowd of sightseers, which had almost doubled in size now, new watchers attracted like ants to a cube of sugar. 'Strachan, get statements from the local coppers who arrived on the scene. They may have noticed something.'

'Yes, sir.'

Danilov looked down at the body once more. A strand of blonde hair hung down over her forehead, framing one of the cornflower-blue eyes. A pretty woman, he thought, vivacious.

'Who took your life?' he asked out loud to the corpse.

A sudden breeze whistled through the trees, blowing Danilov's hat off his head and past the bench with its cold body. The hat rolled on, pushed by the breeze, across the lawn towards the bandstand.

Danilov stood there and watched it go.

CHAPTER 11

'How was your day?'

'Just the same. Busy. Bureaucratic. Corrupt. Nothing new. Did you see Elsie?'

Richard put down his drink. He stared up at the carvings of laurel leaves, acorns and cherubs that adorned the ceiling of the Shanghai Club and decided to come straight out with it. 'She's gone away with another man.'

'Impossible. I don't believe it. She couldn't . . . she wouldn't.'

'I'm afraid it's true. I went to the theatre. They said she didn't turn up for work last night. I also went to her home. Her flatmate said she had gone away.' He paused for a moment and thought about what he was going to say. 'It appears I wasn't the only one.'

'*Rubbish!*' Alfred shouted loudly. Two of the other members turned and stared at them. He lowered his voice. 'It can't be true. Not Elsie. I don't believe it.'

'She left all her clothes behind. Took nothing.'

'Elsie wouldn't have gone without talking to you. She wasn't that sort . . .'

'And what sort was that?' asked Richard.

Alfred had the sense to remain quiet.

'It does seem strange, her vanishing like that.' Richard finished his Scotch and water. 'Not like her at all.'

'Listen. She wouldn't just go off. Something must have happened to her.'

'Like what?'

'I don't know. A lot of kidnappings lately.'

'But Elsie hasn't got any money. And there's been no ransom note.'

'Not that sort of kidnapping. One reads about it all the time. Pretty girl. Kidnapped. Taken to some foreign mansion. Held against her will. You know the sort of stuff I'm talking about.'

'But that's just the stuff for the yellow press like the *Daily Mail*. It doesn't really happen.'

'There is a word for it, isn't there? Shanghaied.'

'I thought that was just for sailors.'

Alfred shrugged his shoulders. 'It doesn't feel right to me. She wouldn't just go off.'

'I think you're right. If I haven't heard from her by tomorrow morning, I'll go to the police. They'll know what to do.'

'Do it. You never know what could have happened to her.'

Richard checked his watch. 'No point in hanging round here. Can I give you a lift anywhere?'

'Let's go to the Lido.'

He got up and nodded to the waiter, who went behind the bar and brought Richard the chit to sign. 'Last night, I was going to ask her to marry me and now she's vanished.'

Alfred guided his friend out of the Long Bar to the door of the club. A doorman leant to one side, pulling open the imposing double doors. The car was already waiting with its engine running.

'I can't believe there was anybody else in Elsie's life. I know there was only me.'

Richard threw his cigarette into the gutter. As he did so a copy of the *North China Daily News* drifted along the road, blown by the wind. In bold black letters, the headline on the cover read:

ANOTHER BODY FOUND

Beneath it, in smaller type, a subhead made it plain to all but the most stupid reader:

THE CHARACTER KILLER STRIKES

CHAPTER 12

Inspector Danilov and Detective Constable Strachan were sitting alone in the detectives' room at Central Police Station. A solitary lamp burned above Danilov's desk. A clock ticked loudly on the wall. Smoke hung in the air, its white trail caught in the light like a silk shroud.

Danilov was slouched in his chair saying nothing.

Strachan was sitting opposite him, tapping his fingers on the table.

The rest of the night shift had been called out to a stabbing on the Bund near Chu Pao Street. An American marine had taken a strong dislike to a British squaddie over a game of darts and knifed him between the ribs. Just another quiet night in Blood Alley.

'Another killing, sir.' Strachan was just trying to make conversation with his boss who had spent the last half hour just sitting there, rolling his pungent cigarettes.

'An acute observation, Stra-chan.'

'Sorry, sir, you were lost in thought, I just thought . . .'

'You just thought you would disturb me?'

'No, sir.'

'You will learn, Detective Stra-chan, that silence can be the most useful weapon in a policeman's arsenal. Silence makes people feel uncomfortable. Just as you felt when you were sitting here with me.'

'Yes, sir, I . . .'

Danilov held his hand out in front of his face and his finger came up to his lips. As he did so, he noticed a yellow note peeping out from under his desk blotter. He picked it up with the tips of his fingers. 'A Lieutenant Masset called. Would like an update on the investigation? Miss Cavendish.'

She even signs it Miss Cavendish, thought Danilov. I wonder what her first name is. Something very English, I'm sure. Daphne. Dorothy. Daisy. Maybe all three.

But who had hidden the note? One of the children, Cartwright, Ford, or Tinkler. Would they never stop playing games? Their childishness was affecting his investigation. He would have to do something. 'Masset is inquiring about our progress, Stra-chan. What shall I tell him?'

'You could tell him there's been another murder, sir.'

'I'll let him know tomorrow morning, I'm sure it's not the news he wants to hear.'

Danilov then lapsed back into silence, staring at a brown mark on his desk. 'It's the same man,' he said quietly. 'The rope marks, the characters on the chest, the personal, close method of killing.'

'The same man who killed Henry Sellars?'

'No. The same man who killed Henry Sellars. And the magistrate. And the Russian prostitute. And the woman tonight.'

'I think I understand, sir.'

'What are the patterns?' He looked across at Strachan. 'What colour was the prostitute's hair?'

Strachan reached for the files that had arrived from the French Garde Municipale that afternoon. He scanned down the form. 'She was blonde too, sir.'

'And the magistrate?'

He took the other file and scanned it too. '*Châtain*. I think that means "chestnut", sir. Reddish-brown.'

Danilov was deflated. 'It does, Stra-chan, your years studying French under Mademoiselle Lafarge were not wasted.'

'Actually, I studied under a large Belgian monk called Georges who weighed 300 pounds and stank of beer. I think he brewed it himself.'

'The Belgians make good beer. They don't make good monks.' Danilov thought again. 'What about the eyes? Both our victims had a beautiful shade of cornflower blue. Most striking.'

'The magistrate had hazel eyes, sir. "*Yeux noisette*," it says here. The Russian prostitute had green eyes.'

'Stra-chan . . .'

'Yes, sir.'

'How much did you understand during our meeting with the French?'

'Quite a lot, sir.'

'You never let on.'

'No, I thought it better not to reveal how much I understood. You never know when silence can come in handy.'

'Silence is golden, Stra-chan.'

'We have the same proverb in English, sir.'

'I know. I was speaking English.'

'Oh, I thought . . .'

'Don't think, Stra-chan, that's my job. So the only link between the victims seems to be the characters carved on their chest and the rope that tied their wrists.'

'That seems to be it, sir. But the characters have been different every time.' Strachan checked his notebook. '"Vengeance" written on the magistrate. "Damnation" on the Russian prostitute. "Justice" on Henry Sellars.

And "Retribution" on our woman in the park. Not common characters, sir. Quite old-fashioned. The sort of language a Mandarin would use in the Imperial examinations, not your normal johnnie's word at all. I had to look it up in the dictionary.'

'Like Shakespeare or Chaucer?'

'Exactly, sir, except a Chinese version.' Strachan thought for a moment. 'I know somebody who could help us. My mother's eldest uncle, Chang. He sat the Imperial examinations in 1910.'

'Not the best time to be a Mandarin.'

'Took him fifteen years of study and he finally passes them just as the Empire begins to crumble. Not much use for a Mandarin in a republic.'

'How can he help?'

'I don't know, sir, but as you said, we're missing something. He may be able to give us a new angle.'

'And what about the scratches on the bottom of the lid?'

'"HATE ALL" – the words of a madman, if you ask me.'

'Luckily, I wasn't asking you. But they are frightening words, Stra-chan. It seems our killer has no love for the human race.'

'Do you want me to check the local asylums, sir? See if anybody has been released lately?'

Danilov became much more active, stubbing his cigarette out in the ashtray. 'Not yet. I think there is a logic in their madness. We just haven't seen it yet. But you can set up a meeting with your uncle. I think we have to learn more about these written characters.' He stood up in front of his desk. 'Did you find out anything about the church? The Children of God, I think it was called.'

'I've got an address, sir. It's across the creek in Hongkew.'

'Meaker's territory.'

'Shall I tell him we're coming, sir?'

Danilov took out his tobacco pouch and began rolling another cigarette. 'No, don't, he won't want to get involved. The man's a waste of oxygen. I worked with him once. Not a good partnership. We'll pay it a visit tomorrow morning.'

'I also checked the club, Paresis Hall, with the local coppers. Well known, it is. Somebody must have been paid off because it's been going strong for a number of years. Attracts tour groups apparently. There to see the local "sights".'

'Hmmm, let's visit there now. You don't have anything else to do, do you?'

Strachan hadn't eaten all day. A warm bowl of dumplings was waiting for him at home. As his mother always said, the one thing that was definitely Chinese about him was his stomach. 'No, sir, nothing else to do.'

'Good, let's get going.' Danilov picked up his hat and coat from the stand next to the door. 'Heard anything from the river people?'

'Not a dicky bird, sir.'

'At least we won't be getting any red herrings from them.'

'Was that a joke, sir?'

'Yes, Stra-chan, we Russians are famous for our sense of humour.'

'Very good, sir, very funny.'

'Let's go and meet our androgynes, shall we? It should be an interesting evening.'

CHAPTER 13

From the outside, the building was just like all the others in the street: three storeys tall with a classic Shikumen gate at the entrance, leading into a small courtyard before the front door.

Inspector Danilov and Detective Constable Strachan were standing at the door with their hats in their hands. A small man had tried to stop them from entering, but they had shown their warrant cards and brushed past him.

It went quiet as soon as they entered. There were twenty people standing at the bar, with another four wooden tables occupied by an assortment of patrons: two Russians with dyed platinum hair obviously taking a break from walking the streets, some Chinese and Western men, and a pair of Chinese girls dressed in ornate *chi paos*. In one corner, a threesome played piano, drums and an upright bass on a stage raised just three inches off the floor, the music providing background noise to fill in the gaps in conversation.

Before they had entered, the patrons had been laughing and joking with each other. Now they were silent, looking straight at Danilov and Strachan.

A six-foot tall woman, dressed in a bright red silk dress with long flowing ruffles, high heels and black stockings, approached them. She was wearing the longest string of pink pearls Danilov had ever seen.

When she opened her mouth, out came a deep, booming voice. 'I don't want any trouble, gentlemen.'

'I'm sorry, Plum, I couldn't stop them.' The small man squeaked from behind the detectives. Danilov realised that the man was a woman.

'Don't worry, Lesley. I'll handle it from here.' Lesley adjusted her purple tie, pulled down her dinner jacket, and went back to her place by the door.

'We have no desire to cause you any trouble . . . madame. We just want a chat.'

'Call me Plum. And you are . . .?'

'Inspector Danilov and Detective Constable Stra-chan.'

'Delighted, I'm sure.' Plum held out her hand towards Danilov. She obviously meant him to kiss it. Instead, he shook it once, before stepping back.

'Come, we'll sit over there. We don't want to disturb the guests.'

She led them to a table in the rear of the room. As they walked through, the other patrons at the bar pulled back or turned their faces away. Danilov walked past an assortment of women dressed as men, men dressed as women and men dressed as men who looked like women. He tried to look straight ahead so that he wouldn't stare at the patrons, but a woman with a moustache got the better of him.

Plum pulled out three chairs at a table next to some stairs leading to the upper storey. On the wall beside the stairs was a large poster with ENTRANCE THROUGH THE REAR written on it, with a large black arrow pointing upstairs.

Strange, thought Danilov.

'Would you like a drink, gentlemen?'

'No, thank you, Miss Plum, we're here on business, I'm afraid.'

'What a shame,' said Plum looking straight at Strachan. 'How can I help you?'

'Do you recognise this person?' Danilov showed her the picture of Henry Sellars.

Plum stared at it for a long time before placing it down on the table. 'It's Harriet. Her hair looks pretty in this shot.'

'Harriet?'

'Harriet Sole. One of our patrons. I don't know her real name. We don't go in much for real names here.'

'What can you tell me about her?' Danilov was conscious of using the female pronoun. He was sure it was the right approach to take.

Plum looked at him, saying nothing. Danilov could hear the bar sounds increase in volume as the patrons gradually forgot the presence of the detectives, and returned to their games and flirting.

'Harriet is dead, Plum. She was murdered. We need you to help us find her murderer.'

Plum's face changed, going from stubborn resistance to shock to horror, all in a few seconds. He could see the veneer was cracked now. Beneath the make-up, she was a lot older than she seemed. Wrinkles led from her eye to the edge of her hair and a flap of flesh beneath her chin wobbled.

'But she was here only two nights ago.'

'Was she with anyone?'

Plum's eyes glanced towards the stairs and up to the second storey.

'We're here to find a murderer not to arrest anybody.'

Plum placed her hands on her lap and inhaled deeply. Then in a soft, deep voice said, 'She was here two nights ago. She may have entertained a few gentlemen upstairs that evening.'

'Do you know who they were?'

'One was a tall man, a European. I hadn't seen him before, but he seemed pleasant. The other was one of her Chinese regulars, Mr Chan. He comes here every two weeks.'

'Names?'

'We don't take names. Here, people can be who they want to be, not a name.'

He decided to take a different tack. 'Can you remember anything about the tall man?'

'Well, he was thin, quite elegant. He had an air of superiority about him. Not my type at all. I only saw him for a few seconds, across the bar. It was a busy night. Harriet was in a good mood. Her Chinese friend had visited her earlier and she obviously liked her tall beau.' Her hand went to her mouth and stifled a sob. 'Harriet dead?' she whispered.

The door opened at the front of the room and a group of people, both men and women, entered, headed by a small Chinese woman.

Plum pulled out a large silk handkerchief and dabbed the corners of her eyes. 'If you will excuse me.'

She got up and approached the group. Soon they were seated at different tables, each attended to by the girls and the boys.

Plum stepped onto the stage and nodded at the band. They stopped playing. She leant into the microphone. 'I'd like to welcome our guests from the liner, *Orestaia*, I do hope you have a wonderfully perverse time in Shanghai.' Her voice, channelled through the wires of the microphone, had a sound like melted chocolate. 'Here's a song I'd like to sing for you. It was one of Harriet's favourites.'

She turned back to the band and whispered something. The bassist put down his instrument and picked up a trumpet.

She began singing, slowly and sensuously, the band providing a soft, unembellished accompaniment:

'Baby face, you've got the cutest little baby face.'

Danilov recognised the lyric but thought it was a much happier, more vibrant song. Plum sang it slowly with a melancholy edge that matched her deep, sad voice, each word enunciated beautifully and mournfully:

'There's not another who can take your place,

'Baby face, my heart poor heart is thumpin',

'You sure have started somethin',

'Baby face, I'm up in heaven when I'm in your fond embrace,

'Uh well I need a shove because I'm in love, with my pretty baby face.'

The trumpet came alive with a plaintive lament to the last 'baby face'. Plum wiped a tear from her eyes, smearing her make-up in the process.

'Baby face, I'm up in heaven . . .'

She stopped singing and just stood there. The band carried on with the melody, finishing the chorus and bringing the song to an end.

The audience clapped loudly. Plum took a deep breath, bowed and walked back to rejoin the table. 'Sorry for the interruption, I have to sing occasionally. It keeps the girls happy.' She wiped a tear from her eye.

'Who are the new arrivals?' asked Danilov.

'As I said, a tour group from one of the cruise ships in the harbour. We often get them here, seeing the joy, gin and jazz of Shanghai. They'll be off to the Lido soon. A few will stay here longer, of course.'

'Enjoying the city of shadows,' said Danilov.

'It's always enjoyable as long as you can return to the light. Or a luxury cruise ship, in their case,' replied Plum.

'It seems everybody knows about your establishment except the police.'

'Oh, I'm sure they know. One of your inspectors owns the place. Charges a fat rent too.'

'I'm sure you can afford it.'

'I can't not afford it. Given my particular taste in dresses.' She waved her long elegant hands over the red satin.

Danilov tapped his fingers on the table. 'What else can you tell me about Henry Sellars, also known as Harriet Sole?'

'Not a lot. We don't ask too many questions, so we don't get told lies. Started coming here about six months ago. Kept her clothes in an upstairs locker and kept herself to herself. Not one of the chatty types. Liked her finery though, Harriet. Loved her blue silk, I remember. A gorgeous girl. An even prettier boy.'

'Could we look in the locker?'

'Be my guest. It's padlocked, but I'm sure your muscular friend could pull it off quickly. I'm sure he's good at that.' She stared at Strachan. He stared at his feet.

She led them up the stairs to another small room above the bar. Four girls were waiting for customers in various stages of undress. They quickly put on some clothes and left as soon as Danilov and Strachan appeared.

'You certainly have a way with the girls,' said Plum from the doorway. She pointed to a locker in the corner. 'That's Harriet.'

At a nod from Danilov, Strachan took the lock in his hands. It was cheap and light. With a sharp tug and a downward pull, it came free from the latch.

Plum clapped her hands from the doorway.

Strachan went red and stepped back. Danilov opened the locker. Hanging inside were two blue silk dresses, obviously expensively tailored, with matching blue court shoes. Next to the dresses was a man's suit with a white shirt hanging inside and a tie draped over it.

'She always wore male clothes outside and changed when she got here.'

'What about the long, blonde hair?' asked Strachan.

'What do you think a hat is for?'

Danilov held up his hand in front of Strachan. 'Were these the clothes she wore when she arrived?'

'Probably. Looks like her suit.'

'Then, she left the club wearing female clothes. Was that normal?'

'Listen, honey, nothing is normal around here.'

The Inspector changed his question. 'Was that usual?'

Plum sighed. 'No, it wasn't. Harriet always wore male clothes outside. She said this was the only place she could be herself.'

Danilov searched the pockets of the suit. In one of them he found a small bible, printed by the Overseas Chinese Missionary Organisation of Missouri. He opened the fly page and read, 'To Henry, from your preacher, may you always find comfort in his words.' He opened the next page and saw a printed sticker: EX LIBRIS. THE CHURCH OF THE REDEEMER, SINZA ROAD, SHANGHAI.

He passed the book back to Strachan and checked the rest of the suit. Nothing. He examined the shelves of the locker. Some talcum powder, a safety razor, a small bottle of Chanel No 5, a brush, a pair of brown brogues and a trilby.

He closed the door of the locker. 'Thank you, Miss Plum, you've been a great help.'

'Always happy to give a hand to the police. Wouldn't you like to stay for a drink?'

'Thank you, but no, we have work to do.'

'And what about you?' Plum looked straight at Strachan. 'The girls would be happy to help you relax.'

'Detective Constable Stra-chan is busy tonight, unfortunately. Perhaps, another time.' He reached inside his jacket and pulled a card from his wallet, giving it to Plum. 'Please ask the other girls if they saw or knew anything about the tall man, or Harriet Sole. It's very important.'

Plum took the card. 'I will, Inspector, but I wouldn't hold my breath if I were you. We spend our lives avoiding the stares of others. In the end, we stop seeing anything at all. Even here. Especially here. A consequence of our situation you see . . .' Her voice trailed off.

'I understand, Miss Plum. But call me if anything comes up, however small or insignificant.'

Danilov put on his hat and said goodbye. Strachan followed the Inspector down the stairs.

'Thank you for rescuing me back there.'

'That's all right. I'll need you to come back on your own tomorrow night though. Take some witness statements from the girls.'

Strachan's face fell.

'We've all got to make some sacrifices in the line of duty.'

As they left, the Inspector said goodbye to the man guarding the door. All he got was a high-pitched squeak in answer.

Back on the street, they could hear the sounds of laughter returning to the club.

Danilov was used to the effect of his presence in certain places. It was almost as if he carried around with him a magic wand that somehow removed all happiness, laughter and gaiety.

He was used to it, but it still left him saddened. Strachan appeared not to notice. He hides it well, thought Danilov. Already, he hides it well.

'What time will I meet you tomorrow, sir?'

Danilov looked at his watch. 'Let's say 7.30 a.m. We should go to the church early. Time to atone for our sins.'

Strachan brushed his hair away from his eyes. 'I don't understand, sir.'

'It was nothing. You'd better get some sleep. Not much chance in a murder enquiry. Good night, Detective Constable Stra-chan.' The Inspector lifted his hat.

'Can I drive you home, sir?'

'No, Stra-chan, I prefer to walk. It gives me time to think. You should try it some time.'

'Walking or thinking, sir?'

'Both, Stra-chan. You should start with the thinking first though. For example, why did Henry Sellars leave his clothes in his locker? And how did he meet our tall man?'

'I don't know, sir.'

'So think about it. Good night,' the Inspector shouted over his shoulder as he drifted off into the shadows.

'Good night, Inspector.'

***

Danilov pulled his hat down lower over his eyes and put his hands into his pockets. Ahead of him the lights of Nanking Road shone bright against a fog of coal smoke.

The streets were still crowded with people, scurrying here and there in search of bargains, food or the denizens of the night. Stalls in all shapes and sizes crowded in on the road; an itinerant barber shaved a man's head beneath the light of a hurricane lamp. Fortune tellers, with the sticks and bones and birds of their trade, called out to all and sundry to find out what lay in store for them in the future. Danilov was tempted to ask one of them who the killer was. He was sure the man would have an answer, it just wouldn't be the one he was looking for.

Across the street, a group of American sailors in their wide-bottomed trousers and white hats poured out of a bar, singing raucously. They staggered on down towards the Bund and Blood Alley, in search of more beer, more love or more fighting.

A rickshaw ran by, his load an overweight merchant, dressed in a white suit. The rickshaw puller wore nothing but a loincloth wrapped around his belly, despite the cold. The merchant was berating him to go faster.

Danilov watched it all as he walked along. Shanghai was a hard place to live if you had nothing. An even harder place to live if you had nobody.

For a moment, he considered going to a nearby opium den that he knew well and that knew him. A bed awaited him there, and the pipes were clean. But not tonight, tonight he had work to do.

He walked on between the stalls that lined either side of the pavement. Firecrackers were going off on his left, sparkling the night skies with their bright colours and rainbow flashes. A conjurer appeared in front of him, keeping six balls in the air, his hands catching and tossing the balls with the speed of a well-greased machine.

He stepped past him and walked on only to find his way blocked by a large circle of people. They surrounded what looked like a fight between two midgets. The fighters pulled left and right, tugging each other round like two martial artists, until one fell upon the other. Then, they were up again, their heads leaning against each other, their legs gripping the road, looking for an advantage. The music ended and the audience clapped loudly. The two midgets stood, one balancing on the head of the other. A shirt was taken off and a single man stood there. He had been the body, the arms and the legs of both midgets.

Danilov clapped the display of agility and nimbleness. And then it occurred to him: the acrobats had found a way of demonstrating a basic human truth. Some people have more than one personality inside themselves, fighting for control. Was this the case with their killer? Could he be living two lives? Walking among them right now?

He sat down at a tea house. The owner rushed over with a pair of chopsticks and a bowl. Danilov indicated that he just wanted tea. He got out his tobacco tin and rolled a thin cigarette.

The investigation was troubling him. There seemed to be too many clues – bound wrists, characters carved into the bodies of the victims. Now, a message scratched into a barrel lid: 'HATE ALL'. What a message of disgust with the world. Nihilism of the worst kind. He had dealt with the Nihilists in Russia, but even they would have balked at such a message. Somehow it felt wrong, out of keeping with the characters that were carved into the bodies.

He took another drag on the cigarette. The waiter arrived with his tea, pouring out a small cupful before departing to return inside his store.

He took a sip of the hot tea. Its smokiness complemented his cigarette perfectly.

He would have to watch Boyle. The man was more concerned with keeping his superiors happy than actually capturing the killer. How he hated these petty bureaucrats. They seemed to be everywhere though, crawling out of whatever cesspit had given birth to them, to infect every place he had ever worked with their small-minded beliefs.

In Shanghai, they were everywhere. He would have to watch himself.

He went over the case once more in his head. What were the patterns? He knew they were there, he just couldn't see them yet. It was like a jigsaw puzzle with all the important pieces missing but just enough on the table to irritate the viewer.

He knew he would make sense of it. It was just a question of time. But how long? And how many murders would occur before he could solve the puzzle?

He hoped Boyle would leave him alone. But he doubted that he would. People like Boyle measured their lives in the reactions of their superiors. The world was good if the boss was happy. The world was bad if the boss was unhappy. Danilov could see the advantages of such a black and white world view. But it wasn't for him. Give him the uncertainty of an investigation. The purity of pitting his wits against a criminal mind.

He finished his tea. Time to go home to Medhurst Apartments. The idea did not appeal to him, but he needed to get some sleep. Perhaps a pipe or two would still his mind long enough for his eyes to close.

And then, maybe he would meet his family again in the dreams that came with the sweet-smelling smoke.

He got up and ambled down the road, past the storytellers recounting the legendary exploits of Zhuge Liang, past the young girls selling their bodies, past the night soil collectors doing their final rounds, and past a blind man with his hand held out, repeating, 'Xie Xie,' to everyone who passed.

Danilov kept his hat pulled down over his eyes and his hands in his pockets, looking, to everybody who passed him, like a man lost in his own solitary world.

CHAPTER 14

Strachan was tired when he got home. His mother was waiting up for him as she always did, bringing him a bowl of pork rib soup before he had even taken off his shoes.

He knew she wanted to hear about his day. What had he done? Who had he met? He remembered she used to do exactly the same thing with his father. Listening attentively as he told her about the people he had met on his beat, the arrests he had made, the thieves he had put away.

As a young boy, Strachan had listened at the door to the parlour as his father recounted the day's events. He thought they didn't know he was standing there, but one day his father had said, 'It must be a wee bit cold out there in the corridor.'

Strachan pretended he didn't hear.

'I said it must be a wee bit cold out there, you wearing naught but a shift and your bare feet.' Then his dad had smiled at him. 'Next time I come home, come in and have a wee drop of soup wi' me. But ask your mother first, won't ye?'

Strachan had asked his mother and was surprised when the answer was yes. Every night, until his father's death, they sat up together, drinking soup and listening to his tales of the beat and the people of Shanghai.

It was a tradition himself and his mother continued to this day. Each time he came home, he was acutely conscious of his father's absence from the seat by the fire. There was a photograph above the mantel, but it wasn't the same. On it, his father stood in his blue uniform, looking neat and tidy against the chaos of the street market behind him. He didn't know who had taken the photograph, just that his mother was proud of it.

When he joined the police, he had sat in front of the photograph just like his mother sat in front of her gods in the kitchen. He had asked his father to help him every day. The photograph had just stared back at him, a look of displeasure on its face. All through school and college, he always felt his father was somehow disappointed in him. He had tried his best, but he felt the unspoken disappointment strongly, as if he could never live up to his own, or his mother's memories, of this man.

Perhaps, he never would.

He lifted the ceramic spoon to his mouth. Danilov had told him to think about the murder of Henry Sellars, or Harriet Sole as she was now known. Why had she left her clothes in her locker? Her dress was missing so she must have been wearing it on the streets. But why do that? The woman in the red dress had said she never wore her female clothes on the streets. It didn't make sense.

Strachan took another long slurp of soup. It was warm and satisfying, the pork slipping off the ribs and dropping into the bowl with a splash.

His mother sat next to him. 'Eat. Eat. It will warm your bones against the cold.'

He took a few more spoonfuls and a large chunk of warm pork.

'How was today? Did you make your father proud?'

She always asked the same question every night. Strachan never knew how to answer her properly. And today, he didn't know how to answer her at all.

***

The smoke of the opium flew through his lungs, folded its wings and nestled in the cavity of his chest. His body relaxed and his toes began to tingle.

He took a long draw on the ebony pipe. Again, the smoke rushed down his throat and into his chest.

His wife was crying. Not sobbing out loud, but he could see from her face, she was holding back her tears. The children thought it was a big adventure; choosing his ties, picking out the right shirts, laying everything topsy-turvy in the bottom of the leather suitcase.

The journey to the station was tense. The children were talking on about their friends and their schools and their drawings and their games. His wife was quiet. Eventually, he could bear it no longer. 'I'll be back soon, you'll see. Won't be away more than a couple of weeks.'

She didn't answer.

Then the children were waving and he was leaning out of the carriage and she was still quiet. Finally, as the train had started moving and the children were running along beside it, she lifted her arm to wave goodbye. But it didn't look like a wave, more a blessing, the sort the priests bestow on the dead.

He took another draw of the pipe. There wasn't much life-giving smoke left, the opium was nearly done. He inhaled and held it deep, pushing it to the very corners of his lungs.

Once again, he enjoyed the familiar ease in every muscle of his body. But the images of death didn't leave him. His wife lying in the street, her clothes dishevelled, her arm bent at a strange angle, pointing directly at him. His children dancing around her body, singing an old nursery rhyme, its words changed:

> Brother Ivan! Hey!
> Brother Ivan! Hey!
> Are you asleep?
> Are you asleep?
> They ring the bell,
> They ring the bell,
> Dead-dead-dead,
> Dead-dead-dead.

Then, with the words of the children's rhyme still ringing in his head, the image of a dead blonde on the 'Beach of Dead Babies' swam into view, its intestines waving in the waters of the creek:

> Henry Sellars, Hey!
> Henry Sellars! Hey!
> She is dead,
> She is dead,
> Floating on the river,
> Floating on the river,
> Dead-dead-dead,
> Dead-dead-dead.

The voices became higher, shriller, taunting him the way children in a playground torment one of their victims:

> Danilov, Danilov, the great detective,
> Can't even find his own family

Danilov, Danilov, the great detective,
Can't even find his own family.

He forced himself to raise his shoulders off the bed. I need more opium, he thought. He looked over at his pipe. Another little ball lay next to it. Immediately, he toasted the opium and placed it in his pipe. His hands were shaking, the lighter dropped from them onto the bed sheet. He searched around desperately for it. His fingers touched the hard metal. Here it is. Immediately, he brought the flame up to the bowl and inhaled.

The smoke coursed through his body and he relaxed once more. His family weren't dead, he knew they were alive. His wife and children had escaped from Minsk. They had gone east. He knew it. They would see the advertisements he had placed in the newspapers. He would be reunited with them. They would be a family again.

As the opium coursed around his body, he lay back on the bed and all was beauty and peace and happiness as his family gathered round him for Sunday dinner:

All smiles.

All happy.

All here.

February 24th 1928.
The 33rd day of the Year of the Earth Dragon.

CHAPTER 15

The preacher was in full flow as Danilov and Strachan arrived at the church. They edged their way into the final pew, drawing some vicious stares from an old Chinese lady with jade-green earrings, and a look of disdain from a freckle-faced boy. It was the early-morning service at 8 a.m., but the church was as packed as a cake of tea.

The preacher noticed nothing, caught in the power of his voice: 'Put to death, therefore, what is earthly on you: sexual morality, impurity, passion, evil desire and covetousness. Thus spake the Lord in Colossians, verse 3, chapter 5.'

The preacher raised his head from the bible, pausing for a moment as if remembering all the times he and the congregation had indulged in such sins.

Then his voice rang out in the rich tones of Ulster, 'Put them to death. Murder them. Cast them out. Throw them from you as the Lord cast out his sins in the garden of Gethsemane.'

There were a few muted cries from the congregation, but he held up his hands to stop them. His eyes closed and his voice rang out again: 'Lord hear us we beseech you. Look on the poor sinners of this city with pity. Do not turn your back on them. We do not fear them, Lord. Not when we have you by our side. For we know they will stand before you on the day of judgement, their sins held in their hands, standing like wanton sheep.'

A young Chinese man stood up at the back of the church. 'They will be judged.' He was joined by two older women, who swayed with their hands in the air, caught in a moment of rapture.

The preacher took the opportunity to pause, gain breath and slowly amble to his right. He stopped in mid-step before the plain altar, ordained with its bare table and single wooden cross, apparently struck by a new thought.

The voice of Ulster rang out again: 'We, the people of Shanghai, reject the temptations of Sodom and the fornication of Gomorrah. We reject the god of Mammon. We reject the lies of the moneychangers in the temple. We reject the false gods of their temples and shrines and heathen images.' He raised himself up to his fullest height and brought his fist down on an imaginary table in front of him. 'We reject all the devil's works. For we know, it is all a shadow. Colossians puts it in a way no man is able: "Which are a shadow of things to come; but the body is of Christ".'

He paused once again, his body seemingly exhausted by the effort of conveying the words. His voice now became a whisper. 'We know they will be punished.'

He pointed at the congregation. 'As the Lord said, "You will be brought down to Hades. For the mighty works done in you had been done in Sodom, it would have remained until this day." But, I tell you, it will be more tolerable on the day of judgement for the land of Sodom than for you.' His eyes and stabbing finger pointed at the members of his congregation, picking out individuals like choosing ripe mangoes on a market stall.

He moved slowly back to his original position in front of the pulpit, his eyes afire with passion. 'The day of judgement is here.' He repeated even louder, 'The day of judgement is here.' His hands rose to the roof of the church, 'The day of judgement is here.'

The congregation, both Chinese and Western, began to take up the cry, 'The day of judgement is here.' Slowly, at first, then more forcefully, as they lost their inhibitions: 'THE DAY OF JUDGEMENT IS HERE!'

From the back of the church, Danilov could hear and feel the rising passion of the congregation. As the shouts rang out to the rafters of the church, a collection box passed in front of him. He passed it on without adding any money to the plate. His neighbour, the old Chinese woman with jade-green earrings, glared at him. She took the plate in her left hand, adding five dollars before passing it on. She stared at the Inspector as she did so. Danilov just looked straight ahead, seeing the audience with their raised hands standing in front of the preacher like soldiers in front of a drill instructor.

On his right, an organ played the opening chords of, 'Onward Christian soldiers, onward as to war.' The preacher began to sing loudly, leading his flock deftly from the chants of judgement to the anthem of struggle.

Strachan was singing quietly along with the song, clearly knowing the lyrics. Danilov nudged his arm and indicated they should leave the church.

The old Chinese woman again glared at him as he slid past her on the way out.

Once outside, Danilov immediately began to roll a cigarette. 'You know the words?'

'Can't ever forget them, sir. I was sent to Saint Ignatius school and then St John's University here in Shanghai. Both run by missionaries, one Catholic, the other Protestant. My mother thought I should receive the best education, whatever the religion.'

'A pragmatic woman.' Danilov pointed at the church with his cigarette. 'Not a lot of love in there.'

'More brimstone and damnation than love. The preacher was splendid though. Fired them up.'

Danilov thought about his own youth in Minsk, attending the Orthodox church with his mother. There, it was the mystery of God that mattered. The delight that came alive with incense and ritual, lifting the senses and elevating the spirit. He did not understand this God of hate and judgement.

The congregation began to stream out of the chapel, past the two detectives. The preacher stood at the door, collecting plate in his hand, encouraging his flock to give a little more. A few dug deeper in their pockets. The old Chinese woman gave another five dollars, glaring at Danilov once more as she did so.

After most of the congregation had gone, the two detectives approached the preacher. He was counting the money collected on the plates, a pile of notes and coins lay on the table in front of him.

'A good collection?' asked Danilov.

The preacher looked up from his counting. 'Not bad, the people have only to look round to see Sodom and Gomorrah are everywhere. They understood the message.'

'And what message is that?'

The preacher blinked once. A slow blink, like that of a reptile. 'I didn't get your name?'

'I'm Inspector Danilov and this is Detective Constable Strachan. You are Mr Renfrew, I presume?'

'It's Dr Renfrew. How can I help you?'

Danilov produced the photograph of Henry Sellars from his inside pocket. 'Do you know this man?'

The preacher put on a pair of wire-rimmed spectacles. He squinted through them for a long time. 'It looks like Henry but his hair is longer and it's dyed blonde.'

'Are you sure?'

The preacher glanced at the photograph again. 'Yes, it's Henry. I knew him well.'

'You used the past tense?'

The preacher slowly took the wire-rimmed glasses off and placed them on the table next to the money. 'What's all this about, Inspector . . .?'

'Danilov.'

'Inspector . . . Danilov. Henry is no longer a part of this church. He has been disowned.'

'Disowned?'

'He broke the covenant he had with the Redeemer, cavorting in an unseemly manner. Dancing.' The preacher's voice rose, once again he seemed to be on stage, railing against the brazen iniquities and blasphemy of Shanghai. 'He betrayed the trust we placed in him, falling prey to the temptations of Mammon. This city offers so many temptations for the young and innocent. Not all can resist them. Henry was one of those who fell by the wayside.'

'What did he do?'

'He stole, Inspector. From this church. From these people. From me. He stole to buy the goods of Mammon. To live the life of an unbeliever. So, he was cast out.' The preacher's fist came crashing down on the desk. The piles of coins collapsed like the tower of Babel.

'When did all this happen?'

The preacher calmed himself. 'Six months ago, last summer. Henry left our home one day and never came back. We found the money missing from the collection box after he had gone.'

'Did you report the theft to the police?'

Once more, the voice boomed out. 'We have no truck with the agents of the devil, sir. The only laws we recognise are those of God himself.'

There was a moment of silence. The preacher calmed himself again and began to re-stack the coins in neat piles.

'Did Henry have a tattoo on his wrist?'

'All the children of the Redeemer bear the sign of the covenant. It's what binds them to the Lord. A mark so that they can be recognised on the day of judgement when they stand before him, asking for judgement on their life. Asking if they have obeyed his laws.'

He pulled up the sleeve of his jacket and showed them another tattoo on the inside of his wrist. 'The word is on their skin, engraved there for the Lord to see.'

'How long was Henry with your church, Dr Renfrew?'

'Henry came to us when he was young, ten years old, placed in our care to teach him the righteous path of the Lord. His parents had seen the marks of a sinner on him.' The preacher sighed. 'We tried to cleanse him, to lead him to see the light, to redeem his everlasting soul.'

Danilov put his hat back on his head. 'Thank you, Dr Renfrew, for your time and your words. One last question, you talked of judgement in your sermon?'

'The day of judgement is upon us, Inspector. As we sit here, we are being judged, our sins examined and weighed. Our wickedness exposed to the light of the Redeemer. We will face his wrath, Inspector. Heed my words, we will all face his wrath.'

***

'Can I help you, sir?' Sergeant Wolfe leant over his desk. The sergeant had spotted the well-dressed, confident man in the crowd of hawkers, rickshaw pullers, pimps, thieves and conmen who surrounded his desk.

'I would like to speak to Chief Inspector Boyle.'

The sergeant was automatically deferential. 'And who shall I say it is, sir?'

'Richard Ayres.'

'Any relation to Councillor Ayres, sir?'

'He's my father.'

The sergeant stood up. 'I'll let him know you're here, sir.' He picked up the phone and rang through to the Chief Inspector. The answer came back quickly. 'Would you come this way, sir?' He led Richard behind the desk, through a double door and into the anteroom of Boyle's office.

Boyle was waiting outside his door to greet him. 'Good morning, Richard, good to see you again. How's your father?'

'Fine, Chief Inspector, working hard as usual.'

Boyle stepped back and allowed Richard to enter his office first. He indicated a seat in front of his desk. He opened a cigar box and offered Richard a Havana. Richard shook his head.

'What can I do for you?'

'It's rather delicate.' He paused for a moment before continuing. 'It's my girlfriend, my fiancée, actually.'

'I didn't know you were engaged. Congratulations.'

'I'm not. We're not. That's to say, we were about to get engaged when she disappeared.'

'Disappeared?'

'Two nights ago. She didn't turn up at the theatre. She's an actress, you see.'

Boyle scratched his bald head. 'I do see. Have you talked to her friends?'

'Of course, they think she's just gone off for a while.'

'Well, she is an actress, Richard. They can be a mite . . .' Boyle searched for the right word, '. . . flighty.'

Richard's hackles went up. 'Elsie's not "flighty". She would have told me if she were going off somewhere.'

Boyle leant back in his chair and crossed his hands in front of his stomach. The girl's just gone off with another man that's all. But this is Councillor Ayres's son, he thought. 'What would you like us to do?' he said in a soothing voice.

'Find her, of course. Perhaps, she's been abducted, shanghaied.'

Boyle laughed. 'That sort of thing only happens in trashy novels, not here in Shanghai and not on my watch. Do you have a photograph of her that I can circulate?'

'We took this last week at the Astor.' He showed the picture of himself and Elsie dancing to the band.

As soon as he saw the photograph, Boyle's face went pale as if it had been illuminated by a flashbulb. 'If you'll excuse me for a moment.' He got up and went outside.

'Get Danilov immediately.'

'I'll see if he's back, sir.'

Boyle went back into his office. The calm, peaceful Chief Inspector had been replaced by a nervous, stammering man. 'Just a minute, Richard, Inspector Danilov will join us. Ah, speak of the devil.'

Danilov appeared in the doorway, his hat still in his hands. 'You wanted to see me, sir?'

'Yes, Danilov. This is Richard Ayres, he's inquiring about his missing fiancée.' Boyle handed the photograph to Danilov.

He took one look at it. 'When was the last time you saw your fiancée, Mr . . .?'

'Ayres. Richard Ayres.'

'The son of Councillor Ayres,' interrupted Boyle.

Danilov ignored him. 'When did you last see her?'

Boyle laughed. 'Our Inspector Danilov is known for his brusque manner, aren't you, Danilov?'

Richard spoke directly to the Inspector. 'Two days ago. Her name is Elsie Everett. We were at the Astor together. She left around 5.30 p.m. Something about having a rehearsal.'

'You haven't seen her since?'

'No. I checked at the theatre. She didn't go there that night. Her flatmate hasn't seen her either. She's just vanished.'

Danilov took out a picture of the girl in the park from inside his jacket. Richard looked at it. 'Yes, that's Elsie.' Then he stared at it more closely. 'But she doesn't have that mark on her face. And her eyes, they are . . .'

It was Danilov who spoke first. 'I'm afraid to tell you, Mr Ayres, we found Miss Everett in the public garden on the Bund yesterday evening. She had been murdered.'

Danilov watched the look on Richard's face. This was the moment of truth. Very few people could fake surprise well. Most of them overacted it, making all the emotions too big, too obvious.

Richard just stared straight ahead. 'But, she can't . . . she was just . . .' he stammered.

Danilov watched him. Surprise followed by disbelief. Classic reactions, they should be completed by acceptance and sorrow, usually tinged with a little self-pity.

'She was murdered some time on the morning of February 23rd, about twelve hours after you last saw her.'

'Do you have to be so blunt, Danilov?' Boyle touched the shoulder of Richard's jacket.

Richard buried his head in his hands. 'My poor Elsie, what are we going to do?' He quickly stifled his sobs, gaining control of himself.

Danilov just sat there, watching.

'We were going to be married. I'd bought her the ring and everything.' He looked up as if a thought has suddenly occurred to him. 'What am I going to do with it?'

Danilov leant forward. 'Where were you on the evening of the 22nd and the day of the 23rd, Mr Ayres?'

'Now, look here Danilov . . .'

Danilov held up his hand. The Chief Inspector stopped speaking.

'Where were you, Mr Ayres?'

Richard glanced up into the eyes of the Inspector staring straight at him. 'I was . . . I was at Ciro's with friends on the evening of the 22nd. Then on the 23rd I went to see Elsie at the theatre and her home, then I went to the office not getting back until the early evening.'

'Someone can confirm this?'

Richard nodded. 'My friends at Ciro's. And the theatre director met me.'

'Good,' said Inspector Danilov. 'Now, this may be painful, but I need you to tell us everything you know about Miss Everett.'

Richard nodded.

Danilov raised his voice. 'Miss Cavendish, could you bring us some tea?' he shouted through the closed door, knowing the secretary would be listening.

***

He watched the preacher leaving Jingling Church, the black bag clutched to his chest, like a virgin guarding her chastity. The man's eyes darted right and left, wary of the snatch thieves that preyed upon the citizens of Shanghai.

He followed him. Li Min was behind in the car, idling the motor, letting it creep forward slowly.

The hunter following its prey.

The preacher turned left and then first right. He passed a one-legged blind beggar leaning on his crutches on the street corner. The beggar had his hand out, murmuring, 'Xie Xie. Xie Xie,' every five seconds, although nobody had put any money in his tin.

The preacher just ignored the outstretched hand, entering a small bank on the street. The Nanking Commercial Bank. The preacher went up to one of the counters and slowly emptied all the coins and notes in front of the cashier, counting every one as he did so.

Patiently, the cashier re-counted it all, writing the total in a book. A smile crossed the man's face as he read the amount.

The preacher came out of the bank, still reading the figures in his book, adding them up in his head.

He was waiting.

The street was empty, with only the blind beggar occupying his place on the corner.

He raced in to stand behind the preacher, thrusting the hessian bag over the man's head. Immediately, the preacher started to struggle, shouting out in his deep Ulster voice.

He wrapped his arms around the man, ignoring the muffled shouts, and pushed him to the edge of the pavement. Li Min accelerated the car and braked heavily with a loud squeal.

Must get those brakes checked soon.

A door opened and, a few moments later, Li Min clamped a cloth soaked in chloroform over the hessian bag where the preacher's mouth should be.

The preacher struggled for ten seconds before his body went limp. Li Min opened the boot of the car and the heavy body was tumbled in the back.

The preacher lay there, faint breathing coming from inside the bag. Luckily, it wasn't far to the courtroom.

Li Min ran round to the driver's seat and started the engine.

He closed the boot, adjusted his necktie and walked round to the rear of the car. He scanned the street. Still empty except for the blind beggar with his hand held out.

But the beggar was looking straight at him, no longer mouthing the words, 'Xie Xie. Xie Xie.' The man wasn't blind, just another faker who inhabited the streets of Shanghai.

He was tempted to kill him, but it was not part of the plan. The preacher was the plan.

He climbed into the rear seat. Li Min accelerated away from the kerb. As they drove past the blind beggar, the man stared at them.

He would have to get rid of the car now. Just to be on the safe side.

It was time to concentrate. Time to try the preacher for his sins.

Yama was needed again.

* * *

'I believe we're dealing with a serial killer, sir.'

'Come on, Danilov, this isn't Victorian London.'

'No, it's modern-day Shanghai. But we are still dealing with a serial killer.' Danilov sighed. 'Four people have been murdered in the last nine days.'

'There is no need to take that tone with me, Danilov.'

Danilov ran his fingers through his hair. 'I'm sorry, sir, but unless we act quickly this man will kill again and again.'

'You were too harsh on young Richard Ayres. He is the son of Councillor Ayres, you know.'

Danilov closed his eyes and forced himself to take two deep breaths. 'He is also the prime suspect in a murder inquiry. He was the last person to see the victim alive. He has no alibi for her time of death. And he had the opportunity to kill her.'

Boyle smiled. 'You are forgetting motive, Danilov. What's his motive, tell me that, hey?'

Danilov looked down at his hands. The fingers of his right hand were beating a tattoo on his leg. 'I don't know, sir. If I knew what the motive for the murders was, I would be closer to catching the killer.'

There was silence between the two of them. The sort of silence that underlined a temporary truce in a war of words.

Boyle spoke first: 'OK. Let's say there is a "serial killer" on the streets of Shanghai. There have been four victims now and all seem to have Chinese characters carved into their bodies. It seems to suggest, and I emphasise "seems", Danilov, that the same man committed all four crimes. What will he do next?'

'That's pretty obvious, sir.'

Boyle waited for the answer.

'He will kill again.'

'You are certain of that?'

'Yes, sir. All my experience tells me this man, and it is a man, will kill again. Brutally. Viciously. And without mercy.'

Boyle's tongue flicked out and licked the left side of his moustache. 'Well, you'd better catch him before he strikes again. If you don't, I can't answer for the consequences.'

Danilov stared down at his hands once more. The fingers had stopped tapping his knee. 'Neither can I, sir.'

***

'Do you need me to go to the Astor, sir?'

'Not yet. Let's go to the mortuary first and see what Dr Fang has to say. You can interview the hotel staff afterwards. Has the barrel lid arrived yet? I'd like the doctor to take a look at it.'

'Not yet, sir. I'll call Lieutenant Masset.'

Danilov sat down at his desk. It was completely empty. Sniggers came from behind him. Cartwright and a few of the other detectives were watching from the door. As he looked up, they beat a hasty retreat. He opened his drawers and found the telephone, his desk diary, pens, pencils, pencil sharpeners and tobacco tin inside.

'This is becoming intolerable, Stra-chan. I must complain to Chief Inspector Boyle.' As he got up from his desk, the phone rang.

Danilov picked it up. 'Central Police.'

'Hello, hello, is that Inspector Danilov?'

He recognised the elegant Russian vowels of the Princess. 'Good morning, Princess. How can I help you?'

'It's the opposite, Inspector. It's how I can help you. Victorov has turned up.'

'The pimp who ran Maria Stepanova?'

'The one and only. Scum like him can't keep away from the bright lights for long.'

'Where is he, Princess?'

'He's sitting in my cafe as we speak, Inspector. He thinks he is getting some work from me but I don't deal with the dregs of the Earth like Victorov.'

'Please keep him there. I'll be there in an hour.'

'Be careful. This one's not to be trusted.'

'Of course. Thank you for your efforts on my behalf.'

'I'm sure they will be remembered, Inspector. And if they are not, I'm sure somebody will remind you.'

'Thank you once again, Princess.' He put the receiver back on the cradle.

Strachan had been listening to the conversation. 'Do you want me there, too, Inspector?'

'Not necessary, Stra-chan, let's see what Dr Fang has to say first.' Danilov picked up his hat from the stand in the corner. His desk was still empty. It would have to wait. There were more important matters to attend to.

But the image of the empty desk haunted him all the way to the morgue. Something would have to be done.

CHAPTER 16

'Good morning, Dr Fang, I'm sorry to be seeing you again so soon.'

'Good afternoon, Inspector.'

Danilov checked his watch. 12.05 p.m. Dr Fang was as accurate as ever. 'You have our latest victim?'

'She arrived last night. We carried out the autopsy this morning at 8 a.m.' The doctor led them through into the white-tiled mortuary. A body lay on the second slab from the door. Danilov did not recognise who it was. The skin of the face had been peeled back in two sections and then rolled up like a ruched rug along the hairline. All that was left of the woman's beauty was blood and muscle and bone.

He remembered something his mother used to tell him long ago: 'A candle is a flame, the woman a glow.' There was no glow left here, the light that had shone from this woman was long gone.

Behind him, Strachan coughed.

'If you are going to be sick, Detective, please do it outside in the bucket, not on my clean floor.'

Strachan glared at Dr Fang. 'I'm not going to be sick, Dr Fang.'

'Please begin, Doctor,' Danilov said.

'The victim's death was caused by a single trauma to the throat, severing the aorta, trachea and Adam's apple. She died almost instantaneously.'

'And the wounds on her body?'

'I counted 137 separate cuts to the arms, hands, legs and feet, and one deep cut to the left side of her face. They were clean, sharp scores caused by an extremely thin knife, scalpel or razor blade. See here, here, and here.' Dr Fang pointed to the slashes. 'Most seem to be on the arms and legs. Very few cuts to the body.' The doctor scratched his head. 'Sometimes, we see similar cuts in knife fights caused by cutthroat razors. But never this many.'

'Would she have bled to death from these cuts?'

'I don't think she would, Inspector. The cuts were all shallow, barely penetrating the epidermis. They would have caused pain, severe pain. Her death was brought about by a deep cut to the throat produced by a completely different weapon.'

Danilov glanced down at the faceless corpse in front of him. Another body, another person who had their life terminated. Four corpses now. One frozen to death. The second drowned in blood. The third nearly severed in two, the genitals removed. And finally, this young woman, her throat cut and multiple slashes across her body. Four different ways to die. Four personal ways to kill. In each case, the killer must have been very close to his victims. Close enough to see the pain in their eyes as they died.

The doctor was speaking.

'I'm sorry, Doctor, could you repeat that?'

Dr Fang sniffed, pushing his glasses back onto the bridge of his nose. 'As I was saying, Inspector, there are two small characters carved into her chest just above the sternum. The instrument used to carve these characters was larger and thicker.'

'Not the same one as caused the cut on the throat or the slashes on the rest of the body?'

'No, definitely not.'

'A knife or a scalpel?'

'I'm not at liberty to say, Inspector. It is up to you to find the instrument. But I will say the wound was definitely caused by a different weapon than the cuts on her body and throat.'

'Thank you, Doctor. We will let you see the weapon as soon as we find it.'

'The character is interesting, Inspector. Not a common character, "retribution", as you know. Rather old-fashioned, I even had to check its meaning in the dictionary. Whoever did it was quite punctilious, though. Each stroke of the character has been cut precisely. The proportions of the strokes are very accurate. Almost as if it was copied from a book.'

'The character looks the same as on Henry Sellars?'

'As a pathologist, I can only say the character was created with a similar instrument. But as a student of Chinese, I would say it was written by the same hand. Or rather, it was carved by the same hand.'

'Thank you, Doctor. Anything else you can tell us?' The smell of formaldehyde was beginning to irritate Danilov. He avoided looking at the faceless corpse.

In another part of the morgue, a telephone rang three times before somebody answered it. So there were other people in here beside the doctor, thought Danilov. Sometimes, it seemed as if the doctor was the only living person here.

Dr Fang sniffed loudly, pushing his glasses up to the bridge of his nose again. He lifted up one of girl's lifeless arms. They were thin and white. 'See here, the marks of the rope. She was bound at one point. The wrists show deep bruising where she struggled against her restraints.' He put the arm down. 'There are also rope marks on her palms,' he turned over the hands for Danilov to see, 'the inside of her thighs and her ankles.'

Danilov could see the marks clearly on her legs. Livid, blue marks, lying along the inside of the thigh and along the inside of the ankles.

'The marks don't go around her thighs or legs. They are only found on the inside.'

'Were they inflicted pre- or post-mortem?'

'Pre-mortem, Inspector. See, the bruising is livid, going from purple into blue. I've seen these sorts of marks before. Usually old scars that have healed and left a mark.'

'Where did you see them, Doctor?'

Dr Fang sniffed. 'It's very strange but they are usually found on men who ply the coastal trade. On the old junks.' He mimed a sailor climbing a rope. 'The men get them from climbing the ropes attached to the rigging. But one sees them less and less these days. The advent of steam power.'

'Thank you, Doctor. Any other reason she would have these marks?'

'There are many reasons, Inspector, none of which I could speculate about.' The doctor sniffed once again. 'A few more things. You will have noticed the corpse has dyed hair just like the previous victim. A slightly darker shade though, not so platinum, but still dyed. And then there are the eyes . . .'

'Cornflower blue.'

'So that is what the shade is called. I looked it up in the dictionary but couldn't find it anywhere.' Dr Fang took a small book out of his top pocket and began writing notes.

Inspector Danilov stared down at the face once more. The cornflower-blue eyes were there sitting in their sockets, staring out lifelessly into the world, shaded by two rolls of skin that formed a small peaked cap along her hairline.

A pretty girl, he thought, a very pretty girl.

His thoughts about Elsie Everett were interrupted by the clatter of the door to the morgue swinging open. A young man's head appeared.

'I've told you so many times, I am not to be interrupted when in the middle of an autopsy.'

'I'm sorry, Dr Fang, this was delivered.' He held up a blue hessian bag. 'The man said it was for Detective Constable Strachan.'

'It's the barrel lid, sir. I asked Lieutenant Masset to send it here.'

'You are being efficient today, Stra-chan. There's hope for you yet. Dr Fang, I wonder if you would mind taking a look at this for us?'

'I've got two stabbings and a coronary thrombosis to deal with before tea-time.'

'I would consider it a great favour if you could examine it, Doctor. I'm sure you'll find it very interesting. Professionally, of course.'

Dr Fang sniffed, enjoying the compliment. 'I'll see if I can find the time.'

'Thank you, Doctor. Come, Stra-chan, you have work to do. And so does the good doctor.'

CHAPTER 17

He loved the sound of a knife sharpening against a steel. There's the ascending harmonic of the rasp of the blade as the edge kisses the metal. Up one side and up the other in a rhythm like the sound of the bossa nova. No downstrokes. We wouldn't want to snag the end, chipping away at its edge, would we?

Even more than the sound, he loved the way the eyes of the guilty were inevitably drawn to the blade. Fascinated, entranced by its shining prospect of pain. He always sharpened the knife in front of them. It did prolong their terror.

The preacher lay on a slab in front of him. His eyes were only focused on the knife. Nothing else existed for him. The man was struggling against the ropes. He didn't blame him. He would struggle too if he were in the preacher's position.

Then he smelt the rich earthy smell of shit. The preacher hadn't been able to control himself. What a shame. It meant Li Min was going to have to clean him again. He did wish they could control themselves more. He would have thought a preacher would have set a better example. After all, he was going to the place he'd always wanted to go, wasn't he?

He touched the edge of the blade with his finger. Nearly there, a few more strokes should do it. Well, it was always better to be safe than sorry. At least, that's what his nanny used to say.

He had tried the preacher that morning, soon after he had got back here. Now, in some courts, it might be seen as strange that he was prosecutor, judge, jury and executioner, but not here. We all know many criminals escape real justice through having clever solicitors. Or corrupt police. Or even incompetent judges. But in his court, there was no such chance to escape. They always enjoyed the certainty of justice.

Sometimes, he even acted for the defence, but not often. The guilt of his accused was usually so clear, he could smell and taste it.

He did have a helper though. Li Min was splendid at the work, a court clerk if you like. Li Min enjoyed bringing the miscreants to justice as much as he did. But it was up to him to see justice was done. That was his role. The role assigned to him.

He tested the edge of the blade with his finger.

Perfect.

The preacher struggled again as he got closer to him. The man saw the knife clearly now. He had been calling it a knife, but it was probably more of a cleaver. The sort butchers used in the market to slice into a piece of beef. It had a marvellous balance, nestling in his hand, crying out to be used.

As he got closer to the preacher, the man struggled even more. He could see the wild fear in the preacher's eyes. Quite an imagination this one. Perhaps it was the man's obsession with the Old Testament that enabled him to imagine what was going to happen next. It was a harsh book. They certainly knew how to deal with criminals.

Only the Chinese had the same sense of justice. A quick judgement and an even quicker execution, that's *what criminals could expect. They had been refining the ways of death for thousands of years. Coming to Shanghai, discovering the Chinese way, had made it all clear to him. This was what he had to do. This was what he was driven to do. They had done wrong. This was what they deserved.*

The blade was in front of the Preacher's eyes now. The man was struggling, but the rope around his forehead held him tight. He could see the blood where the rope had bitten into the skin.

Don't struggle, preacher, you'll only hurt yourself.

He put the point of the knife into the shoulder where the socket met the body. There was a little indentation there to guide him. How thoughtful the gods were. He saw the preacher's face grimace with pain as his mouth struggled to scream against the glue of the duct tape.

Don't struggle, preacher, you'll only hurt yourself.

He pressed the knife deeper into the socket. The blood was flowing now from the wound, drenching the preacher's body. He was wearing an apron, a mask and a surgeon's cap. He didn't want any of the preacher's blood on him. Li Min stepped forward to wipe his brow, so very thoughtful of him.

He pushed the blade in further. He could see the pale whiteness of the bone through the blood. There was a roundness to the ball of the joint where it slotted into the arm socket. What a perfect piece of engineering, so beautifully designed to give a range of movement and strength.

He pushed it deeper and turned the blade. The preacher had gone limp now, unconscious.

Don't sleep, preacher, you'll only hurt yourself.

Li Min stepped forward and threw a bucket of cold water over the preacher's face. The man opened his eyes, looked at him and tried to scream again, his mouth tearing at the glue of the duct tape.

He pressed the knife down and cut through the final tendons that held the arm to the shoulder. The arm pulled away neatly when he removed it from the body. Quite a good job, even if he did say so himself.

He showed the severed arm to the preacher. The man tried to scream but collapsed, unconscious.

The preacher didn't know yet he still had to remove the man's other arm and both legs.

He would do them later after he had eaten a spot of dinner.

CHAPTER 18

Victorov was seated at the table with a glass of tea in front of him. Danilov knew it was him as soon as he entered the cafe. Three days' worth of beard. A dirty black overcoat and the constant shifting of the eyes, first to the left and then to the right, gave it away.

The Princess introduced them. 'Victorov, this is an Inspector from the Shanghai Police. He's here to have a chat with you.'

'But Princess Ostrepova, you promised . . .'

'I promised nothing. Enjoy the tea.'

Danilov sat down on the chair opposite. 'Hello, Victorov, I want to ask you a few questions.'

'The Princess tricked m' into comin' here.' The man spoke with a heavy Moscow accent. Once again, the eyes flicked from left to right, never looking Danilov directly in the face. 'I don' have to answer. Shanghai Police. No power in French Concession.'

For the first time, he stared directly at Danilov, defiance dancing in his eyes, before they darted to the left and right again, like a rat in a sewer.

The Inspector sighed. Time to end this. 'Look, Victorov, you have two choices. Either you answer my questions and walk out of here, free to run wherever you want. Or I call my men to come and drag you back to the International Settlement. By the time the French hear about it, you will be locked up in Ward Road Jail for a couple of years. The Warders take a perverse pleasure in Russian prisoners, I have heard.'

Victorov's eyes had resumed their constant darting this way and that. The Inspector opened his arms wide, hoping the thug would not call his bluff. 'The choice is yours.'

Victorov sat in his chair, rocking backwards and forwards. For one moment, Danilov thought he was going to take a chance and make a dash for the door and freedom. Then, he saw him shrug his shoulders and his head went down. 'What d'ye wanna to know?'

Danilov relaxed and sat back in his chair. 'Victorov. Is that your only name?'

'That's what they call m'. Given names are Ivan Yuri, but everybody calls m' Victorov'

'How did you know Maria Stepanova?'

Victorov inhaled deeply. He picked up the steaming glass of tea and sipped carefully from it. 'We met in Shanghai, in '27. She came from same part of Moscow as m'. Didn't start working for m' then. Still had money.'

'But you helped her spend it?'

The eyes squinted up over the rim of the glass. This man wasn't as tough, now he wasn't facing a woman. 'Money finished. Came to m', begging m' to help her. She wasn't bad looking and wasn't old, what else could she do?'

'So, she went out on the streets or worked the clubs?'

Victorov became offended: 'No, m' girls don't work streets or clubs. Better places to meet men. I set her up in own apartment. Much better for her.'

'And for you. Easier to control and monitor the money and the merchandise.'

A smile spread across Victorov's face like an oil slick spreading on the sea. 'I know m' business.'

'So, you set her up. What then?'

'She got her own men. Usually, by word of mouth. She was good at job was little Maria. One of m' best little earners.'

His grizzled face supped his tea again. The glass was empty. Danilov signalled the waitress to bring him more.

He took another slurp of the fresh tea and wiped the back of his mouth. 'Maria had special man. Came every couple of weeks. An Englishman. Well-dressed, well off. Said name was Mr Thomas. Liked it rough, if you know what m' mean.' He took another slurp of tea. 'Maria found his real name and address one day. He some bigwig in the Shanghai Council, name of Ayres.'

Danilov's brain sparked at the mention of the name, but he kept his voice under control as he asked his next question. He had to keep Victorov talking. 'So, you decided to make a little money on the side.'

'It wasn't m', it was Maria. She wanted get away from Shanghai. Ayres was ticket out of here.'

'What did you do?'

'We waited for Ayres t'come again. Waited till he was in leather costume and I burst in.'

'The outraged boyfriend, who just happened to have a camera at the ready.'

'Outraged husband.' Victorov chuckled. 'Ayres promised would send money. We just had to give him couple of days.'

'And . . .?'

'Two days later, we were called by man. Said he was from Shanghai Police. Like you. Said he had Ayres's money ready.'

'So you sent Maria to get it?'

'She was one they knew. I followed her though. She met a tall, thin man. Well-dressed too. Wealthy. A gentleman.'

'Why do you say that?'

'Because when they met, he gave her his card, all polite and official like. They went into cafe but never came out. I went after them but owner said they had gone out back.' His shoulders slumped forward and all the cockiness seemed to leave the man like air escaping from a balloon. 'Was last time I saw her. Two days later French police found her. Dead.'

'What did you do?'

'I got out of Shanghai. You can't trust police. I would've been set up for murder. I swear I had nothing to do with it.'

'Other than sending her out on her own to face a killer.'

Victorov shrugged his shoulders once more.

'Would you recognise the man she met again?'

'No. Only saw him quickly and was dark. All I remember, tall and well-dressed. His hat covered face most of the time.'

Danilov sighed. He wasn't going to get any more out of this thug. He pointed to the door. 'You've got five seconds to get out of here, Victorov. If I were you, I would run now and keep running. The man you sent Maria to see could be looking for you as we speak. If he is . . .'

Danilov left the last words unspoken. Victorov finished the last of his tea and bolted for the door, slamming it behind him in his rush to get away.

'That man leaves a bad smell wherever he goes.' It was the Princess speaking.

CHAPTER 19

Sergeant Wolfe looked up from his duty book. What a day, he thought. I'll be happy to get home to the missus tonight and put my feet up. He could feel his boots pinching his toes and the ache in his calves from standing. Lord, how he wanted to put his feet up.

It had been a good day though. Nothing had gone wrong. That was important for Sergeant Wolfe. When things went wrong that meant problems from upstairs. And he needed those like he needed a new arsehole. Years of walking the beat and being behind the desk in countless police stations across the International Settlement had taught him one thing: nobody noticed when things went right, they only saw the cock-ups. Avoid Mr Cock-Up and everything was plain sailing.

A young Chinese boy wearing the uniform of the post office was standing in front of him. 'What do you want?' he asked in English before immediately switching to pidgin. 'Lookee, what wan?'

'Telegram.'

'Well, this is a police station not a bleedin' poste restante.'

The post-office boy just stood there. The sergeant asked again 'Who for?'

The boy examined his book. 'Telegram for Danny Love.'

'Danny Love. There ain't no Danny Love here. So piss off back to where you came from.'

The boy reached over and showed the open book to the sergeant. Wolfe scanned down the list of names with his finger until he came to Danilov. 'Inspector Danilov, why didn't you say?' Then he switched back to pidgin. 'Give one piece here.'

'Can give only to number-one man.'

'Now look here, sonny. Me number-one man, you give.'

The boy handed over the telegram reluctantly. 'You sign chit.'

'Me sign your arse off,' replied Wolfe. Another fucking troublemaker, he thought, should have the lot of them thrown in Ward Road Jail. Lord knows, it's big enough.

He glanced at the clock on the wall opposite. Nearly the end of his shift. Soon, he would be able to put his feet up and have a nice cup of tea. He took the book from the young boy and signed an illegible scrawl along the bottom. Work that one out, sonny.

'What you got there, Jim?'

'A telegram for Danilov. You know, George, I think I'm becoming a blooming concierge in a flophouse, not a copper any more. The amount of stuff I do, I should get three times what I get. I'm not paid to run errands and take notes for nobody.'

'I'll give it to him if you want. Save you the trouble.'

Wolfe looked at the telegram and the onion-sheet wrapper in his hand. 'I should give it to him myself. I signed for it.'

'Please yourself. Both Danilov and Strachan are out. Miss Cavendish is on her chocolate break, I wouldn't disturb her if I was you. You could wait for her to come back . . .'

Sergeant Wolfe glanced at the clock on the wall again. The minute hand was just one tick away from the 12. Nearly 4 p.m. The cup of tea was calling his name. He handed over the telegram to Cartwright. 'Make sure he gets it, won't you?'

'You can count on me.'

As Cartwright took the telegram and walked back to the detectives' room, Sergeant Wolfe turned round to see the post-office boy still standing there with his hand held out. 'Fuck off, before I give you a clip around the ear.'

'Fuck you, too, copper. And your mother,' said the boy in perfect English, before running out the door.

Lord save me, thought the sergeant. He stared at the clock on the wall. The minute hand just clicked on to the twelve. Before another tick occurred, the sergeant had already taken off his uniform jacket and was heading to the back office to change.

At his desk in the detectives' room, Cartwright opened the telegram. It was in the usual onion-skin envelope with two lines of text pasted onto a pro-forma sheet, typed in capital letters:

HAVE INFORMATION RE DAUGHTER STOP CALL TSINGTAO 73546 WILLIS STOP

Short and to the point, he thought. What's it mean? A daughter? I didn't know Danilov had a family. Always a bleedin' loner that one.

He checked the telegram again, turning the sheet over to see if there was anything on the other side. He didn't know why he did that, there was never anything on the reverse side of a telegram.

He read the typed information at the top. Standard rate telegram sent from Tsingtao at 12.45. Tsingtao was a former German colony now controlled by Japan, about 300 miles north of Shanghai. Strange it should be coming from there, he thought. But it was on the coastal route between here and Siberia. The telegram was received at the Shanghai Post Office on February 24th at 2.15 p.m. and delivered to the Shanghai Central Police Station at 3.30 p.m. Remarkably efficient, thought Cartwright. For once, something actually worked in China.

'Have information re daughter.' That looks interesting. Was Danilov looking for his daughter? He didn't even know that Danilov had a wife never mind a daughter.

What was he going to do? He could just leave it on Danilov's desk.

But he wouldn't. The bastard didn't deserve it, the way he had humiliated Cartwright in front of all the other detectives. All that stuff about his wife and his boy, it shouldn't have been said. Too clever for his own good was Mister fucking Danilov.

He checked the Tsingtao number. He could ring it and discover what the information was. Have something to get back at Danilov. Show the bleedin' Russian he could be just as clever, knowing stuff the Russian didn't have a clue about. Surprise them all with his little piece of detective work.

He picked up the phone and immediately put it back on its cradle. No, not here. Somebody would have to put through the call, and Miss Cavendish was bound to hear about it. Nosey old arse, that one.

He folded the telegram and its envelope neatly, putting it in the inside pocket of his jacket. For the first time that week, a smile appeared beneath Cartwright's bushy moustache. He might even treat himself to an early pick-me-up, and work out what to do with this little gem of information that had fallen into his lap.

***

It was late in the afternoon by the time Strachan finished at the Astor Hotel.

He had gone in there to be greeted by the sound of the band playing and a horde of revellers, shuffling along to the latest dances from America. It wasn't Strachan's idea of enjoyment. He much preferred a quiet evening at home, eating his mum's cooking and listening to the radio. The loud bonhomie of the dancers did nothing for him. The only time he enjoyed it was when the black singer got on stage and opened with 'Thinking of You', a beautifully sad song that she sang from the heart. The mood didn't last long though. She next launched into 'Sing, Sing, Sing' and immediately the dancers returned to the floor in their swaying masses.

At the end of their tea-dance shift, the staff had been less than co-operative. He couldn't blame them as most of them wanted to go home. Or on to some seedy casino hidden in the depths of the Badlands, out past Bubbling Well Road. Or just to find a quiet place where they could rest their tired feet and enjoy a gossip over a meal and a pot of tea.

He had work to do, so he held those back that had been working on the tea dance when Elsie Everett vanished. He didn't get much from them though. It was as if most of the patrons of the tea dance had been faceless.

'All wearing black jackets.'

'One couple kept bumping into me as I served champagne. *Ta ma de.*'

'He had shiny shoes,' one remembered.

'What did he look like?'

'I dunno. Never saw his face.'

They all remembered one man though. He had been a good tipper. Giving them money every time they brought him a drink and, at the end of the tea dance, he left twenty dollars.

'Twenty dollar. Best tip this week. He was American. Told me that. Here on business, staying Palace Hotel. Number one man, he come again, I kill anyone who stops me serving he.'

The only other people they had remembered were an old Chinese man, dressed in a long robe. The robe was pretty common but to be dressed like that was unusual at the tea dance. 'He only drank tea too. Very strange man.'

A young Chinese guy also caught their eye, or at least, his companions did. 'He very flash. Pretty girls. Number one girls from Madame Wong's house. Verrrrrry expensive each one. He had three. Lucky guy. Dunno why at tea dance, waste too much time.' The waiter then placed his right index finger through a circle formed by his left hand, just so Strachan would get the point.

The chits the guests had signed proved to be more useful. He recognised Richard Ayres's name at once, with its scrawled signature and presumption everyone knew who he was. There were twenty-one other chits, all signed clearly. The manager produced the chit book for Strachan to copy all the addresses.

The American and the two Chinese paid with cash. The manager remembered the younger Chinese man though. 'He been here before. Big spender. Big dick. Left his tie pin here one day. Gold with two diamonds.' He scrambled through his desk, shoving aside a pile of invoices and chits before snatching up a scrap of paper.

'Here it is. Never lose anything.' He handed over the address to Strachan.

'Any reward if you find him?'

'Maybe.'

'We go 50–50. What you say?'

'I say, "I'm arresting you for attempting to bribe a police officer."' Then he smiled.

'Only joking. A joke among friends. You keep all of the reward.'

'There will be no reward.'

This time it was the manager's turn to smile.

Strachan picked up his hat and left there as soon as he could. On his way out, a bellboy ran out to get a taxi for a young, elegant woman who was wearing a dress slit up to the top of her thigh. Every time she stepped forward, the dress revealed the pale skin above her stockings.

The bellboy stood outside the revolving doors of the hotel and put his fingers to his mouth. A sharp, shrill whistle forced a taxi lurking in the shadows to switch on its engine and its headlights. The taxi drew up to the hotel's portico. A hand reached through the driver's window and dropped a coin into the bellboy's hand. He ran around the back of the taxi and opened the rear door for the young woman to enter.

She took a coin from her purse and also placed it into his waiting hand. A broad smile crossed his face as he touched the coin with his fingers.

He closed the door and, as the taxi pulled away from the hotel, he wrote something in a small notepad he had pulled from his pocket.

Strachan walked over and tapped him on the shoulder. 'I want to ask you a few questions.'

'Busy,' the bellboy replied and started to run back into the hotel.

'I'm police, it's about a guest . . .'

'Look, still busy. Many guests here. This hotel you know.'

Strachan pulled a dollar coin from his pocket. The boy's eyes lit up and he went to grab it. Strachan clenched his fist around the coin before the little hand could snatch it away. 'Questions first, money later,' he said.

'No money, no talk.' The bellboy folded his arms across his chest.

Strachan gave him the coin.

'What you wanna know, me busy.'

'On the 22nd, two days ago, a young woman left the hotel.'

'Lots of women leave hotel. Some young, some not so young.' The boy glanced in the direction of the departing taxi.

'This young woman left after the tea dance, around 5.30 p.m. Blonde bobbed hair, silver grey dress, about so high.' Strachan mimed the girl's height above the boy's head.

The boy made a pretence of thinking. 'Lots of women at dance. Hard to remember.'

Strachan produced another coin from his pocket. The boy reached to snatch it again but Strachan closed his fist around it. 'No talk, no money,' he said.

The boy's eyes furrowed and he took off his hat to scratch his head. 'Woman left with man?'

'No, we think she left alone. Around five-thirty.'

The boy's eyes lit up. 'With a shiny dress. Pretty lady?'

'That's her,' Strachan said hopefully.

'No, I don't remember.' The hand came out again and a smile spread across the boy's face.

Strachan gave him the coin. This was proving to be expensive.

'Woman left at 5.35 p.m. Alone. She took taxi.'

'Taxi?'

'Yes, not normal taxi.'

'Why wasn't it "normal"?'

'Didn't want fares. Not normal. All taxi want fare.'

'Didn't want fares?'

'I already said that. Just sat here for one hour. No want fares.'

'So what happened when the lady came out?'

The boy's hand came out again. Reluctantly, Strachan dug into his pocket and pulled out his last coin. He also pulled out the inside lining of his pocket to show there was nothing left.

The boy took the money quickly. 'When she come out, taxi start engine. He pull up and she get in. No tip.'

'Did you see the driver?'

'Chinese man. No hair. Not friendly. No tip either.'

'Did you get the number of the taxi?'

'I take all numbers. Hotel policy.'

Strachan sighed, it was like pulling teeth. 'What was the number?'

The bellboy pulled out his book and flicked through the pages. Strachan could see dense rows and columns of car numbers.

'Hard to remember which one,' said the boy. The hand reached out again, palm upwards.

Strachan sighed and reluctantly reached into his jacket pocket. With his good hand, he pulled out a five-dollar note and held it in front of the wide eyes of the boy, waving it just below his nose.

'If look hard, sure can find.' The boy flicked through his book again. He pointed to a scrawled number.

'Are you sure?'

'Does rice grow on trees?'

Strachan leant over and followed the boy's little finger with its chewed nail. The number was scrawled in pencil: ST 105.

The five-dollar note was snatched from his hand and the book closed as quickly as it had been opened.

'Rice doesn't grow on trees,' he said to the bellboy.

'You very smart. For a policeman,' said the boy as he was swallowed up by the revolving doors.

                              * * *

'Thank you for meeting me so quickly.'

'That's no problem, Inspector,' said Alfred.

'Yes, it bloody is.' Margery took a sip from the cup in front of her. 'Even the bloody coffee is awful.'

'I'm afraid visitors to the station don't normally drink our coffee, Miss Leadbitter.'

'I can see why, Inspector.'

'We're happy to help.' Alfred glanced across at Margery. She snorted and took another sip of coffee, making a face as she did so.

Danilov stared at the two people sitting in front of him. The man, tall and thin, almost ascetic in his looks, but elegantly and expensively dressed. The woman short and sharp, with the most beautiful cheekbones he had ever seen.

'Can we get on with it?' said Margery.

'Of course, madam.' Danilov allowed his fingers to form a steeple before he spoke, as if praying to the god of interviews. 'You have heard of the death of Miss Everett?'

They both nodded.

'Good riddance to bad rubbish, if you want my view . . .'

'Shhhh, Margery, you shouldn't speak like that. Elsie is dead, after all.'

Margery turned to Alfred. 'She was a little gold-digging tramp. If you men didn't have your eyes in your trousers, you would have seen it as sure as night follows day.'

Danilov held his hand up.

She stared at him and took another sip of coffee.

'She died some time in the early morning hours of 23rd February. You were the last people to see her at the Astor House. Can you tell me what you did between those times?'

'You can't be suggesting . . .'

Margery snorted. 'Yes, he is, dear Alfred. He thinks you killed her.'

Danilov held his hand up again. 'I have made come to no conclusions . . . yet.' He let the 'yet' hang in the air for a while. 'Can you tell me where you were that night?'

Alfred's eyes flicked up to the right. 'At home in bed, I think.'

Danilov looked at Margery. 'Can anybody confirm that?'

'He wasn't sleeping with me, if that's what you mean.'

'Thank you, Miss Leadbitter, it's not what I meant.' He turned to Alfred. 'Well?'

'My boy woke up when I got home. It was about two in the morning. We had been out at Ciro's that night. Elsie was supposed to come, but she didn't turn up. We stayed until one and then went home.'

'And you, Miss Leadbitter?'

'I can't remember a thing, Inspector. As high as a kite. I remember having a couple of bottles of Belle Epoque in Ciro's and after that, it's a bit of a blur.'

'So you can't remember . . .?'

'Listen here, Inspector. I didn't like Elsie. She was a not-so-young, gold-digging trollop who had got her hooks into Richard and wasn't about to let go. But I didn't kill her. Wanted to, but didn't, understand?'

'Perfectly, Miss Leadbitter. So nobody saw you come home that night?'

'Nobody.'

'You did go home?'

'Of course, everybody makes it home eventually, don't they?'

Danilov made a steeple with his hands again. 'And you, Mr Wainwright. You say your boy will confirm you went home at two?'

'Well, he must have seen the light come on.'

'But he didn't actually see you come in?'

Alfred looked down at his coffee. 'No, he didn't.'

Danilov stood up quickly. 'Thank you, both, for coming.' He held out his hand.

'Is that all?' asked Alfred.

'For now, Mr Wainwright. Thank you both for your time.' He turned to go, stopped and then turned back. 'Just one more thing, do either of you know a Monsieur Flamini? He's a magistrate in the French Concession.' Danilov glanced from one to the other. Margery was cleaning her nails.

'I've had some dealings with him, Inspector,' said Alfred.

'Have you, Mr Wainwright? And what was it you do?'

'Property, Inspector. I'm in property.'

CHAPTER 20

Strachan was already sitting in the empty detectives' room when Danilov arrived back. 'Sir, I've got the number for the taxi Miss Everett took,' he said excitedly.

'Good, well done.'

'ST 105. Driven by a bald-headed man. Left the hotel at 5.35 p.m. I've already put it out on the wire to the beat constables. Maybe somebody will spot it.'

'Did you find out anything else?'

'The waiters only remembered three of the guests with any certainty. An American, an older Chinese man and a young man, a big spender, apparently. The rest of the guests seem to have been faceless, sir.'

'They often are in those sorts of establishments.'

'Richard Ayres was there, he signed a chit. There are twenty-one other chits. Here are the names and addresses, sir.' Strachan handed over his notebook.

Danilov looked at his colleague. 'You write like a child, Stra-chan. All capitals.'

'It's how we were taught by the monks, sir.'

Danilov sniffed. 'Well at least it's easy to read.' He traced all the names and addresses with his finger. He stopped at one. 'Strange, what was he doing there?'

Strachan tried to peer over his shoulder to see what he had noticed, but the Inspector closed the book quickly.

'And while you're at it, find out who the taxi is registered to, will you? But my bet is that it's a false number plate.'

'Yes, sir. The bellboy told me the taxi was waiting for Miss Everett when she came out of the hotel. It didn't want to take any other fares.'

'The taxi was waiting? Perhaps our killer is not choosing his victims at random, Stra-chan. He's picking them deliberately.' The Inspector took a long drag from his cigarette and exhaled three perfectly round circles of smoke.

'A clever trick, sir.'

'The sign of a misspent youth, Stra-chan. It strikes me our killer or killers has us jumping through hoops, as you English say.'

'I'm Scottish, sir.'

'The Scots don't say the same thing?'

'Well, they do, sir, but . . .'

'Stra-chan. I will never understand your petty English obsession with the minor regions of your country. In Minsk, we say, "It's not the horse that draws the cart but the oats."'

'That seems more appropriate, sir.'

'Were you making a joke, Stra-chan?'

'No, sir.'

Another long period of silence. Finally, Danilov stubbed his cigarette out in the overflowing ashtray. 'We have at least four murders. A French magistrate. A Russian prostitute. An American androgyne and an English actress. There may be more, but these are the ones we know.'

'All different nationalities, sir.'

'But that's to be expected, isn't it? After all, Shanghai has always been a magnet for people from all over the world. No, what's more important is not their nationality, it's what links them. What do they have in common?'

'Well, sir, I think . . .'

'That was a rhetorical question, Stra-chan, I was thinking out loud.'

'I'll keep quiet, sir.'

'That would be a good idea, for the moment.' Danilov rolled another cigarette, filling it with just a few strands of tobacco from the tin. It flared as he lit the end and took the first lungful of smoke. 'This requires the thoughtfulness of tobacco.' He stared at the glowing end of the cigarette. 'Have you ever thought, Stra-chan, that one of the unintended consequences of man's obsession with burning a toxic weed, is his ability to think over a problem?'

Strachan shook his head, careful not to speak.

'I wonder if the man who discovered tobacco realised this effect. The Indians did and that's why they smoked it in the first place.'

Strachan had the good sense to still remain quiet.

'Well, with the aid of the demon weed we will return to our problem.'

Strachan decided that maybe, just maybe, he could now speak. 'There could be others we don't know about.'

'I'm sure there are, Stra-chan But we can only deal with what we know. We can't know what we don't know. And, we certainly can't know what we know we don't know.'

'Yes, sir . . . I know . . . I think.'

Danilov stubbed the cigarette out. 'All had been bound with rope. But the rope is available at any merchants. At least the killer is consistent, is he not, Stra-chan?'

'He is, sir. Always the same way of operating.'

'And most important, all had Chinese characters carved into their bodies with a sharp knife.'

Strachan flicked through his notebook until he found the characters. 'They were "vengeance", "damnation", "justice" and "retribution", sir, in order of the victims' discovery. It suggests our killer is Chinese, sir, using Chinese words.'

'Not necessarily, Strachan, do not jump to conclusions. All it tells us is that the killer, or killers, knows Chinese.' Danilov began to roll another cigarette. 'Or at least knows enough Chinese to copy the character from a book.'

'And enough Chinese to understand what the character means, sir.'

'Yes, there may be something in the meaning of the words. Or their order. Or their usage. I think we need to see your uncle, Stra-chan, as soon as possible.'

'I'll call him right now, sir. How does 11 am suit?'

'It suits very well, Stra-chan. Tailor-made, one could say.'

While Strachan made his call, Danilov stared into space, smoking his cigarette, blowing the ice-blue smoke into the air above his head. Why was the killer killing? Revenge? Excitement? Pleasure? Or all three? He blew another smoke ring. Until they knew why he was killing they weren't going to find him. They had to understand the reasons, understand the patterns, and he would be discovered.

He stubbed the cigarette in the ashtray. It was already full to the brim with ash and used stubs. What about the words on the barrel lid, 'HATE ALL'? Such a strong, violent phrase, frightening in its intensity. Why had the killer written it on the underside of the lid? Why write anything? And then, for a moment, Danilov was struck by the thought that maybe the words were not linked to the killings at all.

He shook his head. They had to be. The coincidence of those words being scratched into a barrel that just happened to be used for a brutal murder was impossible. Dr Fang would be able to tell them more.

'Done, sir. We'll meet Uncle Chang at 11 a.m. tomorrow, in his house.'

'That gives us time to check out the people at the tea dance in the morning. You start with the old Chinese man. A strange place for him to be. I'll look in on the American.'

'He's staying at the Palace Hotel, sir.'

'We'll meet up at your uncle's house. What's the address?'

'Er, 10 Jessfield Road on the western borders, sir. You can't miss it, it's big and dark.'

Danilov carried on staring into the air. 'What are we missing, Stra-chan? We have four bodies, but we have no motive, and no reason for the murders.'

'Does a serial killer need a reason, sir? Isn't killing reason enough?'

'All killers need a reason, Stra-chan. Killing is the one human activity that always has a reason. Whether it's love or jealousy, pride or greed, anger or sadness, we all need a reason to kill another human being. Even a soldier needs a reason, even though it could be he's just scared of his sergeant.'

'Yes, sir. But we don't know why our killer is killing these people. There seems to be no link between any of them.'

'Oh, there is a link, Stra-chan. We just haven't found it yet.' Danilov blew out another long plume of smoke. 'Maybe we are looking at it incorrectly.'

'What do you mean, sir?'

'Well, what if we stop looking at the victims and start looking at our killer?'

'I don't understand, sir.'

'How does our killer know his victims? How does he select them? How does he know these are the people he wants to kill?'

'Well, they are all foreigners, sir, there have been no Chinese victims.'

'Is he preying on foreigners? Why?'

'Could it be political, sir?'

'Political? No, I don't think so. Examine the evidence. There have been no anti-foreign messages attached to the bodies. And the Chinese characters are not linked to any known political movements. No, this is more personal than political. This matters to him personally, it's not in aid of any cause.'

'What about criminal activity?'

'No ransom demands. No evidence of gang activity. No increase in gang-related crimes. The French magistrate may have been corrupt. The Russian prostitute may have had a pimp who was a gang member. But our androgyne certainly wasn't involved with the Triads. I don't think they would welcome a man dressed as a woman into their ranks. Whilst the English actress may have acted criminally on the stage but that's as far as her involvement with crime went.'

'Then it could be racial, sir. Somebody who just hates foreigners.'

'They exist in every culture, Stra-chan, those who hate people who are different, blaming them for the problems in their own society. God knows, the Chinese have enough to blame the foreigners for over the last hundred years, but this is not the wholesale murder of foreigners.

These victims are chosen.' Danilov blew two more perfectly formed circles of blue smoke. 'It's like these particular people were being punished for something.'

Danilov jumped up. 'Come on, Stra-chan, I want to go back to the park where Elsie Everett was found. It will help to look at it again when the crowds are not around.'

'I'll fetch the car, sir.'

'Do you remember which one it is?'

'The black one, sir.'

'You're learning, Stra-chan. One day, you might even become good at this.'

CHAPTER 21

They had barely crossed Nanking Road when the radio on the dashboard buzzed. Strachan picked the receiver up and pressed a button on the side. 'Strachan here, over.'

From the speaker on the inside roof of the car, the crackly voice of the radio operator blasted out. 'A black taxi, licence plate ST 105, has been spotted by a beat constable on Weiheiwei Road, turning into Hart Road, heading towards the French Concession. Over.'

The Inspector pointed to the road on the right. 'Strachan, turn along Sinza Road. We'll head them off at the bottom near Avenue Joffre. This could be the break we were looking for.'

The tyres squealed as Strachan heaved the bulky sedan around the corner. A rickshaw boy jumped out of the way, narrowly avoiding being hit by the car. The rickshaw itself wasn't so lucky.

Strachan glanced in his rearview mirror, seeing the rickshaw boy waving his fist in the air and mouthing obscenities. He pressed harder on the accelerator, honking the horn with his right hand.

'Please don't do that, Stra-chan, you'll give me a headache. We're just two minutes away from the border with the French Concession. We mustn't let them cross over.'

Strachan accelerated even harder, scattering some schoolgirls as they ambled across the road. He changed the gears down and turned left into Hart Road.

'Go down to the corner with Avenue Joffre and stop there.'

Strachan accelerated and the Buick responded well. Hart Road was a wide, spacious street, with plane trees lining its length. On either side, elegant shops displaying the latest fashions from Paris, Rome, New York and London lined the pavement, their windows hidden by a mass of afternoon shoppers.

'Pull in here, Strachan.' The Inspector had seen a space at the side of the road, facing back towards the Settlement.

'The taxi could have passed us already, sir.'

'I think not. The streets are narrow and congested around Weiheiwei Road. As long as we're here, they can't escape into the French Concession. Do you know how to use that thing?' Danilov pointed to the microphone. Strachan nodded. 'Call the Mobile Unit to provide back-up.'

Strachan took hold of the microphone and began speaking. 'Central, over. Come in Central . . .'

Danilov scanned the approaching cars, looking for the licence plate.

A crackly female voice came over the loudspeaker above their heads. It was as if an angel were speaking to them. 'Car 12, come in, over.'

'This is Car 12. Request support from the Mobile Unit. We are at corner of Hart Road and Avenue Joffre. Over.' Strachan let go of the button and listened for a reply.

After an age of hisses, squeaks and static, the voice returned. 'Car 12, Mobile Unit on its way. ETA, eight minutes. Over.'

At the same time, Danilov tapped Strachan's arm. The black taxi with number plate ST 105 was coming towards them. They could see a driver in the front and two passengers in the back.

Strachan jammed his foot on the accelerator. The car surged forward blocking the taxi. It braked sharply, swerving to the left. The driver swore at them.

'Show him who we are, Stra-chan.'

Strachan leant forward and flicked a switch on the dashboard. Suddenly, a loud wailing filled the air, its pitch rising and falling as if a thousand devils had suddenly been jabbed with hot pokers.

The driver's anger turned to fear. He looked behind him and immediately the car reversed backwards, towards a crowd of people standing at the side of the road. There were shouts and screams as they jumped out of the way. One old man wasn't quick enough. His body hit the boot of the taxi and vaulted into the air, landing on the tarmac of the road with a soft thud.

The driver of the taxi fought with the steering wheel, twisting it hard right. It surged forward away from the screaming crowd and back the way it had come.

'Get after them!' ordered Danilov.

Strachan put the car in gear, heaved round on the steering wheel, pulling straight into the oncoming traffic. A delivery van screeched to a halt just inches away from Danilov's door. He could see the badge on the driver's cap: LEE'S LAUNDRY. Then Strachan accelerated away, throwing Danilov over to his right.

The car in front was getting away from them. Strachan changed up and pressed the pedal even harder. The surge of the car threw Danilov back into his seat. He gripped the dashboard to hold himself upright.

The taxi in front weaved in and out of traffic, racing past lorries and cars, first on the inside and then on the outside. Strachan followed exactly in its wake, keeping his eyes on the road and his jaw clenched.

They were coming to the crossroads with Weiheiwei Road. The car paused as if ready to stop, then quickly surged through the traffic, turning right at the junction.

Strachan kept following just thirty feet from the taxi. Behind them, Danilov could hear the squeal of brakes and the loud honk of horns. He peered through the split windscreen. They were going to hit the rear of a truck! Then they swerved out, passing the truck on the inside. A pedestrian crossing the road jumped out of their way, a look of sheer terror animating his face.

Strachan's eyes were fixed on the road, calmly keeping the black Chevrolet taxi in his sights.

In front, the right-hand rear door of the car opened and a small Chinese man dressed in a brown business suit stepped onto the running board. His arm came up and their windscreen cracked with a round bullet hole appearing in the middle. Then Danilov heard the shot. He thought how strange that he would see the shot before hearing it.

Another hole appeared and another. The loud wailing suddenly ceased.

Strachan swerved to the left, narrowly avoiding a cyclist.

'They are shooting at us, sir.'

'I had guessed, Stra-chan.'

The gunman's arm was coming up again. The Chevrolet took a sharp right at the next junction, throwing him off balance. He clung to the top of the door, but it swung closed, smashing into his body, throwing him off the car. He landed with a sickening bounce at the edge of the road, rolling over twice and then hitting a fire hydrant.

As they passed, Danilov could see there wasn't much left of his face. 'Keep going after the taxi,' he commanded.

Strachan accelerated again, throwing Danilov to this left against the handle of the door. A sharp pain stabbed beneath his rib cage. He glanced down; spots of blood were already seeping through his shirt.

The Chevrolet was going much faster now, not caring who, or what, was in its way.

It swung to go right along Myburgh Road, but the back wheels locked and it slid towards one of the plane trees, hitting it full on, throwing a cloud of steam and bits of metal into the air.

The back door opened and a man clambered out. He fired two shots at their car, before running down one of the narrow *lilongs* that led off the street. Pedestrians scattered in front of him.

Strachan braked the car and jumped out. He began to run after the suspect, chasing him into the *lilong*. Danilov shouted after him, 'Let him go,' but Strachan carried on running.

Danilov gingerly stepped out of the car. Strachan was already halfway down the *lilong*, heading back towards Nanking Road; no point in trying to stop him.

He approached the taxi cautiously. In the front seat, a young Chinese man lay draped over the steering wheel, his face a mass of blood and bone, his skull shattered, revealing the pink sheen of the brain.

Behind the man, the back seat was empty except for five brass cartridges littering the floor.

Brakes squealed behind him and there was the sound of running feet – the Mobile Unit had arrived.

He felt the side of his chest. He hoped he hadn't been shot again. The shirt was wet with blood. His fingers traced the outline of his ribs.

Pain. A sharp shooting pain. But no bullet hole. He was lucky this time.

'Get after Stra-chan,' he shouted at a sergeant of the Mobile Unit.

***

Strachan could see the stocky man weaving through a crowd of people up ahead, his dark suit distinctive against the *chi paos* and long Mandarin coats of the shoppers. A woman screamed as she fell over, struck by the man when she didn't get out of his way fast enough.

They were running down a narrow alley, hemmed in on both sides by three-storey buildings housing tenants on every floor. Above Strachan's head, the sky was dense with wet clothing hanging out to dry on long bamboo poles. On the right, a door was open to the street. Inside, an old man, sitting on a bamboo chair, slowly devoured a bowl of rice. As he ran past, the man lifted his head for a moment before returning to his bowl.

Strachan ran faster. The wind stung his face and his feet clattered heavily on the cobblestones. As he ran round the corner, his legs went from under him and he slid into a pile of stinking rubbish lying against a wall.

He picked himself up quickly and ran on, throwing away the remains of a steamed fish that had become stuck to his jacket.

The man ran through the stone exit of the *lilong* and straight across the street. Strachan was closer now, gaining on him. A loud screech as a car braked suddenly.

The man jumped to avoid the thrusting bonnet, landing heavily on his side.

Strachan had him now. He increased his speed, racing under the stone gate and crossing the street.

The man picked himself up and limped heavily up the stairs of the Great World entertainment complex, knocking another young woman out of his way.

Strachan saw a gap in the traffic, darting in between the lorries and cars, sticking out his hand to stop a rickshaw driver. He scurried across Nanking Road after the limping man. He could hear swearing and the screech of brakes behind him.

The man was only fifteen yards ahead.

Strachan charged up the steps, following him through the entrance of Great World. A shot rang out and a bullet clanged against a brass bell to the right of his head. He ducked beneath a counter. Up above him, the bell still sang its song.

The man aimed again, his right arm coming up. Everything was slowing down now for Strachan. He had time to see the man was young, not more than twenty-five, with a round head and crew-cut hair. He was breathing heavily, his chest panting, grabbing for air, like a drunk grabbing a drink.

The pistol was up now, pointing directly at Strachan. A German Mauser, not terribly accurate, thought Strachan as the bullet ripped into the wall an inch from his head, spraying his cheeks and ear with shards of plaster and stone.

He threw himself back behind the counter. A torrent of candies, nuts, dried fruit and pineapple cakes tumbled down on top of him from a shelf above his head. All around him, the screams of the patrons of Great World as they ran for cover. The harsh squeals of the taxi dancers cutting through every other sound.

And then the pain hit him.

He reached up to the left side of his face. It was covered in blood. He touched the lobe of his ear and a stab of pain shot through his body. Vomit welled up in his throat, like he was going to throw up every meal he had ever eaten, and one more, just for luck. He swallowed the saliva that stuck to the roof of his mouth. Got to keep going, can't let him get away. Can't let this bastard get away.

He jerked himself away from the wall and peered around the corner of the counter. The kidnapper was running down the corridor, past the fan tan tables and slot machines.

Shoppers, patrons, taxi dancers, waiters and customers just out to enjoy the entertainment of Great World, scattered in front of the man, as if he were Moses parting the Red Sea. Others just cowered in the shop doorways, staring at the pistol gripped in his hand.

One young man, a waiter, stepped forward to stop the gunman running up the stairs. Another shot rang out and the waiter slumped forward, a large red stain already spreading across his white shirt.

Strachan reached up to the edge of the counter and jerked himself up. He stepped forward, pulling out his gun from the holster beneath his arm. It had a smear of blood on its black barrel.

He raised himself up and stood as still as he could, sighting down the barrel of the Webley. But the man had already disappeared up and around the corner of the stairs.

Strachan lurched on, scattering the people in front of him, shouting, 'Police! Police!' He ran past the young waiter lying in a pool of blood. Nothing could be done for him, he thought. Got to get the bastard who shot him.

He charged up the stairs. As he got to the first landing, he stopped, afraid he would be ambushed by the man again. He climbed slowly up until he could just see over the top of the stairs. The man was running down the corridor towards another staircase at the end.

A sing-song girl wearing the traditional high-collared gown of the courtesan, slit up the leg to the same level as her hip, got in his way. The man threw her to one side. As she fell, she hit her head on the edge of a slot machine.

Strachan ran up the stairs and knelt beside her, feeling for a pulse. There was none, just a small trickle of blood running from her ear. Another shot rang out from the floor above. He lay the girl's head down on the parquet floor, and ran after the thug, determined that he was not going to escape.

He took the stairs two at a time, not caring any more if the man was lying in wait. On the next floor, a stuffed whale hung from the ceiling, its once blue skin now a tired and dusty grey. Ahead, the shadow of the gunman passed across a row of mirrors, suddenly becoming four men as the reflections rebounded on each other.

Strachan raised his Webley but the shadow didn't appear again.

Cautiously, he inched forward. A young girl, no more than sixteen, with a gown that was slit up to the armpits, displaying her black lingerie, put her fingers to her lips and pointed upwards.

Strachan nodded to thank her and ran up the next flight. He reached the top of the stairs. The kidnapper was already running down the corridor.

As he neared the end, the man took a quick look over his shoulder. Again, he turned and fired. Quicker this time, without taking aim.

The shot passed over Strachan's head thudding into the ceiling above him.

More screams from the bystanders. They had come for an exciting day at Shanghai's most famous amusement centre, but this was far more than they had bargained for.

A crowd of people rushed past Strachan, desperate to get down the stairs and away from the noise of the gun. Strachan was thrown to the side against the wall. His ear was aching now, a deep throb.

The man ran up the stairs at the opposite end, two at a time. Strachan got up and charged after him. Nothing was going to stop him. That bastard was going to pay for what he had done.

Outside, the noise of the sirens of the Red Marias, doors being slammed, commands shouted.

Get a bloody move on, Strachan thought as he ran after the gunman.

'Police! Police!' he shouted at the scared people hiding in the shops and doorways.

He ran up the stairs, and around the landing. Another shot crunched into the plaster wall, just to the left of his eye this time. He stumbled forward and fell, landing heavily.

The steps of the kidnapper echoed on the wooden floor ahead of him. More screams from the patrons as they dived out of his way.

Can't let him go. Must keep going.

He saw an open window and leant out to shout at the Red Marias *below*: '*Police! Up here. Up here!*'

The gunman vanished at the top of the next stairs. Suddenly, the shouts of the patrons of Great World were louder now, on the fifth floor, more intense.

Strachan charged after him, not caring any more about the gun. Only wanting to bring the man down and beat him unconscious.

The man ran through the nightclub, bursting between dancing couples. The band stopped playing. The singer stood in front of her microphone. The taxi dancers ceased hustling for business.

Then they saw the gun and all hell broke loose.

People knocked each other over, desperate to get out of the kidnapper's way, caring only to save their own lives. Three women lay sprawled on the floor, their tight *chi paos* shredded above the knee.

Strachan followed him through the carnage of knocked-over tables and cowering dancers. He ran out of the nightclub and up to the next floor. The gunman was charging through a door at the end out onto the open-air cafe on the roof of Great World.

Strachan could feel his heart beating and his chest heaving. There was no pain any more from his ear but he didn't know whether that was good or bad. He stumbled after the man, pushing open the door at the end.

The gunman had knocked over two tables, spilling tea and cakes all over the wooden floor.

Strachan ducked down behind an advertising sign, which read: TSINGTAO. He could certainly do with a beer right now.

The man had run to the edge of the roof. Waitresses were screaming, the customers were running towards the door like lemmings.

The gunman reached the edge of the roof and peered over.

Strachan got up and walked slowly towards him, his Webley extended in front him. The man was starting to panic, running left and right, his chest heaving and his large eyes frantic with fear.

'There's nowhere to go!' shouted Strachan in Shanghainese. 'Just give yourself up!'

The man peered quickly over the parapet once more.

'Go ahead and jump if you want. I will enjoy scraping your brains off Nanking Road.'

Strachan was just twenty feet away now. The man still had his gun. 'Put the gun down.'

The man glanced at the gun as if suddenly realising he was still carrying it. Then he raised it quickly and pointed it straight at the detective, pulling the trigger.

There was a loud click and for a second, they just stared at each other.

Then the man threw his pistol at Strachan. He ducked, but the heavy gun hit him on the side of the head, right next to his damaged ear.

Again, waves of pain rolled over his body. A long stream of blood ran down his face, dripping off his shirt and onto the roof.

He was hit in the chest by something large. The breath exploded from his body. The man was on top of him, raining blows down on his head. Strachan lifted his right arm to protect himself. The man grabbed the gun, trying to wrestle the pistol free from his hands. Strachan fought back, arching his back and pushing off with his legs to topple the man to the side.

They wrestled with the gun, rolling over and over. Their joined hands, with the pistol between them, hit the edge of a table. The pistol slithered along the roof.

Strachan punched the man as hard as he could with his free right hand, connecting just above the temple. The man grunted and fell to the right.

Strachan scrambled to his feet, rushing over to grab the pistol. His feet suddenly went out from under him as the man grabbed his legs. He fell heavily to the floor; pain shot up through his left shoulder.

The man was on top of him, knocking his head against the wooden floor. Banging it again and again. He started to lose consciousness, hearing the crunch of his head against wood echoing in his skull.

For a moment, he thought of his mother. What would she think now? Her precious son, rolling around on the roof of Great World, his head being smacked again and again against the wooden floor.

He kicked up with his legs, feeling them crash into the back of the man.

The weight was off him now. He tried to lift his head, shake the fuzziness out; why was he moving so slowly?

Strachan tried to get up but a blow hit him on the head next to the damaged ear. He grabbed the leg, but a jolt of pain shot through his head and he released his grip.

The man stood up and kicked out again, his boot landing flush on Strachan's chest.

You're not going to get away, Strachan thought, launching himself upwards, ignoring the pain in his shoulder and the throb of his ear.

He dived forward, grabbing hold of the man's leg. His shoulder hit the ground, and a stabbing pain lanced into the joint. Another kick thundered into the top of his head but he hung onto the man's leg, he wasn't ever going to let go.

The man toppled over him, landing heavily.

Strachan flung his body on top of the sprawling man, thrusting his shoulder into the man's chest, forcing the air to shoot out of his lungs in one sharp gasp.

He brought his right elbow up to connect with the man's nose, hearing a soft thud as it struck home. The gunman's head flew back, and he kicked out, trying to dislodge Strachan again.

But the detective pressed down harder, using his left arm to pin the man's body. Another stab of pain through the shoulder but Strachan ignored the pain. He lifted his right elbow and slammed it into the face that stared up at him.

The man's eyes rolled upwards until all that Strachan should see were the whites.

Strachan hit him again with his elbow, this time slashing down vertically. Blood began to fly from the gunman's nose, spurting all over the detective.

Strachan levered himself over the man's body, bending his back as far as it would go and then slamming forward, putting all his weight on the point of his elbow, smashing with all the strength he possessed into the gunman's mouth.

The body beneath him went limp. Strachan could see the man's mouth was a mass of blood, slashed lips and broken teeth.

He lifted himself slowly off the broken body and gingerly got to his feet.

This is not getting any easier, he thought, giving the man a sharp kick in the ribs for good luck. Strachan's luck, not that of the man lying stretched out on the roof of Great World.

'Get your hands up!' shouted a voice from behind him.

Strachan turned slowly. Two constables were waving pistols in his face.

'I said, get your hands up or I fire!'

He tried to put his arms up in the air, but the pain shot through his shoulder. 'Police. Detective Constable Strachan,' he gasped. 'My warrant card is inside my jacket.'

One of the constables kept his pistol and eyes trained on Strachan as he had been taught to do in the Training School. The other reached into Strachan's jacket and pulled out a thin wallet.

He checked the warrant card inside and nodded, finally dropping the pistol to his side. 'It's Stra-chan, is it?'

'The name is pronounced Str*aaa*n.'

The gunman groaned and began to sit up. Strachan walked over and punched him on the top of the head. 'Enjoy the nap.'

He collapsed back onto the roof.

'Make sure this piece of shit doesn't move.'

'Ye shouldnae have let the bastard hurt ye so.'

Strachan looked up to see a tall, burly Inspector with a shock of ginger hair standing at the entrance to the roof.

'I remember ye from ma classes. Should hae done better, laddie.'

Strachan lifted his head and looked at the Inspector more closely. It was Fairbairn, the head of the Mobile Unit and the fighting instructor for the police.

Inspector Fairbairn shook his head at Strachan. 'I'll book ye in for some classes. Looks like ye need 'em.'

Strachan watched as a large globule of blood fell from his ear and landed on his shoe. 'I got the bastard,' he said as he gasped for breath.

'Aye, but this time, it looks like he got you.'

***

'While you were enjoying yourself on the roof of Great World, Stra-chan, I spent my time searching the car.' Danilov placed a large box down on the desk. 'It's being dusted down by the fingerprint team as we speak.'

Strachan stood up and peered into the box. He began to take things out from it one by one. 'Five brass cartridge cases. These must be from the floor of the car, Inspector.'

'Right. These were the shots that nearly killed us. Allow me to compliment you on your driving, Stra-chan.'

'Thank you, sir.'

He felt the side of his chest. 'And remind me never to share a car with you again.'

'Yes, sir.'

Strachan pulled the rest of the objects from the box: a cheap wallet with three dollars inside but no ID, two fedoras, old and used, a coat which had seen better days, a half-eaten packet of sweets, a used handkerchief, a woman's shoe, three dirty rags and, finally, a small bag full of what looked like metal prongs.

'I wonder what these are used for, sir?'

'I think they are house-breaking tools, Stra-chan. It looks like our killer did a bit of burglary on the side. There's one thing left inside. I found it in the boot.'

Strachan reached in and brought out a leather-covered book with the words HOLY BIBLE embossed in gold on the cover. He opened it to the fly leaf: EX LIBRIS. THE CHURCH OF THE REDEEMER, SINZA ROAD, SHANGHAI.

'It's the same one Harriet Sole, I mean Henry Sellars, had in his locker.'

'Right once again, Stra-chan. Where is our man?'

'Downstairs in Room Four, sir.'

'I think it is time to speak to him, don't you?'

***

Inspector Danilov and Detective Constable Strachan entered the interview room without knocking. The man who had been arrested on the roof of Great World was touching a large bump on the top of his head that already protruded through his crew-cut hair. Two yellowish-black circles sat just beneath his eyes whilst a straight cut ran across the bridge of his nose.

He did not look a happy man.

The two detectives sat down at the table without saying a word. Danilov took out his tobacco tin and rolled a cigarette.

The man said something in Mandarin.

'He's just asked if he could have a fucking cigarette, sir.'

'Tell him no, Stra-chan.'

The detective repeated the message. The man spat on the floor. Danilov carried on rolling his cigarette without looking up. He brought it to his mouth and sealed it with his tongue. From his pocket he produced a lighter and lit the end of the roll-up. He took a long, cool drag and blew three smoke rings out into the air of the interview room.

The man watched as the rings widened and eventually dissipated.

Danilov leant forward and placed his tobacco tin at 90 degrees to the edge of the table. He leant back to check if it was in the correct alignment before leaning in again to adjust it to the left slightly.

The man continued to watch the Inspector, his eyes, with their prominent bruises, making him look like a new species of panda.

Finally, when Danilov was satisfied with the position of the tin, he leant back in his chair. His head fell forward on his chest and he appeared to go to sleep.

The man shouted out in Mandarin. 'Look, I know what you're doing. I've been inside before. You can't scare me.'

Danilov's eyes opened slightly. 'Just tell him exactly what I say, Stra-chan.'

'Yes, sir.'

'Please reassure Mr . . .?' He looked at Strachan to translate.

'Lin. He says his name is Lin, sir, Sounds like Jimmy Lin, but his Mandarin is very thick. The aitches sound like Fs and the Ns like Ls. I think he's from Hunan, sir. Probably Changsha.'

'Thank you, Stra-chan. Please reassure Mr Lin that we have no intention of hurting him. On the contrary, we wish to help him.'

Strachan translated the words. The man shouted back.

'He's asking why, sir. Why do you want to help him?'

'Because the other two men who died in the crash were his relatives. We must help him to see them get into the next life properly.'

Again Strachan translated. The man looked at the Inspector suspiciously. 'He's asking why you would do that?'

'Because he is going to tell us why he committed the murders.'

The man listened to Strachan and stared at the Inspector. After a long pause, he shrugged his shoulders.

'He says that if he tells you, will you send his cousins back to their families in Changsha?'

'I give him my word. On the soul of my father.' Danilov touched his heart.

The man spoke again.

'He says they got in his way.'

'How did they get in his way?'

The man shrugged his shoulders. 'They just did, sir.'

'Why did he carve Chinese characters into their bodies?'

The man looked surprised. 'What Chinese characters? He says he shot them.'

'The Chinese characters on the French magistrate, the Russian woman, Henry Sellars and Elsie Everett.'

Strachan translated again. 'He's asking who these foreigners are. He's never heard of them.'

Danilov crushed his cigarette into the ashtray. 'Let's start again. His car was seen leaving the Astor Hotel with one of the victims inside. Elsie Everett. She was later found murdered.'

Strachan translated and the man giggled.

'Why is he laughing, Stra-chan?'

'He says the car isn't his, sir. He stole it. With his friends. They found it on the Bund with the keys inside. Took it for a joy ride. Then we showed up. Now his cousins are dead.'

Danilov held up the bible he had taken from the car. 'How does he explain this? It's the same bible that we found in Henry Sellars's locker.'

The man giggled again.

'He says he doesn't know, sir. They just stole the car.' Strachan thought for a moment. 'I think he's telling the truth. This isn't an educated man. He's just a street thug with bad Mandarin. Can I try something, sir?'

Danilov lit another cigarette and placed the tobacco tin back in its proper place on the table, Jimmy Lin watching him all the time.

Strachan produced his pen and note book from his pocket. He passed it over to Jimmy Lin. 'I've just asked him to write down what happened, sir.'

Jimmy Lin stared at the pen, holding it between his third finger and his thumb.

'This man is illiterate, sir. He can't read or write.'

Danilov sighed a long blue trail of smoke. 'I do know what illiterate means, Stra-chan. Charge him with the murder of the waiter and the taxi dancer. He's not our killer.'

'Yes, sir.'

Danilov got up to go. 'And tell him I will send the bodies of his cousins back to Changsha. I give him my word.'

CHAPTER 22

'Please, sit down. Cigars?' Boyle offered them his box of Havanas. There were only two left. Both Danilov and Strachan declined.

'I just thought I would extend my personal thanks to you both. Catching the murderers so quickly was a bit of a coup for us. Upstairs is very pleased. I'll leave you to phone the French, Danilov. Put them out of their misery. We had to do their detective work for them. Of course, you'll both receive commendations and a note on your records. How's your ear, Strachan?'

'Still sore, sir, but the doctor said it would heal soon. It looks a bit of a fright though.'

'The bandage is rather large. Sure you wouldn't like a few days off?'

'No, thank you, sir. Too much to do at the moment.'

Danilov coughed. 'Sir, the man we are holding in the cells is not the murderer. He's just a small-time car thief.'

'What? What's that?'

'He isn't our killer, sir.'

Boyle scratched the top of his bald head. Flakes of white scalp fell like snow onto his shoulders. 'But . . . but . . . you arrested them. They shot at you. They were driving the killer's car.'

'They stole it from the Bund. The keys had been left inside. Obviously, the killer wanted to get rid of it.

The easiest way was to get somebody to steal it. We've charged the man we are holding with murder. He shot a waiter and a taxi dancer.'

'But he's not the murderer. Not the man who killed Richard Ayres's fiancée?'

Danilov shook his head. 'This man is just a two-bit hood from Hunan. Out to make a quick buck in the big city.'

'What am I going to tell upstairs?'

'I suggest you let them know that our investigations are ongoing, sir.'

'Ongoing? Ongoing?' The Chief Inspector's voice rose an octave. 'Not good enough, Danilov.'

'We're moving as quickly as we can. It's a complex case . . .'

'It seems to me you are spending more time on the French killings than you are on solving the murder of the fiancée of one of the leading members of Shanghai society.'

'I think that's unfair, sir.'

'You do, do you? Have you caught the killer? Have you brought anybody in for questioning yet?'

Danilov slowly shook his head. 'Not at the moment, sir, but—'

'Don't give me any buts, Danilov, I want this case solved. Is that clear? Off the books, out of—'

Before Boyle could finish his sentence there was a knock at the door. It opened and Miss Cavendish entered. 'I do hope I'm not disturbing anything, Chief Inspector, but Mr Allen thought you should see this.'

She laid the latest copy of the *Evening News* on Boyle's desk. Glaring headlines shouted from the front page:

ANOTHER VICTIM FOR THE CHARACTER KILLER

Underneath in a slightly smaller typeface:
POLICE STUMPED

Boyle sighed and ran his fingers through the tuft of hair above his right ear. More dandruff fell on his jacket. 'See what's happening, Danilov? I shudder to think what will happen when I ring upstairs and tell them we haven't caught the killer after all.'

'You caught the killer?' asked Miss Cavendish.

'No,' sneered Boyle, 'Danilov caught a car thief. He thought it was the killer.'

Danilov ignored Boyle, scanning the article beneath the headline. 'How did the reporters get this information? We've been keeping the details of this case under wraps.'

'Never mind that. Just. Solve. The. Case. Do I make myself clear?' Boyle stared at Danilov.

Danilov stared at the flakes of white skin on top of the Chief Inspector's blue pinstripe jacket. 'Very clear, sir,' he answered.

Boyle turned to Miss Cavendish. 'Please thank Mr Allen for the information.'

'He's out at the moment, sir. I'll call him when he gets back.'

Before Boyle could continue his lecture, Danilov stood up. 'Come on, Stra-chan, we have work to do.' He quickly opened the door with Strachan right behind him.

As they closed it, the phone rang on Boyle's desk.

***

The preacher died as he was removing his right leg. What a shame. He would have preferred him to stay alive for a little longer. Perhaps he should have waited before taking it off, let him recover for a while.

It was a messy business. The preacher bled a lot, making the knife slippery to hold as the blood spurted onto the grip. And then there was the smell. He didn't mind the pungent aroma of the blood, a metallic, almost rusty smell. But the preacher himself stank to high heaven, which is where he was aiming to go, of course.

Luckily, he had prepared for every eventuality. He remembered the 6Ps from the army: Proper Preparation Prevents Piss Poor Performance. It was the motto of the staff of the division. Shame it wasn't practised in reality. The staff work throughout the war was piss poor despite his attempts to make it better. They just wouldn't listen to him. Idiots. Generals. Field Marshals. Idiots all of them. They should have been the ones to march across no man's land, holding a rifle above their heads as they stumbled through the muck and shit. But no. They were at HQ safely tucking into a chateaubriand and a Châteauneuf-du-Pape. Criminals. He would have to judge one of them after he'd finished with Shanghai.

He made the final cut through the thigh bone using the cleaver. The knife scraped the bone pleasingly and made a sharp crunch as it chopped through the last spur and embedded itself in the wooden slab.

The body of the preacher lay in front of him in five neat pieces: a torso still with genitals attached. He didn't want to remove those this time, just the two arms and two legs. Not a bad job, even if he did say so himself.

The preacher wouldn't be playing with any more young boys, not any more.

It was interesting what people told him when they knew they were going to die. Henry Sellars couldn't stop babbling about the preacher when he was being cut. He described how he had to take off his shirt and pants and put on a girl's yellow dress. Then he was led to a bare wooden table with just a single cross on it. There, he had to lie on his stomach and face the cross, shouting out his sins to Jesus. The preacher pushing into him. Punishing him nearly every day by bending him over the table with the single cross. He had prayed for it to end, but it never did.

Now it had ended, for both of them. Neither Henry nor the preacher would commit any more crimes. They had both been judged, sentenced and executed. For him, there was no mitigation, no excuse. No feeble justifications for crime. No spurious reasons. Just the crime itself and its judgement. And they had both paid the price.

There were so many criminals to judge and so little time to judge them all.

But his work must continue, day by day.

CHAPTER 23

'*Hello, is anybody there?*' Cartwright was shouting into the mouthpiece of the telephone. He always believed if the voice at the other end of the phone wasn't loud, then he should shout to be heard. The louder one shouted, the more likely it was the other person would be able to understand.

'I can hear you quite clearly,' came an educated voice from the other end of the line. Cartwright thought he detected a slight West Country twang in the word 'clearly'. He prided himself on his ability to spot the various British accents. He could hear the difference between Londoners from above and below the river, Brummies from Aston, Solihull and Edgbaston. Mancunians were easy to spot with the nasal twang that annoyed him so much. And Liverpudlians, well, their drawl was as distinct as a pork pie from a ham sandwich.

Unfortunately, his knowledge of British accents had not been much use to him in his police work in Shanghai. Except at the club's Christmas dinner where his recitation of Kipling's *If* – in the regional accents of Britain – was always well received.

'Hello, are you still there?' came the educated voice with the slight West Country burr.

'Hello!' he shouted back. 'This is Cartwright. Inspector Cartwright of the Shanghai Municipal Police. Is that Willis?'

'Yes, this is Mr Willis.'

The voice now sounded slightly annoyed. Cartwright decided to come straight to the point. 'Sorry for calling so late. I am acting for Inspector Danilov; he's busy at the moment. You sent him a telegram?'

'I did. I noticed his advertisement in the *North China Daily News* regarding his missing family. I believe I have some information about his daughter.'

So Danilov was looking for his family. The bastard kept that quiet. Cartwright waited for Willis to carry on speaking. It was always best to stay silent in interviews like these. Let people tell you everything they know without revealing how little you knew.

'I believe his daughter passed through my mission two weeks ago. I should explain. I run the Welfare Home for Young Women in Tsingtao. We are part of the outreach programme of the London Missionary Society.'

'I've heard of your good work, Mr Willis,' Cartwright lied.

'You have? That's most gratifying to hear, Inspector. Sometimes, I feel most isolated here. The last time I heard from the bishop was almost seven months ago, even though I report to him on our missionary activities every week. We have eleven converts now.'

'That's very exciting news, Mr Willis. However, we were discussing Inspector Danilov's daughter.'

'Yes, yes. A woman arrived at our mission on February 2nd and signed in under that name. She was in a pretty bad state, and it must have been difficult for her during Chinese New Year. She stayed three days. As you know, we don't allow people to stay longer unless they convert. We can't be a hotel for all the world's waifs and strays, can we?'

'No, just the Christian ones,' Cartwright said under his voice.

'What was that? You were faint for a moment.'

'I said of course, you can't, Mr Willis. She stayed at your mission?'

'We run a home for women in trouble. A place where they can enjoy a Christian welcome and Christian education for three days.'

'Women in trouble? Was his daughter pregnant?' he asked.

'Not that sort of trouble, Inspector. Women who are down on their luck, have been thrown out of their homes by their families or their husbands. Those sorts of women. We would never deal with the pregnant ones. I mean, how could we give help to a woman who had got pregnant outside of marriage? The thought is unthinkable and unchristian, Inspector . . .?'

'Thomson. Inspector Thomson,' lied Cartwright, without thinking.

'I thought you said your name was Cart-something?'

'That's the other inspector,' he now said, quickly, 'who is helping Inspector Danilov. So Inspector Danilov's daughter came to your mission?'

'We have been getting many Russians recently. They're still leaving Vladivostok in vast numbers, fleeing the godless communist hordes. As I said, on February 2nd, a young woman signed into our home as Elina Danilova. She said she was going to Shanghai to meet her father who she believed was waiting for her there. Well, as soon as I saw the Inspector's advertisement, I put two and two together. I knew I just had to contact him.'

The phone went silent for a moment, and Cartwright thought the connection had failed, then he heard a soft, 'There was mention of a reward in the advertisement.'

Bloody Danilov, thought Cartwright, giving money away as if he had a bank in his pocket. Obviously, paid far too much that one. 'I'll make sure Inspector Danilov calls you regarding the reward. I feel sure he would want to thank you personally himself. What happened to his daughter?'

'Well, when we asked her to leave after three days, she said she was going to try to catch a ship south to Shanghai. Good luck, I told her. If you don't have any money, none of the shipping lines will take you. But she was adamant she was going that way.'

'So you don't know where she is now?'

'We don't follow every girl who stays at our mission, Inspector.'

'No, that would be too much to ask.'

'I don't think I care for your tone, Inspector Thomson.'

'Thank you for the information, Mr Willis. I'll get Inspector Danilov to call you back regarding the reward. I'm sure he will want to thank you himself for the kind service you gave to his daughter.'

'I'll wait for his call.'

'You do that, me old cock,' said Cartwright as he put the earpiece of the telephone back on the hook. He leant back on the wall of the telephone booth of the Palace Hotel. 'You'll never hear from either of us again, Mr High-and-Mighty Willis.'

And for the second time that day, a broad smile appeared beneath the bushy moustache of Inspector Cartwright. He might even treat himself to another snifter, and work out what he was going to do with this information. Charlie Meaker would be dying to know all about it. Could even be a nice little earner.

CHAPTER 24

Danilov and Strachan returned to the detectives' room. It was empty. Strachan slumped down at his desk and covered his face with his hands. Danilov opened his cigarette tin and began to roll a cigarette.

'We've got no suspects. Nobody we're watching. We've got no idea who the killer is or why he's killing.'

Danilov placed the rolled up cigarette between his lips and lit it. The smoke rushed down his throat, filling his lungs.

'And Chief Inspector Boyle looks like he's about to burst a bloody vessel. My first case and it's all going wrong.'

Danilov brushed a few loose strands of tobacco off the table, closed the tin and placed it at exactly 90 degrees to the desk blotter.

'What do we do, sir?'

Danilov blew out a long stream of smoke up towards the ceiling where it gathered like a cloud around the light bulb. 'Did I ever tell you about my family, Strachan?' he said softly.

Strachan raised his head from the desk. 'No, sir. You asked me not to mention them.'

'My family were the centre of my life when I was living in Minsk. I had a beautiful wife, a loving daughter, and a son who was as bright as a samovar in winter. He beat me at chess.' He took another drag on the cigarette. A stray strand of tobacco stuck on his lips and he removed it with the tips of his fingers. 'But, being the man I am, I didn't really appreciate how lucky I was.'

'We never do, sir.'

Danilov didn't hear him. 'Minsk was descending into chaos but there was a case in Moscow I had to solve. I left my family behind. The train lines were cut and I couldn't get back to them. The day I left Minsk was 12th November 1924. I haven't seen my wife, or Elina, my daughter, or Ivan, my son, since then.'

'You must miss them, sir.'

'I miss them every second of every hour of every day. But there is something I know, Stra-chan.'

'What's that, sir?'

'I know, one day, we will be together again. They are there, out there, somewhere, waiting to be found. It's that belief that keeps me alive. Keeps me going.' He looked across at Strachan. 'We must never give up. If we do, he wins. Don't you see that? This killer has made mistakes, and will make more. We have the clues. We just can't see the patterns yet. But we will get him. He won't stop until we do. We must get him. Do you understand?'

'Yes, sir.'

'We will nail this killer if it's the last thing we do on this Earth. Is that clear?'

'Yes, sir. Sorry about your family, sir. I don't think anybody knows in the . . .'

'Nobody must know, Stra-chan. It's our secret.'

'Yes, sir.'

Danilov stubbed out his cigarette into the ashtray. He stood up. 'It's time to get working. Get on to the newspapers. Find out where they got their information.

They probably won't tell you but it doesn't hurt to try. Once you've finished, interview the young man who was seen at the Astor when Elsie Everett was killed. He's the only one we haven't talked to yet. You have his address?'

'Yes, sir.'

'When you're finished, come back here. I'm going to check up on Richard Ayres and his friends.'

'You don't think he did it, do you? He spent a day looking for her.'

'Everybody is a suspect until nobody is.'

'I don't understand, sir.'

'Everybody is a suspect until we catch the killer.'

'I get it, sir. But that means the whole of Shanghai is a suspect, including you and me and the rest of the police force.'

'Correct, Stra-chan.'

There was a sharp knock on the glass door of the detectives' room. It opened quickly and the duty sergeant stood in the doorway.

'What is it, Sergeant?' asked Danilov.

'You'd better come quickly, sir, there's been another murder.'

So quickly, thought Danilov. So soon after the others?

'It's out by the race course, Inspector.'

'Get the car, Stra-chan.' He picked up his coat and hat from the stand near the door. 'I think this is going to be a long night.'

On his way out of the station, Danilov bumped into a large man dressed in a patchwork of clothes who was blocking the doorway.

He said sorry.

The Giant grunted in return.

CHAPTER 25

The naked body was propped up against the entrance of the main clubhouse of the Shanghai Racing Club. Even from a distance, Danilov could see something wasn't right. He pointed to Strachan's shoes, warning him to watch his step. 'The murder scene, it's staged like a diorama.'

'What do you mean, sir?'

'I mean we are supposed to see it from here. The body is facing us, confronting us. See how it is perfectly aligned with the centre of the door? Sergeant?'

'Yes, sir?'

'Who found the body?'

'One of the grooms, sir. He was walking past here on his way from the stables and he noticed something was wrong.'

'Did he touch anything?'

'Apparently not, sir. Ran to get a trainer. Thought he'd seen a ghost.'

'What time was this?'

'About 9.30 p.m. The clubhouse is locked up at 9 p.m. There was no body there then.'

'Good, very good. We know the exact time the body was placed here.' Danilov took three steps forward.

The strangeness of the naked body was even more apparent now. Through the gloom of the night, its white nakedness stood out against the dark wood of the door. It appeared to be correct: a torso, two arms and two legs, posed like da Vinci's Vitruvian Man in the doorway. But there was a gap between the shoulders and the arms. Not much of one, but Danilov could see the dark, weather-stained wood through the void where the arm should have been.

He walked three more steps forward, checking the gravel in front of the entrance all the time, searching it for any footprints, looking for clues that may have been left behind by the killer. He didn't expect to find any. This man was far too clever, far too meticulous to leave behind such obvious clues. He would find him through his patterns, the way he thought, the way he worked, the way he killed. He would make a mistake, eventually. A small stupid mistake, but it would give him away.

There was nothing on the ground.

The naked body was much closer now. He could see its glaring whiteness, the head staring straight forward at him, the arms outstretched, the legs together, slightly crossed at the feet. It wasn't Vitruvian man at all. It was Christ that was in front of him. A naked Christ.

Danilov shook his head. Concentrate. Concentrate. He was five feet away from the body now. Even in the low light, he could see the arms weren't attached to the body. There was a clean edge where there should have been skin. The white of bone where there should have been a shoulder. No blood though. Strange that. The body seemed to have been washed, deliberately cleaned up to present its best face to the public.

His eyes drifted down over the chest and stomach to the legs. They weren't connected to the torso. He could see the inner muscles, tendons, sinews and bones all clearly displayed like a prime cut of meat in a butcher's shop, somehow not a part of a living animal, just another piece of meat.

Then he examined the face.

He remembered it well in life. It was Dr Renfrew, looking just as he did during his sermon, scowling as he ranted against the iniquities of Shanghai. The lips were pushed back to reveal the teeth, the eyes bulged from the head, a livid burn seared across the forehead. He looked like he was in the middle of one of his sermons, in full flow, speaking to his flock. A voice railing against Sodom and Gomorrah, against evil and wickedness, against the works of the devil in the city of Shanghai.

It was a vision of hell, not of heaven.

It was apparent to Danilov that Dr Renfrew had met the Devil at the gates of Hell, not St Peter at the gates of Heaven.

Despite himself, his hands came up and made the sign of the cross. It was the reaction of a child, the instincts taught in his youth taking over his logical mind. He was a little ashamed of his action and glanced quickly to check if Strachan had seen his moment of weakness. But Strachan was just staring at the body of the preacher, his mouth slightly ajar.

Danilov nudged him with his elbow. 'Call Dr Fang, we have another body for him to examine.' Danilov pointed to the Chinese characters carved into the preacher's chest. 'Our killer has struck again.'

'Yes, sir.'

'What does it say?'

'It's the characters for "revenge", sir.'

'Call Dr Fang now. I want this autopsy done by tomorrow morning.'

Strachan ran back to club where he could use a telephone. Danilov turned back to the preacher.

He could see now that the arms had been balanced on three nails driven into the wood of the door, to keep them stretched out horizontal, whilst the head and torso had been hung from a rope that ran around the neck and fastened to a nail on the lintel. The legs were propped against the door, one foot crossed over the other.

Danilov stepped back five yards. From this position, the body was whole, only the slight gaps between the arms and the shoulders, and the torso and the legs, revealed something was wrong. Then he took four paces to the side. The arms and legs were against the door while the body hung two feet away and at least two feet in front.

'Strange, very strange,' he said out loud.

'What's that, sir?' Strachan had returned silently to his side.

'It's like he's playing a game of perspective with us. From the front, Dr Renfrew looks whole. But when you look closely, really closely, you see it's just . . . what do the French call it?'

'A *trompe l'oeil*?'

'Exactly, Stra-chan, you never cease to amaze me.'

'As I said, sir. Most of the monks at the college were from Belgium. We heard more French than anything else.'

'A *trompe l'oeil*. A piece of fakery to deceive the eyes.' Danilov scratched his nose and then both his ears. 'Perhaps, the killer is reminding us to look more closely, to see behind what we think is true about the victims.'

'But Dr Renfrew was a well-known and well-respected member of the community, sir. A Christian missionary of high standing.'

'Was he? I wonder . . .'

'Anything else, sir?'

'I think we've done all we can here, Stra-chan. What time is it?'

'12.30, sir.'

'It's time to go. We have an early start tomorrow.'

***

Danilov opened the door of his apartment. Its cold modernity depressed him straight away. For a moment, he imagined being greeted by his children, them rushing to give him a hug, him responding with a warm smile, his wife placing a steaming bowl of piroshki on the table.

He closed the door. The clang of the security lock echoed through the apartment. He turned back to see the clock ticking noisily above the fireplace: 1.15. It was late, and he was too tired to eat. He realised he hadn't eaten anything that day, but he didn't care.

He took off his coat and hat, hanging them on the hook behind the door. He walked into the bedroom, sitting down on the edge of the made bed. The opium pipe stared at him from its tray on the side table, the long stem and the carved bowl looking at him as if selecting him out of all the people living in Shanghai.

Tonight, he would not smoke his opium. Tonight, he would keep his mind free from the dreams of the pipe. Tonight, he would just go to bed and fall asleep.

He looked around his bedroom. The bare white walls and single rattan chair sat alone, unloved by anyone, daring him to be alone too, without the succour of his pipe. There had been many nights like this, too many nights, when the bareness of his existence away from his work had troubled him.

He knew he had been separated from his family because he cared more for his work than he did for them. But he couldn't help himself. His work was all he had. It was the only thing that shored up his ruins, preventing the whole rotten edifice of his life from collapsing and falling into the abyss.

He picked up the pipe off the tray. It felt heavy as he balanced it in his hands. A small, black ball of opium was sitting ready on a pin. Left over from last night, he thought, I must have drifted off before I had time to smoke it.

He leant back against the wall behind his bed and brought the stem of the pipe up to his mouth. Just one bowl, to chase away the shadows, he thought.

The lighter flared, and the flame touched the pea of opium in the bowl. Danilov sucked deeply, feeling the warm smoke enter his lungs and expand to drill its way into every nook and cranny in his body, filling it with light and shade, black and white.

He blew the smoke out. For a second, he was as weightless as the smoke, hanging between heaven and hell, dangling in the purgatory of the drug. Then his knees relaxed, his whole body went limp, the stiffness leaving it like a soul leaves a dead man.

He slid further down the bed, letting the soft mattress envelope him. The opium pipe dropped from his hands onto the floor. His eyes fluttered closed.

Just before he was lost to the opium dreams, a voice whispered something deep inside his head. His own voice. 'How does the killer choose his victims?' it said.

Then, he heard the same sentence again, only this time it was in the soft, lilting voice of his wife. 'How does this killer choose his victims?'

The answer came almost immediately. 'He knows all about them, Daddy.' It was his daughter. 'He knows all about them.'

Then his eyes closed and he floated off to a large park. His daughter was running around with a butterfly net, and his wife was sitting on a picnic rug, taking food out of a large, wicker hamper. His son was throwing a ball for the dog to chase. How he missed that dog.

His daughter came running up. She stopped in front of him and said, 'How does he know about them, Daddy? How does he know which ones to kill?'

Then he saw himself, lying on his back staring up at the blue sky, not a care in the world.

In his opium dream, he began to cry.

February 25th 1928.
The 34th day of the Year of the Earth Dragon.

CHAPTER 26

Danilov stood at the front desk of the Palace Hotel. Not the best hotel in Shanghai, he thought, but certainly not the worst. There was at least a pretence at gentility with rich maroon drapes, linoleum floors and uniforms for the staff. The fact that all the uniforms were two sizes too big was of no account to the management. What was more important was that the staff wore them.

A European reservation clerk was pretending to be busy, reading through the seven messages which he had already read a thousand times that day.

'I'd like the room number of a guest.'

The clerk took an age to respond before finally lifting his head. 'I'm sorry, we don't give out the room numbers of our guests to people who just come in off the streets.' He turned back and pretended to sort through the notes left in the room pigeonholes.

Danilov heard a German accent behind the upturned nose and cold exterior. By 'people who came in off the streets', he meant him. He reached out and banged the bell on the desk. Then he hit it again. The tiny bell clanged through the lobby. Three guests turned their heads towards the sound.

'I don't think you understood me, I would like the room number of a guest. An American, big man. Fleshy. Tips well. Checked in about a week ago.'

The clerk coughed like a child, his small white fist coming up to meet the thin lips. 'I don't think sir understood me. We do not give out the room numbers of our guests to just anybody.' He saw Danilov staring at him and added, 'It's hotel policy.'

Danilov pulled his warrant card out from his jacket. 'Listen, I want that room number now, or else you could find yourself staring at a damp wall in Ward Road, charged with obstructing the police. Not a nice place Ward Road. The rooms are not so comfortable, and there's no receptionist on the door. Just a fat warder with a liking for fresh, young meat. Do you know what I mean?'

The clerk nodded. He scrambled for the register. 'I . . . think you are looking for . . . Mr Anderson,' he said without looking up, his shaking finger turning the page.

'An American. Checked in about a week ago.'

The finger stopped moving but still shook as it hovered over a name. 'Room 436.'

'Thank you for your help.' Danilov strode across the lobby. He always hated these places with their veneers of sophistication and gentility. Behind the fake marble, plush velvet and humble subservience was a world of hard work and petty rules.

He stepped into the lift. A young boy, no more than thirteen, pulled the iron gates closed behind him. 'Where to, sir?' he said in remarkably clear English.

'Fourth floor.'

'Going right up, sir.'

Danilov leant back against the far wall, regretting his treatment of the clerk. He should not have shown his temper but there was something about the clerk that enraged him. Being German didn't help. He felt the lift begin to ascend.

'Always wanted to say going right side, not up, but nobody get the joke.' The lift boy was speaking to him. 'Definitely not hotel manager.'

Danilov laughed. The round eyes and face of the boy had collapsed into one big smile with only the pug nose visible.

'Fourth floor, what room?'

'Number 436.'

'So you visiting big American with long arms?'

'Long arms?'

The lift boy mimed reaching deep into a pocket to bring out a tip. Danilov laughed again.

'It's on the right side, third door. Have a good day.' The lift shuddered to a stop, and the boy reached across and opened the iron gates.

'You too.' Danilov reached into his pocket and gave the boy a dollar. The little hand took it faster than a starving man snatches a grain of rice. 'Keep going sideways,' he said over his shoulder.

'You too,' the boy shouted after him.

A long corridor stretched in front of him with doors either side. He counted three doors: 436 in large brass numbers on the white door.

He knocked.

There was no answer and no sound from within. He knocked again, and before he could finish, the door swung open. He was left with his fist hanging in the air.

'What d'ye want?'

A large man stood in the doorway wearing a white vest and blue pinstripe trousers held up by wide red braces. A nest of black hair struggled to escape from the top of the vest whilst a belly strained the fabric below, dragging it over the trousers to form a sheltered porch of fat. The cheeks and chin were covered in white foam. 'What d'ye want?' the man asked again.

Danilov produced his warrant card, holding it up in front of the man's face. His eyes tracked across the card, reading everything that was written there: Danilov's name and number, his rank, the address of Central Police Station and a short note regarding the powers of the Shanghai Municipal Police force. The man continued to read as he reached the Chinese version of the information. Eventually though, he looked back at Danilov.

'So you're a cop?'

Danilov nodded. 'You are Mr Anderson?'

'What d'ye want?'

'I need to ask you some questions.'

'Listen, buddy, you may need to ask, but I dun need to answer. Can't you see I'm busy?' The man placed his hand on the Inspector's shoulder.

Danilov glanced down, seeing the hairy paw on his jacket, noticing the way the hairs grew in profusion across the back of the hand like a garden that had been left untended for a long while. He thought about hitting the man with a straight right to the side of the face, but then he would get his hands covered in soap. 'Just a few questions. We can do it here or down at the station. Up to you.'

The man took his hand off Danilov's shoulder. 'Is this a friendly talk or are you puttin' the squeeze on me?'

'Friendly . . . for now.'

The man stood still, thinking. 'You don't mind if I carry on, do you?'

'Be my guest.'

'"Be my guest." You guys are so weird. In Boston, I'd a been flat on my back with a knee on my chest by now.'

'In Shanghai, we do things slightly differently.'

Anderson walked into the bathroom. Danilov followed him. It was large, almost as large as the detective's bedroom at home. A large globe light above the silver-etched mirror illuminated the whole room.

Anderson stood in front of the mirror and took the cutthroat razor from the shelf. 'Ask away.'

'You were at the Astor House Hotel two days ago?'

'The dance? Heard it was a lotta fun. Thought I'd drop in. Was kind of cute actually, what with the butterflies and flamingos and stuff. But the music was good, and the dancers were better.'

'What time did you go there?'

'I dunno. Around four I guess.' Anderson took a long strip of foam off his left cheek with the razor.

'What time did you leave?'

Anderson stopped shaving and turned to face Danilov. 'Say, what's with all the questions? You know I'm an ex-cop?'

'I didn't know, actually.'

'"I didn't know, actually."' Anderson mimed Danilov's accent. 'You guys are weird. Was in the force for nineteen years before I retired and took the pension.'

'So when did you leave?'

'About two years ago.'

'I meant the dance?'

'I like that. Like a dog with a bone. Around 5.30 p.m., but I wasn't keeping tabs on the time.' He turned back to the mirror and began shaving again.

Danilov noticed the hand was steady as it approached the foam-covered throat.

'I'll ask you again. I can be a dog too. What's this about?' he said as he wiped the foam on a towel.

'A woman was murdered. She was last seen at the Astor House.'

'What's she look like?'

'Why?'

'I'm a cop. Never leaves you. Looking at people, you can't help it. Not after nineteen years anyway.'

'She was blonde, bobbed hair, five feet four inches tall, wearing a tasseled silver dress.'

'Cute?'

Danilov nodded. He could see Anderson's face looking at him, reflected in the mirror.

'With two sloppy looking guys and a viper of a dame?'

Danilov nodded again.

Anderson turned in mid-stroke, with the cutthroat poised just half an inch from his throat. 'Cute dame, great legs. Would've liked her to come up and see my moves, if you get my meaning.'

'Oh, I get you, Mr Anderson. May I ask you what you are doing in Shanghai?'

'You may ask, I may not tell.' Anderson turned back to the mirror and continued to shave.

'Normally, I am a patient, nonviolent man, Mr Anderson, but in your case I will make an exception.'

Before the razor had touched his throat, Danilov had moved, grabbing the hand holding it and kicking Anderson in the back of his knees so that his legs collapsed. His chin hit the side of the sink on the way down, and the head jerked back as if he had been hit by Max Schmeling.

Danilov gripped the hand holding the razor and forced it to the flare of Anderson's nose. 'I'll ask again, Mr Anderson: what are you doing in Shanghai?'

Anderson's eyes focused on the blade. The white lumps of shaving foam with their little slicks of black hair glistened on the sharp edge. The Inspector forced his knee into Anderson's back, thrusting his chin over the sink, the blade just a millimetre away from the nostril.

'I'm a PI. A private investigator. Was hired to come out here.' Anderson's voice quivered, his eyes never leaving the cutthroat razor.

'Why?'

'Murders. In Washington. Two murders. Hired by one of the families.'

Danilov moved the blade away from Anderson's nose slightly, but he kept his grip on his hand as tight as a vice. The fat man's flesh quivered as he pressed his knee on it.

'What's that got to do with Shanghai?'

'Got a lead the killer was here.'

As he had already told Anderson, normally, Danilov disliked violence. The last refuge of the mentally incompetent, he always thought. But the American only understood force. A shame he had to use it. He took the cutthroat from Anderson's hand and pulled his knee from his back. The fat man's body collapsed on the floor.

'That was easy, wasn't it? What was the lead?'

Anderson was breathing heavily, his body slumped beneath the sink. 'The family thought the murderer had gone to Shanghai. I thought it was a good idea.'

'A good idea?'

'To have a month here on the family's dime. Life ain't easy as a gumshoe. It's not all Pinkerton stuff. Anyway, they're rich, they won't miss it.'

'And did you find anything?'

Anderson rubbed his jaw where it had struck the sink, moving his mouth left and right. 'Not much, not yet. Only got here a week ago.'

'And already another woman is murdered, and you just happen to be in the same place at the same time she disappeared. Strange that.'

Anderson lifted himself onto his knees. 'Listen, buddy, I got nuthin to do with those dames. I'm from Boston, not Washington.'

'Don't leave town just yet.' The Inspector took out a card from his wallet. 'If you find out anything, call me. Even if you find out nothing, call me.'

He reached out to the man's face. Anderson flinched.

Danilov wiped off a large blob of shaving cream from the side of his face and showed him his index finger. 'You missed a bit.'

***

The old man lived on Roberts Street on the second floor of a modern apartment. Strachan knocked and it was immediately opened. He was ushered inside and given tea.

The old man sat down opposite him, carrying a brown Pekinese whose colour and demeanour matched his owner. The dog, however, was the one baring its teeth and growling. 'There, there, Xiao Hu Mei, it's just a smelly young man.'

'You are Mr . . .?'

'Kung, the same as the surname of Confucius. We're related you know. In the distant past, of course. A direct line of descent. Would you like to see the lineage?'

'Thank you, Mr Kung, another time perhaps.'

The old man looked disappointed. Strachan realised he didn't get many visitors. Loneliness was a disease of the old. 'I'm here about the murder of a young woman.'

'I didn't do anything like that. I wouldn't do anything like that, would I, Xiao Hu Mei?' He nuzzled his face with the dog.

'I'm sure you wouldn't. She was at the tea dance at the Astor House hotel two days ago. You were there too, I believe?'

'Two days ago?' The old man counted on his fingers. His hands had the liver spots of old age, and scratches from the dog on their back. 'Yes, I was. Clever of you to remember. This one is smart isn't he, Xiao Hu Mei?'

'Do you remember anybody else who was at the dance?'

'We do like to go to the dances, don't we, Xiao Hu Mei? All the young women in their finery. And the men, dressed in black and white. Reminds us of our youth in Peking, before the Boxers, of course. But, we don't drink, do we? You don't like Daddy to smell of silly alcohol, do you?' He leant his head close to the dog and was smothered in wet licks from a small, pink tongue.

Strachan thought this wasn't going very well. He tried again. 'Do you remember anything from the tea dance?'

The old man sat upright. 'I may be old, young man, but I'm not senile. I certainly remember the tea dance. Cost me four dollars and thirty cents. It's ridiculous the price they charge for tea at that hotel. They should be ashamed.'

Strachan was about to close his notebook and say goodbye when the man continued.

'There was someone I remembered quite well because he was like me, he wasn't drinking. Or at least, he was only drinking soda water. He was European, English I would guess from the cut of his jacket. Tall and elegant, dark hair, in his late thirties, I would think. I remember him because he was like me. He wasn't there to dance or drink or listen to the music. He was there watching the people. Just like me. Another watcher.'

Strachan wrote it all down. 'Is there anything else you remember, Mr Kung?'

'I won't go back again, will I, Xiao Hu Mei? Too tiring now.' He took out a pocket watch hanging from a fob around his waist. 'If you'll excuse me, young man, it's time for Xiao Hu Mei's nap now. I usually join her. We're both not as young as we used to be.'

'Thank you very much for your assistance, Mr Kung. This is my card. If you think of anything else, just give me a call.'

'A call? Myself and Xiao Hu Mei don't have a telephone. Nasty things. Make nasty noises that disturb our beauty sleep.'

'If you think of anything else, just come down to the station and ask for Detective Constable Strachan.'

Mr Kung thought for a moment. 'There was one other thing, Constable Strachan, the man had a strange smell, sweet, almost sickly, like a woman's perfume. The older I get, the more sensitive my nose becomes. A bit like you, hey Xiao Hu Mei?' The old man nuzzled the dog once more.

'Are you sure?'

'Inspector, I told you, I may be old but I'm not senile. My mind is as sharp as Xiao Hu Mei's teeth. And my nose is a good as a bloodhound's.'

'Thank you, Mr Kung, you have been extremely helpful.' He finally passed his card over to the old man. The dog, seeing the movement, snapped at his hand, the jaws just missing his index finger.

'There, there, don't be a naughty bunny.' The dog continued to growl at Strachan, its eyes never leaving the young detective.

The old man examined the card. 'Strachan. Your father was European?'

The detective nodded, keeping one eye on the dog.

'Shame that. You speak such beautiful Chinese and have such good manners. Oh, well, we can't all be perfect.' He stood up and hobbled to the door, the dog tucked underneath his arm.

CHAPTER 27

Strachan was already five minutes late. Inspector Danilov was looking at his pocket watch when he came running up.

'Sorry, sir, the interview with the old man took longer than I thought. Very interesting, though.'

'It's 11.05 a.m., Stra-chan, let's not keep your uncle waiting.'

They both walked through the imposing iron gates and were confronted by the black stone of a tall three-storey house. Strachan was always afraid of this house. It reminded him of some haunted place in the pictures, all crenellated bumps and lost towers. Every stone was covered in a layer of black soot as if it had been dipped in bitter chocolate. He never understood why his uncle lived there nor had he ever worked up enough courage to ask. It was just another strange eccentricity of his family, or at least of the part of the family that recognised he existed.

Danilov knocked on the door. Padded feet tumbled down the corridor, muffled by the imposing grandness of the carved mahogany.

'*Shi she?*' came a voice through the door.

'It's the Ah Yi. She's from Peking. Only speaks Mandarin,' Strachan said to the inspector. 'Been with the family for ages but never learned Shanghainese.'

He stepped up to the door and shouted through the letterbox: '*Shi wo*, Ah Yi. Second cousin Da Wei, to see Uncle Chang.'

The door opened immediately, moving smoothly despite its size. A small woman stood there, dressed in black from head to toe. Strachan looked down at her feet. They were the small, butterfly feet of woman who had been hobbled since childhood. He always thought they were like the tiny hooves of a donkey, not a harbinger of sexual promise.

She led them into the front parlour swaying from side to side on her bound feet. It was as if they had stepped back sixty years. Inside, all was dark wood and even darker walls. A large throne-like ironwood chair dominated the centre, faced by four smaller chairs and a mother of pearl inlaid table. All the chairs had matching carvings of vine leaves and peach blossoms on the backs and crawling up the legs. Above the main chair were two stern portraits; an old man and woman, both seated and facing the room. The man wore an ornate hat and an elegantly embroidered Mandarin overcoat.

'My great grandfather,' whispered Strachan.

On the opposite wall, a large character flowed off white paper. Strachan recognised the character for '*shou*', the character that symbolised long life in Chinese, a blessing somebody had sent to his uncle a long time ago. It had worked so far.

'Good morning, Hong Yee, it's a pleasure to see you again.'

Strachan stood straighter and bowed slightly from the waist. His uncle always had this effect on him, making him seem like a seven-year-old boy all over again.

His uncle was wearing the traditional morning coat of blue, with soft wool court shoes. His appearance hadn't changed since the last time Strachan had visited. The hair was still flecked with grey and his beard a brilliant white. There may have been a few more wrinkles around the eyes, but Strachan wasn't sure. The eyes themselves, though, were still as vibrant and alive as ever.

'Good morning, First Uncle,' Strachan stammered.

'I see you have been in the wars, Hong Yee.'

Strachan touched the side of his face. His ear had been re-bandaged this morning by his mother after a lot of fuss. 'It's nothing, Uncle, a small injury.'

His uncle frowned. 'Please offer our guest a seat, Hong Yee, he will think we have no manners.'

Strachan's face began to redden. He reached for one of the smaller chairs and offered it to Inspector Danilov.

'And this is . . .?' said Uncle Chang quietly.

Again, Strachan felt he had embarrassed his uncle, failing, in his clumsy Scottish way, to mimic the elegance of Chinese hospitality.

'This is Inspector Danilov, First Uncle. He's my boss.'

As soon as the word had left his lips, Strachan knew he had made another mistake.

'Boss, such a strange, modern word. So . . . blunt,' he said to nobody in particular, but Strachan knew he had been rebuked. 'Please be seated, Inspector. And please excuse the clumsiness of my nephew. He means well but sometimes . . .' The voice trailed off.

Strachan stood even straighter, making sure his eyes remained fixed on the ground.

Inspector Danilov sat down. Uncle Chang followed him, sitting in the larger chair, his rightful position, adjusting his long Mandarin gown elegantly as he did so, revealing two thin, white wrists with small, almost feminine hands attached to them.

'Danilov, a Russian name, I believe.'

'From Minsk originally. I arrived in Shanghai in 1925.'

'Along with many others from your country. Did you join the police right away?'

'Almost immediately. I had been in the Imperial Russian police, so it seemed the right thing to do.'

'And your family?'

Strachan watched as the Inspector hesitated for a moment, his eyes staring glassily into space. Uncle Chang stayed quiet, respecting the feelings of their guest.

Eventually, Danilov spoke: 'I was separated from my wife and two children.' There was a slight pause. 'I'm still looking for them.'

'War is a terrible thing. And Civil War is the cruellest of all. We, in China, know better than most. If I can be of any help at all, Inspector, please don't hesitate to ask. I still have many friends in the government.'

'Thank you, Mr Chang, for your generous offer.'

'Please call me Hong Lin, Inspector, all my other friends do.'

Strachan felt the meeting was going well. It wasn't often his uncle asked people he had just met to call him by his given names.

'I must admit, Inspector, I wasn't in favour of Hong Yee joining the police force. His present state merely confirms my foreboding.'

'Hong Yee?'

'I'm sorry, David, my nephew.' With a slight wave of the elegant white hand, he indicated Strachan, still standing beside the chair like an errant schoolboy in the headmaster's study. 'The police force is, shall we say, not the normal career of a young man from a good family, but David insisted he wanted to follow in the footsteps of his father.'

'I understand. My father wasn't keen on me joining either. He always used to say "A good police force is one that catches more criminals than it employs".'

A small smile crossed the uncle's lips. 'How correct, Inspector. Unfortunately, it has been the Chinese experience the police have always employed more criminals than they have caught.'

There was a slight tap on the door. It opened slowly, and the old woman entered, followed by two other servants.

'A few snacks to help lighten the conversation, Inspector. I'm afraid they are not as good as those you are used to. It's so difficult to find the right servants these days. Ah Yi is the only one left, and she has looked after me since I was a baby.'

The Ah Yi placed five dishes, each on elaborately designed blue plates, in the centre of the table. She added a small blue and white plate in front of the Inspector and Uncle Chang, placing a pair of silver chopsticks on a rest in the shape of a lotus leaf, next to it.

There were no plate and chopsticks for Strachan. His stomach rumbled. The perfumed aroma of garlic, chili and anchovies filled the air. It was one of Strachan's favourite dishes, the crunch of the fried anchovies complementing the bite of the garlic and chili. The other dishes were no less tasty: crispy tofu, boiled peanuts, dainty little *xiao mai* still in their bamboo steaming basket, and freshly pickled cucumber. His stomach rumbled again.

'Please do not stand on ceremony, Inspector.'

The Inspector picked up the chopsticks, tapping them gently on the table as they became an extension of his fingers. He reached over and picked up a single boiled peanut from the plate. He put it in his mouth and a broad smile of pleasure lit up his face. 'Your food is remarkable, Hong Lin, even a simple peanut becomes a taste of heaven.'

'You are too generous, Inspector. These snacks are a poor imitation of food. I remember back in 1903, before the revolution, a meal in Peking that would put this poor offering to shame, a meal that was the manna of the gods.'

Strachan stood there as the two men occasionally dipped their chopsticks into the dishes, talking of meals they had eaten and meals they had not. Even where one could find the best peaches in China. From Wuxi, at the beginning of August, according to his uncle.

Strachan was beginning to become impatient. There was so much work to do. He was about to interrupt when his uncle placed his chopsticks down on the lotus-shaped rest and leant forward. Inspector Danilov immediately followed suit.

'Have you eaten enough, Inspector, or shall we have some more?' Strachan could see most of the dishes had plenty left on them.

'No, Hong Lin, I've eaten my fill. I fear if I eat any more, your nephew will have to carry me out of here on his shoulders.'

'It has been a pleasure talking to you, Inspector, but I'm sure you haven't come to my home simply to exchange pleasantries and try a few poor snacks. How can I help you?'

'Thank you for the *dian xin*, Mr Chang, they were worthy of your elegant home. However, we have come for something more than your excellent food. I presume your nephew has explained the purpose of our visit?'

'Very poorly, I'm afraid, Inspector, he still has a lot to learn. You are investigating a murder I believe?'

'Five murders to be exact.'

Mr Chang sucked in his breath and pulled on his white beard. 'Somebody has been busy.'

'And will continue to kill, we think.'

'How can I help?'

'Each victim has Chinese characters carved into their body. The first victim was a French magistrate, and he had the characters for "vengeance".' Danilov passed across the photo sent across by the French. Mr Chang looked at it without any emotion on his face. 'The second was a Russian prostitute who had "damnation" carved on her body.'

'All the characters so far have been of the same style, Inspector, quite precise with no indication of personality.'

'That is interesting, Mr Chang. There are two other victims. The third was an androgyne . . .'

'I'm afraid I don't know this word, Inspector.'

'A man who dressed as a woman.'

'Ah, quite a common occurrence. As you know, all opera singers are male, even those playing female roles. I believe some of them continued to play their parts even when they left the stage. Mei Lan Fang at the moment is famous for his ability to mimic the mincing gait and gestures of a woman, though he is without doubt, a man. Such androgynes, as you call them, were highly prized by the emperors as entertainers and for their sexual services.'

The Inspector passed across the photograph of the dead Henry Sellars in the morgue. 'This androgyne was young and American, Mr Chang.'

'The characters for "justice". Most unusual. Archaic even. Related to judgement in Chinese. Judge Bao and all the old writings.'

'The fourth victim was an English actress. She had "retribution" carved on her body.' Danilov spread all four pictures out on the table. 'I'm afraid they are quite explicit.'

'I have seen worse. In 1903, I spent two years as the assistant to a magistrate in Guizhou in southern China. Not a post I enjoyed. Far too many executions.'

'The last murder occurred last night. The victim was butchered into five separate pieces. We are still waiting for the pictures to come back from the lab.'

'The victim also had characters carved into his chest. The characters for "revenge", Uncle.'

Uncle Chang picked up the pictures one by one and examined them closely, stroking his beard as he did so. 'The characters are all interesting, Inspector, all legal in one way or another.'

'Legal?' asked Danilov.

Mr Chang stopped for a moment and stared into mid-air. 'Of course, I have been a fool, old age is creeping up on me and with it the dulling of the wits.' He turned to Danilov. 'Please excuse me, Inspector.'

He got up, carefully arranged his long gown and left the room.

Danilov and Strachan glanced at each other. 'Your uncle is an extremely well read man, Stra-chan.'

'I know, sir. I always feel so stupid whenever I come to see him.'

'Not a feeling you are unused to, it would seem.'

They both lapsed into silence. The clock ticked on the wall. Outside, they could hear the sounds of the Ah Yi brushing the path to the house with a reed brush, singing a soft lullaby to herself, trilling the 'r' in her Peking accent.

Strachan's stomach rumbled once more. The food still smelt delicious, its aromas tempting him to reach out and try a morsel. But he knew his uncle would be ashamed if he did. He stood still, trying to think of anything but food, succeeding only in thinking of food.

The door opened once again, and his uncle appeared in the doorway, carrying a large, old scroll that had obviously seen better days. He walked over to the long painting table, moved some Yuan books to one side, and unrolled the scroll carefully, weighing down one end with a large carved rosewood frog.

'I'm sorry, Inspector, I have been slow this morning. I should have recognised the characters immediately.'

'You know where they come from?'

'It's so obvious once one sees it.' He pointed to the scroll. Strachan could see a hideous small painting of what appeared to be a red devil, surrounded by written characters.

'It's Di Yu and the eighteen courts of hell.'

The Inspector got up and walked over to the painting table. 'I'm afraid it's my turn to say I don't understand.'

'Di Yu is the name for our Chinese underworld. Many people think this idea of an underworld, with souls waiting for justice, originates from Buddhist scripture, but I believe it goes back much further and is much darker. In your Christian cosmology, it would be purgatory. A period of reflection and punishment where we can atone for the sins of our life and prepare for reincarnation.'

'We have a similar idea in the Russian Orthodox church.'

'But, in the West, this purgatory is individual. People simply have to endure it. In the Chinese underworld, there is a god called Yama who sits in judgement on all who come before him.'

'So this Yama punishes people?'

'Yama is the king of the underworld. He has created eighteen courts, the courts of hell, where sinners undergo judgement and punishment depending on their crimes.'

'Crimes?'

Mr Chang pointed to a long list of Chinese characters, each with a small ink painting next to it. 'There's a whole list of crimes. Corruption. Theft. Prostitution. Being unfaithful to your wife.' His finger followed the list down the page.

Strachan looked at the drawings. Men and women were suffering painfully as the devils and their assistants administered the punishments.

Mr Chang continued to translate. 'Dishonesty. Lack of respect for your elders. Being unfaithful to your family. The list goes on and on, Inspector. Some sources seem to suggest there may be as many as 134 different crimes. It's all policed by ten judges, with Yama being the most powerful. Each crime and each court has a particular punishment decreed as the correct retribution for the crime.'

'You think our victims are being punished?'

'See there, Inspector . . .' he pointed to an ink-wash drawing '. . . the Mountain of Knives.' His finger followed the characters as he translated. 'Sinners are made to shed blood by climbing a mountain with sharp knives sticking out.'

Strachan stared straight at Danilov. 'It explains what happened to Elsie Everett.'

'In the eighteen courts of hell, the sinners are subjected to a whole host of punishments, limited only by the capacity of the gods to inflict pain.'

'Or, in our case, Mr Chang, by the capacity of our killer to inflict pain.'

Mr Chang returned to his book and once again his finger traced down a long list of characters. 'Sawing, carving, slicing in half, grinding, crushing by rocks, boiling in oil, being set afire, tongue ripping, eye gouging, skinning, being frozen in ice, pierced by hooks. The list goes on in excruciating detail, Inspector. We Chinese have always been extremely punctilious about the different ways to kill another human being. It is one of our least pleasant characteristics as a race.'

'Each crime has a particular punishment?'

'Indeed.' He returned to the scroll. 'You said one of your victims was frozen?'

'The French magistrate.'

Mr Chang gazed at the scroll, his eyes tracking the lines of characters as they ran down the page. 'Here it is. Being frozen in ice is a punishment reserved for corrupt officials.'

'The Russian prostitute was drowned in pig's blood.'

Once again, Mr Chang's eyes danced down the page as he stroked his beard. 'A punishment doled out to those who sell their bodies.'

'The others were almost severed in two, cut on the Mountain of Knives, and last night, we discovered Dr Renfrew had his body dismembered.'

Uncle Chang scanned through the scroll, his finger tracing the characters downwards. 'Being severed in two is a punishment for the crime of . . . unnaturalness. The Mountain of Knives is reserved for those who have lied and killed. The final one, having the body dismembered, is the punishment for perversity.'

'So it seems our killer is acting as Yama, the god of the underworld, punishing people for crimes they were supposed to have committed here on Earth,' said Danilov.

'Oh, Yama is much more, Inspector. He not only punishes people, he is judge, jury and executioner. He decides who is to be punished and for how long.'

'Crime and punishment. We Russians are familiar with this idea.'

'I believe there is a precedent in the Christian world, too.'

Inspector Danilov raised his eyebrows.

'Didn't your Christian God punish Sodom and Gomorrah for its sins?'

CHAPTER 28

Strachan shifted the gear of the Buick. There was a loud screech as the engine refused to engage.

'Sounds like a herd of strangled cats, Stra-chan.'

'Sorry, sir.'

'Your uncle's information was vital, Stra-chan. It's the first real break we've seen in this case. Up until now, we've had lots of information, quite a few clues, but nothing has coalesced into a cohesive pattern. At least we now know the motivation of our killer. He sees himself as a judge, sitting in a court, trying the miscreants of Shanghai.'

'He's going to be busy here, sir.'

'That's the point, Stra-chan. There were time gaps between the first three murders, but now he has started to kill every day.'

'It's almost as if he feels he's running out of time, sir.'

'I wonder. You could be right, Stra-chan. We're getting close now.'

'Are we, sir?' Strachan scratched his head.

'What did you find out this morning?'

'I met the old man. He described someone he had seen at the tea dance.' Strachan reached into his pocket and passed his notebook to Danilov. The Inspector read it carefully.

'This is good, Stra-chan. But it presumes this man is our killer.'

'He's a suspect, sir. We should check the chits to find out who he was.'

'Perhaps.' Danilov thought for a moment and decided not to tell Strachan about his meetings with Victorov and the American. If his hunch was correct, it was better that he didn't know.

Strachan changed gear once again. 'I didn't realise you had a family, sir.'

Danilov's face went pale. 'My family has nothing to do with you or this investigation, Stra-chan. Is that clear?'

Strachan bit his lip, concentrating on avoiding the dense traffic. 'Yes, sir.'

Danilov turned back to look out of the window. They were crossing Garden Bridge, close to the morgue. As usual, it was dense with rickshaws, wheelbarrows and hawkers pushing their carts. He was sorry he had snapped at Strachan. It was a perfectly reasonable observation, but not one he wanted to deal with right now.

They accelerated to a stop outside the morgue.

Dr Fang was waiting for them at the entrance. 'At last, you're here. I've got a piece of liver waiting for me.' He ushered them through the door.

'Is it fried or steamed?' said Strachan.

'It's stabbed, young man, with a five-inch blade. The liver is a highly sensitive organ which has to be examined quickly if one is to get the best out of it.'

'Sorry, sir, I just thought . . .'

'Thinking is bad for you, Detective. Let me do the thinking while you do the detecting.' He pushed open the door of the mortuary.

Strachan bit his lip once again.

As he entered behind the doctor, Danilov couldn't help but feel an immense sadness. Perhaps it was the white walls or the astringent cleanliness of the place, or even the sharp tang of formaldehyde that produced this reaction in him. When Dr Fang pulled back the white sheet covering the body, Danilov knew what it was that upset him. It was death that inhabited this room. The white-faced solitude of death. All the bodies lying here on their marble slabs, covered by their starched white sheets, would never know the warmth of human contact again. For them, all that remained was the cold embrace of death.

Imagine working in a place like this, day after day, he thought. He glanced at Dr Fang as he bustled about the corpse, arranging his knives and forceps close to the head. What sort of man would spend his life surrounded by the solitude of death? What sort of man would choose to be in the business of death?

The same kind of man who decides to become a detective, he thought ruefully. But, at least in his job he dealt with living people. How can you have a relationship with a corpse?

Dr Fang began speaking: 'This is the 46-year-old man brought here last night.'

The corpse of the preacher lay on the cold, white marble slab of the mortuary. The arms and legs had been placed in their usual positions on the body, but Danilov could still see the gap where the arm didn't quite meet the shoulder, and the leg was separated from the torso.

'The arms and legs have been separated from the body by a large knife with an extremely sharp edge, rather like a butcher's cleaver. The separation was not performed with any professionalism or accuracy, however.'

He sniffed. 'It's the work of an amateur. Quite a good amateur but still an amateur, you'll understand. The cuts are quite clean, and the knife work is solid rather than spectacular.'

'So not a surgeon or a doctor?' he asked.

'No, I don't think so. A butcher not a surgeon. See here . . .' He pointed to the leg. Danilov could see the white of the thigh bone as it shone through the pinkness of the muscle and skin. 'The femur has been sawn through with a blade. It would have been much easier, if one wanted to remove the leg, to simply place the blade in here,' he picked up a scalpel to demonstrate, 'and pop the joint here.'

'Pop?' asked Strachan.

'That's the medical term,' answered Dr Fang.

Danilov coughed. 'Was the victim already dead when this was being done?'

'No, he was still alive. There must have been copious amounts of blood.' Dr Fang pushed his glasses back onto the bridge of his nose. 'I don't normally comment on the manner of a victim's death. I never believe such details are relevant to my investigations. But, in this case, I will make an exception.' There was a slight pause as Dr Fang gathered his thoughts. 'This death was very painful. Excruciatingly painful. The amputations were performed while this man was still alive.'

'Alive?'

'This man would have been conscious. And this work wasn't carried out all at the same time. It was spread out over a number of hours.'

'Why?'

'I couldn't possibly comment, Inspector. The man's motives are none of my concern, simply his actions.'

'Of course, Dr Fang, please continue.'

'From the angle of the cuts, we can conclude the man was right-handed, working from the right-hand side of the body. There are more characters carved into the chest. This time, they read "revenge" as I am sure you are already aware.' The doctor sniffed and pushed his glasses back onto the bridge of his nose. 'However, following the principles of Song Ci, I have undertaken some experiments on a pig's body over the last few days. I believe the knife that carved the characters would look something like this.' From beneath the mortuary table, he produced a short, rather stubby, triangular blade with a sharp point. He placed it next to the skin of Dr Renfrew. The blade seemed to fit exactly into one of the cuts of the stroke on the character. 'The knife is not common. Used by sailors on the Yangtse to splice ropes.'

'Thank you, Dr Fang, you have been diligent. Is there anything else?'

For the first time, the pathologist smiled. 'There are no other marks but we have found this.' He pulled up the torso and turned it over to reveal the back of the left shoulder. 'The body had been washed after the amputations, removing all the blood. He is a clean operator our killer. I remember that the English actress had been washed in exactly the same way. And, of course, our first victim had been cleaned by the waters of the creek, not that they are particularly clean.'

'I don't believe he is being clean, Doctor, I think he is removing any trace of evidence that might remain with the body,' said Danilov.

'If that is the case, Inspector, he must be aware of Locard's theories also. It suggests an educated man who is aware of the latest advances in forensic science.'

'Oh, he's clever all right, too clever perhaps.'

'But cleverness is not everything, is it, Inspector? Sometimes, the truly clever make the simplest mistakes.' The doctor turned the shoulder and pointed to a small red mark with distinctive whorls and ridges. 'In this case, he wasn't as punctilious as he was with our English actress. Do you see it?'

Both Danilov and Strachan leant over the body to get a better view.

'I think the killer reached around with his left hand and gripped the shoulder, whilst his right hand severed the remaining sinews and muscles attaching the arm to the shoulder. Something like this.' The doctor demonstrated what he meant to the two detectives using the small scalpel as a knife.

'I'll call the fingerprint squad right away,' said Strachan.

'I have taken the liberty of calling them already, Inspector.' Dr Fang looked at his watch, 'they should be waiting outside.'

Danilov gestured for Strachan to get the fingerprint team.

'I think it's the left index finger. Fingerprinting from skin is notoriously difficult, but I think your team should be able to get something from this. It's a classic example of Locard's theory. When two humans come into contact there will always be a transfer of some sort. Humans always have relationships, just not the sort we normally think about.'

'Thank you, Dr Fang, your examination has been most useful. I wonder did you have time to look at the lid of the barrel?'

Strachan and the fingerprint team burst through the doors and marched up to the mortuary table. Dr Fang stared down at the wet feet spoiling his pristine white tiles.

He sniffed again and pushed his glasses up onto his nose. 'I did, Inspector. Most interesting.' He walked over to a stainless steel table in the corner. Beneath a white sheet lay the lid, looking as though it was yet another corpse awaiting its autopsy.

'It's made of oak. French oak, I believe, but wood is not really my field. Far too healthy for me, I'm afraid.' He picked up the lid. 'As you will have worked out, there are traces of bitumen all around the edges. A common enough material, used on boats up and down the China coast. The blood stains are pig's blood. It seems to have seeped into the wood, giving this peculiarly pink tinge to the oak.'

'What about the scratches on the inside of the lid, Doctor?'

'Patience, Inspector, I was coming to those. Made with the fingers, I believe. It seems to be the words, "HATE ALL". But the last "L" is noticeably fainter than the rest of the letters.'

'You said, made with the fingers?'

'The nails of the fingers to be precise. And probably a woman's hand.' Dr Fang held up a small glass bottle with a minute fleck of something lying on a white cotton ball in the bottom. 'There are traces of nail polish on this fragment. Scarlet nail polish. Not a colour I would recommend to anybody.'

Danilov scratched his head. 'Let me understand you properly, Doctor, you are saying that a woman made these scratches?'

'I am, Inspector. And given the context, I would be quite confident in stating these scratches were made by the victim.'

'Maria Tatiana Stepanova?'

'Of course, without examining the nails, I can't be a hundred per cent certain but . . .'

'Thank you, Doctor. That is most interesting.'

'It's my pleasure, Inspector. And now, I must return to my liver.'

Danilov looked across at Strachan and the fingerprint technicians carefully taking an impression of the print on Renfrew's shoulder. To find a match was painstaking as they searched the records by hand. And that was pre-supposing they had the killer's fingerprint on file.

This case was becoming more and more complex. He desperately needed time to think and smoke. 'Stra-chan, leave those men to their jobs, they know what they are doing. We need to take a walk.'

***

They both stepped out of the morgue, leaving the sterile smells of death and loneliness behind them. Danilov immediately began to roll a cigarette. 'Walk with me, Stra-chan. I always find a walk and a good smoke clear the mind of the cobwebs. A shot of vodka sometimes helps too.'

'I don't drink, sir.'

'Not at all?'

'No, sir. Never developed a taste for it. I prefer tea.'

'Do you enjoy any of the vices, Stra-chan?'

The detective stared at the back of a lorry laden down with freshly cut bamboo. 'I suppose my one vice is food, sir. I love my food.'

As if by chance, they walked past a row of carts selling all the tastes of China: pungent preserved bean curd, steaming pots of pig's giblets, Cantonese Xiao Mai, a sizzling wok full of Ma Por To Fu, a string of glutinous rice cakes wrapped in lotus leaves dangling from a rattan roof, noodles of all shapes and sizes waiting to be thrown in vats of boiling clear soup, and golden glazed ducks hanging by their necks waiting for the burly cook to chop their heads off.

'You wouldn't like to eat would you, Strachan?'

'After the morgue, a bowl of noodles would settle my stomach, sir.'

Danilov sat down at one of the small bamboo tables that surrounded each stall. The cook ran over and greeted them. 'Can I get anything for you, sir?'

'A cigarette and a pot of tea will be enough for me. I ate my fill at your uncle's. But eat away, Stra-chan. Don't let me put you off.'

Strachan ordered a few dishes from the cook.

'While you are waiting for the food to arrive, let's talk about the case. We now know why the killer is committing his murders. He sees all the people he's killed as criminals who deserve to be punished. That's important, Strachan.'

'Yes, sir.' The tea arrived. The cook set two glasses in front of the detectives and filled them half full. Strachan washed a pair of chopsticks in his glass and threw the tea away. 'Can't be too careful, sir.'

'No, Stra-chan. Not with a deranged killer on the loose. We also know that he carves the characters into his victims to mark them.'

'Just like the preacher, tattooing his disciples, sir.'

'Exactly. Then he puts them on display. He's proud of his work. He believes this is his mission in life. And in death.'

The noodles arrived. Strachan immediately began to assemble them into a nice ball in his bowl and shovel them into his mouth with the same vitality as a stoker feeding coal into the engine of a ship.

'He obviously knows a lot about the secrets of his victims. He knows their lives, their habits, their thoughts. How, Strachan, tell me that?'

Strachan lifted his head from his noodles for a second. 'I don't know, sir.'

'Neither do I, Strachan, not yet. But we will find out.'

'That's good, sir,' said Strachan between spoonfuls of soup. Then the soup spoon stopped halfway to his mouth. 'There's one thing I don't understand?'

'What's that, Stra-chan?'

'Well, sir, if our prostitute was Russian . . .'

'She was. Her name was Maria Tatiana Stepanova.'

'Yes, sir. If she was Russian, why did she write a message in English as she was dying? I mean, you don't get anything more English than "HATE ALL", do you?'

Strachan returned to his bowl of noodles, slurping his soup. Inspector Danilov leant over and planted a kiss on the top of his head. 'Brilliant, Stra-chan. You are brilliant. Why didn't I think of that?'

Strachan looked at his bowl of noodles, pleased with himself. 'It's because you don't eat, sir.'

'I need to see someone and then go back to the station. I've got an idea who the killer is. We're close to Garden Bridge so it should be easy to get a cab. You've still got to finish the interviews of the people at the tea dance, haven't you?'

'Just one more to go, sir – the young man.'

'Well, get a move on, we haven't got all day.'

'Getting a move on, sir.'

CHAPTER 29

'I'm so glad you could see me at such notice.' Danilov took his hat off as he entered the office. The secretary closed the door behind him.

Councillor Ayres continued writing, ignoring the interruption. Richard Ayres stood up from his seat in front of his father's desk and held his hand out. 'Good to see you again, Inspector. Please sit down.'

Richard's father looked up from his documents. Behind him, the view of the Whampoo was stunning. Ships of all shapes and sizes swarming over the river: small bum boats, dirty tramp steamers, elegant yachts, sea-wasted junks, ocean-going liners and, in a row down the centre of the river, a fleet of warships, their decks covered with bunting, their guns pointing towards Shanghai.

Danilov heard a cough.

'How can we help you, Inspector? If it's about this girl, Elsie . . .?'

'Everett . . .' Richard leant forward and interrupted his father.

'Yes. Elsie Everett. My son has told you all he knows. He doesn't have anything else to add.'

'Thank you for making the time to see me. I know you are a busy man, Councillor Ayres.'

'I've given you fifteen minutes and then I have another meeting. With the American Consul.'

'Once again, I thank you for the time. I asked to see you both this time.'

'How I can help with a murder investigation is beyond me.'

'Nonetheless, I'm sure you can, Councillor.' He sat down on the chair next to Richard.

The desk in front of him was extremely tidy. A small stack of documents on the left, another stack on the right, a blotter, two pens and a telephone was all that cluttered the pale oak. There was no ashtray so he decided not to roll a cigarette. Councillor Ayres sat facing them, his back to the view and his face in the shadow of the light from the picture windows.

He turned to Richard. 'Could you tell me about your movements last night, Mr Ayres?'

Richard glanced at his father. 'I went to the Shanghai Club at seven, had a spot to eat. Father joined me at nine. We ate a little more and drank a nightcap at the Long Bar. Then we both went home. A very quiet night, Inspector.'

'Why do you ask?' The words from the Councillor had a hint of menace in them.

'Last night, there was another murder. We believe it was the same man who killed Elsie Everett.'

'You're talking about Dr Renfrew?'

'How do you know who was murdered, Councillor Ayres?'

The Councillor smiled smugly, reached down into his waste paper bin and pulled out a copy of the morning newspaper. He threw it on the desk. 'I would think everybody in Shanghai knows, Inspector, if they read the news.'

The newspaper headline on the table shouted up at Danilov:

CHARACTER KILLER STRIKES STRIKES AGAIN

Somebody was leaking information to the press. The papers seemed to know more about the murders than he did. It was time to wipe the smile off that smug face. 'And where were you last night before 9 p.m., Councillor?'

The face smiled back at him like a tiger who's just spotted a goat tied to a post. 'Are you accusing me of murder, Inspector?'

'No, sir. Just asking a few questions. If you would answer. Please.'

The smile appeared on the Councillor's lips once again. 'If you must know, I was in a Council meeting.'

'You stayed in the Chamber the whole time?'

'The whole time. The meeting went over. Mrs Harbottle insisted on putting a vote on the motion of introducing prohibition into Shanghai. Damn fool woman. It would be the death of the place.'

'So you stayed until 9 p.m.'

'One hundred other people were there. Perhaps, you would like to ask them if I stayed?' He put the cap back on his fountain pen and laid it at the head of the blotter. 'Now, if there is nothing else, Inspector, I need to go to my next meeting.'

He stood up, blocking the light from the windows. A black silhouette against the window, strangling the view of the river and the Bund.

Danilov remained seated. 'There is one more thing, Councillor Ayres.'

'Make it quick.'

'Do you know a Maria Stepanova?'

The Councillor sat back down in his chair. The view of the Whampoo appeared again. Danilov noticed a boat had just left one of the liners packed with tourists eager to spend their money in the shops of Shanghai.

The Councillor's green eyes stared at Danilov for a long time. 'Never heard of her.'

'Are you sure, Councillor? You've never met a woman with that name?'

The smile appeared again. 'Never, Inspector. One of your Russian friends is she?'

'No. Actually, she was found in the French Concession ten days ago. Drowned in a barrel of pig's blood.'

For a second, the smile vanished. Councillor Ayres returned to stacking his papers. 'As I said, never heard of her. Now, if you will excuse me, Inspector, I have another meeting. Richard, will you show the man out?'

Richard got up. 'This way, Inspector.'

Danilov put his hat on and walked to the door. Before he left, he turned back. 'I will check with the one hundred witnesses, Councillor Ayres. I do hope they confirm what you told me.'

He opened the door. A secretary was waiting outside, his coat in her hands.

'Any news about Elsie, Inspector?' Richard asked.

'I'm sorry, Mr Ayres, we are pursuing a few leads but nothing concrete yet. I'll let you know just as soon as I have something.'

'Thank you, Inspector. Elsie didn't deserve to die like that.'

'Nobody deserves to die like that. Not even a Russian prostitute.' He walked out of the wood-panelled office and hurried down the marble stairs. Paintings of Councillor Ayres's predecessors lined the walls.

He needed a cigarette and the fresh coal-scented air of Shanghai. Anything was better than the atmosphere in that office.

* * *

'This man has killed five times already, there can be no more.' Boyle slammed his fist down on the table. 'I'm getting pressure from upstairs to solve this.' Boyle scratched his head just above the left ear. Flakes of his scalp fell like snow onto his shoulders. 'And Dr Renfrew was not without his supporters in the Council, despite his criticism of them.'

As Boyle became more angry, the odour of his cologne filled the room, a mixture of sweetness and sweat.

'It's a difficult case, sir. The killer is clever and sophisticated.'

Boyle slammed his fist down on the table again. 'I don't want to know how clever he is, I want to know how caught he is.'

Inspector Danilov was standing in front of Boyle's desk. There were no offers of cigarettes or cigars this time. In fact, there wasn't even the offer of a seat.

'We have a few leads we are pursuing, sir.'

'A few leads? Is that all? When this man was killing Frenchmen and prostitutes nobody cared too much, but girlfriends of upstanding members of the community, that's a different matter. And now, it's members of the clergy. What is the world coming to, Danilov, when the vicars of Christ are murdered in cold blood on the streets of Shanghai?'

'We think he wasn't murdered on the streets, sir, but in a much more secluded spot.'

'Don't be literal, Danilov, you know what I mean. Such killings are not good for business or our reputation. The Chinese will lose all confidence in us.' Once again, he scratched his head. More flakes of scalp fell onto his shoulders. A red blotch appeared on his head where he had scratched. 'For God's sake, man, I'm even hearing rumours the vicar was dismembered.'

'His arms and legs were amputated, sir. Then he was displayed at the entrance to the Shanghai Racing Club.'

Boyle shook his head. 'I don't want to hear the gory details, Inspector, I just want him caught, is that clear?' Boyle paused and removed a speck of scalp from his desk blotter. 'You have two more days, then I'm calling Charlie Meaker in.'

'Meaker is a fool.'

'He may be a fool but he's a man who gets results.'

'He'll just pin it on anybody who's stupid enough to get in the way. Don't you realise this killer isn't going to stop until he's cleansed the world? He thinks he's Yama, for God's sake, the judge of the underworld.

'I don't want to hear any Chinese mumbo-jumbo from you. The man's just a killer like all the others. Charlie Meaker has some interesting ideas. Thinks the case could be political, wants to get Allen involved.' Boyle lifted his head and stared straight at Inspector Danilov. 'I'm giving you one last chance. Don't let me down.'

'Politics has nothing to do with this. It's personal. He's cleansing Shanghai.'

Boyle stood up. 'You have two days, Inspector Danilov,' he said formally, 'then I'm calling in Meaker to take over. Ye gods, man, even the French have been calling me.'

Danilov knew the interview was over, there was no more point arguing. He picked up his hat from the stand near the door. Boyle pretended to be reading some memos. Danilov thought about turning around and trying once again to explain to his boss that Meaker would get it all wrong. But he knew he was fighting a war which he could not win, Meaker had already seen to that.

Miss Cavendish was waiting for him as he left Boyle's office. 'I couldn't help overhearing, Inspector Danilov, the voices were raised, you see.'

'I understand, Miss Cavendish.' Danilov glanced down at the hat in his hands. The silk band was stained with grease and sweat. It had even begun to seep into the fabric of the hat itself. Had his standards deteriorated so much in Shanghai? What was becoming of him?

'This came for you.' She reached beneath her desk and produced a Manila envelope with 'Internal' stamped across it.

Danilov opened the envelope and saw another move from Allen: Kh1. *He's getting better, but I've still got him, black is ready to move in for the kill.* He quickly wrote 'Qh6 check' and placed the sheet of paper with their moves back into the envelope. 'Would you be so kind as to give this to Mr Allen?'

'Of course, Inspector.'

'I need to send a couple of telegrams.'

'I'll get the post boy to attend to you.'

'Right away, please.'

'He'll be there before you can roll one of your cigarettes.' Miss Cavendish chewed the end of her pencil. 'Are you going to beat him, Inspector?'

For a second, Danilov wasn't certain whether she was talking about the chess match with Allen, or the killer.

He thought for a moment, and answered, 'Yes.'

* * *

'Oh, it's you again, what do you want this time?'

Sergeant Wolfe had glanced up to see the Giant standing in front of his desk, blocking out the light on his log book with his shadow. The Giant spoke a few incomprehensible words in an even more incomprehensible dialect.

Sergeant Wolfe sighed, it wasn't going to be his day. He took the telephone off the hook and rang through to the detectives' room. Danilov answered almost immediately.

'It's that bloomin' Giant. He's here again, after the reward, I bet.'

'What giant?' asked Danilov.

'The one who came in two days ago. George Cartwright interviewed him. About the murder.'

'Which murder? And who interviewed him?'

Sergeant Wolfe sighed again. Sometimes, it was harder dealing with the stupidity of the detectives than the waifs, strays and dog eaters that came into the reception of Central Police Station. He wished he was back at home, sipping a nice cup of tea and putting his feet up in front of the fire. A hot buttered crumpet wouldn't go amiss too. Goes well with a cuppa does a buttered crumpet.

He decided to start again from the beginning with Danilov. 'The Giant. The boatman from the creek. He came in two days ago as a witness to give information about the murder there. You asked people if they had seen anything, remember? George Cartwright interviewed him. Said he was working with you.'

'Working with us?'

'That's right. He wants his reward.'

'George Cartwright wants a reward?'

'No, the bloomin' Giant wants his reward. He's the bloomin' witness, ain't he?'

'But we've heard nothing. Cartwright didn't say a word.'

'Well, your Giant is standing here in front of me.' The Giant was still blocking out his light. 'He's big too. Dunno how he fits in a bloomin' boat.'

'Keep him there. I'm coming now.'

'You'll need an interpreter. Dunno what sort of language he speaks, but it's nothing that nobody else understands. The interpreter from last time is around somewhere. I'll get him for you.'

'I'm on my way.'

'Did you get the telegram as well?'

'What telegram?'

'The telegram that came for you.'

A loud, exasperated sigh at the end of the phone. 'I know nothing of any telegram.'

'What's Cartwright playing at? You can't trust nobody to do nothing these days. Do it yourself, that's my policy. Always has been and always will be.'

'I'm on my way.'

Sergeant Wolfe put the telephone down. By way of sign language and lots of finger pointing, he eventually got the Giant to stand in the corner out of his light. It was going to be another one of those days, he thought. 'Who do I have to kill to get a cup of tea around here?' he shouted to the crowd in front of his desk.

Nobody responded.

* * *

'Good afternoon, my name is Inspector Danilov. You are Mr Hung, the interpreter?'

Danilov gestured for the interpreter and the Giant to sit at the table. The Giant tried to slide his knees under the desk, but they wouldn't fit, so he adjusted his seat before eventually getting comfortable. Danilov was about to start when the Giant moved again, this time putting one foot up on the chair and hunching over his leg. The image of a gargoyle from Notre Dame in Paris flashed through Danilov's head. 'This man lives on the creek?' he asked.

'He does.'

'Ask him to tell me everything he saw.'

'He's already told you everything.'

'I'm sorry but this is the first time I'm meeting this witness.'

'Not you personally. You, the police.' The interpreter waved his arm to indicate the building around them.

Danilov smiled. 'I'm afraid we will have to go through the questions once more. I would like to hear the answers for myself.'

'Well, it's your time and money.'

'Actually, it's the Municipal Council's money. But you are correct, it is my time, so please ask the witness the question.'

The interpreter turned to the Giant and spoke in the flowing tones of the boat people's dialect. The Giant looked surprised and began speaking.

'He says he's already answered these questions and just wants the reward.'

'Please apologise to him and explain if he wants the reward, he has to tell me everything he knows. Tell him, I am the head man who has the money.' Danilov reached into the inside pocket of his jacket and put his wallet on the table. The Giant's eyes became as wide as rickshaw wheels at the sight of the notes sticking out from the edge of the wallet. Immediately, he began speaking, illustrating his tale with his hands as his father had taught him.

Danilov watched the hands as they described waking up in the early morning, drinking tea, stretching, rowing his boat, seeing something strange and then describing two men. The interpreter kept a running commentary of the story like a race-course announcer who already knows the result of the race.

'So there were two men,' interrupted Danilov.

'Yes, a tall European and a short Chinese man. Actually, this man uses the word for land dweller but he means Chinese. That's what they call us.'

'Can he describe them?'

The interpreter trilled away to the Giant, who answered with just a few flowing words. 'The European was tall and white but that's about all he knows. All Europeans look the same to him. The land dweller, the Chinese man, was short and bald.'

'Bald? That's interesting. What about the colour of the clothes the European was wearing?'

'Grey,' answered the interpreter after the Giant spoke, 'like the waters of the creek where it meets the Whampoo river, with thin white stripes.'

'The colour of his hair?'

Again the Giant spoke and the interpreter answered, 'He couldn't see, the European was wearing a hat.'

'Like mine?'

The Giant launched into a long description. 'No, not as dirty as yours and much lighter in colour with a light grey band around the rim.'

Danilov pointed to another hat hanging on the stand. 'Like that?'

The Giant nodded without waiting for the interpreter to translate.

'And what was the colour of his skin?'

'White,' said the interpreter, 'all Europeans look the same to him. Plain white, your colour.' The interpreter pointed at Danilov.

'The height was as tall as him or as short as me?' Danilov stood up.

The Giant stood up too and looked him up and down, measuring him like a tailor measures a prospective customer.

'He says the man was nearly the same height as he is.'

He leant towards the Giant. 'What about the eyes of the tall man? What colour were they?'

The Giant launched into a long monologue full of flowing sounds and sibilant esses.

'He says the European's eyes were green, not the brown of the land dwellers. Green like the ghosts that live in the lily pads or the trees in April. I'm sorry, but these people often use strange descriptions impossible to translate. Their ghosts must be green, I think.'

'Don't worry, we're getting somewhere. Was there anything else? Did he smell anything?'

The Giant imitated the interpreter's sniffing and then his body curled up on the chair in a fit of giggles.

'He says he smelt fish. He always smells fish.'

'But was there any other smell?'

The Giant thought for a moment and then spoke to the interpreter.

'He says there was a strange smell as the boat with the European and the bald land dweller went past him. The breeze had just come off the river and drifted up the creek. It was the smell of flowers that one sees in June. A sweet smell.'

'And what about the bald Chinese man? Was he my height?'

The Giant thought again. 'He was smaller than you, dressed in normal land dweller clothes, not a suit.'

'A Chinese jacket and trousers?'

'Yes, dark blue almost black, he says, the bald man had a scar on his head – he saw that when he bent over.' The Giant collapsed in another outburst of laughter with his shoulders rocking up and down. 'Must have been painful,' he says. 'For some reason, he finds this funny.

But the boat people often find the habits of land dwellers amusing.'

There was a knock at the door. It opened and Miss Cavendish stood in the doorway. 'I'm so sorry to disturb you, Inspector, but the Chief would like to see you as soon as possible.'

'Thank you, Miss Cavendish, I'll be there just as soon as I have finished.'

'He did say it was important.'

'Thank you, Miss Cavendish.'

She nodded and closed the door. The Giant suddenly became agitated. He pointed at the door and a long stream of sibilant esses issued from his mouth.

'He says he smells like her?'

'What? Smells like a woman? Like Miss Cavendish?'

'That's what he said.'

Danilov thought for a moment. 'Was there anything else?'

The interpreter spoke, and the Giant stopped laughing, bringing his large index finger up to his head, before speaking. 'He says the land dweller did all the work, this European just watched as they placed the bundle in the water. When they had finished, they went back to the Rowing Club.'

'The Rowing Club?'

For the first time, the Giant spoke slowly, as if explaining to a three-year-old.

'He says the place on the river used by the long noses and their useless little boats. He can't understand what they do on the river. They don't fish, they don't carry cargo. They just go up and down, wearing thin little vests even in winter.'

'Is he sure they went back to the Rowing Club?'

He watched as the Giant nodded in reply to the interpreter.

Danilov smiled. 'Please thank him for his information, it has been extremely useful.' He reached for his wallet. 'The reward was five dollars, was it not?' He pulled out a ten dollar note and passed it into the large grubby hand of the Giant.

The Giant took it gingerly, holding it carefully with his two sausage-like fingers and smelling it, before carefully folding it into four and placing it deep into his patched trouser pocket.

'You do realise this is more money than he sees in a year?' said the interpreter.

'He deserves every cent,' answered Danilov standing up. 'Please thank him once again.'

The Giant stood up, accidentally knocking the interpreter off his chair. He reached out for Danilov's hand, enfolding it in his own and singing his praises in the soft sibilant esses of the boat people.

Eventually, after an age of thank yous and hand pumping, the Giant was encouraged to leave with his reward.

Danilov hurried back to the detectives' room, crossing the reception area of the station. Finally, they were getting somewhere. The killer was starting to make mistakes.

'Inspector Danilov . . . Inspector Danilov.' Sergeant Wolfe was waving to him from behind his desk. 'Did you get the telegram?' he shouted across the hubbub of the lobby.

'I told you I received no telegram,' shouted Danilov over the people pressing around the sergeant's desk.

'The telegram from Tsingtao. Came yesterday.'

Danilov strode over to the sergeant's desk, elbowing aside two arguing rickshaw drivers. 'What telegram, Sergeant?'

'The telegram I gave George Cartwright. It came yesterday. He said he was going to give it to you.'

Danilov gritted his teeth and marched back to the detectives' office.

The sergeant turned back to see the rickshaw drivers had started throwing ineffectual punches at each other. 'I've had enough, throw them both in the nick and throw away the key.'

Two Chinese constables rushed forward and grabbed the scrawny boxers by the scruff of the neck. 'Any more fighting in my station and you'll all spend the rest of your worthless lives in hell,' he shouted in bad Shanghainese.

The crowd in the lobby all stopped talking and stared at him.

'Thank God. Peace and quiet, finally.'

Then the crowd erupted again; papers being waved in the air, children elbowed out of the way and all the dialects of China being spoken at the same time.

Sergeant Wolfe held his head in his hands and started to bang it on his desk.

* * *

Cartwright was sitting with his feet up on his desk, reading the *North China Daily News*. The door flew open and Danilov charged in. He leapt at Cartwright, kicking his chair from under him so he sprawled backwards on the floor.

'What the . . .?'

Before he could finish his sentence, Danilov had reached down and picked him up by the lapels and pushed him against the wall of the detectives' room, scattering chairs and tables out of his way.

'Why didn't you tell me about the witness?'

'I . . . I . . . didn't have time,' Cartwright stammered.

Danilov slammed him back against the wall again, pushing upwards so Cartwright was standing on tiptoes, handling him as if he were a rag doll. In any other situation, it would have been funny. A small, slightly-built man attacking a much taller, much stronger one and treating him like a puppet.

Again, Danilov pulled Cartwright forward and slammed him back, making sure his head made contact with the wall. There was a loud thud as it did so and, for a moment, Cartwright's eyes glazed over and his feet went from under him. Danilov kept him upright.

'You should have told me,' Danilov snarled.

'I forgot . . . didn't have time.'

'Do you remember now?' The head hit the wall again, and a large crack appeared in the green painted plaster.

Cartwright nodded.

Danilov pushed him harder against the wall. 'Two more people died because of you, you scum.'

He looked past Danilov at the other detectives in the office, appealing for help. 'Nothing to do with me, it's your case.'

Cartwright's head slammed into the wall once again. Danilov reached up with his left hand and gripped Cartwright's windpipe, pushing in with his whole body against the neck. Cartwright's eyes began to bulge, and his tongue stuck out from his open mouth.

Danilov pushed harder, feeling Cartwright's legs kick against his own, enjoying the weakness of the taller, stronger man, watching as the eyes flickered with terror. For a moment, he imagined pushing and pushing and pushing till Cartwright couldn't breathe any more. His hand squeezing the windpipe, grabbing it with his fingers and ripping it out of the neck.

Then the image of his wife flashed in his mind. She was smiling, gesturing for him to come forward and hug her.

He released the pressure and let go of Cartwright's body.

The detective fell forward onto his knees, his breath coming in huge gasps of air. Danilov stepped back but remained standing over the detective.

'Where's my telegram?'

Cartwright was on his hands and feet, desperately trying to suck up all the air in the room.

'Where's my telegram?' demanded Danilov, his fists raised ready to strike Cartwright across the head.

Cartwright looked up, and a wry smile crossed his face. Between lungfuls of air, he began to rearrange his clothes, adjusting his shirt and tie and pulling down his jacket. 'What telegram?'

Danilov's fist hit Cartwright full in the face. At this point, two detectives jumped forward, wrapping their arms around the Inspector. There was no struggle from Danilov.

'The telegram you owe me,' he said through gritted teeth.

Cartwright's hand went to the back of his head, feeling in the grey hair where his skull had hit the wall. He winced and pulled the hand away to see blood covering the fingers. He smiled up at the Inspector.

'Where is it?' snarled Danilov.

Cartwright put his hand out as if to pass him. 'It's in my desk.'

Danilov moved aside. The detectives let go of his arms.

Cartwright stayed on his knees for a while, before slowly getting up and adjusting his jacket and tie once again. He walked over to his desk, slowly and painfully, hanging on to it when he got there, gasping for breath.

'Where's the telegram?

'It's in here.' Cartwright took out his keys from his trouser pocket and, after fumbling with them, finally unlocked the drawer of his desk. The telegram lay there, its pale-green envelope shining brightly amongst the old pens, cigarette butts, erasers, bottles of hair oil, rubber bands and paper clips. Cartwright picked it up with the tips of his fingers and held it up towards Danilov. 'You mean this telegram?'

Danilov stepped forward to grab it, but Cartwright stopped him by wagging his finger. 'No, you don't. This here telegram is very valuable.' Cartwright began to cough and rubbed his throat where Danilov had grabbed him. 'It doesn't contain dollars or gold, but it's still valuable, isn't it?'

Danilov took a step forward to grab it. Cartwright reached into his pocket and brought out his silver lighter. He held the lighter against a corner of the envelope and his thumb hovered over the lever. 'I wouldn't, if I were you. This telegram is valuable because it contains information about your daughter. What was her name?' He pretended to think. 'Elina, that was it. Such a nice ring to it.'

At the sound of his daughter's name, Danilov leapt forward to grab the telegram. In spite of his weight and size, Cartwright was nimble, stepping back and pressing the lever of the lighter. Instantly, a bright yellow and blue flame erupted from the silver box. Cartwright brought the flame to the edge of the envelope. Danilov could see the paper begin to curl from the heat and brown scorch marks scar the light green surface.

The door to the detectives' room opened. 'Danilov. In my office. Now!' Boyle stood in the doorway.

Danilov took another step towards Cartwright. Again the flame of the lighter lifted up towards the corner of the envelope.

'What are you waiting for?' said Cartwright, moving the flame closer.

Danilov looked at the telegram held up by the tips of Cartwright's fingers. The thumb holding down the lever of the lighter, the flame wavering upwards threatening to engulf the pale-green envelope.

Inside was his daughter Elina, trapped there.

'Didn't you hear me? Inside. *Now!*' Boyle turned on his heels and went back to his office.

What was he going to do? He saw the leering smile on Cartwright's face, the flame flickering upward towards the pale-green envelope, the scorch marks already forming on its surface as the paper wrinkled with the heat, and he stepped back, keeping his eyes on Cartwright all the time as he did so.

'Shouldn't you go now, Danilov? Chief Inspector Boyle is waiting.'

Danilov heard the words and the smiling face that produced them. He launched himself at Cartwright. A look of shock passed across Cartwright's face. Danilov's body hit him and they both went down in a heap in the middle of the detectives' office.

Strong arms closed around Danilov and pulled him away. '*No!*' he shouted and tried to struggle free, but the arms dragged him towards the door.

As he was being carried from the detectives' room, Danilov heard Cartwright's laughter, followed by the smell of burning paper.

* * *

'What the hell do you think you're doing, striking another officer?'

'He stole something from me.'

'Stole? Are you accusing another officer of theft, Danilov?'

'A telegram was addressed to me. Cartwright took it.'

'So, is that the pathetic reason for rolling about on the floor, fighting with another officer?'

Danilov bowed his head.

'And that's not all. I've just had a long talk with Councillor Ayres. I call it a talk but it was really me listening and nodding my head, and him talking. Ranting actually.'

'I interviewed him and his son.'

'Accused them of being murderers, didn't you?'

'That's unfair, sir, I questioned them about their whereabouts on the nights of the murder. Councillor Ayres's name has been mentioned in my enquiries.'

'But didn't he have an alibi?'

Danilov's eyes dropped to the floor. 'Yes.'

'Being in the Council Chamber with one hundred of Shanghai's leading citizens is a pretty damn good alibi, even in your book.'

A glass of whisky appeared on the table in front of Danilov. He pushed it back towards the Chief Inspector.

Danilov stayed still, ignoring the pale shimmer of the whisky reflecting through the crystal of the glass.

Boyle sighed and scratched his head. 'That's it, you're suspended. Clear your desk today.'

'But the murders . . . you said you would give me two days.'

'Charlie Meaker will take over the case.'

Danilov forced himself to calm down. He took two deep breaths. 'But we're close to catching the killer, sir. Just a few more days—'

'You're suspended from now, Danilov, clear your desk.' Boyle walked to the door of the office, opened it and stood there.

Miss Cavendish was behind her desk, looking down at her paperwork, pretending not to have heard what had happened.

Danilov pushed his chair back from the desk. 'This man is going to carry on killing until he's stopped. How many deaths will you have on your hands, Chief Inspector Boyle?'

There was no answer.

He straightened up and strode out of the office, past Miss Cavendish, whose head was still buried in her files.

The walk to the detectives' room was long, the longest he had ever taken. He had let Cartwright get to him. Stupid. How could he have been so stupid? Finally, he had sunk to their level.

He stepped into the detectives' room. It went quiet. Suddenly, the reports they were writing, or the doodles they were scribbling, were far more important than Danilov's arrival.

On his desk, everything was neat and tidy, except for an ashtray in the centre of his blotter. The ashtray was full of burnt paper: the blackened remains of an envelope with just a few hints of light green showing through the dark brown ashes.

He reached forward and touched them. They dissolved into a black powder, leaving a dark stain on the tips of his fingers.

He collected his things from the desk. His tobacco tin, a few pens and pencils, his warrant card. The words written on it in dark-blue type: DETECTIVE INSPECTOR PYOTR DANILOV. SHANGHAI MUNICIPAL POLICE.

Looking at these words, seeing them so close, he decided he wasn't going to be beaten by these people. His job was too important. The murderer had to be stopped. Despite Cartwright. Despite Boyle. Despite Shanghai.

Sergeant Wolfe appeared at the door. 'I'm to escort you out of the station, Inspector Danilov. Orders from the Chief.'

Danilov gathered up his few possessions and stuffed them in his pockets. These people weren't going to beat him.

Not this time.

Not ever.

***

The interview with the young man from the Astor had been worse than useless. He had obviously been smoking opium and his mind drifted off after every question that Strachan asked. It was like interviewing a fish only not as helpful.

Strachan decided to give up and head back to the station. He stepped through the door. Instead of the usual greeting, Sergeant Wolfe looked down, finding something terribly urgent to do in his desk diary.

Strange.

He walked past the Sikh guards, through the double doors and into the detectives' room. Again, nobody greeted him. All who were there seemed to be engrossed in their work. Even Cartwright didn't look up and make a joke as he entered.

He looked at the desk next to him. 'Where's Danilov?'

'He's been suspended,' a detective answered, without bothering to look up. 'Attacked George Cartwright, didn't he? Russians . . . don't have the temperament for our work.'

Danilov was suspended? But there was so much to do. What about the case? The killer? What should he do now? He ran his fingers through his thick black hair. Didn't Danilov have a phone at home? Perhaps, he should ring him. Find out what to do.

He went to see Miss Cavendish. 'Do you have Danilov's phone number?'

Her finger went to her lips. She leant forward and whispered theatrically: 'You're not supposed to speak to him. He's been suspended.' She stared past him to the closed door of Boyle's office. 'Between you and me, Inspector Danilov and Chief Inspector Boyle had a argument. It was over Cartwright. I think your Inspector is off the case.'

She picked up her pen and wrote a number down on a pad in front of her, passing it across to Strachan whilst staring at the closed door.

Danilov off the case? What was he going to do? He thought about the old man and his description of the killer. What was he going to do with it?

'Detective Constable Strachan.' A large body with an even larger moustache placed itself in between himself and the door. 'Good to see you again.' The body leant in closer to him, and he could smell the whisky on the breath. It was as if the whiskers were soaked in it so the owner could taste them any time he wanted. 'Well done, good collar, even if I do say so myself.'

Meaker stuck out a meaty hand towards him. Strachan took the hand and shook it, but it didn't let him go. 'I'm here to see Chief Inspector Boyle. To take over Danilov's case, the one from the creek. Apparently, he's cocked it up, the brass are livid.'

Strachan could see Meaker's yellow teeth beneath the bushy whiskers. They looked like large, unkempt gravestones. Once again, he smelt the overpowering stench of whisky.

'You'll be reporting to me. I'm sure we'll get on fine.' He finally released Strachan's hand and stroked his moustache. 'We'll soon have this killer caught, sentenced and executed, won't we? Then, we can go back to our quiet, ordinary lives.' Meaker glanced around him. 'Where is Danilov anyway?'

'I don't know, sir. Inspector Danilov didn't tell me where he was going.'

'Just like Danilov. You know when I worked with him, he wouldn't tell me anything. Can't think why. Probably off enjoying himself with one of his Russian lady friends, you mark my words. Anyway, can't stand around jawing all day, Chief Inspector Boyle is waiting.'

He turned to Miss Cavendish. 'Can I go in now?'

'Please go ahead, Inspector, Chief Inspector Boyle is waiting for you.'

'I'm going to look forward to coming back to Central.' He looked around the office. 'I always feel at home here.'

He knocked on Boyle's glass door. There was a muffled 'Enter', and Meaker strode in.

Strachan whispered to Miss Cavendish, 'Thank you for the number.'

'If you see Inspector Danilov, do tell him we miss him, won't you?'

CHAPTER 30

Danilov had been lying on his bed since his return from the station, staring up into the white blankness of the ceiling. He was so close. He knew who it was. He just needed proof.

His body tensed as he remembered the confrontation with Cartwright. How could he have been so stupid? It was what they wanted him to do. To react, to fight. He had descended to their level, rolling around the floor like a Cossack. He had let them get to him. The children, with their petty jealousies and their stupidity. He had always remained aloof from them, and they had repaid his isolation with a revenge of the worst kind.

Now the only link to his family had been destroyed. The ashes of the envelope and the telegram mixed up with all the cigarette butts and filth of the detectives' office.

What had the telegram contained? Was his family alive or not? Where were they?

He got up from the bed and paced around the room. He must be able to find out.

The phone rang.

He ignored it.

Nobody would be ringing him. Nobody ever rang him. In the year the phone had been installed in his home, it had rung only once. Miss Cavendish wanted to let him know there would be a staff meeting the following day to discuss overtime.

The phone continued to ring. Perhaps it was Miss Cavendish again. Perhaps Boyle had realised his mistake in putting Meaker in charge of the investigation.

He walked over to the table. The telephone rang again, its base and handset rattling with each vibration.

He reached out his hand to pick it up.

No, they would never realise their mistake and, even if they did, it would be a terrible sign of weakness to admit it by ringing him.

He went back inside the bedroom and looked across at the opium pipe. A bowl or two to forget Boyle and Meaker and Cartwright and the whole maggot-filled corpse that was the Shanghai Police. He took the pipe in his hands, looking for his lighter.

He knew who the killer was but he could not prove it. There was circumstantial evidence but no actual proof. This man was far too smart to admit his guilt. And he knew enough about police work not to fall for any tricks that could make him confess. He had to be caught in the act of murder.

But how?

Meaker was running the investigation now not him. He was stuck here at home, whilst the killer was still on the loose in Shanghai.

He looked down at the opium pipe again and raised the lighter to the ivory bowl.

The phone rang again. And again. And again.

He put the pipe back on the bedside table. This was not the time to find solace in the dreams of opium. This was a time for his mind to be sharp. A time to stop the killer.

Despite the jealousy of his colleagues.

Despite the stupidity of his bosses.

Despite the aching loneliness of his life without his family.

Stop the killer.

Why should he just roll over and accept what he was told to do? He wouldn't do it in Russia when ordered by the Tsar, why do it here when the man commanding him was a pipsqueak English colonial?

He'd never given up on an investigation in his life; why start now? What could possibly happen? If he failed, he was in exactly the same position as he was now. If he succeeded, then a deranged killer would be brought to justice.

But how was he going to bring him out into the open?

He had no resources. No Mobile Unit to back him up. No legions of constables to dance to his orders. No way to do anything.

But he knew he had no choice. This killer was never going to stop until he was dead and buried, with a stake driven into his heart.

The phone rang again.

He walked out of his bedroom. The phone was sitting on its small table in the living room.

It rang again, the vibrations making the base shiver against the wood of the table. It was near the edge now, about to fall. He jumped forward and caught it as it fell off the table.

From the listening extension in his hand, a small, tinny voice squeaked. He brought it up to his ear.

Strachan's voice echoed through the wires.

'Hello. Hello, Inspector?'

He raised the phone to his mouth. 'I'm glad you called, Stra-chan. I need you to do something for me.'

February 26th 1928.
The 35th day of the Year of the Earth Dragon.

CHAPTER 31

'Right then, you, let's get a move on.' Meaker was standing at the door of the detectives' room, gesturing for Strachan to follow him.

'Where are we going, sir?'

'I've been looking over the files and the case notes. Good ones from you by the way, nothing from bloody Danilov, of course.'

'Thank you, sir.'

'It strikes me there is one person who could have killed the woman in the creek.'

'It was a man, sir.'

'Man, woman, whatever. Anyway, the one person who had both time and opportunity to do it, was the boatman.'

'Which boatman, sir?'

'The one that came into the station to report what he had seen the morning of the killing. Very clever him comin' here. Steppin' into the mouth of the dragon, as it were.' Meaker chuckled at his own joke and tugged on his moustache.

Strachan smelt the salty tang of whisky as he did so.

'Anyway, George Cartwright told me he tried to pin it on two other people. A tall European and some bald Chinese man. Not a likely story, is it? A European and a bald Chinese in cahoots, murderin' people on the river? Nah, this smacks of the Oriental, I can feel it in my water.'

Strachan decided to fix a smile on his face. Meaker seemed to be ignorant of the fact he was talking to somebody who was half Chinese. On reflection, Strachan decided he was just ignorant. 'What about the other murders, sir?'

'He did them as well. We've got our killer, Strachan. I've asked George Cartwright to put together a team with the Mobile Unit. You'll need to do the paperwork. We'll bring him in, and then, with a bit of gentle persuasion, he'll cough up to everything. What are you waiting for, man? Hop to it. Haven't got all day.'

'What paperwork do you want me to do, sir?'

'You are slow this morning, Strachan. Didn't have our pickled pig's foot, or whatever it is you Chinese eat for breakfast?'

Strachan just stared at him.

'No, well, get on with it, man. Just make it all above board and proper. Can't have any cock-ups at the last minute. I need a cuppa tea and a fag.'

'Yes, sir.'

'Before I forget, make sure you include George Cartwright's name in your notes. I want him to share in the glory for this one.'

'Cartwright, but he . . .'

'You heard me, Strachan, get a bloody move on.'

***

Inspector Danilov sat in the cafe waiting for Strachan to arrive. The Princess recognised his desire to be alone and simply sent a waitress to serve him with a glass of hot tea.

The cafe was empty this morning, save for two chess players hunched over their board. He wondered if they were the same two who had been playing when he last visited here, still absorbed in the same game. Probably were, he laughed to himself, understanding the obsession that chess can become.

He had thought about what he was going to do all night, planned it down to the smallest detail. But he knew that too much was still left to chance. He had no hope of proving who the killer was. The evidence was far too circumstantial. He had to drive him out into the open. Get him to make one more mistake.

The killer had been clever so far, but he had begun to take risks. Killing almost every day now. With every murder, becoming more and more confident.

His plan had to succeed. If it didn't, then the killer would carry on. More lives would be lost. He had no choice. He had to go ahead.

Strachan would bring the final confirmation with him this morning. One piece of paper that would confirm the name of the killer. He knew it wouldn't stand up in a court of law though. The connections, the patterns, were too abstract for the logic of the law. But he knew he was right. This morning would simply confirm it.

Then, it would be time to set his plan in motion.

The chances of success were slim but he could see no other way of trapping the killer. He would have to rely on Strachan doing what was right.

With his suspension, he finally had the freedom to act without asking for permission. He had always been an outsider in every force he had ever worked. In Russia, they had just left him to get on with what he did best: catch criminals. The politics and the political in-fighting he left to others. He had stayed an Inspector for many years whilst others had risen up in the world but he didn't care. He was doing what he knew how to do.

A wave of sadness washed over him.

His family. If he failed, he would never see them again. He would never feel the warmth of their smiles or the tenderness of their hugs.

He quickly pulled himself together. He would have to succeed. Whatever happened, he would have to succeed.

He took another sip of tea. Strachan would be here soon. He had to brief him carefully, make sure he did what he was supposed to do. It all rested on him.

Strachan was going to make a good copper. Just had to be trained in the right way. He reminded him of an older version of his son. The same intensity. The same sense of purpose. The same desire to do it right. If he fell into the hands of the likes of Meaker, well, one could never be sure. The delights of an easy life with plenty of 'extra' money were tempting to any young policeman trying to make his way in the world.

That was life. One could make all the plans one liked, but in the end it all came down to trusting other people. He knew he wasn't very good at that. Never had been. But if he got out of this alive, he would change. Or at least, he would try to change.

Then he realised that he had already changed. This morning, he was going to put his trust, and his life, in Strachan's hands. It was a strange feeling but he knew it was the right thing to do.

The bell rang as the door to the cafe opened. Strachan stood in the doorway.

***

'Thank you for coming, Detective Stra-chan. Nobody followed you?'

'No, sir. I made certain . . . but I don't understand, sir . . .'

Danilov held up his hand. 'You will soon enough. Did you bring them?'

Strachan handed over the two telegrams. 'They came this morning, sir. As you requested, I got in early before Miss Cavendish and took them from her desk.'

'Good.' Danilov checked both the envelopes had been unopened, then he ripped through the seals. Strachan watched as his eyes scanned the contents of the first telegram. He tried to read through the onion-skin paper but all he could make out was three lines of telegram pasted together.

Danilov grunted once then unfolded the second telegram, reading that one as quickly as the first. He placed both telegrams and envelopes in his coat pocket. 'You have done well, Strachan. Now, go on back to the station before anybody misses you.'

'Inspector Meaker is in charge of the investigation now, sir.'

'Chief Inspector Boyle said he would appoint him.'

'He's going to arrest the fisherman. The man who came forward, sir.'

'Him? The Giant? Don't be stupid, man, he can't even write.'

'Inspector Meaker is pretty sure, sir. He's going to bring him in for questioning. He's confident he will admit everything.'

'You would sell your own mother after a little "gentle" persuasion from Charles Meaker.' Danilov shook his head in exasperation. 'It means I'll have to get on with this,' he said softly.

'Sorry, sir. What was that?'

'Nothing, Stra-chan. Just go back to the station. When you are there, don't forget to follow up on the fingerprint from the preacher's body. Whatever Meaker tells you to do, make sure they check the fingerprint against all the files: criminals, police, government employees. The lot.'

'Everyone, sir?'

'Everyone, and do it quickly.'

'Yes, sir, if you say so.'

'I do. I most certainly do, Stra-chan.'

Danilov got up from the table and said goodbye to the Princess.

'What are you going to do, sir?'

'I'm going to feed the wolf.'

'Sir, what should I do?'

'Do what you think is right, Strachan. That's all we can ask anybody.'

Strachan thought for a moment. 'Inspector, that was the first time you have said my name correctly.'

'Did I? How careless of me. I promise I won't make a habit of it, Strachan.' Danilov stubbed out his cigarette, put on his hat and went outside to wave down a taxi.

'Another glass of tea, Detective?' asked the Princess.

'Thank you, Princess Ostrepova, that would be wonderful.'

'And I have some piroshki for you. Inspector Danilov said you might be hungry.' A steaming plate was placed in front of Strachan. He picked one up and began to eat.

What was he going to do?

The fisherman was obviously not the killer but Meaker seemed desperate to charge him. If he went back to the station, they would make sure he was involved. What was it Danilov had said? 'Do what you think is right.' What would his father have done?

He thought for a moment and realised he didn't know. His father's stories were always about arresting this or that criminal, or the things he had seen on the beat. There was nothing about going against his superior officer. Perhaps his father had just followed orders all his life.

He didn't know.

He took another piroshki and bit into it. The sweet pork and its juices ran down his chin and dripped on his jacket. He mopped them up with the napkin. As he did so, he remembered something his father had said one night as they sat in front of the fire. He had been telling them about arresting a man for stabbing his sister that day, when he stopped talking and just stared into the fire. 'My job is to clean up the mess left by others, David. Whatever you do, try not to leave a mess for people like me.'

Strachan put down the glass of tea and rose from the table.

The Princess was beside him immediately. 'Leaving, Detective? You haven't finished your piroshki.'

'I'm sorry, Princess Ostrepova, I have a mess I need to clean up.'

CHAPTER 32

The taxi was taking a long time. Danilov leant forward and tapped the driver on the shoulder. 'Could you go faster?'

'Busy, today. Students.' He pointed through the split windscreen.

Outside, crowds had gathered on the streets. At their head, a group of young people were assembling under a white banner with large characters pasted on to it. They were shouting slogans, their fists thrusting into the air at the end of every line.

Danilov sat back in the leather seats. Life goes on, despite everything. If this didn't go well, he would miss Shanghai. Its life, its teeming streets, its sheer passion for getting on and doing. There were none of the obsessions or abstract reflection of his homeland here. Just keep moving on because nobody knows what tomorrow will bring.

He laughed to himself. That was exactly what he was doing. Moving forward towards a future which he didn't know.

The taxi accelerated in between two rickshaws, just barely missing both.

The driver edged through the crowds that lined the streets. Some were there to watch the march, others simply to do their shopping. A few more to take advantage of both.

He smelt the fragrance of roasting sweet potatoes once more. The man gets around. Then Danilov laughed to himself. There must be more than one of them. Nobody could be that agile, could they?

Up above, the sky was a bright, bright blue. A colour that he had only ever seen on winter days in Shanghai when a breeze had come in from the sea to blow away the smoke that normally shrouded the city.

On a day like this, it was good to be alive. To smell the roasting sweet potatoes, to hear the chatter of the people, to see the colours of the sky. He almost reached forward to tap the driver on his shoulder and tell him to go back to Medhurst Apartments.

But he didn't.

His course was set now. There was no going back.

The taxi stopped again. They were at a junction. People flowed in front of the car: tall ones, short ones, men dressed in Mandarin coats, women in their tight *chi paos*.

They didn't know there was a man out there who wanted to kill them all.

The lights changed colour and the taxi accelerated forward again, only to stop after fifty yards. Up ahead a funeral procession had taken advantage of the gap in the traffic to come out from a side street.

The family of the deceased were dressed in white from head to toe, all looking like refugees from a Ku Klux Klan meeting in America's Deep South. They walked behind the hearse, two drums beating a rhythmic tattoo in counterpoint to the squeals of a herd of trumpets. In front of the hearse, the paid mourners cried and tore their hair out, lamenting the departure of the deceased.

This must have been a rich man, thought Danilov, to have such a procession. Who would mourn him?

Nobody.

His family were missing, he was all alone in this world. Perhaps, in stopping the killer, his life would have some meaning, a final atonement for what he had done.

The driver spat out thorough the open window and said a soft '*Ta ma de*' under his breath. He jerked the wheel to the right and accelerated past the grieving family, past the squealing trumpets, past the horse-drawn hearse, and past the wailing mourners.

The road was clear in front of them now, just a few pedestrians taking their life into their hands by darting across the road.

Danilov eased himself back into the leather seat. Don't think any more. Don't worry. The course has been set. The die cast.

It was time to feed the wolf.

* * *

'*Come into my parlour, said the spider to the fly.*' He spoke out loud and Li Min had glanced up from his ropes. The view through the window had surprised him for a moment. Danilov was getting out from a taxi outside the Rowing Club.

How had he got so close?

He underestimated Danilov it seemed. Well, he wouldn't do that any more. He intended to leave him to be punished until later but such an opportunity would not present itself again. The gods were helping him in their unique way.

Danilov was standing there alone. Such a tempting target. He must have decided to continue the investigation despite being suspended.

Fool.

Nobody in the Shanghai Police cared for justice. They just wanted an easy life with a fat pension and a comfortable retirement in Margate at the end of it.

Danilov was different. Now it was time for him to go. Perhaps they would begin to understand the necessity of his work after he got rid of the Inspector. Striking at the heart of the police force would make them all realise they couldn't hide any more. If they had done wrong, they would be punished.

It was that simple. Whether you were a prostitute, or one of Shanghai's elite, he would bring you down.

'Come into my parlour, said the spider to the fly,' he said out loud again.

Well, here was the fly and it was time for the spider to act.

Danilov should have been later but no matter. His time had come. He had committed a crime and would be punished like all the rest.

'Come, Li Min, we have work to do.'

***

The taxi driver pulled up beside the Shanghai Rowing Club. 'You want me wait?'

'No, thank you. I'll look after myself.'

'Taxis not many round here.'

'I'm fine, thank you.'

'Tree dollar fifty.'

Danilov gave him five dollars. The taxi driver pretended to search for change. But Danilov was already out of the taxi, staring up at the mock-Tudor facade of the building. He barely noticed the taxi pulling away in a cloud of blue exhaust.

The streets were quiet despite being in the centre of the busiest city on Earth. Not a person, not a policeman, could be seen. They must all be at the demonstration, he thought.

No matter.

He walked to the entrance of the club. It was locked. He leant forward to look through the dirt-encrusted windows. His own reflection stared back in the glass. Was that really him?

He shielded his eyes and stared into the club. It seemed deserted.

He stepped back and examined the upper storeys. There were no signs of life. Should he wait or go in? He checked his watch. Can't stay here not doing anything. He had to move, had to get it over with.

On the left was a rusty half-door set into a wall. He pushed it and was surprised when it opened without a noise.

The courtyard of the Shanghai Rowing Club stood in front of him. He walked through the door and past a large potted plant guarding the entrance. He was dimly aware of a movement on his left, just out of the periphery of his vision. A blur of blue, a sweep of an arm coming towards him. His instinctive reaction was to duck and avoid the arm, but the man was too quick for him.

A hand grabbed him around the back of the neck, and a wet cloth covered his mouth and nose. He smelt the pungent aroma of chloroform on the rag. The hand clamped tighter around his mouth, and he tried not to breathe. He kicked backwards with the heel of his shoe and it connected with the hard peak of a knee. For a second, the grip relaxed and he heard a grunt from behind him. Then, other arms encircled his and the rag was clamped tighter to his mouth and nose.

He threw his head backwards and felt it connect with the bridge of a nose. This time the rag came free from his mouth. He started to shout and struggled against the other arms holding him. For a second, the grip on him relaxed, then it tightened again, and the rag clamped over his nose once more.

He breathed in.

His legs lost all their strength, and his body collapsed, as he went as limp as a sock full of borscht.

The arm released him, and he fell. A strange slow-motion fall where he could see everything that was happening to him, but was unable to prevent any of it.

The ground came up to meet him. His head bounced once, twice, three times, then settled into the earth, blending into the soft ground. He was aware of a beetle, a twig between its jaws, making its way home in front of his eyes.

Above him, a bald Chinese man slowly came into focus and then disappeared from view after shaking the Inspector's shoulders.

'He's out like a bowl of noodles,' said the man with a voice like a grind of gears.

Behind him, a tall European man stood adjusting the sleeves of his jacket.

Then blackness.

CHAPTER 33

Strachan knocked on the door of the Fingerprint Lab. There was a long silence before somebody inside shouted, 'Go away.'

Strachan knocked again, this time harder and longer.

The voice inside shouted back, louder and longer. 'It's lunchtime, we're closed. Come back after two.'

Strachan knocked on the door with his fist now. 'I need to see you now. Urgent.'

A loud '*Ta ma de*' came from inside the room. The door opened and a fat man with glasses, dressed in a white overcoat, stood in the entrance. He was eating a white *bao*. 'Can't you see? We're closed. Lunchtime.'

He tried to shut the door but Strachan inserted his foot between it and the jamb. He put his shoulder against the door and it gave way. 'Now, I'm going to say this once and once only. Are you listening?'

The fat man nodded his head. A chunk of *bao* fell from his open mouth.

'You got a fingerprint yesterday from a body in the morgue. I need to know the results. Now.'

The fat man swallowed his food. 'Yesterday, we won't have done it yet.'

'It was a rush job. Urgent. For Inspector Danilov.'

A look of recognition passed across the podgy face and the eyes became small slits behind the glasses. 'Oh, that one. Danilov promised us ten dollars if we did it for him quickly.' He stuck out a pudgy hand.

Strachan dug deep in his pockets. He counted the coins. 'I've got eight. Danilov will give you the rest when he sees you.'

The fat man took the money from Strachan's hand and placed his half-eaten *bao* down on the desk. Strachan noticed it was Char Shao, his favourite.

The technician went behind the counter. 'We had to work a lot on this one. Danilov asked us to compare it with all the criminals in our files as well as the fingerprints of police officers and government officials. Do you know how many sets of prints that is?'

Strachan shook his head.

'A lot. A bloody lot, let me tell you.' He began to search through the stack of papers, files, used chopsticks, used soup bowls and uneaten *bao* on the counter. 'I know I put it here somewhere. Where is it?' He moved a bamboo container, left over from yesterday's lunch. 'Here it is.' He held up a piece of paper with two matching pictures of a fingerprint on it. Red lines radiated from the pictures in the same places.

Strachan reached for it, but the technician snatched it back. 'Danilov also said he would treat us to a meal at Romanov's. I've never eaten Russian food.'

Strachan reached for the paper again. 'If Inspector Danilov said so, I'm sure he'll keep his promise.'

The technician handed over the paper and Strachan saw the name written at the top. His face went white. He looked at it again. 'Are you sure this is the man whose fingerprint matched the one we found on the corpse?'

The technician frowned. 'Look, whoever you are. I know my job. That patent print matched in twenty-two different areas. We only need twelve matches for it to stand up in a court of law. It has very distinctive whorls and arches. Plus there's a bridge that I haven't seen often at all. It's a good match, even . . .'

But Strachan was already out of the door.

He had to tell Danilov whose name was written at the top of the paper.

***

The ropes bit into Danilov's wrists. He tensed his arms and tried to loosen the bindings, but the more he fought against them, the tighter they seemed to get.

He shouted as loud as he could. A shout of rage and defiance. He listened for a response but nothing came back. He knew he was in a cell and, for some strange reason, he thought he was underground. He wasn't sure why he sensed this, perhaps it was the way the sounds were absorbed and swallowed up. A dead sound with no echoes, as if everything was solid around him.

He kicked out with his feet but the ropes were just as strong around his legs. He shouted again. His voice sounded hoarse to his ears and, once again, the walls absorbed everything.

He wasn't sitting in the dark though. There was a small light behind him that gave a brown glow through the cell. It was like the light of early dawn in Minsk when the sun is still below the horizon but its rays are reaching out to the world.

The room was empty. There was nothing there but him, the chair he was tied to, and the black walls.

He shouted once again, louder this time.

A crack of light appeared vertically in the wall opposite him and began to get wider. A black shadow stood in the doorway, its height dominating the entrance.

Then it spoke: 'Shouting will only make your voice hoarse, Inspector Danilov. Nobody can hear you down here.'

So he was underground. The voice was cultured, elegant and vaguely familiar.

The black shadow stepped into the cell, closing the door behind him. The only light now was coming from behind Danilov. He stared into the gloom at the thing in front of him. For a few moments, it appeared to have no face, just darkness where eyes and ears and nose should be. Like the shadow of a man with the shadow of a face.

Then it spoke again: 'It's your time, Danilov. I've been waiting for this moment for a long while but I didn't think it would come so soon.'

Danilov could see a little more clearly now. The man was dressed from head to toe in black. On his head he wore a mask, but one without definition, just a dull matt-black skin that covered his face and absorbed the light. He saw the man's eyes. Green. Emerald green.

'I can see you like my mask, Inspector, you do recognise it, of course?'

Danilov let his head drop to his chest. 'It's Yama, I presume. The god of the underworld.' Every time the man spoke, he caught a whiff of something. Warm, earthy, but with a hint of sweetness in it. Just as the boatman had said.

'You are probably wondering why you are here?'

Danilov lifted his head and stared straight into the eyes of the black mask. He shook his head.

'An eye for an eye.'

'Another saying?'

'This one from the bible, I think. A terribly judgemental book.'

'What's that to do with me?'

'Everything, Inspector. Today, you are to be judged.'

'By you?'

'Today, I'm your judge, your jury, your prosecutor and your executioner.'

'So, you've already decided I'm guilty?'

The man took a step to the side. 'I didn't decide, Inspector, you did, long ago.' The man's body was close to him now. The sweet smell was even stronger. He tried to lash out, struggling against the ropes that bound his wrists.

'That won't help you, Inspector. The others found that out too.'

The door opened behind the man and another shape was silhouetted in the doorway.

'Do come in, Li Min. My colleague will be the clerk of the court. As you see, we always try to follow the correct procedures for a trial. Shall we begin?'

Li Min moved into the room. For a second, before he closed the door, a shaft of light caught the top of his head and the livid red scar that arched over it.

'Please read out the charges.'

The Chinese man produced a sheet of thick manuscript paper. 'Pyotr Alexandrevich Danilov, you are charged that on the 12th November, 1924, you deserted your family, leaving them to face the depredations of the revolutionary authorities alone.'

'Danilov, you realise in the eighth court of hell, desertion of your family is a very serious offence, to be punished by the gouging out of your eyes, if you are found guilty.'

'How does the prisoner plead?' said Li Min, his pen poised over the manuscript waiting for the answer.

Danilov remained quiet, slowly working his wrists against the ropes that bound him.

'I think you can write down the prisoner pleads guilty, Li Min. After all, the evidence is rather damning.'

'I didn't desert my family, I had a job to do.'

'Please change the plea, Li Min, the prisoner has changed his mind.'

'Not guilty now, sir?'

The mask turned towards Danilov. He could see the green eyes staring at him from the blackness. 'That's right, Li Min, the Inspector pleads not guilty.'

'When will the trial be, sir?'

'I think now is as good a time as any, don't you agree, Li Min?'

The Chinese man nodded.

'Does the Inspector need time to think about his defence?'

Danilov remained quiet.

'No, well, let the trial begin.'

'Before we do,' Danilov raised his voice, 'I would like you to remove your mask. I have the right to see my accuser.'

'You have no rights in my court, only responsibilities and punishments. I'm not on trial here, Inspector Danilov, you are. Request denied.'

The scratching of pen against parchment cut through the silence.

The ropes bit against Danilov's wrists as he strained against them. He would endure the pain. He had to endure the pain.

The mask sighed. 'Let's examine the evidence, shall we? Firstly, you deserted your family in Minsk. Is it true the city was in a state of anarchy?'

'The government was looking at undesirable elements in the city.'

'Just "undesirable elements". So there was no danger?'

There was the sound of pen on parchment again. A scratching, irritating sound that came from Li Min as he wrote down all that was being said. Danilov lifted his head. 'There didn't seem to be any. I was a member of the police. I'd never been involved in politics.'

'Not involved?' The shadow laughed behind his mask. 'You say you were not involved?'

'In Minsk, the Red Army and the Soviets were seen as liberators, welcomed by the people.'

'And did the Red Army have an equally warm welcome for former officials of the regime?'

Danilov's head went down and looked at the feet of his jailer. He was wearing brown brogues beneath his black gown. 'No, they didn't.'

'Didn't they have a history of reprisals against the former officials of the Tsar and the Mensheviks?'

'Yes but . . .'

'And didn't those reprisals also include members of the families of those officials?'

'Yes, sometimes. But you have to understand there was no danger at that time.'

'So you left the city?'

The pen had been scratching all his answers on to a parchment. For a moment, it stopped, waiting for his response.

'I went to Moscow.'

'Why?'

Danilov struggled against the restraints again, trying to keep his movement away from the eyes of the man in the mask. 'I had a case. A murderer had fled there. We went after him.'

'What had the murderer done?'

'He had killed his mother and father.'

'So, you abandoned your family to bring the killer of another family to justice?'

'I didn't abandon my family.'

'But you left them.' The man held his arms out wide as if appealing to a non-existent jury.

'I went to do my work.'

'How long were you away?'

'Five weeks,' said Danilov quietly.

The scratching of the pen got louder and then stopped. 'I didn't hear you?'

'Five weeks. I was away five weeks.'

Danilov could hear the noise of the fountain pen as it scratched his words on the parchment.

'Five weeks to catch a killer?'

'He escaped.'

'So you captured him once, he escaped and you stayed on in Moscow to catch him again?'

'Yes.' The bald-headed Chinese man stopped writing and looked down at him.

The mask continued. 'Meanwhile, the situation in Minsk changed, didn't it?'

'I tried to get back, but . . .'

'The purge began. Officials were being arrested, their families persecuted.'

'Yes, the town was isolated, even the trains stopped running. I couldn't return.'

'And your family?'

Danilov looked down at his hands tied to the arms of the chair. 'They were caught up in it all. With two other families, they decided to leave the city and go south.'

'They fled south.' More scratching from the pen of the Chinese man. 'And what did you do?' the man in the mask asked softly, the hand coming up to scratch the outside of the mask where the nose should have been.

'I followed them.'

'No. What did you do before you followed them?'

'I don't understand.'

'I think you do, Inspector. Didn't you arrest the killer in Moscow first?'

'Yes, but that was my job, to catch the killer. That was why I was there. And the news was so confused from Minsk. Nobody knew what was happening.' Danilov paused to catch his breath. 'I followed as soon as I could,' he said quietly.

'Wasn't there a woman too?'

'A woman?'

'The sister of the man you were chasing.'

'Her? Yes, she was in Moscow too.'

'Didn't you stay on in Moscow because of her?'

'Yes . . . I mean, no. It wasn't like that.'

'Like what?'

Danilov raised his voice. 'You are insinuating that I stayed on in Moscow because of her.'

'Well, didn't you?'

'She asked me to stay to catch her brother. She didn't trust the police in Moscow.'

'So you stayed.'

'Yes.'

'For five weeks.'

'Yes.'

'Whilst your family were forced to flee from a purge in Minsk.'

The answer when it came was soft, a whisper: 'Yes.'

Danilov's interrogator turned to the bald-headed Chinese man. 'I think the case is proven, don't you, Li Min?'

'Haven't you ever made a mistake? Haven't you wished you could roll back time and change what you did? Acted differently, made different choices?' Danilov shouted at the mask. Then he dropped his head onto his chest. 'If I had my time back, I would have stayed with Maria and Ivan and Elina.'

The man's voice was firm, almost strident. 'The only mistake I made, Danilov, was not starting my work earlier. I thought the system would punish those who had committed crimes. But I was wrong. Even worse, I found it rewarded them.'

Danilov lifted his head again, aware of the change in the man's voice. 'So that's when you started killing?'

'I didn't "start killing" as you say. I began to judge those who had done wrong, to bring them before the court. To punish them for the crimes I knew they had committed, but the courts of Shanghai refused to do anything about.'

Danilov waited for a while and then he said, 'I know who you are. I've known for a while. You made too many mistakes.'

CHAPTER 34

Strachan had rung the Inspector's home from three different places. Each time, there had been no answer.

He tried to remember what Danilov had said to him. Something about 'feeding the wolf'. He thought at the time it was another one of his Russian sayings. But he now wondered if it was a bit more obvious, more direct. Had Danilov gone to find the killer himself?

Strachan looked at the paper from the fingerprint lab again. The name couldn't be right, could it? The thought was outlandish. A man who had risen so high was the killer?

He was close to the station now. He folded the paper from the fingerprint lab carefully and put it in his inside pocket.

What should he do? Danilov had vanished. Perhaps he should let Meaker know? But Meaker was hell-bent on arresting the boatman. He wouldn't be interested.

How about Chief Inspector Boyle?

He imagined Boyle's reaction. 'You must be mistaken, Strachan. Check it again, boy. Who do you think you are? Making such outrageous accusations against a senior member of Shanghai society.' His father had warned him all about the establishment and how it stuck together to protect its own.

He waved at Sergeant Wolfe as he walked through the foyer. Got to behave like nothing happened. Just another day on the job. He had to avoid Meaker though. He didn't want to get involved with his arrest of the boatman.

He peered through the glass door of the detectives' office to make sure neither Meaker nor Cartwright were hanging around.

Miss Cavendish would know how to get hold of Danilov. She knew everything in Central Police Station. She even knew his mother's name. If there was one person who would know where Danilov had gone to, it would be her.

Unless, of course, he had gone to confront the killer. A shudder went down Strachan's spine at the thought.

She was behind her desk as usual, sucking on the Parma Violets that she loved so much. Their floral scent surrounded her like a bouquet of flowers. As he approached her desk, she put her fingers to her lips and pointed to Boyle's door. 'They're both in there,' she whispered.

'Who?'

'Chief Inspector Boyle and Inspector Meaker. Planning the arrest of the boatman. Mum's the word. I didn't tell you.'

'I've been trying to get hold of Inspector Danilov, do you know where he is?'

'He rang me earlier today and asked me to give you this message. You are to go to 76, Nansoochow Road, as soon as you can.'

'Where's that?' He leant over and took the address from her.

'It's the Rowing Club, Detective Strachan. I had a wonderfully elegant evening there back in '07, dancing in the open air in front of the creek. The lights were so beautiful and the music . . .' Miss Cavendish trailed off, lost in her memories of young beaux and Strauss waltzes.

Strachan snatched his hat off her table. 'Thank you, Miss Cavendish, you've been a great help.'

'But it will be closed now, nobody uses it any more,' said Miss Cavendish to the closing door.

It opened again a second later, and Strachan rushed back in. 'Can you get the Mobile Unit to go to the address? I think we'll need them.'

'Of course, I'll use Chief Inspector Boyle's name. They'll jump if they think the request is from him.'

But again, she was talking to empty space. Strachan had already gone.

***

'So you think you know who I am, Danilov?'

'How many people have you tried in your courts, Mr Allen?' Danilov stared straight into the green eyes behind the mask.

The pen stopped scribbling across the page. In the cell, time stood still for a moment.

'You were always too clever, Danilov, that was another of your failings. Cleverness is all right as long as it's hidden. We British have been taught that in our public schools for years. The tall poppy gets its head chopped off. Better to hide away in the middle of everything, hiding behind a veneer of banality, of cigars and chums, of small talk and even smaller ideas.'

'You were different?'

'I've always been different. But I've always known how to play the game. To hide behind a mask.' Allen reached up and slowly removed the face of Yama. 'It's always so hot in this bloody thing, but people do like a bit of theatre even when they're facing death. How did you know it was me, Danilov?'

'One of your victims told me.'

'One of my victims? But they were all dead.'

'Not all of them. Maria Stepanova was still alive when you put her in the barrel of pig's blood.'

'The scratches on the inside of the lid?'

Danilov nodded his head.

'I should have arranged your trial earlier, Danilov. I underestimated you.' Allen loosened his black jacket to reveal a green, white and red tattoo etched into his chest. The face of Judge Yama in all his glory.

Danilov stared at the tattoo. Allen had kept many things hidden beneath his veneer of civilisation. 'At first I was confused, there were so many different things going on. Chinese characters, rope bindings, blue eyes. But it was the extremely personal nature of the killings that first struck me. The killer was always up close at the moment of death, enjoying the process of the extinction of life. These deaths meant something to him.'

'Yes, they did.'

'What they meant was confirmed by Mr Chang. You took the persona of Yama to judge people.'

'Not a persona, Danilov. I am Yama.'

'Becoming Yama gave the killings meaning. But what exactly did they mean, that's what I asked myself? What were the patterns in your crimes?'

'I didn't commit any crimes. I made judgements.'

Danilov carried on regardless. 'Two witnesses at least gave me a sketch of your identity.'

'That I was tall and European? That could fit ninety per cent of the men in the Settlement.'

'True, but how did the killer choose his victims? He obviously knew a lot about them. He had to be able to get the information from somewhere. It became obvious to me only someone in the police, judiciary or high up in government, would have access to this information. Victorov's story led me to suspect Councillor Ayres for a while but it couldn't have been him, no opportunity to kill the preacher and display his body.'

'You met our Russian blackmailer? You have been a busy soul. Councillor Ayres was a silly man about that Russian whore. He told me about it and asked me to sort it out.'

'Did he expect you to kill her?'

'No, just pay her off. And make sure she stayed paid off. You know he rang me after your visit to his office? Stupid man. I told him Victorov killed her for the blackmail money.'

'He believed you?'

'He wanted to believe me.'

'I thought so. But, in the end, it was two mistakes that gave you away.'

'Mistakes?'

'The first was putting the prostitute into the barrel whilst she was still alive.'

'And the second?'

'It was your smell.'

'You're lying, Danilov. How can a smell give anyone away?'

'Your smell. The boatman reported it to me. It was your trademark. The scent of Parma Violets that you used to cover your breath. At first, I thought it was a strong cologne that the killer was wearing but Miss Cavendish showed me the truth.'

'Miss Cavendish?'

'You gave her some of your French sweets. Your Parma Violets. A distinctive aroma when they are chewed. The fisherman recognised the smell. And you left a packet in the taxi which you used to kidnap Elsie Everett.'

'You have been diligent, Danilov. But it's all circumstantial. You can't prove anything. And, as you may have noticed, you are in my courtroom now.'

'You worked in Washington before Shanghai, didn't you?'

'Yes, hated it and hated Americans. Far too direct for me.'

'You killed there?'

'She deserved it. Selfish, rotten, corrupt woman.'

'Did you know a private detective followed you here?'

'Anderson? A waste of oxygen. It was easy to keep him in girls and drink.'

'I sent a telegram to the Embassy in Washington yesterday.'

'You have been a busy little Russian, haven't you?'

'The only thing I don't understand is how you chose your victims?'

'They weren't victims. They chose themselves. Being in Intelligence has its advantages. Reports crossed my desk all the time. But nothing was ever done. These people were committing crimes and getting away with them.'

'Crimes? What had Henry Sellars done wrong? And Elsie Everett was just an actress and not a very good one.'

'Henry Sellars stole from a church collection box. You should have seen how proud she was the night she died. Stepping out for the first time on the streets of Shanghai in her blue dress, leaning on my arm. Unfortunately for her, it was also her last time. As for Elsie Everett, she was the worst. I received a request from Scotland Yard to detain her. She had murdered one of her rivals. This actress had actually won the part in Shanghai not Elsie, so she was removed. Pushed in front of a subway train, if my memory serves me right. I thought I would save them the trouble, and the expense, of repatriating her. She appeared all sweet and innocent, did Elsie, but beneath the act was a tough bitch. She died well, though. Surprised me with her strength.'

'And the preacher?'

'For many years, he made the lives of young boys, including Henry Sellars, unbearable. He deserved to die.'

'And me?' Danilov stared Allen in the face. 'I made a mistake. Work had engulfed my life, I had lost track of what was important.'

Allen held his hand up. 'You are guilty of deserting your family and you live your guilt every day. You know you do.'

Danilov remained quiet.

Allen checked his watch. 'The court session has ended, Danilov. I hope you enjoy your knowledge in the underworld. I'm sure it will be useful there. The jury has examined the evidence and found you guilty.'

Li Min scribbled in his book, ending his sentence with a lavish full stop.

'The sentence of this judge is that you will be taken to your place of execution where your eyes will be gouged out. That being the punishment suffered by all those who desert their families.'

'I was only doing my job,' said Danilov.

'And I am only doing mine.'

Allen looked at his watch again. 'It's four o'clock now, let's carry out the execution in an hour. We can enjoy a pot of tea first. A trial always makes me thirsty. All the talking you know. Meanwhile, Inspector, enjoy your last hours on Earth. I'm afraid we don't go in for any of that "last meal for the condemned man" rubbish in my courts. Experience has taught us death is usually less messy on an empty stomach. We'll see you at five.'

Li Min rolled his manuscript up like a scroll and opened the door, flooding the cell with light.

Danilov took the chance to take a good look around him. The cell was about twenty feet square with black painted walls and no windows. The light source was a small hurricane lamp, set against the wall behind him.

For the first time, his head sunk to his chest. There seemed to be no way out of here.

CHAPTER 35

He didn't know how long he sat with his head on his chest, slumped forward in his prison of a chair. Sweat dripped from his forehead. Blood flowed from the cuts in his wrist and ran down his fingers. He could feel its sticky embrace covering his hands.

He lifted his head and summoned one last burst of effort, straining his arms against the ropes, feeling them bite into the wounds already there. He rocked back and forth, twisting his body from side to side, the ropes biting deeper into his wrists. There was some movement now. They didn't grip his wrists as tightly as before.

He redoubled his efforts, ignoring the shafts of pain searing through his arms. The ropes give a little more. His arms and wrists could twist now, separate from the ropes, their grip no longer holding him like a vice. One last effort. The sweat ran down into his eyes. He wanted to wipe it away, to rid himself of its salty sting.

He jerked at the ropes, twisting his forearm to create space. He pivoted his elbow against the arm of the chair, gaining a little leverage at the expense of a vast amount of pain. Gritting his teeth, he forced his arms to revolt against the bite of the ropes.

One rope began to come loose. He could feel the skin of his right arm sliding through it. He twisted his arm harder now, forcing the rope to stretch, desperate to work it free.

'You'll never escape. Nobody ever does.'

The voice came from above and to his left. Danilov froze like a child caught doing something wrong. Slowly, he searched the wall with his eyes, not moving his body.

'Li Min was a sailor in a previous life. Knows how to tie somebody up properly.'

Danilov searched for the source of the voice. His eyes scanned the black wall, looking for movement or a patch of light that would give away its position.

'I wouldn't waste my time if I were you. You have so little of it left.'

There it was, in the far left-hand corner, a slightly paler shade of black. If he squinted, he could just make out two faint crescents of white, almost like paint splashes, which were the whites of Allen's eyes. Faint glimmers of white in a death-black wall.

'I see you've found my little observation post. Just like the trenches. The Germans eventually found us too, sitting out there all alone in no man's land. The others used to hate being a spotter. I loved it. Hiding in full sight. Story of my life. I started in the Staff, of course. Now, they were real criminals, sending men to their deaths like pigs to the butcher. I found my calling as a spotter though. All alone, with nothing but the mud and the rats for company. And the corpses. One mustn't forget the corpses.'

The voice was stronger now, more obviously that of Allen, less concerned with concealment.

'I think I began to discover who I was during the war. I began to see the evil men do to each other. I was like a larva with only a sense of what it was. It took the violence of war for the larva to pupate, to find a sense of meaning. It took Shanghai, and ten years of sorrow, to bring the larva to full awareness of what it was to do with its life.'

'The war was a long time ago.'

'Perhaps for you. For me, it was just yesterday.'

Danilov's head slumped forward, his body held in place by the rope. The sweat and blood dripped off his brow and fingers onto the floor, pooling at his feet, forming a rich, sticky mess.

'You see, for those of us who were there, unlike you, we live it every day. Oh, we may bury it beneath an orgy of sex or champagne or dancing, but it's always there, buried deep in our bones. A part of us, you see, a desperate part of us.'

'I never went to the Front.'

'You were lucky.'

Danilov lifted his head. 'Lucky?'

'Yes, lucky. The war was horrific yet beautiful. Nobody ever understands its beauty.'

'Beauty? The war destroyed my country, killed my Tsar, brought famine and destruction to my city,' Danilov sucked in a deep breath of the foetid air of the cell, 'and destroyed my family.' The eyes blinked behind the darkness of the wall. Was he laughing at him?

'Oh, didn't I tell you? Your family is still alive. Well, at least part of it is.'

Danilov sat bolt upright. 'What? How do you know? Where are they?' He twisted and jerked against the ropes again, struggling to free himself.

'You had a telegram from a Mr Willis in Tsingtao. An answer to your advertisement. Cartwright took it.'

'I know.'

A soft chuckle came from behind the wall.

'Cartwright . . . you have been using Cartwright, haven't you?'

'Not directly. But Charles Meaker was so very keen to return to Central, and he controlled Cartwright.' The voice trailed off leaving Danilov to work out the rest.

'You've been watching my investigation all this time?'

'I just wanted to make sure I knew what you were doing. It's knowing the moves your opponent is going to make before he makes them. Like chess, only with people.'

'Just pawns, aren't we?'

'Like flies to the gods . . .'

'Cartwright told you everything I was doing?'

'Him and Miss Cavendish. She didn't know, of course. But she's such a terrible gossip. I find a few sweets always loosens her tongue.'

'And Stra-chan?'

'Such an innocent, isn't he? Shame. Under you he would have the makings of a halfway decent copper. Pity we're never going to find out. Meaker will probably be his new boss.'

'So it was time to get rid of me.'

'You were getting a little too close, asking the wrong sort of questions.'

'Time to kill me off?'

'Oh no, you did that yourself, Danilov, the day you deserted your wife and children. I am merely the agent of Di Yu, punishing those who transgress.'

There was a loud snap as the small window high on the black wall closed.

Danilov was left staring at the wall. 'Where are my family?' he shouted. 'Where are my family?'

His body slumped forward again, the sweat running down his forehead into his eyes. He pulled against the ropes, twisting his body for extra leverage.

His right arm came free.

***

Strachan parked the Buick around the corner from the Rowing Club on Yuanmingyuan Road. There was no point letting the killer know he was there. Not until the back-up arrived in their Red Marias.

He walked to the Rowing Club, the sun fighting with its late afternoon strength to cast strong shadows across the buildings. He passed one of the new Art Deco buildings that was finished yet still not occupied. The streets were deserted. This wasn't the Shanghai he knew, full of lights and noise and people and smells. Here, everything was as quiet as a funeral parlour with no bodies.

A mist was creeping off the creek and drifting around the dark buildings of the club, shrouding the mock-Tudor frontage and the black and white boathouse. Strachan sniffed the air. The unmistakable reek of salted fish assaulted his nostrils, carried on the mist from the boats on the river.

He crept around the building trying to remain hidden from view. So like the British to build something like this, as if it were located on the Thames at Henley rather than here, in the middle of the biggest Chinese city in the world.

He stared down at the flotsam and jetsam floating off the launch ramp of the Rowing Club. Over there, they had found the body of Henry Sellars, stretched out on the 'Beach of Dead Babies', his stomach ripped apart. It seemed so long ago. A lifetime and an age away.

He turned back to the building. Should he go in, or wait for help to arrive? It looked empty and deserted, but the killer might be inside right now.

And if the killer came out before the Mobile Unit arrived, what was Strachan going to do? He could try to ambush him, but there was nowhere to hide on the open street.

Better to catch him unawares inside, when Strachan would be in control. Besides, the Inspector was probably in there too. What if he had already been captured by the killer? A shudder went down Strachan's spine.

He stood on tiptoes and peered through the window of the boathouse. The waters of an indoor swimming pool reflected into dancing shadows on the walls. He could stand here waiting for help to come, or he could go in and check it out for himself. In for a penny, in for a pound, he thought. Was that one of Danilov's Russian idioms or something he had picked up at school?

He didn't care.

He smashed his revolver against the glass. The sound seemed so loud in the silence of the street. He stopped and looked around, waiting for a reaction.

Inside, the building nothing moved. Outside, the streets were empty, the only sound the waves lapping against the launch ramp of the club, and the muffled chug of some ancient motor as it struggled against the tides of the Whampoo.

He cleared the remaining glass from the window, reached inside and drew back the bolt. He pushed the window open and climbed in. His boots made a loud crunch as they landed on the broken glass on the inside of the building.

Once again, he froze and listened for any reaction.

Nothing.

He stepped forward, carefully checking where he put his feet, the revolver clenched in his right hand. A vehicle drove past outside, its headlights briefly illuminating the shadows in the boathouse, throwing blue light onto the walls.

He was five feet from a shimmering swimming pool. The smell of the water – a mixture of chlorine and damp bath towels – took him back to his childhood, swimming with his father, laughing, being wrapped up in a giant swathe of Lancashire cloth, teeth chattering with the cold.

Mustn't think about that now, not now.

The shadows of the reflected water danced on the wall in front of him. He jerked back as something brushed against his face, striking out with the butt end of the gun. The back of his hand touched the crinkled leaves of a palm frond.

He slumped forward, breathing deeply. Pull yourself together.

He stepped past the palm tree and peered through the stained glass windows of the double door leading to the club itself. He remembered the layout from when he visited with his father. But he hadn't been here for years, not since his father had died.

The doors led to a large open lobby, a restaurant and smoking room to one side and upstairs, more rooms for reading and relaxing.

He pushed the door open with his left hand. It moved smoothly, without a squeak. It was as dark as the devil's soul in the club. He stood there listening, smelling the years of tobacco smoke and whisky and whiskers.

He stepped through, letting the door swing shut behind him. It made a wooden thunk as it closed against the other door. Once again, he froze and listened.

Letting his eyes slowly become accustomed to the gloom, he scanned the room. A large oil painting of a dead grouse on the opposite wall, while beneath his feet a thick maroon carpet cushioned his steps. There were other prints and etchings on the wood-panelled walls, all depicting long lost hunting scenes in England.

To his left, the carpeted stairs rose to the next floor. He began to climb upwards, stopping after each step to listen for any noise that might show the killer was in the building, lying in wait for him.

But all he ever heard was his own breathing.

He reached the landing. Above him, the portrait of a pompous European, proprietorial in its whiskered face and smug smile, stared down as if wondering what this half-Chinese interloper was doing in his club.

Then a scream pierced the silence.

* * *

Danilov kept his eyes on the spy hole in the wall as he undid the rope tying his left arm to the chair. His fingers fumbled on the complex knot. He worked his fingers into it and pulled one of the strands. It began to give.

The spy hole opened and he immediately put his right arm back on the chair, letting his head fall forward as if he were unconscious.

What was he going to do next? There were only two of them as far as he could see, but both were more powerful than he was and neither had spent the last five hours without food and water, tied to a chair.

The spy hole snapped shut again. He opened one eye and stared at the wall were the sliding panel should be. He could see nothing but a black, blank wall.

He began tugging at the rope binding his left wrist again, working his fingers into the strands. It was coming free. He could feel his left wrist had more movement now, it wasn't as tightly gripped as before.

He pulled at the knot but his fingers felt like coarse German sausages. The rope was taking an age to untie with one hand. In the pictures, the hero always freed himself in three seconds, but this wasn't a film, this was real.

He strained his left wrist against the rope. The bindings were looser now. Just a few more tugs at the strands of the rope and he would be free. He pulled at the rope with his right hand, working his left wrist up and down. It slid from under the rope, taking a layer of skin with it. The pain shot through his arm, he almost cried out but stifled it to a quiet groan.

He held up his arms, massaging the hands together, desperately trying to bring life and energy back into the fingers. My feet, he thought, I still have to untie my feet.

He kicked against the restraints, and the chair rocked backwards and forwards. He brought his hands down and began to work on the ropes tying his ankles to the chair. It was easier now, even though the rope was tied tightly. Two hands worked on the knot, searching for a way to loosen it.

He kicked out with his right foot again. This time the knot gave slightly. His fingers found the strand that would come loose. He pulled and pulled, alternatively straining and relaxing his ankle against the leg of the chair. The foot began to work itself free.

There was the rattle of a key in the door, turning in the lock. He sat bolt upright, returning his hands to their tied position on the arms of the chair.

The door swung open, light shafting in from the corridor. Danilov shut his eyes.

'Ah, good to see you are with us again, old chap. But I would open my eyes if I were you. It does make Li Min's job easier, and it will certainly be far less painful for you.'

Allen hadn't bothered to wear the mask this time. He stood in front of Danilov with his long, patrician face, Roman nose and tight jaw, every inch the stern judge passing sentence.

Despite himself, Danilov opened his eyes. The bald Chinese man had followed Allen into the cell, still carrying his notebook and pen, but now he also had a canvas bag over his arm.

'Li Min will do the honours.' Allen's voice was almost jovial, like a schoolboy asking a new boy to cut the cake.

'Pyotr Alexandrevich Danilov,' Li Min read from his book, 'you have been tried and found guilty by this court of deserting your family in time of war.'

'I'm not guilty,' shouted Danilov.

'I'm afraid it's a little too late for pleading, Inspector. Please carry on, Li Min.'

'You have been sentenced in accordance with the assigned punishment for this heinous crime. Your eyes will be gouged from your head whilst you are still conscious. You will then be left to bleed until you are dead.'

Danilov could hear his own breathing, short and sharp and rasping. Allen and Li Min were silent, waiting for a reaction from him, but he refused to give them any more pleasure.

'It is customary at times like these for the guilty party to say a few last words before the sentence is carried out. But as you, Danilov, have shown neither remorse nor guilt for your actions, I am going to dispense with tradition. Such a waste of time and effort, don't you think?'

Danilov stayed quiet, thinking furiously. When could he act? When could he do something?

'Carry out the sentence, Li Min. Let's not keep the Inspector waiting any longer. The suspense is killing him.'

Li Min placed his book and fountain pen on the floor. Danilov could see the neat handwriting of the notes, covering the two open pages. The pen was a Parker, filled with purple ink. Its black body and open nib lay there on the words, on his sentence of death. Such a strange colour to use, he thought.

Li Min reached into his canvas bag and pulled out a long piece of old leather. It was shaped like a thick headband with a buckle at one end. In the middle were two spikes, sharpened to glittering points. They glinted savagely in the light from the open door.

'I thought we would use silver on you, Inspector. It's a far more elegant way to die than cold steel, don't you agree?'

Danilov stayed quiet, every muscle in his body waiting for the moment when he could act. The bald Chinese man walked around the chair and out of sight, carrying the leather headband like a priest carrying a chasuble. The scratch of leather on metal as the headband was released from its clasp. Li Min's soft footsteps as he stepped forward, leaning in closer to fasten it around Danilov's head.

He felt the heavy touch of the hard leather on his forehead.

Now, now was the time.

He reached down and grabbed the fountain pen from the top of the book, bringing it up in an arc over his head, stabbing backwards with all his strength.

The pen dug deep into flesh. A scream burst over Danilov's head. Warm liquid squirted over his hand. He pulled the pen out and stabbed backwards again, harder this time, as hard as he could.

Another scream pierced the air. Li Min staggered in front of him, the Parker pen buried deep in his right eye.

* * *

Strachan heard another scream, this time even louder. Where had it come from?

He rushed down to the bottom of the stairs. He stopped and listened. There were the muffled sounds of somebody in pain, moaning like a ghost. It seemed to come from within the wooden walls.

He put his ear to the panels. There it was. A keening moan, like a dog with a broken leg.

He rushed into the lounge of the club. The moans were slightly louder now, and they seemed to be coming from below. He got down on his knees and listened once again, but the thick maroon carpet dissipated the sound.

A door at the end of the room was half open. He ran to it and flung it out of his way. More shouts now. Much louder. Coming from beneath his feet.

He ran down a short corridor and entered the kitchen. Pots and pans hung from the hooks above a long range. On a long table in the middle sat a tea pot, milk jug and two empty tea cups.

There was more shouting from below. The sounds of fighting. Another shout. Was that Danilov's voice? He ran to the back of the kitchen, hurdling one of the chairs in his way.

He was in a larder now. Bags of sugar and flour, assorted tins of fish and beans, bottles of oil and jars of soy sauce lined the shelves. There were more shouts. The loud crack of a gun being fired, another shout, indistinct and muffled. It was the Inspector.

'Danilov,' he shouted back.

There was a shout in return, muffled, indistinct. He shouted back but there was no answer this time.

He banged on the wooden wall. It shook but stayed intact. He stopped and listened.

Nothing.

Silence.

He banged harder. The wood sounded hollow; there was nothing behind it. He slammed the edge of his fist against one of the panels. It shook, but held solid.

He stepped back to the door of the larder and then jumped at the wall with his feet. The panel cracked in the centre. He kicked again and again, each kick becoming more and more violent as the wood splintered.

There was a space behind. Empty space.

He reached in and tore the wood away with his hands. 'Inspector Danilov,' he shouted into the void.

There was no answer.

CHAPTER 36

Li Min screamed again and fell moaning to the floor. Danilov reached down to his left leg. Got to get it free. His fingers struggled with the knot, clumsily undoing the first few strands of rope.

Allen just stood there, transfixed by the moaning Li Min lying on the floor. Danilov's fingers worked faster, the knot was coming loose, just a few more pulls.

Allen suddenly came alive, roared at the top of his voice, and launched himself at Danilov, hitting him square in the chest. Danilov felt his arms being knocked upwards, away from his foot. The chair toppled over backwards.

Allen was on top of him, hitting down with the leather belt across his face. The silver points snagged the skin beneath his eye. Blood poured from the cut.

He kicked out with his right foot and caught Allen just below the knee. A loud crack as a bone snapped. A sharp gasp came from Allen's mouth.

Danilov tried to roll away from the chair but his left foot was still tied to its leg. He jerked himself over onto his left side and reached down to his foot. The knot tore into his ankle. He managed to undo another strand, just one more and he would be free. He kicked hard with his left leg and there was movement.

Allen was getting slowly to his feet, one leg dragging beneath him. He still had the leather belt in his hand. He steadied himself for a few moments against the wall and then lashed out with the belt again, the silver points cutting into the upper part of Danilov's arm.

Ignore the pain.

His fingers carried on tugging and pulling at the knot around his foot. It was coming loose. The belt swooshed down again, catching him where his neck joined his shoulder, ripping into the soft flesh beneath his clavicle.

Ignore the pain.

He twisted and tugged at the rope gripping his ankle. It began to come loose. The brown leather of the belt was coming straight towards his face. In slow motion, he could see the silver points, the holes of the belt and even the grain of the leather coming closer. It caught his jaw on the right. His head snapped backwards and his whole body, and the chair, rolled over. He spat out a tooth through a mouthful of blood.

Ignore the pain.

He kicked out his left leg. It was free. The room went darker. He looked up. Allen was limping through the doorway blocking the light from the corridor.

Danilov kicked away the remains of the chair and rolled over onto his knees. He spat another tooth and a mouthful of blood out onto the floor of the cell.

Got to get to his feet. Got to go after Allen.

He tried to stand up but immediately fell backwards.

Slowly, take it slowly. He reached out to the wall and used it to lever himself up. Allen was nowhere to be seen.

He staggered to the doorway and was immediately stunned by the light. His name was being called from above. At least, he thought it was his name, but it was faint and so far away. He shouted back. 'Here, down, here.'

His head was spinning. He leant on the side of the door to steady himself for a moment. Allen was getting away, got to go after him.

He staggered through the doorway into a long corridor, lit by two bulbs hanging from the ceiling. He leant into the walls for support. His legs wobbled beneath him, as if he was learning how to walk all over again. He stopped, leaning into the wall, taking deep breaths, calming his body, focusing his mind.

Got to find him.

He lurched down the corridor, bumping from wall to wall. A door was open at the end. He stepped through it and there was a loud bang, followed by a crunch as the bullet struck the stone door surround.

Danilov ducked back behind the doorway. He took two deep breaths and quickly stuck his head out, searching for Allen.

There he was, on the path by the creek, limping towards Garden Bridge.

A mist was rolling over the creek. A cold mist, flavoured with all the smells of rubbish and shit and rotting fish. A few boats chugged past on the creek, the rest having put away their nets and cargo, tying up for the night.

His name was being shouted again. Still behind him, but closer now. He couldn't stop and wait for whoever it was. He ran after Allen.

Mustn't let him get away.

After three steps, his feet became entangled in a heap of discarded nets and rubbish. He tumbled over, banging his left knee on the edge of the road.

Don't let him get away. Can't let him get away.

He picked himself up and lurched after Allen. He could see him eighty yards away, climbing up the stairs leading to the Garden Bridge, leaning on the balustrade as he limped upwards.

Can't let him get away.

He heard his name being called again. It was Strachan's voice. He shouted over his shoulder. 'This way, over here.'

Allen turned as he shouted, levelled his pistol, firing another shot. The bullet whistled past Danilov's right shoulder. He ducked again, far too late. No point in trying to get out of the way of a bullet that had already been fired.

He got up and staggered after Allen. He felt stronger now as the adrenalin surged through his body. He was getting closer, nearer with every step.

The sirens of the Red Marias blared in the distance, faint but getting louder with every second.

He mustn't let Allen get across the bridge. In the chaos of the lanes and *lilongs* on the other side, he could escape and kill again.

Allen was nearing the top of the stairs that led onto the bridge. People scattered as they saw the gun. Women screamed, men shouted, rickshaw pullers raced to the other side of the road, pulling for all their lives were worth.

Danilov shouted up at Allen: 'Can you hear them?'

The sirens of the Red Marias were closer now, their klaxons cutting through the mist, the sound echoing off the walls of the warehouses. 'You can't get away. No point in running.'

He was at the bottom of the stairs. He began to climb upwards, getting closer to Allen with every step.

Allen was on the bridge, lurching from side to side. He fired at a car that had stopped next to him. The driver stamped on the accelerator and the car surged away, scattering the rickshaw drivers in front of it.

Danilov was at the top of the stairs. Allen was halfway across the bridge, limping slowly.

'You can't get away.'

As he shouted at Allen, a Red Maria pulled across the bridge at the far end, blocking it completely.

Allen stopped, twisting left and right, looking for another route to get away from the shouts of Danilov and the screams of the klaxons.

'You can't get away, Allen. It's finished. You're finished.'

Allen's head swivelled around, first staring at Danilov, then down the bridge to the Red Marias that blocked his exit.

There were footsteps behind Danilov. Strachan was there, breathing heavily, his Webley nestled in his fist.

'About time, Strachan. Good to see you.'

'Yes, sir, thought you might need a hand.'

'I need a gun more.'

Strachan handed over his Webley.

Allen had backed himself into the middle of the bridge, against the wrought-iron balustrade, the pistol gripped in his hand.

'Time to finish this.' Danilov stepped forward. Allen backed further along the iron railing. He swung round and stared down into the murky waters below, turning back to face Danilov.

'It's all over, Mr Allen.' Danilov stepped forward with his hand outstretched. 'Give me the gun.'

Allen twisted right and left, terror in his green eyes. The police had decamped from the Red Marias and had formed a line at the end of the bridge, advancing across it, pistols drawn.

Danilov moved closer. 'Checkmate,' he said softly.

Allen seemed to calm down, took a deep breath and a sad smile crossed his face. 'There are still so many of them to be judged, Danilov. So many who need punishment.'

Danilov moved closer, his arm still outstretched. 'It's over, Allen. No more Yama. No more trials. No more judgements. No more executions.'

Allen looked at the gun in his hand, smiled and brought it up to his temple.

Strachan shouted 'No', and jumped towards Allen, his arms outstretched.

Allen lowered the pistol from his head and pointed it straight at Strachan. There was a flash. The bullet left the barrel in a gush of smoke and flame, zipped straight towards Strachan, pushing through the air, piercing his clothes and into his body.

Strachan stopped for a moment and just stood there. His arm moved up to touch the red spot of blood that had begun to stain his white shirt. Then, his knees just crumpled and he fell sideways, landing on his left side, his arms outstretched.

Danilov raised the Webley and two loud bangs came from it.

Too loud.

Allen's body jerked as if two bolts of electricity had surged up from the paving of the bridge and shot through his torso, exiting out of the top of his skull. Two red blotches opened in his chest, getting larger and larger. He was thrown back against the iron balustrade and stood there, staring straight at Danilov, as if not believing what had just happened.

Another loud bang from Danilov's revolver. Allen's body launched itself up and over the metal railing of the bridge, flying through the air and out of sight.

The smoking revolver lay heavy in Danilov's hand. He let it fall from his fingers and onto the tarmac.

Where Allen had once stood was just emptiness. He saw again Allen's eyes as the bullet struck his body. Their sense of surprise, betrayal almost, and then the body falling over the balustrade of the bridge.

He sank to his knees. He was tired. Of life. Of the police. Of everything.

Then he smelt a sweet aroma wafting across his face and nose like a silk scarf.

Sweet potato. The sweet potatoes of Shanghai. How he loved that smell.

A moan came from the body lying next to him.

Strachan. Strachan was alive. His mouth was moving but only a deep moan came from his lips. Danilov crawled beside him, shouting as loud as he could for help from the other policemen.

Strachan was looking at him, his brown eyes strangely calm.

Then they closed.

A constable ran to his side.

'Get an ambulance.'

The constable hesitated.

'Now, man, hurry.'

The man's eyes flicked across to the Red Maria. 'The radio's down.'

Danilov picked up Strachan's body, cradling it in his arms like Mary in a *Pietà* holding the body of Christ.

A crowd had already gathered to witness the shooting. The constables were running around. A few were checking the river, looking for the tall man's body.

Others were pushing back the crowd. A few others just ran around doing nothing.

Danilov looked down at Strachan. He couldn't see or hear any breathing. He had to do something quickly or Strachan was finished. He couldn't wait for an ambulance.

Then he knew.

He started to run across the bridge, through the startled constables and onto the Hongkew side. The crowd scrambled to get out of his way.

He ran as fast as he could, his shoes clanging down the metal steps at the other side, onto the road.

He elbowed his way through the crowd at the end of the bridge, using Strachan's legs as a battering ram. The crowd was quick to get out of the way. As he ran, his mind raced back to Minsk. He was fifteen years old. The dark walls of a crematorium. His father's casket vanishing behind the curtains. Him standing there, not crying, not knowing what to do. Just feeling an immense sense of loss. He would never hear his father's voice again. Never talk to him. Never hold his hand. Then the curtains pulled across and his father was gone.

Forever.

He ran faster. He wasn't going to stand in front of Strachan's coffin as it vanished behind a curtain.

He darted across a road, hearing the squeal of brakes behind him. The morgue was up on the left. Dr Fang would know what to do. He must know what to do.

He kicked open the wooden doors, rushing in. Strachan was still not breathing, not moving. 'Help. Help me.' His shout echoed against the white-tiled walls.

Dr Fang appeared in his white coat, coming from his lab. 'What's all the noise? This—'

'It's Strachan, he's been shot.'

Fang threw away the towel in his hands and ran to Danilov. 'Here, put him in here.'

Danilov pushed his way into the main morgue. At the front was an empty, white marble slab.

'Put him here. Call for an ambulance.'

'It'll be too late. He's not breathing.'

Dr Fang examined Strachan. He leant over and put his ear to his mouth. Then he lifted up the eyelids and looked into his eyes.

'He's lost a lot of blood.' Danilov lifted his arms. They were covered in Strachan's blood. 'You have to do something.'

'I'm a pathologist not a doctor. I deal with the dead not the living. He needs an ambulance.'

'It's too late. He'll die if you don't do something.'

Dr Fang stared at the body of Strachan lying on his marble table. He hesitated for a moment, his hand hovering over Strachan's body.

'You've got to do something.'

Dr Fang turned his back on the body. 'Get his collar open. Quickly,' he shouted over his shoulder.

Danilov struggled with Strachan's shirt. His hands, covered in blood, seemed to slide over the cloth.

'Just rip it off.' Dr Fang was standing there with a scalpel in his hand.

Danilov grabbed the tie and shirt and ripped them open. Dr Fang handed him a pen. 'Take the barrel. Just the barrel and wash it in hot water.'

Danilov nodded. He ran to the sink and ran the water. Over his shoulder, he could see Dr Fang lean over Strachan with the scalpel. He seemed to hesitate for a moment, then he plunged the knife into Strachan's throat.

'The barrel, I need the barrel now.'

He ran back to the mortuary table. Dr Fang snatched the barrel of the pen from Danilov's hand.

Blood was oozing from the cut in Strachan's Adam's apple. Dr Fang inserted the end of the barrel into the young detective's throat. He bent down and placed his lips around the barrel and began to blow.

He stopped, stood up and examined the chest. 'Place your hands here. Tell me when you feel it inflate.' He pointed to the centre of Strachan's chest.

He bent over once again, blowing into the barrel that stuck out from Strachan's throat.

Danilov looked down at the chest.

Nothing happened.

Dr Fang blew again, this time slightly harder.

Again nothing.

'Press down on the chest with your hands, just above the sternum.'

'What?'

'Press down with your hands on the chest just here.' He pointed where Strachan's heart was.

Danilov began to press down.

'Harder, man, use your strength.'

Danilov used his body weight and leant into Strachan's body, pressing, once, twice, three times.

'Stop,' shouted Dr Fang. He bent over the barrel and blew into it three times, each time stepping back to look at the chest. 'Again. This time, press harder.'

Danilov put his hands over Strachan's heart and pressed down.

CHAPTER 37

'Sit down, Inspector Danilov.' Boyle reached for his box and offered a cigarette. Danilov lifted his bandaged right arm.

The Chief Inspector scratched his nose. 'Oh, I suppose not, given the circumstances.'

Danilov stared at the wall behind the Chief Inspector's head. The old print of a Chinese street scene had been replaced by a new one. It was of a horse race, the lead horse a white charger, beating two other horses by a short head. The horse's neck was lengthened unnaturally, its whole body straining for the line. Danilov could read the caption beneath: FAISALABAD WINNING THE GOLD CUP IN 1870.

Boyle coughed. 'Look here, Danilov, I just wanted to congratulate you on solving the case. The Director of Criminal Investigation is over the moon, to use a rather quaint modern phrase.'

Danilov's arm still hurt, throbbing like the engine of a car. He would have to smoke another pipe in the afternoon to help with the pain. He craved the opium even more now. It dulled the pain in his arm and the pain in his heart at the same time. 'Thank you.'

'A couple of things have been troubling me though.' He scratched his bald head. This time, Danilov couldn't see any flakes of scalp drifting down onto the suit. 'The most important is how did you know it was Allen?'

'He made mistakes. All criminals do. Two major ones in his case.'

Boyle leant forward. 'Which were?'

'He gave Miss Cavendish some sweets.'

'I don't understand. What has Miss Cavendish got to do with this?'

'One of the witnesses, the boatman, reported smelling a strange smell when Allen passed him on river. I thought it was probably a distinctive cologne.'

'Like my "4711". Picked up a case in France when I was there.'

'Precisely. Except it wasn't. When Miss Cavendish came into the interview room, she was chewing the sweets that Allen had given her. The boatman recognised the smell right away. When I found the same sweets in the stolen taxi, then it all fell into place.'

Boyle scratched his head again. 'And the second mistake?'

'He allowed one of the victims to tell me who he was.'

Danilov was going to leave it at that but Boyle pressed on. 'I don't understand. How could a dead person tell you the name of the killer?'

Danilov sighed. 'It was the last thing Maria Tatiana Stepanova did before she died. She scratched the words "HATE ALL" into the base of the lid with her fingernails.'

He imagined her last moments, gasping for breath, the smell of the pig's blood, its slimy wet stickiness touching her naked body. 'I thought the killer had done it. Another warning. Dr Fang showed me the truth. She scratched it with her nails. The strength of will and presence of mind to write those words at that moment . . .'

'But weren't the words "HATE ALL"?'

'That's right. At first, I thought it was English.'

'"HATE ALL" sounds pretty English to me.'

'That's just it. The word "HATE" wasn't English at all. Why would a dying Russian woman write in English? Strachan pointed it out to me and all the pieces of the jigsaw puzzle clicked into place. She was writing in her own language. Russian. I should have realised it much earlier. In Cyrillic, the word "HATE" is used when you are giving something to somebody. She was giving us her killer.'

'What about "ALL"?'

'That's the saddest part. She was giving us his name. But she died before she could finish writing it. Once I realised that, I knew who our killer was. Proving it though was a different matter.'

'That's why you went to find him?'

'We had to bring him out into the open.'

'A dangerous game.'

'I think it would have been more dangerous not to go.'

Boyle scratched his head. A red lesion appeared on the skin. 'Very clever.'

'I should have spotted it much earlier. May have been able to save the life of Dr Renfrew if I had. Mr Allen was . . .' he searched for the right words.

'We are well aware of that Mr Allen was . . .' he searched for the right words, '. . . a misguided man.'

'Misguided? He murdered at least five people. Probably more.' Danilov reached across and took a cigarette out from the box with his left hand. Boyle reached over and lit it for him. He inhaled the rich tobacco. 'It will all come out in the trial.'

'Allen is dead. There will be no trial.' Boyle knitted his arms across his chest and stared at Danilov.

'But there has to be a trial.'

'Li Min has already been handed over to the Chinese authorities in Chapei.' He glanced down at his watch. 'He was due to be executed this morning. I'm sure his head no longer rests on his shoulders.'

Danilov just sat there, his yellow pallor even more pronounced. The cigarette burned uselessly in his hand, its blue smoke rising up to stain the ceiling.

'Allen is already dead, and now the Chinese man has joined him in his own version of hell. No point in stirring things up unnecessarily, is there?'

'But justice—'

'Justice is a fickle mistress. She changes her affections depending on the mood of the day or of the time.' Boyle threw up his hands in exasperation. 'Danilov, you're a man of the world, you know how these things work.'

'But he murdered five people . . .'

Boyle sighed, combing back the tuft of hair above his ear with his hand. 'Sometimes, I just don't understand you. How do you think a police force of one hundred and fifty Europeans, a few Russians, Sikhs and Japanese manages to control a city with a Chinese population of four million people?'

Danilov stayed quiet, his cigarette beginning to burn his fingers.

'It's an illusion, that's all it is. We have managed to convince four million people only we can manage their affairs to ensure they enjoy the freedom to make money, make children and make a life. We do it all because they respect us. Respect our prestige as natural rulers. That prestige must be maintained at all costs.'

Boyle sat back in his chair and knitted his fingers in front of him. 'Look here,' he said more softly, 'the Chinese may be right in their idea of what life means and we may be wrong. But if we admit they are right, and we are wrong, then we undermine the whole moral basis for our government in Shanghai. We are only here because they think we are bringing them the benefits of Western civilisation. They only allow us to rule because they believe they will benefit from that civilisation.'

'But Western civilisation is maintained by the rule of law.'

'Not in Shanghai it isn't. It's maintained by the perception that the rule of law applies. In actual fact, the Chinese carry on doing what they have always been doing for centuries. We simply provide a veneer of respectability.'

'And in return?'

'And in return we have a standard of life unknown in the West. A life of luxury and servants and money and all those things none of us could afford if we were not attached to the great tit of Shanghai. Remember, Shanghai was founded as a commercial venture. It's still that even today.' Boyle sat forward. 'And when the Russians, your countrymen, were looking for somewhere safe to run to, they came here, to the haven that is the International and the French settlements. Here, they found freedom.'

'The freedom to become killers and prostitutes and drivers and pimps.'

'And policemen. We don't mollycoddle people here in Shanghai, you either sink or swim.'

'Or die.'

'Or die.' Boyle sat back, his argument finished. 'Can't you see? Our prestige, the veneer that keeps us in power, must be maintained – otherwise we have nothing.'

'What about the French? Or Richard Ayres? Doesn't he have the right to see his fiancée's murderer brought to justice?'

'The French are happy that Allen is dead. Saves them the cost of a trial. Mr Ayres is an intelligent young man.

He understands what's at stake. His father represents many of the commercial interests I mentioned earlier. Unfortunately, his fiancée will be forgotten just as quickly as one of her roles.' He shrugged his shoulders. 'It's just the way of the world.'

Danilov felt the cigarette burning his fingers. He stubbed it out in the ashtray. 'Allen's crimes will go unpunished?'

Boyle leant forward again; his eyes had changed, become harder, more focused. 'He's dead, isn't he? You killed him. He's been punished by you.'

Danilov's head went down.

'He deserved to die,' Boyle said softly, 'you and your family deserve to carry on living.'

Danilov lifted his head at the mention of his family.

'You are separated from them?'

'How do you know?'

'Allen kept a file on you. He was a most efficient Intelligence officer. You recently placed an advertisement in the *North China Daily News* looking for them?'

Danilov nodded.

'And received a telegram in response to the advertisement?'

'You know all this, Cartwright burnt it.'

Boyle sighed. 'Inspector Cartwright is not the brightest hammer in the toolbox. We will be sending him out to police the Badlands for a few years. I doubt whether he will survive it, few do.'

'And that's supposed to make me feel better.'

'No, not at all.' Boyle opened the drawer to his desk. 'But what if we could show you what was in the telegram?'

'It was burnt. I know Cartwright burnt it.'

'You may be interested to discover our Intelligence division, formerly headed by Mr Allen, keeps copies of all telegrams coming into the Shanghai Post Office. It's a matter of security.'

Danilov sat back in his chair. 'That's how Allen knew.'

'Knew what?'

'The name of my daughter. He knew her name was Elina. He had seen the telegram.'

'Probably. It took some persuasion, but I managed to get our Intelligence johnnies to give me a copy.'

'A copy?'

'Of the telegram.' Boyle reached into his drawer and pulled out a light green envelope. Danilov could see the words 'Shanghai Post Office and Telegram' typed in both English and Chinese on the front. Stamped across the top was a large square box with the word 'COPY' in bold letters. The ink was breaking up, the red lines of the stamp bleeding into the pale green of the envelope.

Danilov leant across and took another Turkish cigarette from the box. This time Boyle didn't reach over and light it. 'In exchange for what?'

'In exchange for all the good work you did in solving this heinous series of murders.'

'And in exchange for my silence.'

Boyle remained quiet.

Danilov brought the unlit cigarette up to his mouth. He fumbled with the lighter in his left hand before finally getting the flame to touch the tip of the cigarette. There was a brief flare as it finally lit. 'And Detective Constable Strachan?'

'Detective Sergeant Strachan will continue to work with you. He's going to be a good copper. Takes after his father.' He picked up the pale green envelope and put it down on Danilov's side of the table.

He stared at it for a moment before crushing the cigarette out into the ashtray. 'Thank you, Chief Inspector Boyle, for your time.' He took one more look at the pale green envelope lying there on the mahogany of the table and reached out to put it in his pocket.

'Inspector Danilov, if I were you, I would open the envelope at eight o'clock this evening. That would be a good time.'

Danilov opened the door and walked out.

***

Strachan relaxed in his armchair pulled up in front of the fireplace. His mother passed him a steaming bowl of *Hong Dao Sa*. The sweet, maroon soup with its soft balls of red bean had always been one of his favourites. He lifted the porcelain spoon to his mouth and drank. It was warm and sweet and comforting, just what he needed tonight.

He was feeling better but he had lost weight. Two weeks surviving on cold hospital soup had not done him a world of good.

He fingered the raised edge of the scar that ran down his throat. It still hurt sometimes and coughing was a nightmare he avoided as much as the hospital food. The gun shot was not as serious as they thought. It was the shock that had nearly killed him.

He remembered very little from the bridge. He had felt no pain as the bullet entered his chest, but his legs didn't seem to want to go forward. The bridge had rushed up to meet him. Its concrete and metal floor kissing his face. In slow motion, he had seen Danilov raise his Webley, two loud bangs coming from it. Then all was a series of images: the iron stanchions of the bridge, black against the grey of the sky, like the bars of a prison. Danilov above him, his mouth moving but no sound coming from his lips.

He had woken up hospital, his whole body aching.

He had finally been released from that particular prison early that morning. Danilov had picked him up and brought him home. They hadn't said a word until the driver had parked the car in the small space next to his building. He didn't know what say. What do you say to a man who saved your life?

As he got out of the car, all he could think of was, 'Thank you, Inspector Danilov.'

The Inspector nodded. 'It was all Dr Fang's work. You are one of the few men who can say that they came to life in a morgue.'

'I suppose that's something to tell the children.'

'It will make a great story for them. And thank you, Detective Sergeant Strachan.'

'I did nothing.'

'You misunderstand. I'm thanking you for turning up.' He took a few deep breaths and continued, 'I had to bring him out into the open, you see, otherwise we would never have caught him.'

'Bring him out?' Strachan thought for a moment. 'You mean you were the bait to trap him?'

Danilov nodded. 'I thought the killer was Allen. The Parma Violets and Maria Stepanova let me know. Then the telegram you gave me confirmed it. He served in Washington for two years before he was posted to Shanghai. But there was no time. He was certain to kill again and all the evidence we had against him was circumstantial. He would have been able to deny everything. And who would believe a couple of detectives against the word of the Head of Intelligence?'

'Why didn't you tell me?'

'Wouldn't have been much of a bait if everybody knew. Allen had too many informants.' Danilov coughed three times, covering his mouth with his handkerchief. 'So thank you for coming.'

'What would have happened if I hadn't checked the fingerprint or talked with Miss Cavendish?'

'But I knew you would. You've got the makings of a good policeman, if you can train your mind.'

'Look for the patterns.'

'That's it. They tell us everything we want to know. And one other thing.'

'What's that?'

'Learn to trust people. The right people. They won't let you down.' He nodded to the driver. The car moved away from the kerb and Strachan was left standing all alone outside his home.

He took another mouthful of the warm, sweet soup. He looked up at the photograph of his father that hung above the fireplace. For so long it had been there, staring down at him, chastising him for what he had failed or forgotten to do.

Strachan knew it was all in his imagination but, tonight, the look on the face in the photograph was different, less judgemental, more forgiving. The photograph seemed to say to him that he had done well, he hadn't let his father down.

The investigation still haunted him: the viciousness of the killings, the pale body floating in the water of the creek, the loneliness of death in the mortuary, and the fight with Jimmy Lin.

He shuddered at the memories and looked up at the picture of his father again. The look on his face seemed almost proud now.

Strachan knew this was impossible. No photograph ever changed. It was fixed, immutable, as certain as his father's death all those years ago. But nonetheless, here, this night, in front of the coal fire with its amber glow, in front of the picture, he knew it had changed.

He glanced at it once more and for the first time in his short life, he was at peace.

Behind him, his mother entered the room. He took another large mouthful of the warm red-bean soup and turned towards her. 'I forgot to tell you I've been promoted. I'm Detective Sergeant Strachan now.'

***

Danilov arrived home, took his hat and coat off, and hung them behind the door as he always did. The apartment echoed with emptiness as it always did. Cold oozed from its bare walls as it always did.

Ever since the meeting with Boyle, the envelope had sat like a dead weight in his pocket. He took it out and stared at the pale green cover, with its red stamp and neatly typed address.

He checked the clock on the mantlepiece. It was 7.50. What had Boyle said? Open the envelope at 8 pm. He didn't think Boyle had such a flair for the dramatic but this afternoon's meeting had shown a different side to the Chief Inspector. Gone was the bumbling colonial and, in its place, a harder, more determined bureaucrat had emerged.

'Perhaps I underestimated him,' he said out loud to the clock. The minute hand ticked over to 7.51.

He went into the bedroom. The bed was unmade, an old shirt, its collar frayed, lay draped across the chair. On the bedside table, the pipe, lighter, pipe cleaners and pins for the opium lay on the tray where he had used them the night before. A small pea-sized ball of opium remained unused in the saucer. Enough for two pipes, he thought, before I have to go and see the Princess again.

Enough for this evening.

He lay on the bed without taking off his shoes. The telegram was in his right hand. It was still sealed, the gum seeping out where the triangular flap of the envelope met the main body.

He placed it next to the opium pipe on the tray and stared at both of them.

He had waited for this moment for so long. What if the telegram said his daughter was dead? What if it said she had died recently, so close to finding him? What if it told him about the death of his wife and son?

He slid his thumb beneath the seal of the envelope. Tonight, the opium could wait. Tonight belonged to his real family, not to the family of his dreams.

He pulled out the thin sheet of paper and unfolded it. The words were exactly the same as a typical telegram. Teletype that had been pasted onto a standard sheet. The words were blurry and he forced his eyes to focus.

HAVE INFORMATION RE DAUGHTER STOP CALL TSINGTAO 73546 WILLIS STOP

The number jumped at him off the page. Should he ring now or wait? What if this man, Willis, told him Elina was dead?

The opium pipe lay on its side on the tray. Perhaps just one pipe to help him get through this time, just in case it was bad news, news he didn't want to hear.

Danilov put the telegram down and began to reach for his pipe. Just before he touched its ebony hardness, he stopped.

Tonight belonged to his real family, not to the family of his dreams. His real family. His real daughter. His Elina.

He walked into the living room. The minute hand was just reaching eight o'clock.

The phone rang.

Its sharp trill shocked him. He jumped backwards.

It rang again. And again.

He thought about the pipe of opium lying beside his bed, the warmth of the smoke in his lungs, the comfort of his dreams.

Another ring.

But this night belonged to his family, wherever they were, whatever had happened.

He reached out to lift the receiver off the hook and placed it close to his ear. 'This is Inspector Danilov,' he said into the mouthpiece, conscious that his voice sounded frail and unsure.

'This is Willis.' A tinny voice echoing in his ear. 'Just a minute, I have someone for you.'

There was a loud rustling down the line and then a small, quiet voice said, 'Papa.'

For the first time in a very long time, Inspector Danilov didn't have an answer.

EPILOGUE

I was here for at least two weeks before I regained consciousness.

A time of nightmares. Struggling under water. Gasping for breath. Kicking against the grasp of the river.

Survive, my mind had shouted.

Survive.

I don't know why the old couple plucked me out of the water. They didn't speak any English and I didn't understand a word of the gibberish they spoke to me. All I know is that every time they look at my tattoo, the old lady whispers something under her breath. A prayer? An incantation? A spell?

I remember them pulling me aboard their boat. Pain. Much pain. The stench of fish. The rolling of the boat. The chatter of seagulls.

And then nothing.

I woke up once as the old woman was pressing something down against my chest. I fought against her but someone held me down.

I lost consciousness again.

When I awoke, my chest ached and my breathing came in shallow gasps. A hand reached out to touch my face. In it, a cold cloth, stinking of fish.

The coolness of the cloth soothed my brow. A warm coolness like the kiss of a seal.

I lay there in the dark of the boat, tossing from side to side as the waves struck the side, hearing the constant throb of the engine and smelling the salt in the air.

On the wall, I saw a calendar. The dates changing as the fisherman tore off the red leaves.

Two more weeks passed before I could sit up.

The old man came in and fed me a thin, watery soup with the eyes of fish floating in it, and green fronds of soft seaweed.

He stared at the tattoo on my chest.

I took a few mouthfuls and collapsed again.

I just lay there, staring at the dark, salt-stained wood above my head.

I made so many mistakes, disappointing Di Yu, failing in my assigned task. I know now that he has forgiven me. Understood my hubris.

I underestimated Danilov.

It won't happen again. I know now what I have to do. Di Yu has told me the importance of this new work. Nobody will stop me this time.

Now, I had to rest and build up my strength. I will have to kill the old couple eventually. A shame. But nothing must get in the way of my work.

Nothing.

Next time, I will be smarter, more determined, more ruthless. Nothing will get in my way.

Allen was now dead.

Long live Yama.

ACKNOWLEDGEMENTS

To my editor, Clio Cornish, thank you for being so enthusiastic and passionate about the idea of a Russian detective in the Shanghai of the 1920s. To the people of Shanghai, thank you for a wonderful two years in your amazing city. To my wife, Sharon, thank you for making this possible. To my daughter, Eve, thank you for making this impossible. To everybody else, I hope you enjoyed reading the adventures of Inspector Danilov. Find out more at writermjlee.com